The Wingbreaker

The Sundered Stone Book 1

Megan G. Mossgrove

For Mrs. Fuller, who read *The Odyssey* aloud my freshman
year.
"NO-BO-DY"
Thank you.

And for Soru, the bestest dapple-pawed pup that ever crossed
that rainbow bridge.

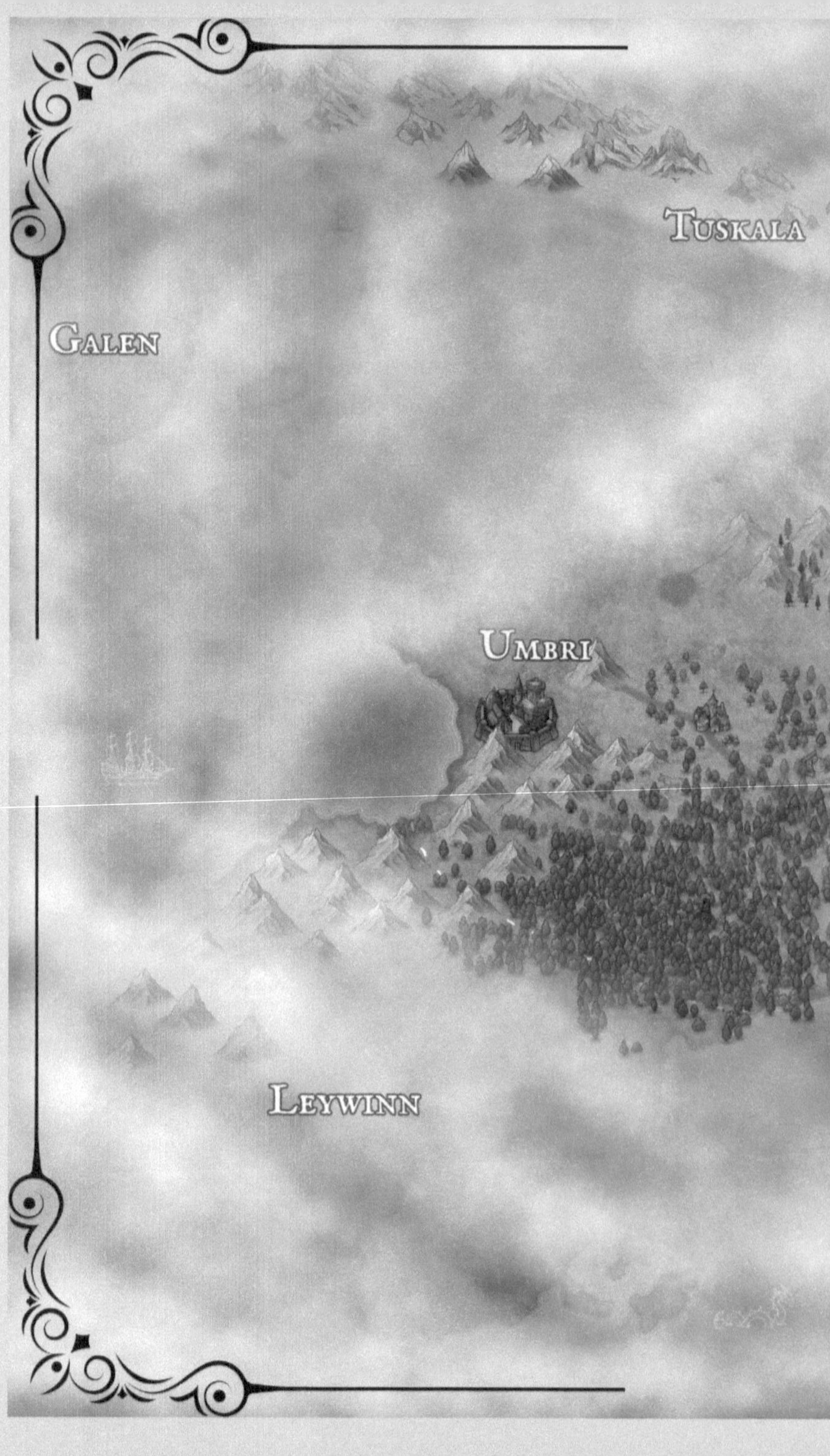

Tuskala
Galen
Umbri
Leywinn

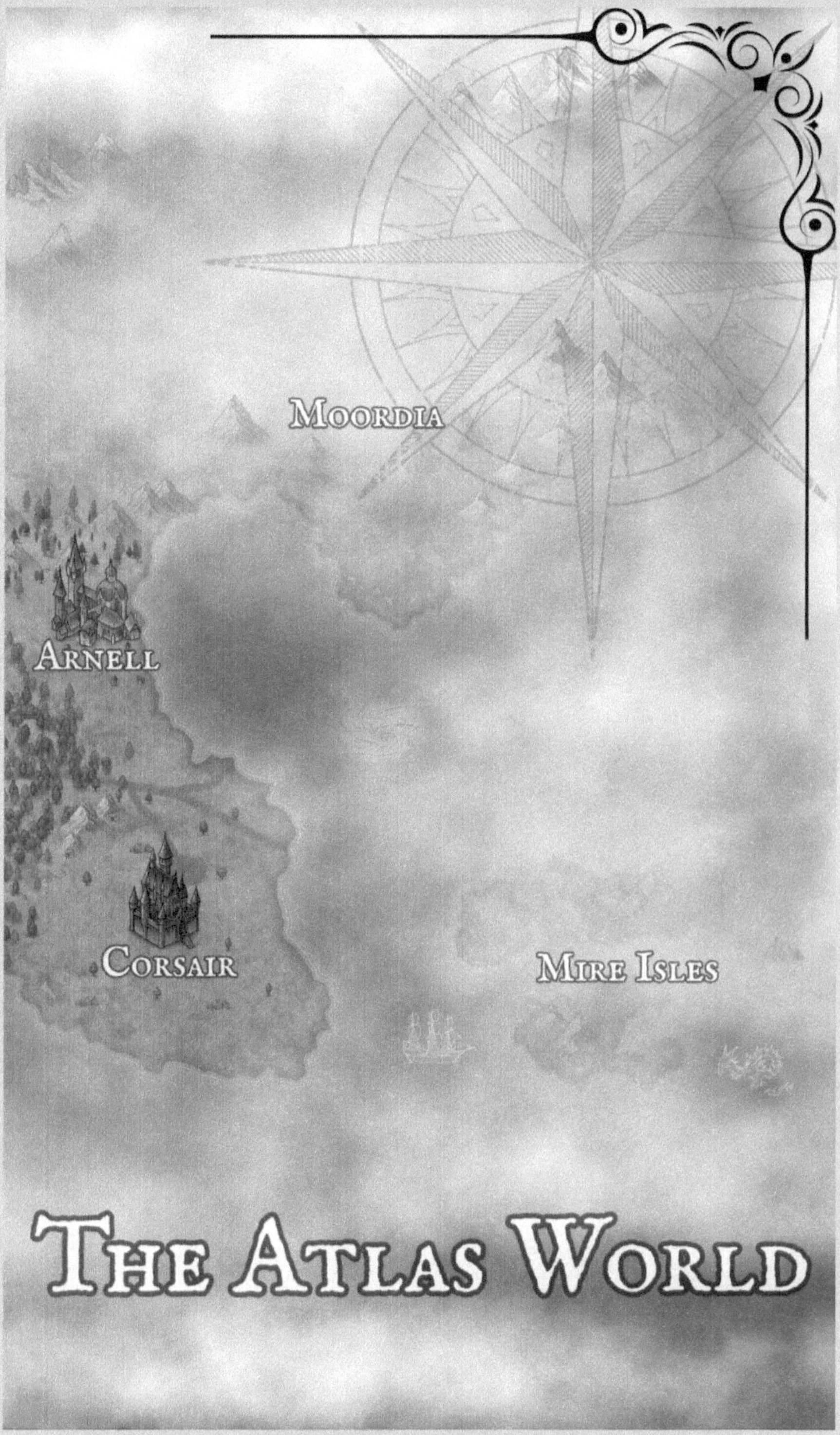

THE ATLAS WORLD

what would it be like
to know you?

not the beauty i see
but the one
            underneath
tucked away
in that cocoon of fiery temper

id temper you

i think

but not in the way you temper yourself

with those flames
that burn you
and burn you
and burn you

i want to know
what's in your mind
that makes you think
they're supposed to

i want to know
so
when i speak
you hear me

when i tuck your hair back
grip reckless hope in my hands
And press my head into yours

when i use the breath that we share
to whisper the truth
into that echoing place
the one in your mind that's never harbored a
soft word.

you don't have to be the kindling

to be the fire that protects you.

Chapter One

GODS, SHE HATED THE way he stared down at her. Early morning illuminated the stained-glass window beyond the throne and ribbed the peaks of his crown, casting jagged shadows over his face. Were he made of stone, Leo might hope his expression would yield with time. As it was, she was forced, as always, to meet the king's steely look with one of her own, willing him to see what he needed to see.

"Fine." The word was soft. His lips hardly moved, as if they fought to clamp down. His chin raised a fraction, shoulders solidifying. Olive-skinned knuckles went white against rippled armrests carved to capture the light and glimmer as though the very sea were enchanted into them. Familiar trepidation skittered down her belly into her legs, heart already quickening under threat of his irritation. "But with an escort."

The words weren't soft anymore.

While relief sealed away easily, Leo's ire had always been more challenging to rein in. Her lips rebelled against the pleasant, practiced smile. If necessary, she could slip away from an escort, but there shouldn't be a need for one at the traveler's market.

Though, admittedly, that wasn't where she was going.

His mother-of-pearl throne was elevated three steps higher than the dais, forcing Arnell's subjects to crane their necks to meet his eyes. She leapt out of her own—the lowest of four and firmly flush with the floor—to press a kiss to her father's grizzled cheek. "I'll be back before dinner," she said, her voice too bright as he rumbled his affirmation. She flew down the center of the giant room before he could change his mind. The echo of hurried footsteps and the weight of his gaze followed until the castle door closed, sealing shut between them.

Outside, the courtyard buzzed with clattering deliveries, tromping horses, and rickety wagon wheels. Leo relished the salty spring air and the cloudless sky, breath puffing in white clouds.

Before assembling her escort, the guards sent a messenger to confirm. One jogged over, shaking his head.

"I'm sorry, Your Highness. It's the King's orders."

"Ellroy, how many times must I ask you to call me Leo?"

The man grinned, his smile and the coral uniform that denoted the castle guard always striking against his dark skin and coiled hair.

"Properly addressing the royal family," he said, "is also the King's orders. We'll get his confirmation and have an escort for you soon."

"I'm always glad to have company."

A lie, of course, but there was no use burdening him with anything more than pleasantries. The silence stretched.

"I 'eard he took the beast down with 'is bare hands," said a guard on the opposite side of the arching gate.

The fae with him laughed. "Heard wrong then," she said. "He used a blade. Faced the beast head on and staked it in the heart."

Ellroy had to lean down to whisper in her ear. "I heard he brought it down with his white-feathered arrows."

Leo lifted an eyebrow. "If he hadn't slain the griffin yet, where'd the white feathers come from?" Her serious tone was immediately betrayed by the crack of a smile.

He cocked his head. "I couldn't say. Perhaps it was a chicken."

"Perhaps," Leo conceded, smiling wide, and he broke into a laugh. New and old rumors of the neighboring kingdom's champion made their way around once or twice a year. The slaying of the griffin Ptolemus gave the man his name, The Wingbreaker, and the story went differently every time it was told.

Ellroy cleared his throat. "That must be it. Chicken feather arrows all along. You know what they say, Princess Madeline: 'never meet your heroes.'"

She huffed a laugh, but sobered as the King's permission was confirmed and a few less-familiar guards set themselves in a triangle around her. She offered Ellroy a nod of farewell, and he bowed before the guards led her into the city.

Subdued, Leo followed them along the cobblestone road, regretting the curious eyes that searched for evidence of who she was. The creamy blue cloak wasn't terribly out of place in Arnell—the city prided itself on its vibrant color—but the escort brought more scrutiny than it was worth. If anything, having them around singled her out as a target.

When they made it to the bottleneck between the road and the market square, Leo took her chance. The notorious space was dominated by a sea of bodies flowing in and out. All manner of races called Arnell their home. Pointed ears and uncanny grace revealed fae blood. Humans moved with more vivacity, a hurriedness that came from cramming life into a mere hundred years. Some bloodlines were so mixed they defied any single category. A fae with islands of shimmering blue scales on her face followed behind a dwarf whose beard was so long it was a wonder he didn't step on it.

A giant-kin led a line of carts that cleaved through the crowd, heading their way. Leo threw herself forward, pretending to fall in its path. People exclaimed and cursed, forced to step over her. She crawled frantically, nearly losing a finger to a merciless wheel. Once on the other side, she crouched alongside the line of carts on their opposite side. A couple of older fae children craned their necks to watch her plight, their mouths dropped open in surprise. She gave them a conspiratorial smile and hurried down the nearest sideroad, hoping to find somewhere to regroup before continuing her task. The road was quiet. One building seemed to be some sort of trinket store, and one farther on had a sign that read "Aspen Inn."

Heart racing, she eased the door open and slipped inside.

"Welcome. Sit anywhere you like," the innkeeper said. His tone was warm enough to quell her jolt of surprise. Orcs were few in Arnell, usually only passing through, but he looked perfectly at home behind the counter. Few tables were occupied at this hour, and she took shelter at one on the wall facing the door. He took drinks to a booth in the opposite corner, exchanging familiar greetings with a woman cozied up to her lover, their arm draped over her in comfortable affection.

Before long, a human server came to ask for her order. There was still time before she was supposed to pick up the grimoire. All she had to do was lie low until the guards moved on.

"Whatever is freshest today—and congratulations," Leo said, beaming at the roundness of the woman's belly.

The woman offered a pretty smile that didn't quite reach her doleful eyes. Wisps of chestnut hair had already escaped the bun she'd pinned low under one rounded ear.

As the woman walked away, Leo scoured the room for anyone who might be paying undue attention.

"I've a table in the back, if you prefer," the orc rumbled, sending her heart thumping with surprised fear. The sleeveless tunic he wore put the breadth of his green arms on display. His black hair was short on the sides, the top pulled into a tie. She swallowed, unnerved by the offer, but he smiled, his lower tusks jutting up past either side of his mouth and dimpling his cheeks under a neat beard.

Just then, the doorbell tinkled, and she ducked her head at the sound of jangling armor. Had they seen her come in? She should have already been moving. What she sought was too valuable to lose.

As they peered around, the innkeeper stepped in their line of sight and jerked his chin toward the kitchen. She relented, and he kept behind her as they walked, concealing her from view with his bulk.

For an inn and tavern, it held surprisingly little space for cooking. A long stove covered the short exterior wall, fitted with various tops and slats to serve. The serving woman labored over a massive pot and gave them only a cursory glance. Next to her, an open door let in a welcome breeze. Dishes nested haphazardly high in a deep double sink and an icebox stood in one corner. The orc motioned to a small table beside yet another door—likely a storage room. A meal waited, steaming.

Bewildered, Leo glanced sideways at him.

"I can tell when a patron would rather remain unidentified, Princess Madeline," he said. The assurance only increased her confusion, but he gave her another easy smile. "Feel free to sneak out the back when you're done. Food's on me."

Chapter Two

THE CARAVAN HAD LITTLE trouble on its way to Arnell. There were monsters, to be sure, but few creatures would attack a group as large and well-armed as theirs. Large-scale brigandry seemed to have died out. The Three Kingdoms had been in relative peace for centuries, and with the economic boom that followed open trade, people had grown used to a certain standard of living. Rare was the defected soldier turned bandit. Rare were those who couldn't find help in a time of need. Rare, too, were the whisperings of war. Yet, the latter was precisely why Fael found himself walking alongside the Umbri tradespeople as their wagons filed through the city's gates.

He needed to meet with his contact.

Arnell was . . . colorful. By now, he knew to expect it, but still he marveled upon entering the market square.

Their trade district sprawled open, framed on three sides by tall, thin buildings. A few boasted signs designating artisans renowned enough to have earned a permanent spot in the market. Many others catered to the tradespeople themselves: taverns and inns that would be full come nighttime. Temporary stalls and wagons situated themselves in rows at the center, bursting with goods. The briny smell of the sea coated everything, and the brisk air deterred few on the sunny spring morning.

Fael followed the Umbri merchants to an open spot, where they began unrolling and stacking with efficiency borne of experience. Before long, the overwhelmingly floral scent of soaps and oils drew the crowd's attention, and he nodded silently to the tradespeople and the other escorts as his goodbye.

Fael perused the wares as he made his way to the edge of the square, his honest interest waxing and waning. The crowded stalls displayed a hodgepodge of goods: embroidered fabrics, jewelry, stationery, pelts, weapons, spices. Before long, he munched on a sweet pie and his pockets held a or two; he'd found it useful to carry a few small tokens that might garner the goodwill of an innkeeper or maid, whose ears were often open. Usually, he would avoid a market, or any city, as crowded as this one, but there was little choice.

Many kept their distance, warned off by his habitual hard expression, but some earned a hard shoulder for their distraction. He checked his pockets after each one. The market would be a thieves' haven despite its whimsical colors.

Thankfully, the street just off the main marketplace saw less traffic. Here, the buildings were different from the bright, cheery structures that greeted those entering the city. These were modest, though not unkempt, and, as always, the low-burning hearth in the Aspen Inn offered a warm welcome.

The innkeeper eyed him. "Wolf, I was beginning to think you'd forgotten about me."

Fael grinned, tossing a tinkling coin purse on the counter. "Satyr, I couldn't forget you if I tried." An orc stood out, even in a kingdom's capital. Usually, they kept to Tuskala in the north, though a few lucky cities on the continent boasted an orc blacksmith or two. Rumor claimed their people had mastered metal craft before the written word—and Tuskalans claimed their blades were the finest on the continent. Fael agreed, having been awarded one upon his promotion to scoutmaster—its edge was the finest he'd ever seen. And he'd put it to good use.

Other than Satyr, Fael had never heard of an orc who had left home to seek the life of an innkeeper, though there was more to the male than what met the eye. The bag of coins disappeared in an instant, replaced by a tall wooden stein—foam spilling over its edge.

"You overpaid." The orc's eyes gleamed as he smiled, letting the rest of his teeth join the pair of large lower tusks that book-ended his mouth.

Fael took a moment to drain the cup. "I was hoping you'd help me with something," he said, pushing the stein back toward the innkeeper. Satyr's eyes flickered around the room as he pocketed the small parchment tucked on one side.

The orc nodded. "Let me fill that for you."

<hr>

Fael stepped onto the side road. He'd deposited his armor and weapons in the room at the inn, leaving only a green tunic, brown trousers, and a nondescript dagger that wouldn't draw a second look. Now that it was closer to lunchtime, the low roar of the crowd carried over from the market square. He went in the opposite direction, his pliable shoes making no sound on the cobbled road.

One could learn a lot about a city in its taverns and markets. These alluring spaces, lovingly tended, put the hopes and passion of its people on display. A bustling square would always be filled with the finely dressed, with shy lovers, with rosy-cheeked children squealing at colorful displays, with hopeful merchants peddling goods aided by the aroma of fresh pastries or savory stews. The best any city offered. A shiny, almost gaudy, surface.

Fael sought something else.

When on the hunt for information, it was better to look from the bottom up—to first ask those who had nothing to lose and everything to gain. Beggars, street sweeps, and the like would be too cowed or too grateful to mention his curiosity to anyone.

He followed the increasingly smaller paved streets down to packed earthen alleyways so cramped he could brush his outstretched hands on either side. Two cloaked figures passed by, one trailing the other. The first, a woman with impossibly long red hair, swiveled her head around, as if trying to get her bearings, while the second moved—no—*stalked* behind. Fael's steps faltered, years of bloodshed-honed instinct rearing its head.

The woman didn't make it to the mouth of the alleyway.

The figure behind her reached up to wrap their hands around her hood and ripped it back, twisting as they did so. The woman's knees buckled, and she fell with a violent gasp. Her desperate hands struggled against the restriction at her throat, breath cut down to a wheeze, but she froze in fear as the attacker spoke.

"I need your coin purse—" The voice broke, panicked. *Young.* "Please," it trembled, "toss it behind us on the ground, miss."

"Let her go," Fael called, annoyed. Had the attacker not realized there was a witness?

The woman cried out as her attacker yanked them around, angling himself towards Fael with her in between. The boy's hood fell, revealing red tipped ears and plump, ruddy cheeks. His free hand angled a short blade under her ribs. "This has nothing to do with you, sir!" His voice had risen an octave, but his eyes glistened with tears and angry determination.

Shit. He was hardly more than a child.

Fael drew his dagger with practiced ease. "I'm only going to give you one warning."

"Don't." The woman's strangled plea barely made it past the noose of her cloak. She batted away her tangled hair, fumbling with something at her waist. Once the purse relented, she tossed it behind them. The boy threw her forward in a rush and she fell onto her hands.

It gave Fael a perfect shot.

As the young thief turned, Fael threw the dagger, slicing the boy's calf to bring him down rather than impaling him.

Fael approached warily, but the thief didn't try to stand. Blood bloomed on his pants and he clutched his leg, biting back a sob.

Fael kept his face neutral. "Do you know what happens to thieves in—" The words were cut off by a second, unlikely attack.

The woman shoved him. "How dare you!" she snapped, all teeth. "You could have killed him!"

Fael blinked, struggling to form a coherent response. She'd already knelt to examine the boy's leg.

"He's fine," Fael said.

The woman stabbed at him with an accusing finger. "*Don't*." The word was a command. The thief, to his credit, tried to rein in his tears, but when she put a gentle hand to his face, they began anew.

"I'm so sorry," he babbled, "I'm so sorry. It's my sister. She's sick and my Da got taken—"

"Hush," she whispered. "Just be quiet for a moment. I need to think. It's—it's going to be alright."

Fael looked to the sky in disbelief when the young man closed his eyes and rested his head on her palm. She took a few deep breaths, and he mirrored her, his trembling easing with every long exhale. Fael scooped up his dagger and tucked it away. The woman murmured under her breath, but he couldn't hear—

Then he saw the magic.

With one hand, she held the boy's face, and the other glowed over the wound, the light dancing across his leg and up her arm. In a matter of moments, his pained expression eased, and the woman sat back with a heavy sigh.

"I'll fetch a guard," Fael declared to no one, though doing so would come with its own risks for him. There was little chance he would be recognized, but being roped into answering tricky questions by Arnell's guard hardly made it onto his list of plans for the day.

The woman stood and wavered, her head bowing into a hand as she swayed. A few steps brought Fael close enough to anchor each of her elbows, the soft fabric of her gown wrinkling under his callused fingers. He was close enough now that his fae senses caught her scent, something warm and slightly floral.

"No." She clenched his arms, steadying herself before looking up at him.

Her eyes glowed faintly, the magic illuminating them as it took its time leaving her body. It was unnerving and otherworldly, and his breath caught, sticking tight in his chest. She smiled gently at whatever expression he wore, as if to put him at ease, but it only made the sudden tightness clench into something unbearable. Made her radiant. He'd let himself get too close. *Too close.* Well past the point of being polite.

He didn't flee.

He *didn't.* He released her and backed away, his heart racing faster than his feet, but he didn't flee. Not when he couldn't tear his gaze from hers.

She looked away first.

He sucked in a breath. Gods, what was wrong with him?

She was moving now, scrambling after the boy who edged away, getting faster the farther he ran.

"Wait!" she called, following, brandishing her purse. The boy hesitated.

She began to count coins and Fael's heart was in his throat as he watched her hand a few over, a hesitant smile tugging at her lips. The thief hugged her. *Hugged her.* And she laughed, breathless from the ferocity of it. The boy tucked the coins into his pocket, but his face blanched when he noticed Fael glowering, and he fled, rounding the corner to disappear into the maze of streets.

"Why are you even here?" he asked the woman, irritation rising as the concern ebbed away. "You could have been killed."

She whipped her head to him and, too late, he thought to check his tone. He rarely dealt with civilians. Instead of wilting, though, she squared herself to him.

"I'd have deserved it for my foolishness, I suppose?" she asked, and her tone left him wondering if she didn't believe exactly that.

It also left him to wonder how exactly he'd become the bad guy.

"This is no place for those who can't protect themselves."

She folded her arms, and his eyes tracked the blood on her sleeve. She looked down and stilled, her face growing pallid as she contemplated the stain. "I got lost." Her voice was softer now, not weak, but distant.

"Then allow me to accompany you."

Her eyes snapped back to him. "Just to the main road," she said, tugging at the collar of her cloak as if it might seize her again.

Fael nodded. Of its own volition, his hand rose to run calloused fingers over the angry red of her neck. There was a good chance it would bruise, unless she could heal it herself.

She watched him curiously, brow wrinkled in a silent question.

Satisfied there was no permanent damage, his attention moved from his wayward fingers to the look in her eyes, but whatever it was, it was banished as she ducked her head and took a graceful step back. Fael's traitorous feet followed, matching the movement, his hand still in the air.

When she looked back up, her almond-colored eyes were clouded. The vibrant magical glow had dissipated. Her lips parted in surprise at his boldness and her cheeks flushed a pretty pink from the adrenaline, or the fear, or maybe—

"Forgive me. I seem to have forgotten myself," Fael said, wrenching his hand down and taking a quick step back. Heat crept up his neck, but he tried to hide it by offering a courtly bow. When he straightened, she'd regained her composure as well, spine set, fatigue pushed away. She inclined her head with graceful forgiveness as he offered an arm. She leaned on it a bit more heavily than expected.

"Did the boy hurt you?" Fael asked, eyeing her fine dress for blood. He clenched his fists until they hurt, trying to ground himself amidst the anger that prowled around him. Young or not, he would track the thief down if—

"No. I'm quite alright," she said, tossing her hood over her head, weariness seeping from every word. "I've never healed before. Not even a paper cut. I'm afraid I may have overextended myself."

Fael didn't know what to say. Few fae were gifted with healing magic, and those that were served their crown without question. It was compulsory. With her fine clothes and that heavy purse, she must be from a noble family or paid handsomely, but if she had never healed before, it meant she'd hidden the talent her entire life. The injury wouldn't have killed the boy; to out herself over a thief with a superficial wound made no sense—one who attacked her especially.

The streets opened and became more populated as they walked. She didn't speak, only clutched his arm with surprising strength, betraying her unease. Before long, the sounds of the city solidified into a raucous din, and the chaos of the main avenue opened before them.

"I'm happy to walk you home," he said as they came to a stop. She was too rattled for him to leave her alone in good conscience. Left would take them to the lower district and the market, right to the upper district. The castle dominated that side, its spires piercing the sky, so unlike the stalwart, defensible stone castle of his home.

She huffed a laugh, and his own lips tugged in return. After hailing a carriage, she gave him a coy smile. Stepping forward in a rush, she rose on the tips of her toes, bracing herself against his chest with a hand. There was a moment's hesitation, as if giving him the chance to pull away. Instead, he battered down the urge to hook an arm around her waist. Lavender and vanilla. That's what she smelled like. The soft scent surrounded him and if breath were an option, he would have taken it, the delicate aroma a relief from the onslaught of the seaside city. As it was, the air stalled in his lungs. What was she—?

She pressed her lips to his cheek, and a seed of heat bloomed from the touch, chasing away the chill of the breezy market-to-castle avenue.

Then she turned to leave.

"Wait."

Why he said it, he didn't know. She paused but didn't turn around, merely offered him a look over her shoulder.

"What's your name?" It didn't matter. He'd be gone by week's end.

"Leo," she said. "Though—" Her lips curled into a wry half-smile. "It doesn't matter, does it?"

He blinked. "What?"

Leo didn't answer or meet his gaze again. She tugged her hood down low, its shadow obscuring her face and that blazing red hair. Fael's spirits dropped with every step she took, but he didn't try to stop her, and the wheels of the carriage rumbled their disapproval over stone as they carried her away.

—◈—

Fael returned to the inn and sat watching Satyr effortlessly manage the dinner crowd. While he waited, a server approached. "You ordered the special?" she asked, her voice lilting with some accent he couldn't place.

He hadn't. He hadn't ordered anything.

After an awkward beat, she raised a pointed eyebrow and placed the plate down.

"Enjoy," she crooned, draping a hand over her rounded belly as she walked away.

The room brimmed with people and the smell of lamb stew. Several tables had the look of soldiers. Most were human and fae, but one corner booth swallowed a dwarf who blushed across from a fae male. Nothing unusual.

Reluctantly, Fael had grown to expect a certain level of notice at home. He was . . . well known in the area. But here? Without his cloak or weapons, he should be indistinguishable. He was a name. A title—not a face. But if anyone recognized him, it may not end well.

He appraised the stew, eyeing the green bits. Peas.

He *hated* peas.

Maybe someone meant to poison him after all.

Satyr appeared at his shoulder, carrying a huge tray laden with generously plated meals. "Let me know if I can get you anything else," he said, motioning his chin to the stew as he passed by.

Understanding dawned, and Fael pushed the plate forward. A slip of parchment peeked out underneath.

His contact had come through.

. . . Every dwarf is a sailor, born of the Undersea.
We are the mountain, and its rivers are our veins.

*-Excerpt of The Chronicles of The Dread Pirate
Longbeard*

Chapter Three

At first, Leo was able to ride the waves of conflicting emotions with detached practice. She took a deep breath and dropped her head back onto the wooden seat of the carriage, pressing cool fingers into cheeks that were too warm. He'd been a hero plucked from common tales of the continent: brave and tall, with golden hair that fell over broad shoulders, every movement too graceful, too intense, to mistake his fae heritage. She'd write him, letting his memory inspire a character who could slay the beasts her mind found too easy to create.

As they had walked, she'd wrestled with her resolve, exhaustion and propriety keeping her from studying him in earnest. Had anyone ever looked at her with that level of genuine concern? It didn't matter. She'd never see him again. She'd ruined that chance by concealing who she was.

Honesty would have ruined it all the same.

Another bolt of fear strangled her embarrassment and gave rise to self-loathing. She'd been attacked. Of course, there was some level of risk to slipping away from her guard, but surely the precaution wasn't necessary within Arnell. Beyond its borders, she might have been spirited away by foreigners for ransom. Unlikely. The current political climate was calm.

But politics hadn't motivated this.

It had been a crime of opportunity. Completely random. Most of the time it was simple to keep to populated areas—the market, the library, the main avenue. Today, she'd ventured deeper than usual and gotten lost on the way back. Foolish. She was lucky that things hadn't gone worse. Leo tucked trembling hands over her stomach, nausea pouring salt into the wound of her unsteady existence.

If the boy's sister needed a healer, they should have been able to get help easily. The Crown employed every healer of an eligible age. If a sick person didn't have the coin to pay, there were ways to barter or trade in labor, while the Crown furnished the coin for the healer's wages.

It made little sense.

The healing magic had drained her, as if she'd poured her own wellness into the boy's wound. It was surprising, but the spell had worked. The entire experience flooded back in a rush of random images: the pinch of the knife, her fingers struggling too slowly to untie the purse at her belt, the boy's sobbing as blood warmed her palm.

Oh, gods. It had dried on her hand and the cuff of her gown. She pulled out a kerchief and spit into it as best she could. The red merely became pink. Already they were approaching home. If anyone noticed, they would no doubt bring word to her brother, or worse, her father. Leo scrubbed until she realized, with mounting horror, that there was the blood of another person on her body, and that she could have been killed in an obscure back alley by a desperate child. Her father would have burned down the entire street. A whole swath of streets, if the attacker didn't come forward.

And if he did?

She swallowed against the bile that climbed into her throat. Would she have gone out this morning had she known she might trade her life for it? That she may have condemned a child to torture and hanging?

The carriage distorted as shock and belated fear somersaulted one after the other. The tips of her fingers began to tingle as her breath sawed in and out, too shallow. She let her head fall forward, cradling it in her hands. The carriage lurched on the uneven street, throwing her sideways. Leo tried to fight against the racing in her chest, against her mutinous throat, as it was again constricted by a cloak intent on strangling her. After warring with the clasp, she tossed it viciously to the floor.

When the carriage stopped, there was only a moment to prepare before the door opened and the driver thrust a hand through the doorway. Quickly gathering the cloak and draping it over her bloodied cuff, she allowed him to help her down the step, and alighted into harsh daylight, endeavoring to focus on a sun that did its best to warm the chill of spring. An eternity and several breaths later, she forced her shoulders and panic down with as much dignity as she could manage.

The driver still waited, hovering uncertainly, but she thanked him and fled the question in his pinched eyebrows. She was likely making a fool out of herself. Still, she kept her back straight, head high. If anyone from the castle saw her walking along the side grounds now, they would have no cause for concern. She lived here, after all.

The castle's kitchen garden wasn't far. Black butterflies with blue spotted wings fluttered over the flowers. She went to those with long petals and bold cones. *Echinacea.* Beautiful, useful, and the perfect way to get back to her rooms without suspicion. She harvested a few of the flower heads, then sought the familiar spray of white blooms to grab a handful of them as well. The smell alone helped calm her. With harvest in hand, she aimed herself at the servant's entrance, passing the kitchen garden proper. Spring vegetables and greens stood in rows, dutifully awaiting their future in bowls and on plates. The more rebellious ones had gone to seed, their flowers shooting up with a pride that belied the now-bitter taste of their leaves. The bumble bees liked those the most.

Leo did too.

She pushed the servants' entrance open and managed a small smile. A woman hummed as she checked the oven, her blonde hair tied back, except for a few stray wisps curling around her face in sweaty rings. Something smelled divine.

"Elaine, would you mind brewing these for me?" Leo asked as the cook smiled, unsurprised. She'd grown used to Leo's unexpected visits long ago.

"Of course." Elaine took stock of the flowers, her lips pinching. "Are you feeling alright?"

Leo nodded, but Elaine pushed a stool under her, anyway. Humming again, the cook poured steaming water over the flowers and set to work procuring a cloth napkin and a small plate on which she placed a freshly iced cinnamon bun.

She grinned, watching Leo scoop up the pastry with enthusiasm. "Impeccable timing. These are for the morning."

"They're so good," mumbled Leo over a mouth already full of crumbs. She all but slumped over the plate, suddenly ravenous. It disappeared embarrassingly fast, leaving her sucking on sticky fingers. Delicious food held its own kind of magic.

Magic.

I healed someone today. The urge to celebrate was tempered by the thought on its heels.

I could have died today.

Evidence of that, of course, remained under her folded cloak. It simply wouldn't do to make it this far, only to have sweet Elaine crowing for the healers.

With a bracing exhale, Leo stood and, avoiding the cook's eyes, accepted the finished tea with a grateful nod. The brew rippled in her hand and she sipped, trying not to spill while ascending the servants' stairwell to the third floor. The coral reef colors of the grand hallway coaxed her forward. Sea green walls and towering, salmon-hued curtains over massive windows gave her the distinct impression of living in a fairy tale. For a long time, she'd loved that. Now it only served as a reminder that she didn't fit the part. Rash, flippant. Worse, Arnell's princess carried not a drop of the royal power in her veins. If she did, today would have gone differently. Once in the hallway, she frowned. There was a guard posted outside her door.

A voice thundered through the space, making her stomach drop through her feet.

"MADELINE LEONORA."

Her already exhausted heart fluttered weakly as she closed her eyes in the tense silence. Steeling herself, she turned, adopting a saccharin smile.

"Father! What—" He wasn't there.

Her suspicion rose, justified quickly by the echo of her brother's laugh as he stepped out from an alcove wearing an infuriating grin.

"Callum Theodore!" She tried to muster the same stern bravado as he, but relief softened its edges. She collapsed, groaning into her hands. "You scared me!"

"As well, you should be scared! I heard Talus asking the maids after you in a panic. You should know to be home well before your abandoned escorts."

Leo glanced through the windows at the sinking sun. It was difficult to note the time in the narrower streets, where just a sliver of sky peeked through. Plus, she'd gotten lost on the way back. Going alone was foolish, but unavoidable. She couldn't have brought an escort to retrieve what she needed. Then, of course, there was the attack.

The bloody cuff peeled reluctantly away from her wrist as she flexed it under the cloak.

Callum continued, eyes sparkling with mischief, "You know, I won't always be here to hide the evidence of your trysts—wait, why is there a guard at your door?"

"I appreciate your service," Leo said, shoving at his arm to hide the dread still curling in her stomach. "There's a guard here on and off. I'm assuming you aren't burdened with one?"

"I don't keep a guard unless we're hosting."

"Well, maybe it's early preparation for our guests."

"They won't be here for days," he argued.

Leo bristled at his tone. What did he expect her to say? She certainly didn't manage their rotation.

"Please, Callum. What did you tell the guard when they came asking for me?" The chance of her father finding out she'd slipped away in the city was a calculated, necessary risk, but that didn't mean she looked forward to another .. . passionate lecture. Any optimism rested with the idea that the escort she escaped would be as loath as she to face the king's wrath.

"I told them the king wanted your help to decide decorations for the Corsair visit."

"And if they ask him about it?"

He chuckled wryly. "They won't."

Leo had to agree. Her father was a hurricane, but never more so than over guest preparations. He'd had centuries to master the art of fae hospitality and, while not unkind to the workers in the castle, could be strict and obsessive. It was best to stay out of his way.

The last Leo had heard, they were painting and re-papering the whole of the second floor.

"You really should have told me you were going out."

"I was fine, Callum," she said, more irritated because her words weren't necessarily true.

"What was it this time? A sweeping romance? A gruesome murder? More riveting alternate history texts?"

"It's not alternate history," she scoffed. "And it's none of your concern."

Gasping in a parody of a scandalized court lady, he wailed, "Oh, sweet Leonora. My disappointment knows no bounds. It *is* a sweeping romance, isn't it? An especially dirty one, if you won't admit to it! 'Oh Fabio! I beg you! Allow me to mount your horse and your—'"

Leo avoided making eye contact with the guard as they made it to her room. Her skin warmed not only for the words, but for the unbidden memory of a face etched with concern—a gentle touch.

She slammed and bolted her door against his echoing laughter.

While circumstances doomed her to spiral into a pit of embarrassment at some point, her chambermaid stood in her room now, silhouetted against the bright window that overlooked Arnell. She stood by an open drawer, a damning piece of parchment in one hand.

"Amara?" The contents of Leo's mahogany desk lay strewn across it, and she crossed the room in an instant, snatching the parchment away. "What are you looking for?"

The woman swallowed, her face white. "Your Highness, I was just looking for ink, so I might leave you a note."

Leo reached across to tidy the mess. The inkwell remained undisturbed in the corner, where it always sat. There was only one reason Amara would intrude in such a way. The hurt and frustration leaked out in a sudden, sharp bite of stacked parchment slammed against wood. The woman reared back a step.

"Well, I'm here now." Leo plastered on a smile that hurt her face. She looked pointedly at the paper and ink already spread on the desk, ignored. "So, what's the message?"

The maid's eyes widened. "I . . . The king was looking for you."

"Odd. I was with him just now." In Callum's version of the truth, anyway.

"Your highness, my deepest apologies. I must have been mistaken."

"Oh? And who paid you for this *mistake*?" Leo asked, her voice wavering in its control. Many of ill repute regarded the castle workers as important eyes and ears, willing to toss a coin into the fountain of gossip. But the next question came out before the maid could answer. "And for how long?" Leo's voice rose, whetting itself with anger—and shame. All the maid could have found were her own attempts at storytelling, but the truth in the words were meant for her and her alone.

"Just this once. I swear it, Your Highness," Amara pleaded, her voice thin. "I was only to look, to report on any information for the ball. It was harmless—"

Leo scoffed. "You've yet to say who hired you"

"A man, my lady. I think he works the gardens—please."

"Sit down."

"Your Highness, *please*—"

"You could have died for this, Amara!" Leo shouted. "Now sit."

The woman sat stiffly on the desk chair, silently weeping, her hands clasped too tight to wipe the tears away.

What had the man hoped to gain? At best, there would be an opportunity to sell any information for the favor of some noble or another. There was no end to the inane curiosity and entitled nosiness in the court. Was the princess seeing anyone romantically? Was her brother? What color dress would she wear to greet Corsair?

One benefit of being the spare was that few bothered to press her for information that was of any importance.

Leo tossed her cloak on the bed and began to ink a letter, the sound of the quill scribbling across the parchment underlying Amara's sniffling.

"Here," she said, flinging it to the maid when it was done. "Take this. Let it dry before you fold it. When you meet the man, let him know I look forward to seeking him out. And you're both no longer employed here."

The woman held back a body-wracking sob and nodded her head. She stood to leave, but Leo held out a hand.

"What was your price, Amara? How much did he pay you?"

"He offered me a pearl."

Leo watched the maid carefully, trying to discern if the confession were true. The pearls harvested off the reef were precious—and heavily controlled by the crown. After a moment, she shook her head. It didn't matter. "Get out."

Leo bolted the door and fell back onto the bed. The day had a far-off quality, as if it happened to someone else entirely, or like she'd read it in a book. Surely, it had been years since this morning?

This morning—

She sat up and attacked her cloak, searching for the inside pocket. With a triumphant flourish, she tossed the garment aside, and it puddled, forlorn, on the bright braided rugs that crisscrossed the floor. She grinned at the prize—an old hand-written journal—but she couldn't explore it yet.

Forcing slow breaths, she methodically unlaced the front of her dress, careful not to let her attention linger too long on the darkened sleeve. The knife had torn the gown at her ribs. Grimacing, she peeled the soft fabric away to reveal the chemise underneath, speckled with tiny crimson spots.

She threw all of it into the fire.

After donning a long, forest green nightshirt, Leo had to pull open her windows to clear the smoke, letting the playful cold and the rhythmic crash of the sea pour into the room. She leaned against the frame, drinking it in, eager for both. Before long, the cold won out, and she retreated to burrow into fluffy white pillows and silky sheets, finally opening the book she had suffered so much for. On the cover, in the long, graceful script that filled every page, lay the author's name.

S. Wilford Abadacus

Chapter Four

To whom it may concern:

I'm neither impressed nor perturbed by your tactless attempts to intrude where you are not welcome. Regardless of your motivation, you'll find no information of any import that you might buy or barter. Sending someone to rifle through my things is not only useless, but hopelessly indelicate. Perhaps if you spent as much time in court as you do paying others to do your dirty work, you might learn some subtlety. I'll take your interest as a sort of crass flattery and bid you a good day, though I cannot honestly wish you better luck in your future .

M

FAEL FOLDED THE LETTER with a grim chuckle.

The princess was as arrogant as he would expect. That wouldn't be the information his king sought, though. There were whispers that the King of Corsair pursued a match between his son, Prince Dimitri Nathair, and Princess Madeline Leonora Galentya of Arnell. The union would be a devastating blow against Fael's homeland—Umbri—the smallest kingdom on the continent. Leywinn in the south was the largest, but rapid expansion of the forest border had cut it off centuries ago. If Arnell and Corsair became staunch allies, rather than participants in a tentative peace, Umbri wouldn't stand a chance if trouble broke out between them. Worse still, it could squeeze Umbri out of trade, killing the kingdom slowly rather than all at once.

As scoutmaster, it was Fael's job to investigate, and sometimes handle, these situations.

His targets rarely had the opportunity to learn about it though.

Sighing, he leaned back in the bed on the Aspen Inn's second story. The lumpy mattress smelled like clean linens, thank the gods. He tossed the letter on the nightstand with the rest of the correspondence.

A dockmaster had been imprisoned for accepting bribes to allow merchants to smuggle heavily taxed goods, leaving his wife and two children destitute. Some noble whose name he didn't bother to remember had dallied in an ugly affair with the daughter of another house. The most useful information he'd received was that the King of Arnell had ordered an obscene amount of paint in the last month. It would seem, at the very least, they wanted to impress Corsair during their visit.

Fael believed the rumors of alliance through marriage to be false. As an unspoken rule, Corsair's royals didn't take fae brides, valuing the purity of their human line.

Investigation of the princess herself had not gone as planned, though his contact said she was missing all morning and returned to her rooms with a ruined sleeve, likely from painting. It was worth noting if she'd been directly involved in preparations—or a princess. That kind of labor spoke to an emotional investment. Not a good sign.

Fael's room had no desk. It housed a single bed with a cotton blanket under a layer of rough wool, a hardwood chest of drawers that doubled as a nightstand, a ceramic wash basin, a fireplace, and a woven basket for clothes if he wanted them cleaned—for an extra fee. He removed a vase of daffodils from the nightstand, their scent lingering as he inked a note to his king. When it was done, he dug through his pack and gingerly removed a quartz circle the size of his palm—a sending stone inlaid with a golden griffin. King Treveri had presented the priceless gift to him when he'd been promoted.

It warmed as he spoke the enchantment. Fael lifted the parchment, entranced, as he always was by the magic's glow. Once caught, the letter hung, suspended, until he spoke the name of the receiver. Upon securing its destination, it spun before disappearing with a soft pop.

The ink would still be wet when the intelligence arrived with his king.

He sent a second message with a smirk, imagining the look on the princess's face, but the satisfaction resolved into steady determination. Time was short. He'd be able to get loads of gossip out of the castle workers once the delegation from Corsair arrived, but by then it would be too late. He meant to stop an engagement, not watch it happen.

<hr>

Fael spent the next morning gathering information from those driving the train of goods that had flooded the castle courtyard, which was a staggering sight when viewed up close. The gateway and the large castle door both arched to a delicate point. A large fountain dominated the space, crystal clear water flowing over its many tiers. A female statue reached to the top, tipping an intricate pot over the smallest bowl, filling until it spilled into the rest. The castle itself, similarly tiered, had white stone spires jutting to ever-more ambitious heights, all outdone by one that lorded over the rest. The pearl-pink caps atop each tower were iridescent in the sun, blinding. Weathered carvings looked down from between large windows, depicting several races that lived on the continent: fae, humans, dwarves, giant-kin, orcs. Sections of stairs led into the castle itself, but drivers lined their carts on the cobbled road, waiting to deposit goods at a series of small servants' doors down the side.

His efforts revealed that the Corsair delegation planned to arrive the very next day. Dressed as he was, in the same neutral trousers and well-worn tunic, he flitted about in the chaos without suspicion, lending help to those unloading wagons. While his body worked, his ears remained open.

"It's going to be quite the party, eh?!"

"You! Move your cart down this way!"

"I do hope you're being careful."

"I'm always *careful*."

Fael let his eyes wander, his hands never stopping. The speakers were a curvaceous, rosy-cheeked human woman, and a shorter figure, cloaked in dandelion yellow. They stood off to the far edge of the courtyard near the servants' entrance. Only the strength of his fae hearing allowed him to eavesdrop.

"Besides, I promise to bring something back for you! I heard the Umbri traders brought extra infused olive oil because of how much we bought last time. Or maybe a few ribbons for your hair. It's so pretty and you're always having to wear it up when you work—"

"Go, *my lady.*" The cook shooed the cloaked figure, sending a nervous glance through the door behind her. "If you're not back before sundown this time, I swear I'll send Prince Callum after you."

"I wouldn't dream of missing dinner."

The cook shook her head but swelled with pride before stepping back into the kitchen, shouting orders as she did so.

Fael kept the cloaked woman in his peripheral vision, making a show of checking goods and horses as he went. She kept her hood low and spoke to no one else as she paced through the line of deliveries, using the disorganization to slip past the guards posted at the entrance to the courtyard.

He followed at a distance, but she didn't check over her shoulder. Foolish, if she was indeed the princess. People crowded the walkways along the main road, but her distinct cloak stood out like a brightly colored bird.

Soon, they made it to the bustling market square, and it became harder to keep track of her. All the men and most of the women were taller than her, and instead of marching through them, she weaved her way around and in between. That fact alone made him doubt his suspicions. A royal would do nothing but barrel through.

Too big in stature to navigate the bustling crowd, Fael didn't quite manage the same grace, riling people to complaint as he pushed past.

With frequent stops to admire the stalls, she made her way to the Umbri carts. Here, traders stacked their items in neat rows, drawing many eyes to the fragrant lotions and soaps. Meticulously labeled oils stood in groups: some for the hair, some for the skin, some even for eating. A fae woman, surrounded by colorful beeswax candles, leaned over a pot, dropping in the long wicks. The next stall shimmered with bolts of silk from Dagada. A few garments hung, already exquisitely tailored, demonstrating the unmatched quality. Rare was a noble lady who did not swoon over the stuff; rarer still was the man who could afford to buy it for her.

He caught up to his target as she brushed light fingers over the garments. The young merchant watched warily. She pointed at a few bolts and waved him forward, speaking in a low voice. The man's face split with a surprised smile, his eyes scintillating in the glow of her coin.

"It's truly an honor, my lady. Please give the princess my most humble thanks, and do let me know if her Royal Highness finds our product lacking. I personally guarantee her satisfaction. Nothing, absolutely nothing, makes the silk happier than to be worn by a beautiful woman." He caught her hand and pressed a kiss to it. "Though, if I may be so bold, I'd wager the silks would be equally happy on yourself as they would be on any queen."

Fael rolled his eyes.

Unfortunately, the young Dagadan merchant didn't recognize Fael as one of the escorts that guarded the Umbri caravan, but his sharp eyes didn't miss the scoutmaster's attention. He dropped the woman's hand in a rush, misreading the situation. "Apologies, my lord."

The princess looked over her shoulder.

They both reared back, but he recovered first and set his body square against her confusion and the rising anger that followed. The lips that brushed his cheek before were now set in a thin line. Almond eyes pinned him with a glare and even then, they sent a shockwave through him. Her cloak billowed as she flew to meet him, righteous with indignation.

"Are you working for Fael, too?" She shot a hand into her bag, producing the letter he'd written in response to hers.

"'To whom I owe my deepest apologies,'" she read, her voice lilting with mockery. "'Princess, I truly regret my garish first impression. I assure you, my contact acted outside their orders. If they had consulted me first, we would have avoided the embarrassment of getting caught. I assure you it will not happen again. Fael.'"

She shoved the letter into his chest. "So much for that. Tell him his *contacts* are woefully incompetent. Not only am I being watched and followed, but I now must suffer the knowledge of being so. And to think I fancied you a rescuer when you are naught but a child-murdering—"

Fael found his tongue then. "*Murdering?*" he said in a fierce whisper. "He robbed you! He held you at knifepoint. I barely even grazed him. He robbed a princess. You! You are the princess!" The information refused to settle in his mind.

"The king would have tortured and hung him for that crime. And you—" His throat thickened, but a rush of exasperation cleared it. Growing louder, he plowed on. "Why are you even in the city without a guard? I can hardly believe your *father*"—his teeth chomped down on the word—"would let his daughter traipse around alone. You were *mugged yesterday!*"

"Keep it down!" she said in a fierce whisper. The silk merchant tried hard to look busy. Curious heads craned in their direction. In a parody of the walk they had taken the day before, the princess grabbed his arm and began to drag him back toward the mouth of the market square.

"So, you were following me yesterday. Was protection part of your orders or would your employer have preferred you'd not intervened?"

Fael stared straight ahead—how was her grip so strong? "My employment then and now remains the same, Princess Madeline."

"It's Leo."

"So you said. You're quite attached to your little alias."

"It's not an alias," she said. They were off the main road now, but still she pulled him forward.

He let her.

"Tell me, why were you alone in the most desperate part of your city?" he said. "Arrogant as you are, you have to know you'd fetch a handsome ransom. Many of your people would turn on you if the price was right."

She didn't look at him either. "No, they wouldn't."

Right. Arrogant and naïve.

They ascended a set of stairs into an opulent stone building. Inside, rows upon rows of bookshelves stood at attention amid whispers and sparkling book dust that glittered in beams of light that pierced through high-cut windows.

Releasing him, she approached the elderly woman behind the counter. The librarian beamed in recognition, and the princess responded with her own infectious smile.

His feelings should be clear. Here was his target. She'd had plenty of time to turn him in, and yet, she clearly had as much a reason to keep these events secret as he did. Essentially, she'd handed him the means to blackmail her. By the end of this encounter, he would have plenty to report to his king.

And then he would never see her again.

The princess dug in her bag and placed a lotion bar and sweet pastry on the counter. Delighted, the white-haired librarian embraced her, and Fael averted his eyes when, over the princess's shoulder, the old woman pierced him with a discerning look.

The princess thanked the woman as they made another trade. When his target returned, she was clutching a book to her chest. "Come on," she said.

After several rows, the books grew dustier and more aged, but her feet carried her confidently toward a nondescript door that she had to unlock before entering.

The room was . . . tiny. A well-worn daybed sat against one side, complete with plush sea-green bedding. A massive, cushioned armchair dominated the opposite corner. Books filled any other available space. A low table spilled over with them. Some were open to a page, others closed with a marker of ribbon to hold its place. There were stacks of parchment too, half-filled with scribbles. Others were crumbled, discarded on the floor.

If the princess was nervous about shutting herself alone in a room with a man, it didn't show. She tossed the book the librarian had given her, *Noble Bloodlines of Arnell*, onto the nearest stack and sat primly in the seat. In any other situation, he would have laughed at the way it dwarfed her. As it was, he schooled his face into neutrality as she unlaced her cloak and let it fall.

Her hair was twisted behind her head, highlighting full cheeks and the delicate lines of her neck. She wore a simple gown and no jewelry. After the previous day's disaster, it appeared she'd at least tried to avoid drawing attention to herself today.

She assessed him as well. Did she recognize, as he had with her, that his simple garb was a measure against interested eyes? Her gaze remained detached and cool, the playfulness from the day before having died, felled by a cruel twist of fate. She nodded with authority, a decision having formed in her eyes. She motioned for him to sit.

The daybed creaked under his weight, and he quickly drew his hands away from the blanket, its softness alien, too gauzy for his callused hands.

Trying to reclaim the situation, Fael said, "I suppose you're curious about my intentions.

"I am," she said, not bothering to look up as she paged through a plain leather-bound book. "Ah ha!" Whatever she found elicited a grin. He fought the urge to smile back as she wielded it against him. Too late, his instincts politely pointed out the gleam in her eye was unlikely to be joy in having him here.

When she next spoke, her eyes glittered, her skin brightened, and her voice took on ethereal overtones that made the room feel too small. An impossible wind ruffled exposed pages.

Fael grimaced as the spell laced his feet to the floor.

Godsdamned *wizards.*

Chapter Five

THE SOLDIER GLARED.

Leo didn't have the simple fae magic of the earth, nor was she gifted with exceptional senses or athletic ability. These traits were passed down sporadically through generations, diluted over time by the intermingling of human bloodlines.

Then there was the Blood of Kings. Arnell's royal family claimed dragons bestowed the elemental magic upon their bloodline—proof of their divine right to rule. While fae gifts sometimes skipped entire generations, the Blood of Kings remained constant, with hundreds of years' worth of Arnell royals displaying some level of skill. Naturally, her brother, the heir apparent, had inherited that gift of elemental magic.

Leo had not.

Less natural methods existed, though. Some sought power by becoming warlocks, binding themselves to magical beings. This was taboo; while the patron may be a god, more often it was some nefarious creature that lent its power for a price. In the stories, it hardly ended well, the bargain often being an uneven one.

Leo had opted for study.

Years and years and years of study. She'd spent a desperate decade searching for more instruction after fate put a wizard's journal in her hands, but any relevant texts had been purged or hoarded long ago. Wizardry was infinitely more challenging than becoming a warlock, requiring one to tap into the very essence of the world. It was nearly impossible to learn without a master.

But the spell had worked.

It pulled at a spot low in her belly as it drew—and kept drawing. A flutter of unease tickled her stomach. Healing the boy wasn't the first spell she'd been successful with—she'd used the fire spell before. To disastrous effect. This one, according to the author of the journal, was an experimental binding charm. Concentration was vital, otherwise it would fail, which wouldn't do. She wasn't leaving this room without answers.

"Who is Fael?" Leo tried to sound intimidating, but her tone came out flat, her mind otherwise occupied.

The soldier crossed his arms and leaned back against the wall with a heavy sigh. It gave her no small amount of satisfaction that his feet strained lightly as he adjusted, refusing to leave the floor.

"I am Fael," he said, looking for all the world like a bored schoolboy.

Leo wavered, the connection weakening as her concentration slipped. With a startled gasp, she poured more magic into it, willing it to stay in place. The other spells she'd tried hadn't required a constant draw.

She'd suspected the Fael behind Amara's snooping was a noble. Perhaps he merely worked for one?

"Why are you sending your contacts to go through my rooms? Why are you following me?"

"For information." He'd set his eyes against the wall over her shoulder.

"What kind of information?"

"Why don't you tell me, *Princess,*" he said, adding her title like an insult. He retrieved a coin from his pocket and began flipping and catching it with one hand, his eyes never leaving hers. The corner of his mouth twitched.

Heat crawled up her neck and into her cheeks at his tone and nonchalance. There was one man on the continent she feared enough to let a comment like that go without reprimand, and it certainly wasn't this two-bit failure of an information broker. Whether or not he'd saved her life.

"One word," she growled as sweat beaded on the back of her neck. The spell continued to take. "One word from me, and those ladies out there will know I'm in trouble. The entirety of Arnell's garrison will pour into this library. You'll be in chains before I let you move an inch and then the king will find very creative ways of getting these questions answered."

He stared her down. The top half of his hair was tied back, accentuating the cut of his jaw and a thin scar that striped out from under one ear to touch his cheek. A stray lock of gold and honey brown hair fell out of its tie. The way his scar twitched as a muscle feathered in his jaw belied the mask of indifference.

"You healed the thief," he said at last.

"He was a child."

"You don't have it in you to hurt me."

With a cry of exasperation, she clamped down on the spell as it wobbled again. A few breaths later, she gave Fael the most predatory smile she could manage.

"Fine," she said. "I'll do the talking."

By nobility standards, Leo was boring. She spent an acceptable amount of time making small talk with the ladies of the court. She attended brunches, learned floral design, and played the piano quite terribly. When left to her own pursuits, she read books or scoured the library for any insight into wizard history. Her dabbling in magic was a closely guarded secret for many reasons, but it was a harmless, eccentric hobby. Just books. All that to say—What could he possibly want?

"Let me guess," she said. "You're embroiled in court blackmail and need dirt on me in exchange for . . . what, exactly?

He finally looked at her, and she raised an eyebrow. His face remained expressionless, his voice silent. She persisted.

"You're trying to discover the color scheme of the Corsair Ball for a noblewoman who can't bear to be a single half-step behind?"

The corner of his mouth twitched, and the gleam in his eye made her shift in her seat.

"Did my brother hire you?" There was no way to hide the uncertainty in her voice now. "To prove I should keep my guard with me?"

Leaning forward, he braced his elbows on his knees. The ends of his shoulder length hair fell forward, softening the lines of his face.

"You're quite bold. . . when you aren't afraid for your life," he said quietly, glancing down to study the coin in his hand. He flipped and caught it in one smooth motion before meeting her eyes again.

Embarrassment rushed in with the memory of how she'd so foolishly, kissed his cheek the day before. It took great effort to draw herself up and set her shoulders. When did she get so tired?

"Well . . ." she said awkwardly, "I can't imagine most people are at their best in a situation like that."

"I am." He grinned and the mirth in his eyes transformed him from handsome to devastating. Her heart lifted, and she grinned back before catching herself.

"Now," he said, suddenly cheerful, "I believe it's my turn to ask questions."

He plunked a boot on her book table with a loud thunk.

Leo jumped to her feet, startled, but the room spun with the sudden movement.

"No, no, Your Highness." He shook a finger at her. "I'm armed. And your soldiers wouldn't get here in time."

The threat hung in the air for a moment before he motioned for her to sit.

She was a fool. A damned fool.

"When did I lose the spell?" she asked, deflating into the chair, bringing her legs up and hugging them to her torso.

Abruptly overcome by utter exhaustion, she rested her head against her knees.

"About the time you stopped being righteously pissed off." He unstrapped a dagger from his belt and set it on the table. That woke her up. A little. She swallowed against the dryness in her mouth.

"You don't have it in you to hurt me," she said, throwing his words back at him. Not at all sure that they were true. This was a mistake. She should have known she couldn't handle this.

He cocked his head. Sunlight streamed from a high window cut in the outer wall, catching in his eyes. It was an odd time to notice how remarkably green they were, like the first buds on a tree as winter turns to spring.

"No? The child murderer won't hurt you?"

"You protected me." It was thin logic at best.

"The way you tell it, I was the aggressor."

"I'll admit I didn't properly thank you."

"You did *improperly* thank me, though," he said with a wolfish grin.

Heat blossomed over her face. Clearly, he was trying to throw her off-center.

"Make no mistake, I'm not complaining." He laced his fingers together behind his head and leaned back again. The casual, almost cocky movement pulled at the short sleeves of his shirt and put a surprising expanse of arm muscles on full display.

"Tell me," he continued. "Why were you running around alone, in back alleys, with no escort?"

"Is that really what your employer wants to know?"

"Consider it a personal interest."

Gods, she was tired. "I went to buy an old grimoire." It wasn't illegal to own, only looked down upon. Strongly. Her skin pebbled at the chill of the room. There may be people she didn't want to know about her academic pursuits, namely her father, but Fael wouldn't want the king to know they had spoken. Would he? She blinked hard. Her eyes wouldn't stay focused. Something was wrong.

"If you think I'll let you ransom me, you'll be disappointed." The words didn't have nearly enough bite.

"Ransom, Princess? I have no need for coin." Before she could speak again, he pushed forward. "Interested parties seek information on the strengthening alliance between Arnell and Corsair."

Leo gathered her cloak, shivering, and angled herself against the tall sides of the chair in a huff. She tucked the fabric over her body like a blanket and closed her eyes, suddenly nauseous.

"What are you doing?"

She startled awake. The room spun. Had she fallen asleep?

"I'm not feeling well," Leo said, but she wasn't sure the words left her mouth correctly, because he stepped over the table and knelt close, scrutinizing her with evident concern.

She blinked in surprise. Gone was the cocky, effortlessly threatening sneak. Gone was the stoic soldier. This was the man who gingerly touched her hurts yesterday—as if certain the act alone could draw away the sting.

She reached out, wondering if she'd fallen into a hazy, frigid dream. She cupped his face, tracing a thumb over soft lips.

His eyes, green and wild, stayed locked on her own. The discernment ached, in a way. Like he saw more than she wanted him to see.

Too soon, he sat back on his heels, pulling away.

She blinked.

"Princess." Fael wrapped a rough hand around her shoulder and shook. "Stay awake." A command. One she tried to follow, but opening her eyes was a heroic task. Another shudder wracked her body.

He scooped up her hand and held it, then pressed cool fingers to the side of her head, her cheek, and cursed. "You're burning up." Fear tried to register, but she couldn't pin it down. Burning up. Hadn't she read about this?

He left again, and she slipped deeper, vaguely registering the sensation of being lifted, enveloped in warmth. Straddling the line between wakefulness and fevered sleep, she felt the muted panic. A pounding heart. The feeling too distant to be hers, but her traitorous body responded to it, anyway. The next few moments rang with clarity, her ears bolstered by the racing organ in her chest, sprinting along in a familiar gallop.

"Could magic cause this? Last time she was tired, but—"

"You can't stay here." The voice was pained but held no space for argument.

The grip on her tightened. "I know."

"I can send for you if we receive any information, but you have to go." Voices echoed and multiplied. "Now."

The stone floor was ice.

"I'll see you again, Princess." A whisper, so close she could feel the promise on her skin.

Leo shivered as he pulled away, and her heart began to slow.

they dance
helpless
caught in currents
twirling in pairs and in groups and
the beast
it rages
clings to its ways
and its wants and its bones and
they are feathers

falling

all of them

Chapter Six

SWARMS OF PEOPLE BUSTLED around as Fael watched from a distance. Soldiers, and one nervous man, presumably the healer, discreetly carried her to a confiscated carriage. Two men on horseback went ahead to clear the way and, with a lash, the horse's eyes went white with panic before they bolted for the castle.

Satyr gave him a sharp look when he blew the door open, turning every eye in the room. Without preamble, he pulled the orc aside, offering no unnecessary details. The male argued the castle had nearly caught his man bribing the maid the first time. This time, Fael assured him, no one needed to do anything more suspicious than inquire after the princess's health and report if there were changes and, this time, Fael would pay double.

One point had swayed the orc more than the other.

Upstairs, Fael reported the news to his king.

She's ill and has taken to bed. All reports indicate she has no knowledge of an impending engagement.

Investigation into other family members is ongoing. Visitors arrive in the morning, with a party to be held at the end of the week.

Fael tossed the letter over the sending stone and dropped his face in his hands as the correspondence popped away. Everything had imploded fantastically, but there was no reason for his king to know that. Yet.

The woman was a fool. An arrogant, naïve fool. She needn't have restrained him. Surely, she didn't believe he would hurt her.

Of course she did.

Of course, she believed he would hurt her just as he hurt the child who would have killed her for her purse. She caught him both intruding upon her rooms and following her about the city. She had no reason to believe he hadn't been following her the day before as well. And he'd all but told her she would be worth kidnapping.

At home, no one second guessed his motives. They knew him. But here? What made him a hero in Umbri made him a threat in Arnell.

Fael sighed.

As much as he hated to admit to it, his skills no longer lay in tracking prey. In anticipating their next move. In discerning events from the clues abandoned and leading men into the skirmishes that followed. His promotion hadn't been unwelcome, but it had taken him out of that sort of action for years. Now he managed scouts from a distance. Delegating, planning, writing reports. At this point, gathering information only required finding the right people and giving them enough incentive to loosen their lips. Blackmail, coin, favors—everyone had their price. But his curiosity about a sharp-tongued princess had evolved into something he could no longer manage.

She wouldn't keep their clandestine meetings to herself, not when each time they were together, yet another threat presented itself.

Fael cringed at the memory. He'd underestimated her and lost complete control of the situation. Then, like a desperate and embarrassed child, he'd all but told her he would stab her if given the opportunity, and she called his bluff. Worse, he'd been too busy gloating at his perceived victory that he failed to notice the light in her eyes dying. Before, she was exhausted by the healing. After a battle, when the adrenaline fades, it can be like that.

Today was more than exhaustion. The color in her eyes paled, clouded like the dead. Her skin had become sallow and burned like fire—truly hot enough that, where their arms met as he carried her, there were patches of red skin, as if scorched by the sun.

His mouth, too, held the mark of her. He poked at the small hurt on his bottom lip. In her delirium, she'd studied him. Touched him. Even knowing the gentleness was unintended—even understanding that, at the door of death, hallucinations beckon you to step across the threshold—he was greedily, twistedly grateful for a glimpse into another life. One where they weren't on opposite sides. Grateful, too, for the burn—physical proof of the way he'd been branded. Twice. He rubbed at his cheek, but it only magnified the memory. He cursed himself.

The librarian had assumed they were together. She'd asked no questions, merely sent him away. They were both conscious of how it would look if the princess was found in town without her guard—and alone with a man.

Was he the first male she'd hidden? What other secrets did the librarian keep for the princess? Clearly the magic had been no surprise, either. Strange that his contacts turned up little about her life while searching the castle, yet here was an entire second persona he'd stumbled into by chance.

She'd be better by morning. The finest healers in this kingdom would attend to her—she was royalty, after all.

Princess Madeline Leonora Galentya

Leo.

He knew little about magic. Neither he nor his mother had it. His father's brood had only a few, including his *legitimate* children. Fael's fae blood manifested in other ways. Sharper senses, exceptional speed.

The magic Leo used wasn't fae magic. A healer could extinguish their pool of it and, while they weren't unaffected, it certainly didn't burn up their bodies. He once watched a girl sing an enchantment over a pear tree. She didn't appear to be giving parts of herself away in the exchange.

So, it might truly be wizard magic. At one point in time, all kingdoms used to employ a court wizard. They'd tried to mass produce them in the Great War, to disastrous effect. Many died or disappeared at the conclusion of the war, and the fear they inspired took on legendary status. He'd never met one, despite his occupation. Being caught off guard was the least of his worries. Fael hadn't felt this kind of helplessness in decades.

He'd forgotten the fear that accompanied it.

His mind continued to wander in circles as the sun set. Satyr sent up food. The roast and vegetables remained untouched, but he took the chance on the fruit-filled pastry—its presence a sure sign the orc recognized Fael's day hadn't gone as planned. Even his lack of appetite wouldn't convince him to waste a good pie. Alas, it soured in his stomach. His body deemed his racing thoughts more important than idle digestion and so, woe upon woe, Fael laid in bed with an ache in his head, his stomach, and his heart.

Fael waited across the street from the library, watching for any hint of news through the watery grey of the morning. When the librarian arrived to open the doors, he trotted over, but she shook her head.

"Nothing yet, I'm afraid."

Fael didn't need further explanation. Reason whispered that it was too soon to know if or when word would arrive, but it didn't stop the churning in his gut. With an appreciative nod, he turned on a heel and headed back to his work.

Corsair's royal procession arrived midmorning—and didn't spare the fanfare. Three carriages, each more gilded than the last, rolled along to the blaring of trumpets. Crowds lined the market and main street on either side, hoping to get a glimpse of the human royalty. Corsair's king remained tucked away, but its prince sat by the driver of the final carriage, wearing beautifully wrought plate armor. The chest piece displayed a fierce dragon head. One shoulder guard rose in vicious spikes. A cloak clung to the other, its royal blue out of place in this world of soft colors. He nodded to the crowd with a polite smile, and ladies waved their kerchiefs in return.

The prince's guards offered no such niceties. Their eyes roamed with distrust over the crowd. Fael marked their uniforms, planning to seek them out later. Most soldiers, fresh off the road, would gather in some watering hole or another. It was a ritual Fael knew well.

The procession passed, and market business resumed with exuberance.

Fael fought his way to the Umbri stalls to ask the merchants to glean whatever rumors they could about the Corsair visit. It was a long shot, but he hadn't been successful in his station by leaving avenues unexplored.

By afternoon, he gave in to the urge to return to the library. A different woman sat behind the desk now. A few patrons perused the shelves, but none paid him any mind. He wandered, taking a circuitous route to the small room the princess used. After a few quick glances around, he tried the handle.

It was unlocked. He stole inside, stopping short as the door clicked shut behind him.

It was exactly as they'd left it.

A half-empty cup of tea sat next to a plate littered with crumbs. Books lay marked or opened as if she might return any moment. He rifled through the parchment on the table: detailed notes on the research she had done, with names of book titles and their authors. There were several scribbled pages detailing the Wizards of Menhir, the ancient god Atlas, and Gallen—a kingdom far in the north. One page just read "Research S. Wilford Abadacus." The books—strewn over the table, stacked on the floor—bore titles such as *Leywinn History Volume* III, *Gods and Giants, One and the Same, Verdas Merlin Harringbon, a Wizard's Life Before Death*. He grinned at a racier one, *Wallflower, Blooming*, stashed underneath a larger, dustier volume. On the cover, jealous ladies watched a blushing woman shyly accept the hand of a muscular, well-dressed man.

On the chair, the book with the worn leather binding lay discarded. She'd read the spell from it. Maybe it would give him some clue about her ailment. Or about her at all.

As he left, a soft voice called out to him. Had they caught him pilfering the book? He hesitated, but turned to find the white-haired librarian approaching.

"You forgot this," she said. Her eyes were crinkled with a smile. Something tight inside of Fael started to ease.

"Thank you." Fael bowed deeply, accepting and clutching the folded parchment over his heart.

Once out the door, he stopped at the top of the stairs to unfold it, happy to find the princess's remarkably unladylike script.

I feel I must thank you for your help. As of this morning, I am well. I hope I'll be awarded the opportunity to thank you—properly, of course—though my obvious indiscretion and current obligation mean it's unlikely I'll be around for a while. Try not to get lost without someone to follow around.

-Leo

P.S. Things have tightened. I cannot guarantee the lives of those caught where they aren't supposed to be.

Chapter Seven

THE SUN POURED IN through Leo's seaside window, as if to congratulate her for surviving the night. She remembered nothing of the evening before. The healers claimed that she had arrived at the castle's infirmary barely clinging to life. That three of them exhausted their reserves holding back death itself, and, for hours, she'd remained unresponsive.

Mid-morning, soon after she woke, Callum arrived with two sticky buns. He'd choked back tears when she bit into hers with relish.

"Proof enough you'll be back to normal in no time," he said.

Guilt spiked, twisting in her gut alongside hunger. She'd made the wrong choice at every turn, yet still couldn't fathom how things had gone *that* badly. Callum lectured her about leaving the castle without her guard again. He'd recited a disturbing list of poisons and a spiderweb of people who might benefit from and conspire for her death. Though he seemed adamant, she wondered if anyone would really resort to such a thing.

She didn't tell him about the magic. Admitting to it would mean she'd never have the opportunity to try again. Wizards weren't persecuted as they had been in previous years, but only because none but the wizards of Menhir far to the north openly practiced. In Arnell, in any of the Three Kingdoms, it was socially forbidden.

Leo drew a breath to tell him about Fael, but held her tongue, knowing he would compile similar information and conspiracy against the man. The fact of his involvement would unravel too many lives. They would find the boy who attacked her and likely kill him. They'd track down Amara. They'd discover Leo's secret space at the library. The whole place would be upended. Margerie, the librarian, might lose her position. In fact, the king may shut the entire library down altogether.

Fael had saved her life, twice. Eventually, she would find the noble who'd hired him and give them the suspicion *they* were due. The visit would enlighten her about any alliance brewing between Corsair and Arnell. Perhaps everyone would know by the end of the week and this whole mess would be over. Surely, the soldier would think twice before agreeing to any future subterfuge.

Fael's motivation remained a mystery. Maybe he was being blackmailed. Or promised a promotion. It didn't matter. It wasn't the first time someone had gone through her things.

It was just the first time she'd caught them in the act.

While there were few ways she could move up or down in political standing, she needed to be cautious. For a long time, she'd avoided those who would befriend her to elevate themselves, but her reclusiveness was not weakness, and she didn't need Callum or her father to step in. She could bear the nosey nobles.

Callum stood at attention as their father entered.

He'd dressed in more finery than usual. The salmon-colored cloak and accents of his attire highlighted the olive skin and dark hair he and Callum both shared. Her mother, who was fair-haired and fair skinned, used to joke she'd simply made a copy of both her and her husband. "Except for this," she would say, tugging at Leo's fire red hair. None could say from where she'd inherited it.

The king's dark beard was shaved in clean lines, its sharpness echoing the rigidity of his face. At two-hundred and eighty years old, he was gracefully turning gray and wore permanent crow's feet around his eyes. He looked more worn than usual, and her stomach flipped as their eyes met. He fell to his knees at her bedside, gently taking her face in his hands.

"Father, I—" the words cracked in her throat.

He swept his thumbs over her wet cheeks and pulled her in. Callum stood vigil as she sobbed, overwhelmed both by the rare show of affection, and by the sudden relief that the king wasn't raging about her trip to the library.

"Madeline," he said, after a time. She stilled, already bracing herself, but he only pressed a kiss to her forehead before taking her hands and standing over her.

"I suspect I know why they targeted you, and I am taking every step possible to prevent it from happening again. The next few days may move quickly, but please know every decision is to ensure your safety, and the safety of this kingdom.

This morning, your brother and I will welcome the Corsairian king. They'll expect your presence at dinner. I ask you, as I've asked everyone else involved, to keep this incident to yourself. No use setting our visitors on edge."

She nodded, because she was supposed to. How would she be well enough for dinner?

He left.

"You shouldn't go," her brother said once the door snicked shut.

"I'll be fine, Callum."

"You think it's a good idea?"

Leo scoffed. "I think this visit has been planned for months and he wants to make a good impression."

"You nearly *died*."

"Exactly. And it's lucky he didn't throw me in irons while I was still unconscious."

"In *irons*?" Callum half-laughed, but Leo sunk further into the pillows, refusing to meet his gaze. He hadn't witnessed the last time their father went into a rage over her recklessness.

He sighed. "Just promise if you aren't feeling up to it, you'll tell him."

"I will." She wouldn't.

Her brother pressed a kiss into her hair before he left.

Still sniffing, she pouted at the now-empty plate on her bed. Her stomach grumbled.

By the time attendants arrived to dress her, she'd dispatched two letters to the library and inhaled an un-princessly amount of food. After calling for the kitchen the third time, Elaine herself carted up a rolling table with enough to feed three, explaining that Callum had finally relented and told her what happened. The woman embraced her, clearly relieved Leo had a good appetite.

"Have some," Leo said, with her mouth full. "I won't eat all of it."

"I just wanted to make sure I brought enough of a few different things. In case you were in the mood for something specific." She'd loaded the table with bowls of brightly colored berries and whipped cream, greasy cuts of pork, hot porridge, rolls, honey, cheese sandwiches, creamy tomato soup, and an entire roasted chicken.

"Well, at least stay while I eat?"

The cook worried at her lip. "There's still a lot to do. The king is hounding us about everything being perfect." She stiffened. "Oh, sorry, Your Highness."

"Elaine," Leo said around a sweet blackberry, "I complain to you about my father all the time. And I've never heard a harsher word than 'hounding' come out of your mouth. I have accused him of worse. In his presence."

The cook eased onto the mattress and tucked a few stray strands of hair back into her bun.

"All the same."

"Oh!" Leo shot up, intending to retrieve the package by the door. Instead, her head dipped in sudden dizziness. After it passed, she walked on shaky legs. "I got you these." She brandished the silk ribbons from the market.

Elaine scurried over to help, her face pinched with worry.

"I can't accept those," she said, looping an arm around Leo's waist and guiding her back to the bed.

Leo had known Elaine for fifteen years, and in all that time she hadn't changed a bit.

"Nonsense. Sit." The word was a command, edged with warning that they'd had this fight a million times and if her friend felt like wasting time, Leo would have it all over again. Elaine relented, and Leo batted her hands away when she tried to untie her hair herself. Leo brushed it out and weaved a silky, shimmering pink ribbon into a long braid that spilled over the woman's shoulder, the ends dangling to her waistline.

"Beautiful," the princess said when she finished, giving her friend's shoulders a squeeze before shooing her toward the mirror.

Though Leo was much older, they looked similar in age. Elaine was quite human. The proof lay in the arch of her ears, and the hint of soft lines that came from a life of laughing. She was generously curved, with plump cheeks to match. Her porcelain skin glowed in her reflection. She reached a hand up to brush the Dagadan silk. The pink in her blonde hair brought out a femininity the cook rarely allowed herself to wear. Leo beamed.

"Things like this," her friend said, voice laced with uncertainty, "aren't meant for people like me."

Leo's smile fell, and she pursed her lips, considering. "It's true they might fall in your way while you work. Perhaps if you wore them so they fell down your back?"

One side of Elaine's lips lifted, and she shook her head. After a moment's consideration, she seemed to draw herself up. "You're right." She spun away from the mirror and tugged at the luxurious silk. "Down the back would be better."

The princess redid the braid, and the cook returned to her duties, her step a little lighter than before.

⸺⬦⸺

Leo's formal attendance at dinner meant hours of preparation. Due to lingering weakness, the attendants made all the necessary preparations while she sat in bed. The princess closed her eyes against the overwhelming sensation of several hands working over her at once. Practiced fingers braided each side of her long hair and twisted the entirety into an intricate knot at the back of her neck. Golden-wrought flowers with enchanting detail studded each pin used to secure it. One woman lined her eyes and oiled her lashes. Another rouged her cheeks and tinted her lips. Two more buffed her skin and moisturized her within an inch of her life.

Despite the caged-in feeling that mounted with every touch, she gasped when she beheld the dress brought in for the evening. A team of tailors must have worked on it since she'd ordered the material the day before. Its simple design boasted no embellishments—it didn't need any. The salmon colored Dagadan silk shimmered with an otherworldly radiance. Its front and back mirrored each other with a V-shaped cut and wide straps at the shoulders. The waist narrowed before relaxing into a generous floor-length skirt, cut so the back would train behind her.

While the silk itself was softer than any fabric she'd ever owned, the corset was unforgiving and, as they pulled the laces tighter, she mourned. Hungry or not this evening, she wouldn't be eating. One attendant held her steady as they draped the dress over her head, and she stood to let it fall around her. As they secured the many buttons, another woman fitted her earrings, each a sapphire teardrop suspended on a thin golden chain. Then, finally, the crown.

Arnell was a kingdom besotted with the sea. Its harvest fed their people. Its reefs guarded their eastern coast. The colors of the city shone in loving mimicry of life beneath the waves.

Her crown, too, reflected that love. Lines of pearls anchored on the bottom branched up on delicate, golden threads. Clusters of jewels and shining nacre shone at the roots of the pearl-studded filigree.

With relief, she thanked the women and bid them goodbye. One threw a pinched look at the mess of crumby food trays on her way out the door.

Leo glanced in the mirror, satisfied. It would be best to get a head-start lest she need a few moments to catch her breath. There was no sneaking through the shortcut of the servants' stairwell, either. She cursed, for the first time regretting having moved into the rooms farthest from the stairs. She made her way down with small, measured steps. Did the guards flanking her know why she moved so slowly? None offered to help.

By the time she reached the bottom, her arms shook from clutching the banister.

"Leo!" Callum rushed to her, offering an arm. "You're early. I was just coming to walk you down." He ushered her to sit with him on a bench outside the dining hall.

"Cute tassels." Leo wiggled her fingers in the swinging threads attached to the epaulets on his shoulders. Her brother tugged at his lapels and threw his chin in the air, striking what he apparently thought was a princely, dignified pose.

"The crowd outside the castle this morning thought my tassels were *very* cute." He wriggled his eyebrows.

She grinned. "The caterpillars over your eyeballs are lucky the crowd isn't afraid of insects."

He fell backwards onto her, a hand clasped over his heart. "You wound me."

Strengthened by a flash of irritation, she pushed him away. "You'll wrinkle my dress. Don't be so dramatic."

The prince relented and became regrettably serious. He leaned forward, elbows on his knees, one hand picking at the fingernails of another.

"How are you?" he asked, his face tight.

Leo adjusted her skirts. Every part of her body ached. And she was more tired than she'd ever been in her life. Not to mention she was starving and not at all looking forward to an insufferably boring dinner locked in the impossible corset they strapped her into.

"Much better," she said with a smile, willing as much life into it as she could muster.

"I'll need a debriefing of the days leading up to your illness. I know Father says he has a plan, but I feel like I'll be able to get more relevant information out of you than he will, all things considered."

Leo gave a noncommittal shrug to hide a bolt of anxiety as she nodded down the hall to where their father now approached. The two of them stood in unison to give the king a formal curtsy and bow.

"You look stunning." His eyes gleamed with pride as he took Leo's hand and gave her a spin. "Absolutely radiant. Arnell has no greater treasure."

Leo couldn't help her embarrassed smile, always crumbling under her father's pride. No matter how distant he'd been in the years following her mother's death, no matter how distracted or angry—a few kind words from him melted away her bitterness. The charisma suited him, and many sought the warmth of his favor, though his irritation was equally potent.

"I do hope you are as pleased with Prince Dimitri as he will be with you," the king continued.

"I'm certain the prince will be a lovely dinner guest," the princess conceded with a nod.

Soon they were ushered into the dining hall, where they stood as a guard announced their visitors.

"Presenting the Crown Prince of Corsair—Prince Dimitri Nathair, and His Royal Majesty King Mardain Nathair."

They each wore black pants and white ruffled shirts. The younger, the prince, wore a royal blue coat that fell to his knees. His father, a rather round man, wore a similar jacket, his long enough to trail on the ground. Medals and ribbons decorated one of his shoulders, broadcasting that Leo would, indeed, find this dinner quite boring. The prince's hair was lighter than his father's, nearly as blonde as Elaine's, but both men kept it combed back in a similar style, accentuating their sharp chins and noses.

Leo curtsied, perhaps a little too low, and her legs threatened to give out. After a breathless moment, she made it back up, grateful that her brother had stepped in front of her to throw his hand into the prince's in greeting. A man stood behind the prince, too, and she wiped the strain from her face as he watched with a puzzled frown. She gave what she hoped was a disarming smile and nodded politely before turning to the prince.

Prince Dimitri took her hand and pressed a swift kiss to it.

"Princess Madeline. I should be honored to share the company of such a beautiful woman," he said, a bit too cool.

Assessing him warily, Leo met the challenge. "And I am grateful to finally meet you, Prince Dimitri. The anticipation of your arrival has simply been too exhausting to bear any longer."

They exchanged impassive stares, each waiting for the other to look away.

The prince finally did, but only to hide his smirk. He moved to the table, where their fathers were already in animated conversation. Leo tried not to let her body slump once she was spared the weight of his attention.

This was going to be so much worse than she imagined. What issue could he have with her already?

She hastily composed herself as the second man—she'd forgotten about him—stepped to her side.

He bowed. "I am Lord Sebastian, the prince's cousin and," he paused, searching for the right word, "advisor. I'm afraid I must apologize for him. The journey, more specifically its company, was quite"—another pause, heavy with consideration—"arduous. I do hope you won't hold his frigid demeanor against him. Let it be proof of his nerves, nothing more."

"Of course. I can only imagine how grueling the journey must've been. I'm sure you're all exhausted." She chanced a sly look, grateful that she wasn't the only one who noticed the prince's lack of tact. "Though I must ask—was his father the arduous company, or was it you?"

He barked a surprised laugh, but smothered it as heads turned their way. His mid-length hair was shaggy and black as obsidian. In fact, Lord Sebastian embraced the color from head to toe. The result was admittedly striking. His eyes, too, were dark. From a respectful distance, she couldn't tell their color, but they swam with enough depth to elicit her curiosity. His grin broke wider when she cocked her head at him, her brow pinching before she had the good sense to hide it.

The sharp angle of his ears revealed fae blood.

Well, that was intriguing, at least.

Chapter Eight

"Leo!" her brother called, "I know you've eaten plenty today, but the rest of us are aching to start dinner." While the other men laughed politely, she and Lord Sebastian found their seats.

The meal was lavish, of course. Her stomach grumbled, but there was no room for mercy, or anything else, in the clutches of her corset.

"So. Leo, is it? Like the lion?" Lord Sebastian asked, shoveling a large portion of fish and rice into his mouth.

"Yes. It's a shortened version of my middle name," she said, as a servant spooned food onto her plate. She sampled the fish sauce, tempted by the savory aroma. Of course, it was delicious. Elaine wouldn't rest until the dish was perfect. Leo pushed her food around, trying to give the appearance of eating.

Prince Dimitri suddenly leapt in his seat and sent a swift glare at the lord. Leo had the distinct impression he'd been assaulted under the table. "Yes," he said in her general direction, "that's interesting."

Rather than dignifying this with a response, she raised an eyebrow at Lord Sebastian, who shrugged innocently.

The prince jumped again, this time drawing the attention of the rest of the table.

"Princess Madeline," he managed through gritted teeth. "I find myself terribly afflicted with the need to ask you," his face made its way from a grimace to a pained smile, "to tell me about yourself."

Temporarily suffocated by the awkward attention, Leo patted a napkin to her mouth.

"Oh. Um. I enjoy reading," she said cautiously.

"She enjoys reading!" Prince Dimitri said with feigned exuberance.

"And she's incredibly beautiful," Lord Sebastian prodded.

"Beautiful doesn't begin to describe it, Sebastian," the prince argued with courtly grace. "The jewels of Corsair are positively dimmed by her radiance." He looked directly at her, then. "Tell me, do you enjoy wearing them?"

"The earrings," the lord cut in, with a pointed look, "were a gift. We like to think of sapphires as the heart of Corsair, and there's no woman more suited to them."

Leo reached a hand to one. "They're stunning. I'm honored by your gift, and your words."

A lie. She felt battered by both the things that were said, and those that were not. Any vestige of energy she still had dissolved with the effort of parsing through the contradictory meanings. Today was not the day for vicious games—and Prince Dimitri was rude beyond arrogance. It seemed the rumors were true—the human royalty of Corsair held prejudice against fae.

She glanced, again, to the pointed ears of the prince's cousin.

Where Leo's bloodline was interspersed with fae and human alike, Corsair hadn't had a fae-touched ruler in hundreds of years. Generations of humans had been born, ruled, and died while her father ruled Arnell without contest. Leo wasn't sure what to make of Prince Dimitri's visit, or the surprise of his fae cousin.

If her mother were here, she'd easily slip into the role of royal host—at one moment, grace incarnate, and at the next, indulgent and playful. Her mother would have loved the mushrooms in the sauce, would have loved to meet Elaine, too. She'd lived a good life, but without fae blood in her veins, it had been a short one.

Leo blinked as her father cleared his throat. He raised a chalice before calling down to their side of the table.

"How are you getting along with Prince Dimitri, then, Madeline? He's a fine man." The king continued without waiting for an answer. "A man among men, if his generals are to be believed." He swirled the wine in his cup. "They say he has a unique mind for strategy and has single-handedly masterminded their successes in skirmishes along their Leywinn border."

Leo lifted her wine. "Let us hope your exceptional talents for organized combat aren't so often needed, Prince Dimitri."

Only her brother lifted his glass to hers. The others remained silent. She sipped the drink gingerly.

"I'm afraid we may need it in the times to come, Madeline," her father continued. "Brewing tensions are unmistakable. Skirmishes with beasts on the Leywinn border are becoming increasingly common in all three kingdoms. And recent stories of broken lawstones bring worry. Worry that our kingdoms are being subtly weakened and will only avoid extinction if we band together."

"You truly believe Leywinn would attack?" Leo asked, "To what end?"

It was the Corsarian king who answered, "We cannot hope to understand the motivations of those so far removed from us. They've kept to themselves long enough that we've let down our guard, and perhaps that was the goal all along."

"But they retained the most territory after the great war," Leo argued. Why was this the first time she was hearing about this?

"Useless territory," her father said, "thick with rapidly expanding forest. And then there's the beasts—"

"I'll not speculate on their motives," the foreign king interrupted. "The fact remains that no scout has ever returned. Just yesterday I received word that another of our lawstones has broken. The village, unprotected by its spirit, was attacked. Those who stayed behind to fight are naught but bloodstains. The entire place is uninhabitable."

"We've yet to see it in Arnell," her brother said, clearly having had this argument with their father before.

"Nevertheless, we must prepare for the worst," their father said. "Prince Dimitri has presented a fine enough proposal that we'd be foolish not to consider it."

The prince of Corsair straightened as the entirety of the table looked at him.

"I propose an alliance between Corsair and Arnell," he said slowly, pondering a flake of fish speared on his fork. His eyes shifted, pinning Leo to her seat. "Through marriage."

The surprise that thundered through her was akin to terror, and her heart leapt into a gallop.

"This is why they're here?" She turned accusing eyes on her father.

It was Prince Dimitri who answered. "It is. This arrangement would benefit both our kingdoms. Civilizations have used arranged marriages this way since the beginning of time. It's the simplest guarantee of goodwill for both parties, Princess. I can give you anything you want, anything you'd have here and more. And, before it crosses your mind, rest assured I'd forsake all right to the marital bed and—if it made our arrangement more palatable to you—I'd support, nay, welcome your discreet involvement with a lover." The pinched smile returned. His human ears bobbed with the effort. "Or two."

Chairs raked against the hard stone floor. Leo and her brother stood in unison.

"Father, do you honestly believe she should marry this intolerable child?" Her brother's voice rose. "Why would you hide your intentions?"

"Remember who you're talking to, boy," their father growled.

It was too much. She backed toward the door. "I'm okay, Callum, really. I'm terribly sorry." Leo pressed her hands over her stomach to hide their trembling. "I've been ill, and it seems it's catching up to me." Her chest could hardly move, bound as it was. Her lungs struggled for air. Her vision wavered—a tunnel of darkness threatening to close in.

A cacophony of voices followed as she exited the dining room. Once clear of the threshold, she ran, weak legs spurred on by the savage beating in her chest.

Get away. Get away. Get away.

On and on it chanted.

⎯⎯◈⎯⎯

Elaine found her. The cook with the ribboned hair coaxed Leo from the servants' stairwell she'd used as an emergency sanctuary—breathing and praying to any god that would listen to placate the organ in her chest that pumped fear through her veins instead of blood.

Her eyes welled over when the scent of chamomile and echinacea hit her. Graciously, Elaine didn't ask why. The cook passed her a kerchief and placed a small serving of glazed fruit cake alongside the brewing tea.

"I can't eat it." Leo sniffed. "This damned corset won't show me any mercy. I'd hardly get a bite down before it all came back up."

Elaine laughed, and Leo forced a small smile.

"They want me to marry that prince, Elaine."

"Can you say no? Your father wouldn't force you into it, right?"

"I don't know," Leo whispered, fresh tears threatening. She took a deep, shuddering breath. "I'm just so tired."

Her friend gave her an appraising look that was obviously left wanting. "You're almost as pale as you were fresh out of your sickbed. Your mind and body need more time to heal. Now isn't the time for proposals, romantic or otherwise." She clicked her tongue. "Go right to bed. And stay there."

"I will. But will you make a tray for me to take? Whatever extra you have? I managed little at dinner."

Unfortunately, another guard watched her room. Leo sighed, as irritated as she was grateful that he opened the door so she didn't accidentally cover her silk dress with soup—crab, if she could trust her still-stuffy nose. The hearth burned low, illuminating the room in half-shadows. Shivering as the adrenaline faded, she sacrificed a few logs to ward against the cool night to come.

In her periphery, a light wavered, catching her attention. She frowned toward the other side of her room.

"You wear that confused face quite often, Cub."

Lord Sebastian. Laying in her bed. His fingers primly turning the page of the book he'd pilfered. A little orb of light floated over his shoulder.

"Don't get me wrong," he continued, without looking up. "It's rather adorable."

Leo opened her mouth to yell, to scream for a guard and bring the might of a castle down on yet another twisted situation she had no interest in dealing with tonight.

"Ah ah—" he lifted a hand and snapped. Her ears popped, and the air in the room changed, stilled.

"That was a ward spell." His eyes were still tracking in his book. "They won't hear you. Rest assured, I'm only here to talk. You're safe with me." He looked up at her then, and his eyes glowed with the telltale sign of a wizard's magic.

Safe? Leo doubted that very much.

"What do you want?" she said, taking a step back toward the iron poker resting by the fireplace.

"To help you." The book flew out of his hand and across the room on an enchanted current.

S. Wilford Abadacus's signature decorated the cover. She snatched it out of the air, clutched it to her chest, eyes flickering around the room as she tried to remember where she'd placed the other grimoire—the first one. She must have left it behind at the library. At least he wouldn't be able to find it.

The lord approached, carrying a tray. "I brought you some food. Hunger is part of the cost of using magic." He nodded to her own tray of food and placed the second next to it. "The body demands its due."

"I'm certain I have no idea what you're talking about. Now I must ask you to leave."

"I'll leave. *If*," he emphasized the word, "you can tell me your plan to manage the burn out. How did you survive it? I'm terribly curious. You know you shouldn't have lived, don't you?" She simply stared. "Forgive my manners." He swept an arm toward the couch. "Please, sit."

She did, and instead of taking the chair or the cushion next to her, he simply sat on the floor, his back resting against the sofa, facing the fireplace.

She closed her eyes and let her head fall back against the pillows.

Lord Sebastian nudged her leg with his shoulder. "You should eat. I can see you dimming."

"I can't eat."

"Why? Not because of the engagement?" He sounded worried.

"What? No. Because of this corset!" she snapped, irritated at being reminded of yet another way her life had spiraled out of control. She let her head fall back again.

His shoulder bumped her knee. "That's not going to be good enough, Cub," he said gently. "Would you like for me to loosen it for you?"

"They're bold in Corsair, are they?"

The lord laughed. "I believe that is my particular vice. Here. Allow me to give you some space."

A short time later, they'd returned, and he sat on the floor. He offered a piece of bread over his shoulder, imploring her to eat.

"When you draw magic," he said, "it's supposed to be from the world. It's not supposed to be fueled by your life force. That's one of the first and most important lessons apprentice wizards learn. And you don't even have a spell focus, so if you did pull correctly, you'd have a hard time keeping it controlled. Even the most experienced wizards use a focus."

She shook her head. "I *know* you can draw magic from the world. What I don't understand is *how*. And plenty of wizards make do without a focus." Leo let herself tilt sideways onto the lush pillows. Sebastian still sat with his back to her.

"And you know that, do you?"

"I've read the stories."

"The stories are about wizards who are trained. And becoming history often serves to embellish our heroes"

"Regardless, I'm making do. I don't have a focus, and you wizards are so precious with your secrets that I haven't learned how to get one."

"We are *precious* for a reason. A focus is earned."

She rolled her eyes at the ceiling. "How?"

"That's not the right question, Cub." She could hear the smile in his voice. "You should be asking, who can I apprentice myself to so that I have a shot at not dying next time I cast a spell?"

"I can't apprentice myself to you because in a week you'll be leaving for Corsair, and I'll be staying here as a free and unmarried woman."

The wizard was silent for a moment.

"Well," he said, as if he held any authority over the matter at all. "Apprentice for a week, then."

they do not know
that i can hear them—
the best of us
and the worst.

i am both,
yet,
i am neither.

and though i know
i am only a Stone
i plant myself
into those spaces
that could never fit

and
woe upon woe
i grow
am carved

away

Chapter Nine

FAEL READ THE CORRESPONDENCE a few times over, despite its simplicity. The evening's report brought the news—castle workers confirmed Arnell and Corsair were negotiating a marriage alliance. The princess, by several accounts, seemed surprised—though one source used the word devastated, having passed her hiding in a stairwell in hysterics. Fael crumpled the parchment and shook his head, trying to dislodge the image. Why her father would spring it on her the moment she rose from her sick bed escaped him—the involved parties must be desperate, indeed.

Grim, he forwarded the information to his king. His Majesty hadn't responded thus far, and with luck there'd be no word until the debriefing back in Umbri.

His optimism was shattered with a soft pop.

Fael tore open the letter, unease gnawing at his stomach.

Regal script flowed across the page, the beauty of the rendering so at odds with its violent request.

Remove her from the board.

He crumpled the paper and let it fall to the floor.

Chapter Ten

THERE WAS A KNOCK at the door. "Your Highness. The king is here to see you."

Leo's stomach plummeted. "Just a moment!" she called, remembering too late that the spell blocked all sound from the room. Lord Sebastian had already risen.

"If anyone finds you in here—"

"They won't. I'll return later this evening?"

Leo threw off her shoes and moved to her bed to rumple the blankets. "We can discuss this evening just as soon as we—" The air softened, and when she whirled around the lord was nowhere to be seen.

The guard knocked again. "Your Highness?"

Rather than respond, Leo leapt into bed and pulled the blankets up to her chin. Her door cracked open.

"Madeline?"

The rugs muffled her father's footsteps. "I know," he said, either knowing or suspecting that she feigned sleep, "that you don't want to talk to me. I know you believe I have kept this alliance from you out of malice, or worse, indifference. But," Leo clenched her hands into her pillow, flinching as his voice rose with the word. "May I remind you that at every instance, you have fought. You've fought curfews, escorts. You've fought the boundaries I've placed to ensure you find information and entertainment suited for your station. You've ignored my every advice on maneuvering in the court and instead choose to isolate yourself, lock yourself away, as if a prisoner. Imagine if I'd told you months ago. We'd have had months of hostility. Even on our best days, I cannot convince you to act with the caution and awareness your role demands. And on our worst . . ."

She said nothing. Willing the memory away.

He sighed before going on. "Seeing as how someone poisoned you, I'm left to believe there are outside forces threatened by this arrangement. It only serves to strengthen my belief that this is the right course of action. You'll be safe in Corsair once the alliance is secured. In time, you'd become its queen. The human prince has, perhaps, fifty years of life left. *Fifty years.* A small price to pay for a kingdom."

Leo remained still, the silence stretching as she bit her lip to hold in the fight he expected, the one that was eager to spill past her closed lips.

When she didn't speak, he cleared his throat. His next words were a steely command. "This is your duty. You're sixty years old. It's time to grow up, Madeline."

⬥

Long past sundown, her ears popped, the sensation accompanied by a familiar change in the air.

"Good evening, Cub."

"It's Leo," she said, smoothing her blankets over her lap to hide her surprise.

"Or shall it be Madeline Leonora Nathair, future queen of Corsair?"

"Perhaps. Though likely not."

"Ah. You abhor the prospect of mentorship so much?"

She gave him the look the comment deserved. "Why are you here?"

"First, we are going to fix that burn out. Then, you're going to learn what you need to ensure it doesn't happen again."

"I'm not going with you back to Corsair."

"No. Madeline . . ." He studied her for a moment. "There's no one here who knows you're trying to learn, is there? No one who has taught you?"

She shook her head. It wasn't worth telling when those who knew would only get dragged under if she were caught.

"Then let me help."

"And if I don't?" It was an opportunity she'd likely never get again, but it didn't seem right to trust anyone from Corsair after how dinner had gone.

"Then you may never fully recover."

There was a beat of silence.

A sudden grin belied his seriousness. "Before we begin, let us agree to keep our meetings . . . private. That won't be a problem, will it?"

She shook her head, studying the lace on the edge of her blanket.

"Good." He dropped to the floor unceremoniously and crossed his long legs. "Join me."

Leo, embarrassed by her thick nightgown, inched out of the bed. To his credit, he didn't bat an eye.

"Now," he said, all business, "close your eyes."

A light flared. "Keep them closed," he ordered when she peeked at the orb of light he'd created. "Alright. Take deep breaths. Focus. Right here." She tensed at a poke to her belly.

"It really is easier if you close your eyes," he admonished, giving her a lopsided smile. A shining sphere of light bobbed over his shoulder and the bracelet on his wrist glowed faintly, too.

Closing her eyes, Leo tried to focus her breathing where he still pressed his fingers to her navel.

"Good. Keep going." He sat back. "I'm going to move this light. Stay focused on that point. Try to feel any kind of tug."

She did. Just out of reach, she felt something. Like the binding spell pulling at her, but instead of a transfer of energy, it was . . . awareness of it.

"I feel it."

"You do?"

"Yes. It's . . . faint, but I think." She raised a hand, pointing. "It's there, now."

"Excellent!"

Leo opened her eyes, surprised at her own prideful grin. The light was exactly where she pointed.

"Well done. Now do it again." The words held a challenge. The light was half as bright now.

Again, she closed her eyes and concentrated on deepening her breathing. It was fainter this time, but she got it.

"Again," the lord demanded, the light half as bright.

Over and over, each time fainter than the last.

One hour stretched to two, and two to three. Her back ached and eventually she simply lay down on the floor, and Sebastian followed suit. Her head at one end, his on the other. She threaded her fingers together over her abdomen and listened to his quiet instruction.

"Keep your eyes closed," he murmured after she finally located the last light, one that was nearly invisible. "I just need you to do it one more time."

She breathed. And waited. Breathed. Waited. A cavernous space opened inside her, empty, her essence depleted. Once there, she pushed her awareness out, questing. The sounds of the room faded. The crackling fire and the rhythm of her own breathing became distant, secondary.

She gasped when she felt it.

It brushed lovingly against her skin. Hummed low in her ears. It was dense where Sebastian lay, but its presence permeated the entire room. She felt its welcome, an invitation.

"Pull," Sebastian murmured, "Imagine yourself breathing it in. Fill that space. Then release it."

Leo inhaled deeply, willing the magic to pool in her belly.

Nothing happened.

She imagined drawing it into her lungs. She imagined gathering it in her hands. She ordered it to obey. She pleaded. The power remained unmoved.

"It's not working," Leo said.

"Patience, Cub. Here." He placed a warm hand on her leg. Her awareness of the magic flickered, distracted, but a sudden thrum of connection pulsed to life, blazingly bright compared to the last few orbs she'd hunted. Unlike the binding spell in the library, it poured *into* her. Warmth pooled in her belly, tingling like butterflies. She felt her skin flush with health and the edge of her tiredness evaporated.

Sebastian lifted his hand back behind his head and the connection cut off, letting the room dim to near-darkness again.

"That's what it feels like. Try to pull on it like that."

It took an agonizingly long time to sink back down—now too aware of the lord's presence. If he noticed, he said nothing. When the magic curled around her again, she recalled the sensation of connection and visualized opening up to it. Imitating it, welcoming it. Like a lock clicking open, it began to flow into her.

"That's it."

Leo hardly heard him.

The emptiness inside began to fill, doing what no amount of sleep or food could. She became heavier, more corporeal. A ghost returned to form. The excess glowed on her bare skin, in her eyes. Already sitting up, Sebastian leaned against the bed, grinning down. She joined him, equally unguarded. It was impossible to muffle this feeling, this relief. It transcended station, propriety, and unfortunate circumstances.

Sebastian's eyes roved over her, and he stood, offering a hand. Instead of letting go, he bowed and pressed a kiss to her knuckles. The midnight suit was irreparably wrinkled, but his dark eyes glittered in the enchanted light. "It's very nice to meet you, Leo."

She groaned when the maid threw open the curtains.

"Good morning, Your Highness," Clara said, a pinch too brightly.

Leo buried her face into the pillows in response.

"What's it today, then?" the princess said, resigned. The king had allowed one full day of rest after everything fell apart. Undoubtedly, he had plans for her now.

"Brunch. In the garden . . . With Prince Dimitri." The maid stared at the ground, clasping stiff hands in front of a spotless apron. Clearly, she expected the princess to be upset by the news.

"Ah. Well, then." Leo adopted a bit of false cheer herself, trying to put the woman at ease. Trying not to think of the way everyone in the entire castle must have heard about her fantastic meltdown. "Would you mind helping me dress?"

Walking to the garden that morning was a far cry from the exhausted trek to the dining room before. Those she passed exchanged greetings with a bow or a curtsy, and she offered a smile and a word to each in return. Her lilac cloak swayed over a sunflower yellow dress that had a high neckline and long sleeves. Clara had braided her hair over one shoulder with a silk ribbon to match. She felt beautiful . . . and alive, which was probably more important.

It was going to be a good day. Considering Father's advice wouldn't hurt: weigh the worth of a life here against the worth of an apprenticeship she should never have had the opportunity to claim. If the cost was unbearable, she'd say no. If the thought of being wed to a stranger turned her stomach sour, she'd only have to become more familiar with him before deciding.

The private courtyard bloomed with daffodils and a few early tulips. Peonies budded up, some cracking above spears of proud snapdragons. Guards stood here and there—far enough away for privacy but close enough to watch for trouble, whatever shape it may take. Lord Sebastian and Prince Dimitri waited next to a small tea table set with juice and an array of breakfast pastries. They cut off their conversation as Leo approached.

"Princess Madeline." The prince nodded in greeting. "I'm glad to see you are well." Today he wore gray dress pants and a well-fitted jacket to match. His hair was different too, fluffy with waves instead of combed back. It made him look . . . young.

"As am I, Your Highness." Sebastian bowed. He'd decorated his usual black attire with a single sprig of blue forget-me-nots.

"I was afraid you'd be ill for the entirety of our visit and we'd be left woefully devoid of your sunny charms."

"I was worried over my illness as well," Leo said, raising an eyebrow at the lord, "but it seems I've made a miraculous recovery."

The prince, already filling a crystal cup, missed his cousin's smirk. He motioned for the princess to join him.

"How old are you, Prince Dimitri?" she asked, as she took the second chair.

"I'm twenty-two. And you?"

Leo tucked her hands into her lap. "I'm sixty-three."

The prince choked on his juice. Sebastian, who'd remained standing a few feet away, cut in smoothly, "I'm a few years from one-hundred. You shouldn't assume age on looks alone when it comes to the fae. Isn't that right, Prince Dimitri?"

"Quite right," he coughed into his napkin.

Neither brought up marriage or the alliance as they ate. Lord Sebastian remained to the side, a dutiful chaperone. Apparently, Prince Dimitri claimed an extensive book collection as well.

"Strategy, history, anything I can get my hands on that will help me rule Corsair when it is my time," he said. "I've recently found myself studying the monsters of the continent. One can never be too careful."

She mentioned her current read, about a tavern girl and an injured foreign lord who didn't speak the local language. Prince Dimitri quickly pointed out he, personally, found reading purely for pleasure a waste of time. The lord winced, and

Leo fell into silence, similarly rankled by the judgment in his tone.

The dinnerware clinked for a while before Sebastian tried steering them in a different direction. "Why don't you tell her about Corsair, Dimitri?"

"Corsair!" he said, leaning forward. "It's beautiful. Its people are many, and strong. We are bordered on one side by the Leywinn forests and on two more by the sea, but reefs do not burden our shores as they do here. Large merchant vessels leave every day, headed for other coasts on the far side of the continent. We do a lot of trade with the Mire Islands, too." He ran a finger over the rim of his cup. "Unfortunately, our landscape is littered with ruins left over from the Great War. Some towns have collapsed tunnels underneath—the Silk Roads. Though they were dug by the Dagadan fae, many human women and children survived the slaughter during the battle of Corenth by fleeing through them when the fae finally overran the city. We have by now, of course, collapsed any that would present a threat should the humans and fae go to war again."

Lord Sebastian, who had his back to them, cleared his throat.

The prince gave her a frozen smile and sat back.

Leo took advantage of his silence. "Many fae fought on the side of humans during the war. It was a war of kingdoms, not of races."

The prince's lips pressed into a bloodless line. After a moment, he raised a hand and waved it with a flourish. "Why don't you tell me about Arnell?"

She did, though, even to her own ears her narrative sounded forced and awkward, shadowed by the fear he might gather up her favorite details of the city and sneer at what he held. She couldn't tell him about the library and rising literacy rates, she couldn't tell him of the reef or its spoils, she couldn't tell him of the wandering traders that made every market different from the last. So she recited facts: her father had been king for two hundred years, his first wife and son were killed in an assassination shortly after he was crowned—nearly a hundred years before Leo was born. Then, instead of bringing up her own human mother, she talked of the white woods and mountain mines in the north. All the while, he sat nearly motionless, staring over her shoulder, absorbed in his own thoughts.

Mercifully, brunch ended. The group took their leave of one another, promising, with forced smiles, to meet again soon.

Leo sought out Callum, but after having no luck at his rooms, or with the staff, she had to leave a note to be delivered when he returned.

The rest of the day dragged on. After sleeping away so many hours in recent memory, she found there was an unbearable amount of time in the day, especially with a guard at her door, reporting her movements. She missed the city.

Bored, Leo took a late lunch in her room and sat to pen a message to the soldier. He buzzed around her thoughts like an incessant, handsome gnat.

Fael.

However, her efforts were soon scattered in a crumpled mess on the floor. Leo had no good reason to write to him.

He'd have no reason to expect another note from her and, therefore, wouldn't check for them at the library. At first she thought to let him know she'd fully recovered, but it looked trivial and self-absorbed on the page. Then she began with wry congratulations on knowing more about the impending proposal than she—it was obvious now he'd been trying to pin her into confessing to the engagement with his questions, but that line of thinking led to other puzzles. Who he worked for. Why? She crumpled the latest attempt and tossed it toward the wastebasket in frustration. It seemed prudent after recent events that she not willfully deliver information into unknown hands. Optimism be damned.

No matter how curious about him she may be.

Chapter Eleven

THE NEXT DAY BROUGHT much of the same, except a blustery wind greeted Leo outside, the chill taking any hope for cheer out of their garden meal. Lord Sebastian suggested, and the prince agreed, that they'd not earn her good graces by forcing her to rough it for the small prize of their company. They genuinely delighted her then, when Sebastian lifted one end of the table, and Prince Dimitri the other. Servants scrambled about, rescuing pitchers and platters of pastries that threatened to fall. Once safe indoors, the trio carried on as though it were a perfectly normal affair for a royal pair to share a meal in the middle of the corridor. Visitors bowed and made it a polite distance away before exclaiming their confusion in bursts of hushed whispers. Her eccentric nature was surely reaching legendary proportions.

Later that afternoon, Callum knocked on her door.

"I got your message," Callum said as she ushered him in. The guard still stood watch.

"Sorry it took me so long. Father has had me answering inane correspondence and fraternizing with King Nathair. It's as if he thinks if he drowns me in boredom, I'll forget how he sprung this on us."

"So, you didn't know, at all?" Leo asked. She couldn't keep the accusation out of her voice.

"Of course I didn't, Madeline," he pleaded. "If I did, I would have talked him out of it. An official alliance with Corsair would be for show at this point. We already engage in open trade."

"But what if there's a war?" She wrapped her arms around herself and sat on the armchair by the fire.

Callum scoffed. "Leywinn is gone. Dead. Somehow disappeared after the war—it's the only thing that makes sense. Even with the forest in the way, they could have sailed the coasts to trade or send word. We've heard nothing. There is no proof Leywinn will attack."

"And the lawstones?"

He shook his head. "There's plenty we don't know about the lawstones. Maybe they degrade over time. That's not our concern right now. You will not marry Prince Dimitri. Marriage alliances are archaic. It's unnecessary."

"I suspect my brother telling me who I cannot marry is equally archaic."

"If you want him, he's ripe for the taking," his voice took on an edge of humor. "And open to the idea of any future lovers, it seems."

She dropped her face into her hands, her stomach sinking. "I can't believe he said that in front of Father."

He chuckled. "He's young . . . and very foolish." Callum sank into the couch, sighing as he leaned back. "Tell him you're flattered and send him on his way."

"Father wants me to marry him."

"When have you ever taken Father's commands so seriously?"

Leo winced as her mind was flooded with the answer.

Ah. There it is. Now we're past that useless obstinance. You're surprised that I've struck you, when any other under this crown would be lashed for such deliberate disobedience. I can assure you, Princess Madeline, your guard will be. Get out, and try not to hurt anyone else with your carelessness.

"Leo."

She blinked back to the present and grinned at him, even as her fingers threatened to go numb over a racing heart.

❖

In the evening, after the castle was quiet with sleep, Leo waited for her mentor, no longer surprised when he appeared without warning.

"When are you going to teach me how to do that?" she said when he popped in. The evening before, he'd made her spend the entire night willing the magic forward again and again, until she could sense it at will.

"Ah. Come home with me, Cub, and I'll teach you everything I know." He bowed.

She raised an eyebrow.

"So touchy," he teased. "Moving yourself with magic is incredibly complex. I was an apprentice for twenty years before my instructor allowed me to try. I managed to magic myself right into a wall. And I do mean *into* the wall. It took them hours to find me, though I have often wondered if they let me remain stuck on purpose to highlight the danger of failure. But"—he emphasized the word—"I do want to try something new today."

"You've progressed quickly," he continued. "My theory is that the burn out made you more attuned to the force that is in and around us. Most apprentices have never been through a similar experience, or lived through it, at least. When one is whole and complete, it may be difficult to distinguish between themselves and the magic. But with you—well . . ." He ran a hand through his hair. "We are never more aware of something than when it's ripped away. With that . . . and our timeline in mind, I wanted to explore this with you." He produced S. Wilford Abadacus's spell book from his inside coat pocket. "I've taken the liberty of adding some notes of advice and caution. There is much in this book you must never try, not without proper instruction and guidance. I've also added a few pages to the end. Some entry level spells I thought you'd find useful."

Leo flipped to the back and gave him a coy grin. "Your handwriting is terrible." She laughed.

Sebastian reached a hand back to squeeze his neck, a sheepish look on his face.

"Oh, don't worry." She stepped to her desk. "Mine too—see?" Leo grabbed the parchment she'd been working on and flashed it to him with a grin. Lightning fast, he snatched it from her hand, smiling like the devil himself. Her stomach plummeted through the floor as he devoured the words.

"The soldier's eyes burned, and her body burned with them." The lord read with an over-the-top drama that set her cheeks aflame.

"Hey!"

Leo was too slow. He vanished and reappeared on the other side of her bed before she could grab it from his hands. With a sound that was half delight, half indignant screech, she pursued, relieved the silence spell separated them from the rest of the castle.

"His warm hands cradled her face, their breath mingling," Sebastian continued. "He beheld her, searching—always searching—but for what?"

Just as Leo reached for him, he appeared on top of her bed.

"Sebastian!" She laughed. It was half a whine, her face molten with shame and absurdity.

"She hoped beyond hope he would find what he sought," he went on, clutching a hand to his chest, "but with a sinking heart she realized—she was but a girl. A foolish girl, one crippled by fear, one the very heavens had deemed unworthy of its gifts. She had no right to hope."

Leo ducked her head and closed her arms around herself, giving up the chase.

The lord's voice quieted, the mirth evaporating. "And so, she turned away . . . and buried the secret wish that he'd find salvation in her embrace."

When he transported again, it was to sit on the side of her bed.

He shook his head, smiling sadly. "Ashamed? Unworthy? It took me a long time to learn these feelings are nothing but rot growing in the gap between who we are and who we think we should be."

Leo forced a bitter laugh. Gods, she was such a child. "It's just a story. Don't make anything of it."

He lifted the parchment and sent it back to her desk like a feather on a phantom wind.

"I'm sorry, Cub."

"I said it's fine." She crossed the room to stand in front of the fire.

A single sprig of forget-me-nots drifted over and bumped against her arm, insistent.

She plucked it out of the air and placed it behind her ear, tamping down the corners of her mouth.

"Okay." She turned to face him, arms crossed. He stood behind the sofa now, hands in his pockets. "I suppose I could forgive you," she lifted an imperious eyebrow. "But you must swear to forget everything that's just happened," his face was indecipherable, "and you must teach me how to do that."

⬦

It turned out moving things with magic was hard. She'd hardly managed a wiggle out of the crumpled parchment they practiced on.

"You have to shape it," Sebastian kept saying. "Imagine it's an extension of your body. Visualize what you want to happen. Picture a breeze lifting the parchment."

Over and over, she chanted, only growing more frustrated.

After the hundredth time, he suggested they move on to something easier, but she declined. Her teeth ached from gritting them.

"You need to at least recenter yourself, Cub." He ran a hand through his hair. It stuck up wildly from the habit, the only evidence he grew impatient. "Powerful emotions impede your concentration. It's especially dangerous to cast a spell when under their influence, as it warps your intent."

But she had just a few more days with her new instructor and would soon be left to her own study again—probably forever.

Leo sunk down into the magic for the umpteenth time, no longer feeling awed by its presence. She opened herself to it and chanted the spell.

Nothing happened.

The lord placed a reassuring hand on her knee. "We will practice more tomorrow. For now, you need a break."

No, she didn't. She needed to do this. Their time together was slipping away right before her eyes. She sunk down again, filling her lungs until they ached. The sharp, satisfying image of the parchment bursting into the air on a gust of wind came into focus. Fearing she'd lose it, she ignored the words that accompanied the spell. Instead, choosing to throw her awareness over the entire room, snaring the magic like a fish in a net.

Then she pulled as hard as she could.

Everything exploded.

Blackness leached away, replaced by mottled color. The room was sloped and out of focus, her head angled sharply against the wood of her bed frame. She leaned onto her arms and squeezed her eyes shut, trying to clear the spots in her vision. The couch and table tilted precariously, upended. The desk was bare, its burden of ink and books scattered at its feet. Sebastian stood from where he'd landed, inches from shattering through the sea-side window.

The lord surveyed the upheaval. "Tell me, Princess." He moved, a storm cloud rolling across the room. "Do you wish to die?"

Leo glared at him from where she lay on the ground, the movement sharpening the ache in her head.

Sebastian met her on his knees, clawing her face into one hand. She hissed as he wrenched her up, so close the heat of him seeped through her nightgown. Expecting to flounder, she gripped his arm, but his hold was iron. The force of her conjured gale had snuffed any light in the room. The embers in the hearth flickered, casting eerie shadows over his face and making his wide eyes wild. Curiously, the frenzy didn't reach the quiet words that caressed her cheek.

"Because that," he murmured, "is a fantastic way to kill yourself."

The hand that held her trembled—with restraint or emotion Leo didn't know, but she didn't back down, only endured with a long-practiced, lifeless stare.

He blinked, and the intensity washed out of him like a tide. In an instant, the hard lines of his face softened. His touch went feather light, and he opened his mouth, as if to speak, but his attention trailed over her face—caught on her lips.

His jaw slammed shut as he ripped his eyes up to the question in hers.

Abruptly, Sebastian let go and stood, forcing her to catch herself on an arm. A small sound escaped her as pain shot through her neck and the ache spread, spearing into her head.

For a moment he stared her down, jaw clenched. Then he sighed, in a single moment, moving from warring waves to cold, dispassionate sea, the emotion tucked away as easily as the hands in his pockets.

Leo looked away, the fire in her doused by icy indifference.

"I'm trying to help. You shouldn't fight me."

That's what her father always said, too.

He waved an arm and the room knit itself back together. The air softened.

And he was gone.

The bed seemed miles away. Her head pounded in time with her ragged heart, and every movement sent spikes of pain down her back. Just as she settled, a knock split the air, and she jumped, jarring her injury even more. A woman in white robes entered, carrying a tray of supplies.

"I was told you needed assistance, Your Highness?" she said, cheery for such a late hour. "And I was to bring you this." She handed Leo a warm cup before surveying her. The healer tsked as she ran cool, glowing hands over Leo's neck, but the enchanted light didn't reach her eyes. It never did for the gifted fae. Already, Leo's pain leached away, and she sampled the tea. Steam licked over the rim, tickling her nose with the scent of chamomile and echinacea.

⸻ ◈ ⸻

Morning found the princess beaming at pastries and a thin vase of forget-me-nots. She'd almost pushed them off when she woke, stretching a toe against the edge of the tray placed on her bed. Relief and shame jumbled together. How would she face him at brunch today?

She needn't have worried. When Leo arrived at the gardens, Prince Dimitri stood alone, their usual table absent. Offering her an arm, he asked if they might walk together, ignoring the guards that moved to fall in line behind them.

"I thought to surprise you today," he said, and guided her through the rows of evergreen hedges and blooming spring bulbs to a perfect picnic scene; a blanket topped with fruit and several sliced sandwiches. He, or the servants, had taken care to spread it in glorious sunlight. The kind that warmed your bones if the wind wasn't chill and insistent. Leo swept her attention over the site, finding Lord Sebastian notably absent. Had she misinterpreted his apology from this morning?

"Do you like it?" the prince asked, following her look. "We could ask for a proper table if you prefer."

"No. Of course not." She squeezed his arm. "This is lovely." It really was.

Dimitri removed his coat before he sat, producing a tiny box from the inside pocket before tossing it to the side. Today, he wore a simple white tunic over brown trousers. The short sleeves showed off an intricate band on his forearm, woven with several gilded threads of metal. His leg jiggled as he tossed the box between each of his hands and Leo placed her sandwich back on the plate, suddenly afflicted by a most curious twirling sensation where her stomach used to be.

"Princess Madeline, I realize that I—" He coughed. "I—Well. You have to know this is not how I ever imagined getting married," he said with a strained laugh. Dismayed, she opened her mouth to speak, but he raised a defensive hand, cutting her off. "But," he said cautiously. "My behavior reflects me. My issues. It is not indicative of what I think of you." He contemplated the box. "I have been . . . under a great deal of pressure to secure this alliance. While it's framed as my idea, I feel I've hardly had any choice at all. I brought this." He thrust the box to her and motioned for her to open it. "As a show of good will."

The brilliant, tear drop cut sapphire set into a jewel studded band was the last thing she'd expected.

"I am serious about this, Madeline. I want this. I do not expect us to move forward as lovers, but as partners. And one day, perhaps, as friends?"

She shut the box and cleared her throat, unsure if the rapid beating in her chest was spurred on by fear or nervous admiration. "It's beautiful."

"It was my mother's," Dimitri said, though he avoided looking at her. "I don't expect you to answer now, but hold on to it. Consider it. Please. I meant what I said about leaving you to your own devices, after. People in our positions, we have to make sacrifices. I wish there were another way. All I can do is make it as painless as possible. Starting now." He gave the ground a half-smile, one arm rested against a bent knee, his other leg stretched out before him.

Leo threaded her fingers through his hand, and he looked up, surprised. She squeezed. "Thank you," she said, before letting go to slip the box into her pocket.

They ate in shy silence for a while, the possibility of becoming husband and wife creating tension in their relative isolation.

"My mother also passed. About thirty years ago," Leo said, scraping the dirt beside her with a finger. Her attendants would be horrified at what it did to her nails. "My father hasn't been the same since. She was the glue that held us together. Since she's been gone, we've—" She shrugged. "We've drifted apart. Callum is learning to be king. Father is . . . who he is—" She cleared her throat, already cursing herself for bringing it up. "I'm not sure where I fit in. I want to do something. Something great." Her face flared with the admission.

Dimitri contemplated her, a troubled look on his face. Of course, he didn't know about the deal with Sebastian. Leo tugged at the turquoise dress that puddled around her, then looked to the rows of budded flowers that still waited to bloom.

"Maybe this is it."

Chapter Twelve

SEBASTIAN GROANED AND LAID back against the sofa pillows. "How your body regularly processes this much sugar escapes me."

Leo polished off the fluffy, glazed confection she held and grabbed another. She'd asked Elaine to prepare enough treats to feed a small army, and the cook had taken her at her word. The low table before them groaned under the weight of the mountain of goods piled high. Beyond it, the hearth popped merrily, keeping the chill of the evening at bay.

"You should thank me." She covered her mouth with a hand as she spoke. "I did this for you."

"It would appear," he said, his eyebrows vanishing into his hairline. "You did this for you."

She rolled her eyes. "You apologized with sweets; I'm apologizing with sweets!"

"Yes, but I've witnessed your love affair with sugar each morning during your dally with the prince. How was it yesterday? Torture without me?"

"It—" Leo wiped her hands with a cloth, not sure how to go on. "It was fine. Good, maybe. I'm considering it—the situation, that is." She swallowed, her throat quite dry. "He had a ring." She washed the statement down with a long, long sip of tea.

Sebastian didn't sit up. "A glowing review for my cousin, I assure you. People are not his strong suit, women especially. And you're a fae. It surprised me as much as any when they suggested this alliance."

What would it mean to marry a man disturbed by fae blood? According to her father, in fifty years she could be queen of an entire people who despised the fae.

"You're a fae," she said.

He didn't look at her. "I am a weapon."

Leo had to concede. Once upon a time court wizards were customary. Typical fae magic had little value in combat, except for healers of course. Wizards were few, and often fae of noble birth, seeing as the craft required a human's lifetime of study, as well as the privilege of access to books and teachers. Those that made it through their apprenticeship usually served royalty directly, with unallied wizards posing a threat to all. Too much power. Too much risk.

The wanton destruction of the great war brought prejudice—many blamed the weapons for the decisions of the kings that wielded them. In the following years, the witch hunt appeared to wipe wizards from the three kingdoms. A small enclave practiced far to the north, but fresh fear and old hatred prevented any similar institutions making themselves known elsewhere. Hundreds of years had passed, and little but luck, a chunk of coin, and voracious reading had allowed Leo a glimpse into the craft.

"Did you apprentice to someone?" she asked.

"Yes. In Gallen. I began before King Nathair's time. It was quite the scandal that a royal had the child of a fae man. It was—" he paused and draped a lazy arm over his eyes. "It was not an easy childhood, despite—or perhaps because of—my royal relations. When I was young, my father sought to send me away, to protect me. He would have preferred I go to his immediate family, but my mother, having grown up enduring the vicious teeth of the court, knew that if I were to return, I would need teeth of my own. She is the one who suggested they send me away. My father had the relevant, distant connections and so I went, terrified, of course. My mother thought I'd come back and be her retribution. Powerful, long living royalty. I never saw her again. When I returned, she and the king I knew were dead, and his son an old man.

"Superficially, I was welcomed as a valuable asset. Human memories are short. I watched the young prince, Dimitri, grow up, entertaining him with my tricks. For now my—my skills are not common knowledge. The king likes the ace up his sleeve, but won't openly admit to it until it becomes necessary. When the prince takes the throne, I feel Corsair will take measurable steps to normalizing fae and magic there. My presence in his life has made him more open than his father, believe it or not, if only for practical military uses. If I can remain close to court, I may continue to belay the prejudice in Dimitri's heirs as well. Of course, with you as their mother, they'd be well on their way without my help."

The growing melancholy inside her evaporated, and the room grew hot with the mention of the prince's heirs. Leo banished the realization of her intimate involvement in that process if she accepted the apprenticeship and, with it, the sapphire ring in her pocket.

Sensing Leo's discomfort, Sebastian reached for the grimoire on the floor.

"Sorry. It's not a terribly happy tale, is it?" he mused, flipping through the pages.

"It's not that, Seb. I was—"

"*Seb?*" The book hid his expression.

"Is that acceptable?"

"I've been called worse. Remind me where you found this book?" He passed it to her, open toward the back. His scratchy handwriting graced the top of the page. "Book Light"

"It was passed down in an estate." Leo took a deep breath, secretly relieved he hadn't suggested they continue working on the movement spell. As the magic flowed into her, she willed it down her arms. The glow took a circuitous route before pooling in her palm.

"*Luminos.*" The word was ethereal.

Leo beamed. The illuminated orb bobbed happily back at her. It was similar to the ones he used in their first lesson. An almost imperceptible cord of energy anchored it to her. Delighted, she cast again, and again, until the touch of magic lingered over her skin. Their brightness fluctuated as she experimented.

"Excellent," Sebastian said. "Can you move them?"

Leo conveyed the command and the lights eagerly obeyed, dancing across the room until a familiar pop shattered her concentration, and they winked out of existence. She and Sebastian turned simultaneously to the letter in her lap.

Flushing with embarrassment, she tucked it primly under the couch pillow beside her. Sebastian flipped through the spell book again, failing to hide the wicked grin on his face.

"There is ever more to you than meets the eye, Cub," he said. "Though I'll admit fault for not recognizing the odds of a secret lover were high."

"And what, Lord Sebastian, is that supposed to mean? I'm afraid you misread the situation."

He hummed in disbelief. "Only that your writing betrays a romantic heart."

"I'm still mad at you about that."

"I'm still mad you misused the tools I've given you and almost got yourself killed." Her stomach dropped as he looked her over. "How's your head?"

"Better than it was." Her knuckles went white gripping the book, the unresolved conflict making her more tense than it should have. She turned to face where he lay back, glaring down at him. "You sent a healer. I guess you were too angry to heal me yourself?"

He stilled, and instead of giving her the fight she expected, his eyes went bottomless, drinking in her sarcastic tone, her anger, and she wished she could reel it back in, if only to stop him from taking it.

"I am sorry," he whispered. He set a sightless gaze against the ceiling. "Intent is everything in magic, especially when you aren't implicitly stating a goal by using an incantation. Powerful emotions muddle intent, as I was trying to tell you. Anger is one that corrupts your intent, yes—but, even more so, is fear."

Lacing his fingers together, he sat up. When he looked at her a line had formed between his brows, his eyes tumultuous and—

Blue, but impossibly dark, like the night sky, or the deepest parts of the ocean. Waves of emotion crested and broke as he looked at her, raw, consuming. His sudden vulnerability clawed at her insides, as if it were her own heart on display.

"I am not a teacher," he said, and the pain in the words leaked out, making her chest ache. "My beginning was so long ago I worry I'm rushing yours. *I* let you take on more than you were ready for. *I allowed* myself to be swayed and didn't realize the signs you were pushing too hard until it was too late. I feel both that I'm damning you with hasty and incompetent instruction and that I've no choice in the matter at all. I'm drawn to—" He paused, dropping his head. "To this. When I realized you were practicing without a teacher, barreling forward when you've hardly a toe in the sea of knowledge and experience you should have, I felt I *must* teach you while I'm here. The magic is eager for you. I've never seen it respond to another with the same ease and fervor. But to trust that I must hurry now, to trust this nebulous compulsion inside me, is to trust that our paths will diverge. Watching you hurt yourself because I've pushed you along, and feeling assured it was the only option, terrified me. And yes," His eyes met hers again, with a hint of a challenge. "I was angry with you, but I was furious with myself. All that to say . . . It's unwise to wield magic thus affected."

Leo swallowed, her throat tight. "It wasn't your fault." She'd been so eager for a teacher she hadn't stopped to consider the wisdom of the path they were on. She had no other option. "As for our paths diverging . . . maybe they won't. Perhaps I'll return to Corsair and continue my studies." A growing part of her enjoyed Sebastian's company, perhaps more than she'd realized. "As long as you care enough to be bothered if I die, then you're a fine teacher. I'd go so far as to admit I've grown similarly fond of you, Lord Sebastian." She shouldered him and turned her face up, batting her eyelashes. "I'd be sorely disappointed if I got you killed."

He grinned, the shadows falling from his face. Shaking his head, he fell back on the sofa, and she laughed as he draped his arm back over his face. "Every moment here is sweet agony, Cub."

"Now who has the romantic heart?" she asked, poking his ribs.

He pointed, firmly, without looking, at the book she held. Once she knew the incantations by heart, she wouldn't need it anymore. She'd memorized the healing spell from the first book she'd found, and a fire spell as well—although it had proven disastrous the only time she tried. Fire would take on a life of its own. Once conjured, it could live without siphoning magic from the caster, if it found fuel.

While he feigned agony, she studied the spell, 'To Ward Sounds,' and attempted to cast. Sebastian waved an arm in her peripheral. His lips moved, but she couldn't hear him. The crackling fire burned in silence. This spell pulled harder than the lights, using more energy. She released it.

"Try to put the ward around the both of us."

When she did, he pointed out the part of the enchantment that a word or two could change depending on if you want to exclude outside sounds or prevent your own sounds from being overheard.

"This spell is a shield, of a kind. So, it's often modified to contain or repel many things. Sound is only one use. Rain, wind, weapons, the magic of other wizards—anything you can think of. It's important to know it drains your power as it does its work. If an arrow hits it, your magic will take a hit too. Being drained faster than you can pull means the spell will feed on your life force. You know what that's like. So always let go before that happens."

"I've some experience with fire and healing spells, but why would a binding spell burn the magic up so fast?"

He grinned. "Why, little Cub, were you using a binding spell?"

"It's Leo," she said, though her face flushed hot, embarrassed by his delight. "And what if I was able to get a focus?" She glanced at the leather bracelet he wore. The moon-colored stone that hung from it like a charm glowed when he used magic.

"A binding spell draws continuously, which I'm sure you noticed. It will take until it is dismissed. A healing spell could have burned you out just as easily, depending on how severe the wound was."

"So I don't *need* a focus. I just need to use more manageable spells."

"Technically, that's correct. A focus is always helpful but will be imperative for large spells—and battle magic. When you don't have time to say the words, a spell focus filters your intent and ensures you're only expending as much magic as you need to. Using a spell focus can make you dependent on it, though. Many argue it's better to learn how to respect and manage the power before relying on a crutch. That way of thinking is considered archaic now. It takes a powerful, experienced wizard to use substantial amounts of magic without one. Either way, now that you know how to channel it, with practice, you'll access deeper stores within yourself, be able to hold more, be able to draw it in faster. But casting with any amount of power is a risk, even with a focus. It takes an amount of self-control few ever find in their lifetime."

Leo practiced changing the ward spell around, and Sebastian checked its soundness by tossing cookie chunks that would halt midair and drop just inches from her body.

After declaring it adequate, he ended their lesson but didn't miss the chance to smirk at the note that still waited as he disappeared.

Leo reached for the letter the instant she was alone.

I look forward to seeing you at the ball. I have something that is yours and thought to return it then. I hope you are well. My contacts say your engagement was quite a shock. I agree—Prince Dimitri would be a terrible match for you; humans do so despise magic.

how can I be
who i want to be
when half of me

is you

Chapter Thirteen

⟶

A soldier with an invitation? You must have high contacts, indeed. I certainly hope you like dancing. I'm sure you'll have no trouble finding me.

L

Fael smothered a smile as he walked back to the Aspen Inn. He hated balls and, worse, was woefully unprepared for one. Battle? Yes. Dancing? No. But the princess would meet with him—out of curiosity, if nothing else.

Satyr guffawed, his belly heaving, when Fael explained the situation. Of course, he didn't know his role as an assassin, just that he desperately needed a rush order of appropriate attire.

By lunchtime, he'd made his request at a tailor far up the main avenue toward the castle, a heap of coin smoothing over their indignation. The crowded upper streets buzzed with excitement. Meaningless chatter and overbearing perfumes engulfed him, and, not for the first time, he wished for the quiet woods of his home. After being measured and pricked of his life, Fael made his way to an apothecary. An elderly, spindly man guided Fael to a popular herb used for aching joints, citing the dosage carefully to avoid poisoning. Fael thanked him noncommittally, hoping, if questioned, the man would remember him only in passing.

Though he much preferred to dirty his hands with the blood of beasts rather than the blood of people, he'd been elbow deep in both for a long time, and should have realized this was the direction his king was headed. While Fael had been ordered to take the lives of a few unsavory nobles or criminal village leaders, he'd targeted none as high ranking as the princess. Or as undeserving.

Not that he knew her. Not beyond a vanilla scent and almond eyes. Not beyond the horror on her face when she saw the boy's blood staining her sleeve. It was a damn shame to have to kill someone who found the idea of blood on their hands so abhorrent.

He'd decided, in the middle of a restless night, that he wouldn't spill her blood like an animal. Her death may be deemed necessary, but she'd done no wrong. The king's lace-flower would be painless. It acted like alcohol at first, then caused unconsciousness before stopping the heart. He'd have to lure her out of the party, and he hoped her book would be bait enough. The plan helped him accept what he had to do. She wouldn't suffer. Not in a marriage she didn't want, and not in death.

It was the best he could do.

Chapter Fourteen

"I'VE DECIDED I'LL TELL my father I'll agree to the marriage."

She and Sebastian sat cross-legged on the floor behind the sofa, facing each other. Thankfully, the morning with the prince had gone well, relaxed. Her marriage to him would be brief, but her apprenticeship with the lord would fill a need she'd had all her life. Sebastian looked up from the grimoire. For a moment, something illuminated his dark eyes. Something hopeful, quickly guarded by the now-familiar, flirtatious persona.

"The prince is an unbearably lucky man. Though I fear he has no idea what he's gotten himself into." He returned his attention to the book, idly flipping a page. "Do you think he'd be jealous of our secret meetings?"

"Should he be?" Her tone came out startlingly suggestive, and his attention snapped back to her with predatory focus. She gave him the same indolent smirk he so loved to employ and his eyes flashed with something unreadable, but it was over before it started. Unable to bear the weight of his full attention for long, Leo burst into an embarrassed laugh, cheeks flushing. In an instant, he softened and grinned.

"You've been spending too much time with me, Cub."

"I hope to spend a great deal more," she said matter-of-factly, her attention firmly fixed on imaginary fuzz dotting the hem of her pristine nightgown.

"Come," Sebastian stood and pulled her up after him, hooking an arm around her waist.

"What are you—" Her breath caught in her throat as he pulled the two of them together. His lips were parted softly, eyes burning under heavy lids. The heat in her face speared curiously down to her belly. Her nightgown, modest though it was, had little structure to shield her from the warmth or feel of him, and Leo understood intimately that it did even less to shield him from the softness of her.

"I want to show you something," he said, his voice rough. Then his lips moved, and she caught her hands in his jacket as they lifted from the floor and spun. He braced her head against his chest as they gained speed. First, they were weightless, then formless. Both squeezed and impossibly scattered. Just when it seemed they would never make it back to solid ground, it stopped, leaving her stomach twisting. When their feet touched the floor, a chill breeze whispered its welcome.

They were outside. Sebastian hesitated for a breath before sliding his arms from her and tucking his hands in his pockets.

They'd landed on a balcony that jutted out from the highest tower of the castle. Behind them was a large set of double doors that led to one of the tower-rooms, but it was impossible to tell which one. Across the rail of the balcony lay an endless expanse of ocean. The stars overwhelmed the moonless night and reflected on the dark, still water, giving the impression of standing in the night sky. Leaning against the railing, Leo breathed in the salty air, drinking in the sight. Awe and anxiety wrestled within her. Delight and disorientation. As if she stood on the edge of eternity. One slip and she'd be lost to it.

She shivered.

Sebastian stepped beside her. His cheeks remained tipped with pink and, as they stood alone in the sky, with her city sleeping before her, and the familiar song of the waves bringing comfort in the face of new beginnings, she had the overwhelming feeling she was exactly where she needed to be.

The breeze coaxed another shiver through her body and the lord slipped a warm arm around her.

"We should go. It's colder than I expected."

Leo turned to him, unsure how to explain that she wasn't ready to leave. By the way he looked at her, though, it was apparent that he felt the same way. She sucked in a breath as he dragged their bodies together, eyes never leaving hers. The touch sent a thrill of sensation down to the tips of her toes. Sebastian traced an idle thumb over her jaw, down her neck, and threaded a careful hand into her hair. Slowly, with agonizing patience, he leaned in, and she tipped her head back, eyes closed, wholly consumed by the fire beneath her skin.

Then the screams began.

Leo ripped away, feet slapping the hard stone as she sprinted for the double doors. Beyond, her father cried out, the sound urging her faster.

An arm's length from the door, the air itself snaked around her, winding and binding until she was completely immobile. She could only dart her eyes around, searching for the attacker. Sebastian put a hand on her back as he passed, and the surrounding air stilled. Fear beat wildly in her chest.

Muffled voices came from beyond the door. Sebastian slowly eased it open, and the words became clear.

"I'm sorry it's come to this, but we need your assurance that our alliance will go forward without question." It was Prince Dimitri.

"I've impressed upon her the importance of this decision. She will—" Her father hissed, the sound turning to anguished groans.

"You did well, but the prince prefers certainty." An evil, distorted voice, a male and female speaking in otherworldly tandem, made her skin prickle in alarm.

Dimitri's voice was ice. "Do it, and be done."

A sinister red light bathed the room and illuminated the crack in the doorway. Again, her father cried out and Leo threw herself desperately against Sebastian's enchantment, silently pleading with the lord. He gave her a look over his shoulder, eyebrows furrowed. The glow of his bracelet flared in time with her struggle, and she remained stuck. Her stomach hollowed out completely. Why was he just watching? Why was he stopping her from helping him?

Dimitri continued, "King Galentya, I want your assurance that you will do everything in your power to secure our alliance."

Her father's voice was tired, but amiable. "Of course, Prince Dimitri, my daughter will see that it is the correct decision, in time."

"I look forward to the announcement tomorrow. Princess Madeline and I will leave the morning after to prepare for a wedding in Corsair. I trust you'll ensure she remains true to your promises."

"As you say, Prince. Your father will be very proud."

Besides the pounding of her heart, there was only silence as the skin-crawling feeling ebbed away. Sebastian turned with haste and grabbed each of her shoulders. They spun, quick and jarring, and appeared in her rooms again. The violent sensation left her queasy, and she fought the urge to double over as the binding magic released her.

Leo fisted her hands against their trembling and scowled. "Who was that voice?"

"I don't know." He didn't look at her. There was no way he didn't know. It had to be someone from the delegation.

"What *do* you know?" Leo asked. The accusation filled the space between them.

A bitter scoff guarded the hurt in his eyes. "If I wanted to magic you into the marriage, I surely could have figured out how to do it myself."

That didn't answer the question. She crossed her arms—feeble armor. She squeezed tight, trying and failing to hold in the wave of fear and suspicion. "And did you? Did you charm me into . . . this?"

He flinched like she'd hit him. Anger, fear, and guilt fought a brief, torrential war inside of her, but she rallied, realizing she would do far worse things for the ones she loved. She pulled on that thought, nursed it, coaxed it, until the anger grew hot enough to burn away anything in its way. "We could have stopped him." Her voice rose. "If you truly don't know what's going on then why did you stop me?"

"Why shouldn't I have stopped you?" he shouted and began to pace, throwing a hand through his hair in frustration. "Again and again, you underestimate or disregard the danger of a situation."

"I thought he was dying." She nearly choked on the words.

"And you thought you could stop a king's attacker? You're—" He cut off the words, but his hands still moved, indicating . . . all of her. No Blood of Kings. Middling magical talent. Weak. "You should have gone in the opposite direction. You should have been afraid."

"Of course I was afraid," she hissed. "I was afraid for him. I couldn't have lived with myself if I didn't try."

"You very well wouldn't have lived at all if you did." He was angry again, that same frenzied look in his eye. Maybe he didn't know exactly what was going on, but he seemed to suspect plenty.

She'd really entertained the idea of going to Corsair. It was the opportunity of a lifetime. Learning magic would mean she'd never have to be afraid again. No more restrictive escorts or whispering nobility. Rumor claimed being born without the Blood of Kings meant she was cursed. Others said she couldn't be her father's daughter.

They'd put some kind of enchantment on him. One that was supposed to ensure he compelled her to marry Dimitri. But who was the woman, and how had Dimitri hidden her all this time? It didn't add up.

Leo turned away, unwilling to share the tears that fell freely now. "Get out."

The force of Sebastian's consideration weighed on her, but she refused to meet it. Instead, she curled onto the bed, pulled the thick blankets over her entire body, and wished she could use magic to fill the aching hole in her chest.

Chapter Fifteen

Leo sent the message at first light.

Not all is as it seems. Come armed. Bring your cloak.

It was madness—that life was so easily upended; that, in the time it took for one day to turn to another, everything could change. She wasn't sure if the soldier could use the small amount of information against her, but he seemed as good an option as any for what she needed. It's not that she trusted him, rather, that there was no way to trust anyone else. Prince Dimitri could have had anyone in the castle enchanted the way her father had been. If the king could be overtaken, then she may not be able to trust even Callum.

Attendants would be in and out of her rooms all day, which meant the best chance of escape would be during the ball while distraction reigned. With any luck, she'd be well on her way by the time anyone noticed. She didn't have a destination yet, but it would be a mistake to play into Corsair's hands. Staying would mean she would be on the way to Corsair by morning and she'd never get another chance to flee. But what about once she was gone?

If she remained hidden long enough, they would leave. And if they hurt her father or Callum, they would never get what they wanted. The question became how long would they remain in Arnell—how long would they hunt her?

She would stay away until they returned to their own kingdom or the enchantment on her father wore off, whichever came first. A spell like that wouldn't work over any kind of distance, according to what Sebastian had taught her.

Leo shoved down the wave of emotion that rushed in, threatening to drag her under.

She called for food, and more food, to all the world looking dreadfully wasteful as she ate only what wouldn't do well on the road.

The thought of leaving was both terrifying and exhilarating. In a brief moment of solitude, she gathered what she could into a pillow covering. It wasn't much. She groaned—that was the least of her problems. Where would she put it? If left in the stairwell, someone might pick it up or wonder about it. She added the simplest dress she could find, and the flint and steel kept by her fireplace, then tossed the sack under her bed. Maybe she would find time to get back to her rooms.

Inspiration struck, and she called for more food. When the tray arrived, she asked that they send Elaine up—with haste. When the cook arrived, sweat beaded at her temples and her face was flushed red with exertion. Leo ushered her to the sofa and urged her to sit, pushing a cup of water into her hand.

"I really musn't stay long, Your Highness." She drained the cup with a grateful sigh. "The chatter is moving through the servants like a wildfire. There's to be a wedding?" The cook gave her a small, sweet smile. "I'm going to miss you."

Leo struggled to speak past the tightening of her throat. "I'm going to miss you, too." She squeezed her friend's hands. "I need you to do something for me." Falling to her hands and knees, she scrambled to retrieve the items. She twisted the first pillow cover over the food, then grabbed another and fit the food bag in, along with the rest of the items. On a whim, she added a few pieces of jewelry that she might be able to sell.

"Don't." The cook's skin was no longer red. Its color had drained entirely. "Don't put the jewels in there. I—I can't be caught with them."

"You're right, I'm sorry." Leo shook her head and dug out the jewels, chastising herself for being completely oblivious. Food, clothes, these things Elaine could explain away, but the jewels of a princess would land her in a dungeon cell, or worse.

Leo pressed the bag into her hands. "Just keep this down in the kitchen for me, please. If all goes well, I'll come for it by the end of the night. Don't mention it to anyone, okay?"

The cook hefted the weight of it. "You're running away? Because of the engagement?"

Leo opened her mouth, but the woman stopped her with a hand. "I suppose the less I know, the better," she said with a sad smile. "These walls have never kept you in. I can't imagine why theirs would be any different."

Attendants spilled into the room with their trays of brushes and oils and cosmetics. "Just . . . Be careful, Elaine." Leo crushed her friend in an embrace and ushered her out before sitting to be poked and prodded. Time oozed by, tortuously slow. Her fears mounted. Unanswered questions swirled in her head. More than once, she had to excuse herself to manage her breath as her anxiety threatened to steal it away. Her attendants offered minor comforts and regaled her with tales of their worries leading up to their own ceremonies. Leo smiled politely and allowed them to believe she found comfort in their reassurance.

Once her skin was scrubbed and oiled and painted and powdered with all manner of cosmetics, they pulled her hair back and twisted it with several elaborate silver pins. One steady breath later, she turned to face the dress that hung from her wardrobe. It was the color of sapphires and nearly as radiant, with gauzy off-shoulder sleeves and a heart-shaped neckline that tapered at the waist before spilling into luxurious waves. Silver embroidery snaked up one side and around the bodice, with a multitude of tiny pearls sewn in.

After strapping into another blasted corset, no less than three attendants helped her into the gown. Fresh anxiety circled in.

How would she get out of this dress?

Leo pressed a hand to her stomach, willing away a fresh wave of nausea. It only doubled as they adorned her with the assigned jewelry: trailing sapphire earrings and a gaudy sapphire necklace, boasting a center gem the size of a robin's egg. Its weight hung like a collar around her neck.

With that image stark and disturbing in her mind, she dismissed everyone, intent to use any remaining time to settle her nerves. She tucked Abadacus's spell book into her satchel and labored to pull up her skirts to loop it around her waist. Its bulk hung awkwardly at the bottom of a leg, but maybe the movement of walking and dancing would disguise it. A breath later, someone rapped on the door.

"Enter." Her voice sounded odd, but she made a show of admiring her dress in the long mirror by the wardrobe, only turning once her visitor shut the door behind them.

"Callum!" she threw herself into his chest and wrapped him in a fierce hug. "You're okay!"

He folded a gentlemanly arm around her back and squeezed before stepping back to peer down at her.

"Why wouldn't I be okay?"

She looked him over for any enchantment, but the assessment was interrupted by another knock. Her father entered. Before, she'd basked in the light in his eyes. Today, she hesitated when he held his hands out to her. "My beautiful princess." Warily, she let him spin her around. "You're doing your kingdom a great service today."

Leo's stomach flipped as she stepped back, hooking one arm with the sweaty palm of another. She had to be sure. "And if I'd rather not move forward with the marriage?" She stole a quick look at Callum, who immediately turned his attention to their father.

"You said she'd accepted." His tone wasn't quite accusing, but it was close.

Their king seemed to grow several inches taller as he moved from warmth to cold stone. His eyes settled on Leo, and dread pooled in her gut. "Leave us." He didn't spare a glance at Callum. Fear burrowed into her gut.

"No, no!" She forced a laugh. "Don't go!" Leo clawed her fingers into her brother's wrist to stop him before turning pleading eyes on her father. "I know you believe it's best I marry the prince. I understand that." She wrapped her arms around his waist, and let her face rest on his chest, as if she were still a little girl. "I'm just so afraid to leave." She let the truth of that color her words. "I need to be sure I'm making the right choice."

The king took her face in his hands and gave her a hard look. After a moment, he softened and pressed a kiss to her forehead. "You are." He backed away and offered an arm. "Come, it's time to present Madeline Leonora—future Queen of Corsair."

Tables framed the cleared center of the throne room, each smothered with a heavy blue table cloth and topped with glittering silver adornments. Towering, floor-to-ceiling windows illuminated it all, catching in the nacre embellishments inlaid on the walls. Leo sat to the left of the queen's empty throne. Callum, elevated one step, sat to the king's right. Glittering nobles poured in, the announcer's voice a muffled monologue.

"Stop , Princess Madeline." Her father didn't look in her direction when he spoke. He leaned back, at home on his throne, his chin resting thoughtfully on a loose fist. Leo tried, as she always did, to mirror his confident exterior, but her foot tapped with a mind of its own.

When the king stood, the assembly quieted. "Welcome! Welcome. Today we gather to celebrate our first step in being an allied people. Princess Madeline has accepted a proposal from the esteemed Dimitri Nathair, Crown Prince of Corsair." The crowd applauded politely. Her father reached back for her, and her legs trembled as they carried her to his side. "From this moment forward, may our people look to our Corsarian neighbors as friends." His voice rose and fell with the confidence earned over centuries of practice. "Greeting them with open hearts. Their strength, joined with ours, secures a mighty future. Soon, Princess Madeline will travel to Corsair to marry. And I'll remind myself that her absence does not mean I've lost a daughter." The word echoed into the space. He let it fade before he turned with a sweeping arm. "It means I have gained a son."

The doors to the side of the dais opened and Dimitri appeared, flanked by a sea of royal blue. The faceless delegation made their way to stand in the front row of the crowd. King Mardain Nathair remained standing at the back while his son strode forward. Admittedly, she and Dimitri would have made quite the pair. He was resplendent in white pants, a blue tunic, and a stiff, knee length cape embroidered with pearls to match her gown. The boyish waves were slicked back again. The king took Prince Dimitri's hand and pressed it into hers, and together they weathered the cheers and whistles of the people.

To her horror, the nobles began forming a long line to offer their congratulations, each hoping for an opportunity to speak with the royal couple. As the prince led her down the marble stairs, she had to be careful not to kick the satchel hidden in her skirt. Soon, the sea of faces and well wishes washed together in a blur. The prince avoided her attention, and she avoided his. Dark bags ringed his sunken eyes despite his attendant's obvious attempt at lightening them with cosmetics. Rouge hid the pallid look of his cheeks and gave life to his bloodless lips. In any other state of mind, or if he were a different person, Leo might have inquired. But he was an unknown, an enemy. And still the ball went on.

The monotony of the greetings only increased her anxiety. Each person bowed as they spoke, and she'd offer a mechanical nod before they parted to join the spinning dancers or mingle in the little puddles of gossip.

"Princess." The low voice rocked her out of her apathy.

Fael wore a long white cloak, far finer than the one he'd worn before. It enveloped his broad shoulders and clasped tightly at the neck, nearly obscuring his front. Golden thread lined the edges, its quality so apparent it might actually be genuine gold. Startled out of her fear, she smiled, something like relief spilling over.

So far, so good.

The corners of his mouth twitched, as if he fought the urge to smile back. The expression disappeared as he bowed. "I believe you requested a dance?" His eyes flicked to the prince beside her, who, after an hour of entertaining, looked through him with disinterest.

She bowed her head, accepting. "I'll find you." As he swept away, the true art of the embroidery on his cloak revealed itself in such a dazzling display that her breath caught. The whirling, masterful design came together in ribbons of gold until, in the center, they pooled into the silhouette of a roaring griffin.

its my favorite color—
green.
though they claim that it is
red.

i'm good at it—
the killing.
One,
for many.

the forest doesn't mind—
i am only One of those
here
that nourish her
with what she always planned to reclaim.

i don't feel it anymore—
the red
the silky scarlet
that binds my hands.
that strangles my soul.

that ruins the green.

i will be the One.

Chapter Sixteen

THE CROWD PARTED TO allow the princess and her betrothed their first dance. It was odd, Fael decided, to have spent so little time with someone yet to know, without reason, without doubt, that the saccharine smile they presented was an absolute falsehood. She danced with the prince like he was a lion, and his arms, like jaws, might snap down to snare her at any moment. Around the ballroom, ostentatious dresses and suits cradled crooning nobles, too self-absorbed to see, or perhaps to care, that their princess was being led, gracefully, into one trap or another. These events were a different kind of hunt. Here, it became more challenging to tell who was predator and who was prey.

Fael sniffed at a flute of champagne. In his other hand, he held a second, already dosed with the king's laceflower. The ballroom filled with polite applause as the regal dance ended, and he tracked the movements of his target as she made a graceful escape. Graceful, until she fumbled, caught for a moment in a small bulk that swung under her dress. On cue, the princess feigned another one of those smiles at a lord who helped steady her, then declined his obvious offer to dance.

While her head swiveled over the crowd, Fael felt a trouble-some sense of satisfaction that she'd declined another man to seek him out.

His fist tightened on the tainted drink. A deep breath later, he pushed his legs to move. The air was cool in the royal gardens, and she gulped it down.

"Princess."

She jumped like a startled rabbit. He tamped down hard on his instincts as she turned to him. Dread widened her eyes, but faded when she recognized him. "Fael." She sighed his name, relieved. Without hesitation, she looped their arms and grabbed a glass out of his hand. His heart constricted as she downed it at once.

It must have shown on his face. "I'm sorry, was that one yours?" She placed a demure hand over her lips, but her eyes sparkled over the hidden smile.

He shut his gaping mouth, let the realization sink in, and nodded.

"Come. Walk with me." She tugged, and he followed, al-lowing the tainted champagne to pour from the remaining glass as they went. He couldn't, very well, drink it himself. A few other couples strolled the gardens. Some sent curious looks their way, and Fael began to re-strategize. His role as the Umbri scoutmaster wasn't common knowledge, but she did specifically ask for him to bring his cloak, so he had to assume she knew who he was. Others might know too. If there wasn't an opportune moment to finish the task tonight, he would have to wait, otherwise he'd start the war Umbri sought to avoid.

Her eyes darted around the garden.

"What's wrong?" He tried not to ask, but her nervous energy grated over him.

"I'd rather not say just yet. But I find myself in great need of a distraction. Tell me about yourself?"

Since it was likely a trap, he said nothing, and the princess laughed. Bright and a little strained. Afraid. She may know who he was, but did she know why he was here? Possibly—she seemed to find entertainment in things she should fear.

Like the magic. It might present a problem. If she had the chance to use it.

She led them on a meandering path before doubling back to an open door. Heat and noise poured out of it.

"Elaine," the princess shouted, throwing her voice with an odd lilt. Someone tossed a sack out with shocking abruptness. After retrieving it, they continued touring the gardens, following the pathways to its outer edge. As the way grew steadily darker, Fael had a mind to wonder if she led him into another trap of her own. She stopped near a small grove of flowering bushes and pulled a dress out of the sack.

"Are you going to tell me what your warning was about? Why I came armed tonight?" Not that he needed too much encouragement to leave his rush order of more appropriate clothes behind.

The princess tossed the sack aside and stepped into the bushes, concealing herself.

"My father's been . . . encouraged to force me into the marriage." Her voice sounded labored, like she fought against something.

"That is not unusual for someone in your position, is it?"

"You don't understand. There's something . . ." She huffed in frustration. "You brought a knife, right?"

He palmed it with the blade flat against his forearm and extended it into the bush. A knife was not how she'd kill him either, he imagined—her reaction to blood was proof enough of that. He could disarm her with a finger either way.

Her hands were hot and clumsy when she pulled it free. "There's something wrong with the prince of Corsair." She seemed to struggle again. "I can't get this off."

"You can't get what off?"

She stepped out again, her dress askew. "I need your help. Otherwise, I'll end up stabbing myself." She offered him the knife.

Fael looked around in alarm. "What are you doing?" he said in a startled whisper.

The skin of her neck bobbed as she swallowed. "I'm getting out of here. But first I need to change. They sewed me into this dress, and you need to help me get it off."

He stilled. "Do I?"

She stepped into his space. "Yes."

The royal entitlement set his teeth grinding. "And if I don't?"

She slipped the tip of the knife between the front of her dress and the skin of her breasts. "Then you'll be carrying me to the castle half-naked and bleeding out."

He pinned her with a glare and wrapped his fist over the knife, pushing hers away. She'd delivered herself to him, a lamb to slaughter. Put the knife to her own chest. Though he wished she would, the princess didn't shy from his ire. Almond eyes set against him with obvious challenge, so at odds with the way the gentle scent of lavender and vanilla washed over him. Fael pressed the blade with intention, slitting the hard fabric, before cursing himself. He flipped the blade and braced his hands on either side of the tear. His hands likely felt too abrasive against the impossible softness of her skin. "You really should be more careful," he murmured, and with a deafening rip, he tore the top in two.

The princess blinked, her cheeks suddenly flushed. "You ripped it."

Fael couldn't help a satisfied smirk as he sheathed the weapon. "You're welcome."

Once she'd scrambled back into the bushes, he checked the perimeter for any other surprises, depositing the empty glass in the bushes.

After a moment, she stepped into view. Clothed, thankfully. The blue fabric of the first dress tangled in her legs. She kicked and prodded until it was concealed in the foliage. "Originally, I thought I'd ask for your cloak—all mine are in beautiful colors—not exactly subtle. But . . ."

Subtle was the last thing one would call his cloak. So she hadn't expected this one after all, hadn't figured out who he was. He didn't let the relief show.

"You're running?" Fael asked. He'd absently drawn his stone from his pocket and flipped it once before tucking it away. The princess's eyes tracked the movement. She seemed more relaxed now; whatever plan she had was going well, but her chin lifted at his dubious tone. The steel in her eye dared him to voice the challenge.

He held his hands up, playing the wolf cowed by the mouse. Her hair fell, long and mussed, down to her navel as she removed the jeweled pins. With graceful audacity, the princess stepped close enough to take the dagger from his belt. He crossed his arms, watching in increasing horror, as she took the auburn length into a fist above her collarbone and, mouth set in a grim line, sawed away at it with his dagger.

"You can go." She tucked his blade in her belt, completely unsheathed—and tossed the shorn hair with the hidden dress. Fael followed her to a bare part of the garden wall. Heaving the pillowcase bag over before her, she scaled it like a cat. His eyebrows rose in reluctant admiration. Obviously, it wasn't the first time she'd used this way to get out. Should he follow? If she was running, the threat of the marriage alliance would be over. Arrogant male laughter interrupted his thoughts and strangled her cry of alarm. Fael leapt into motion, taking a running start at the wall. His feet brought him up one step, two steps, and he lunged, arms stretched high overhead, so the tips of his fingers caught the top. He wrenched himself up with a groan, his muscles burning like fire until he settled, kneeling, on the foot-wide ledge.

A handful of human soldiers were scattered in the alley. One held the princess with an arm behind her back and a hand pinned over her mouth. A couple men flanked the Corsarian prince as he stood before her, not a speck on his ballroom attire. Another figure stood behind them, the dark to the prince's light. His hands were in his pockets, casual, but helplessness revealed itself the tightness of his shoulders, the set of his jaw. He didn't like this. But apparently had reason to believe he couldn't stop it.

Fael had no such qualms.

Standing, he shrugged his cloak over his shoulders, revealing the leather he wore, the sword at his side, and the bow in his hands. He plucked three arrows from the quiver on his belt and three soldiers fell—white griffin feathers buried in their throats. Panicked shouts echoed against the wall, and Fael welcomed the familiar narrowing of focus. He dropped into the confusion, rolling to break the impact. A sharp pain flared in his hip as he rolled over the sending stone in his pocket, but he came up behind the guard holding the princess and swung. The man skittered sideways, avoiding the fist aimed at his kidneys. In panic he released her, and that was all the window Fael needed. Stepping in front of her, he unsheathed his sword. Camhaoir's blade caught the torchlight and glittered, promising death.

In a moment of silence, the prince stepped forward, eyes shining over an arrogant smirk. He stopped his men with one hand and drew a thin sword with the other.

"Dimitri, get back!" None acknowledged the man with the dark hair.

The prince lunged. Fael had height and reach on him—and the prince was human—but the match wasn't so easily decided. Fael had underestimated his opponent's strength and speed. The prince matched Fael blow for blow, and they leapt back from each other, breath ragged. The prince's smirk grew into a grin at Fael's obvious confusion. They lept again, metal ringing. Neither gained the upper hand.

It shouldn't be possible.

Changing tactics, Fael feinted, turning his sword back at the last moment to drag Camhaoir over the man's ribs. The prince lept back, one hand clutching his bloodied side. The dark-haired man spoke to him in hushed tones. Fael glared, hoping he'd step into the fight next. Instead, the two remaining guards circled around, trying to flank him.

But before they could engage again, the prince cried out and dropped his sword. All attention turned to the deafening clatter of metal on stone. He doubled over, clawing at his left arm. Fael used the distraction to haul the princess to him. Her wild heart beat against his chest. He pressed his mouth to her ear. "I'm going to distract the two moving behind us. When you see an opportunity, run."

The princess didn't acknowledge the words, didn't look away from the prince. Her face drained of color. Something was wrong.

"Do you feel that?" Her voice trembled.

An unnatural stillness blanketed the cramped street. Like prey gone silent with the approach of a predator. A lightning bolt of fear made its jagged way through him when he saw why. The prince stood tall now, a distorted, too-big smile on his face. He held his arms out as if unaccustomed to their weight. Torchlight flickered in eyes that were flooded black. Fael was caught for a moment, unable to look away as their ravening gleam assessed friend and foe alike. Dimitri's eerie grin widened into something monstrous when it found Leo.

"How nice to finally meet you." A female voice reverberated on top of the prince's. The wrongness of it prickled the hair on Fael's neck. The creature's smile fell as its eyes roved over him. What was it? It casually surveyed Dimitri's body. "I can see why you have doubts, but I'm afraid I can't allow him to fail. Dimitri won't suit me for long. I have other plans for him." It flicked two fingers into the air and a knife of pure darkness shot toward them. He shoved the princess to the side and rolled the other way. To his horror, she recovered swiftly and ran toward the prince.

"Stay behind me!"

He couldn't have heard that correctly.

A soft wall of light bloomed in front of her. Magic. Hoping he understood, he drew his bow and loosed an arrow at the creature's heart. The bolt sailed smoothly past the barrier but fell out of the air before it hit its mark, as if it hit a wall. The dark-haired man shouted at the princess to stop. Fael loosed an arrow at him too, but the man waved a hand, and the arrow broke on a wall of hard air that surrounded him. Another magic user. This could get bad.

"Leo, let it go! You can't sustain it!"

Feminine laughter bubbled out from the prince, and darkness pooled in his hand. The woman wearing his body tossed it lazily at the light wall, not bothering to aim. A second wall appeared in front of Leo's, brighter and more tangible. The black magic shattered it, and the second wizard flinched. That was Fael's chance. He was going to make sure she made it out of this city.

He drew two arrows and aimed one at the prince's neck and, a second later, at the wizard's chest.

It worked.

Focused on defending the possessed prince, the wizard had dropped his magical barrier.

But he looked up as Leo shouted a warning. The wall of light before her suddenly dissipated.

"I grow weary of this." The creature lifted both arms over its head. It drew the shadows of the alley into the space between them, where they convulsed and formed into a trio of black daggers. They each shot in different directions. Fael dropped his bow and drew his sword, flicking the dark blade away in the same motion, superior sight and speed saving him as it had many times before. This time, however, his sword appeared to consume the attack, and runes along its blade glowed white-hot.

A second dagger arced back toward the princess on the opposite side, too fast. He leapt, but there was no way he could make it in time. Suddenly, a solid wall of light covered the front of her body and the dagger shattered against it. The wall crumbled, and the wizard fell to a knee, wincing, heedless of the blade that now speared for him.

At that moment, many things happened at once.

The princess and the wizard screamed in tandem, and he toppled forward. The prince shuddered and turned human eyes on the man's limp form before racing to him.

Leo ran to where the prince cradled the fallen wizard, but her betrothed bared his teeth in warning. "Go," he said, his voice hoarse. Heedless of the danger, she knelt, placing her hands on the wizard's chest.

"I can help him—"

Fael gripped the back of her dress and pulled her behind him as the prince lunged, intercepting the swinging blade with his own. He held the man's stare, offering a final, silent warning.

He may as well have been looking at a corpse.

The moonlight washed out the prince's sunken eyes and yellow skin. Whatever that creature was, it was consuming him.

"Go!" The prince's snarl echoed down the alleyway; his body curled possessively around the man on the ground. One of the remaining guards stepped toward them, sword at the ready. "All of you," Prince Dimitri ordered, blood soaking into his shirt, tarnishing the royal blue, "carry Lord Sebastian to the castle infirmary. Now!"

The human guards exchanged dubious looks but did as ordered. The princess stared, arms hooked around her midsection, until long after they retreated around the corner. Why had the wizard protected both her and the prince, when he'd made no move to stop her capture? A few people passed the mouth of the alleyway. They needed to get out. When she showed no signs of moving, Fael placed a hand on her shoulder. She ripped away, holding his dagger at the ready.

"Easy." He held his arms out, placating. It was hard to come out of your first fight. If he was being honest, it only got marginally easier with experience. The princess shoved the weapon through her belt. It would shred her clothes, or worse, if he didn't get her a proper sheath for it. She wiped her eyes on a sleeve, then her attention caught on the men he'd killed.

"We should get moving." Fael said, stepping in the way of the scene.

She hesitated. "I don't need your help."

"Yeah. I can see that." He shoved his sword into its scabbard and crossed his arms, mirroring the glare she gave him. "Wanna try again?"

"You're not safe with me. They'll send guards out as soon as they make it back." She walked, aiming for a thin road that would take them further into the city.

Fael gathered his cloak and bow, a new plan forming. Circumstances had changed. New information needed to be considered. Waiting, for now, was the prudent choice. And the alliance had been foiled, after all. That had been his task.

Remove her from the board.

Getting her out of the city, away from the cursed prince, would be good enough. She would be out of the picture, unable to play the part they'd set for her—and his king would want to know about the corrupted Corsarian prince. The princess would be safe in Umbri, out of enemy hands, and perhaps more valuable as a bargaining chip. The logic was flimsy at best, and something in him shied from the idea.

When did he start worrying about his target's safety?

A small voice in his mind sneered at the reluctance—and his failure.

She's a noble. If she knew who you were, she wouldn't spare you any mercy.

He pushed the thought away.

When he caught up to her, she trembled, face noticeably wan despite the darkness, enough so that he didn't resist the urge to place a steady hand on her back.

"Perhaps, Princess . . . But I think you'll be safer with me."

At least for now.

. . . The journey's value is lost to warlocks, and they suffer immeasurably for it. Darkness knows to seek the incompetent, the lazy, and the short-lived. If you, reader, take any wisdom from me, take this: let yourself not be coaxed into a bargain. Let your power come from a mind that is yours and yours alone.

-The Journal of S. Wilford Abudacus

Chapter Seventeen

LEO WALKED BLINDLY, CLENCHING and unclenching her hands, trying to smother the heat that lingered from Sebastian's body. She squeezed her eyes shut, willing the image of him falling to his knees, of him lying limp in his cousin's arms, to leave her. Instead, it muddled with the screams of her father and a warped voice—its mocking laughter.

It's so nice to finally meet you.

In the darkness, a familiar series of streets flashed by. The man at her side held her elbow with a steady hand, the other at her waist, an anchor. He glanced over, concern breaking through stoic resolve. Then there was a door, and rich smells that assaulted her aggravated stomach. The room was packed with people, their faces blurred in her tunnel vision. Excited voices and braying laughter pursued her as the man half-carried her up a set of stairs.

A bed. A bucket. She retched, her body's valiant attempt to purge her stomach and mind in one go. A massive orc stood in the doorway with a tray that was dwarfed by the hands that held it. The soldier moved the bucket to a corner with an air of detached efficiency, but her cheeks burned all the same.

"I didn't expect to see you again." The orc's voice rumbled in her chest.

Leo breathed, trying to focus on the sensation. There was nothing left for conversation. All focus was trained on not retching. On fighting the way her head swam. How did Prince Dimitri know how to find her? What creature had he allowed into his body? Was it related to the marriage? And Sebastian . . . The dead men in the street, breathing and laughing just moments before she'd gotten away at the cost of their lives. None of it seemed real.

Fael was busy packing, shoving a stack of papers with familiar handwriting and a journal from the nightstand into his leather bag.

"Wolf," the orc said. The word was a command.

Conceding, Fael moved to sit next to her on the bed. His shoulder pressed against hers, warm. She let the contact tether her as she struggled to ground herself.

It was an effort to focus on the firmness of the bed, the blankets in her hands, so coarse compared to the ones in her room. The smokey, warm air in her lungs. Inch by inch, she pushed down the thoughts that formed as her heart finally considered slowing down.

Fael was holding out his other arm, where blood dried over an open gash. She heaved and, graciously, he turned so his back was to her while the wound was dressed.

"We will need a carriage to pick us up here," he said. "Can you find someone . . . discreet?"

"All of my people are discreet." Grinning, the orc caught her eye. His hands never faltered as they cleaned and wrapped the injury. Perturbed, she returned the gesture half-heartedly. Clearly, he was more than a simple innkeeper. When he finished, he shouted out the doorway and then murmured to a young man who carried an armful of linens.

"You got hurt." Her voice was rough. The room they were in was long and narrow. Her sack lay by the door, the bed hugged a side wall with a table at the head, and one small window guarded against the cold on the opposite end. A set of fine clothes lay discarded on the floor.

"I've had worse. See? Like it never happened." The soldier threw her a quick smile before tugging his cloak over the evidence that remained on his sleeve, but, as with the orc, Leo found it hard to accept the comfort it offered. Some worry lay behind it, something strained.

The soldier embraced his friend, and they shared a look she couldn't decipher.

"I appreciate your help, and I wanted to ask you something." Fael drew his sword and laid it across his palm.

Satyr took it, his eyes lighting up in admiration. "This is fine work. Tuskalan, surely?"

Though it was pretty, Leo would have to take the innkeeper's word on its quality. She could cut herself with a butter-knife.

"It . . . glowed today." Fael said, "I think it reacted to magic."

"Magic? Fae magic?"

"No." Leo answered. "It seems our visiting prince is more talented than he first let on."

Satyr lifted his eyebrows at Fael. "You attacked Corsair's prince?"

Fael began unstrapping his leathers. "He attacked *her*," he said, tossing a chin at Leo.

"I'm not sure he was in control of his body," she said, keeping her eyes fixed to the floor as the soldier undressed. "Whatever came over him. It was dark magic. Perhaps a curse . . . I fear it was a shade . . . but a bargain with a shade must be freely accepted so . . ." She trailed off, unsure if the prince would want to be freed. Unsure if it was even possible.

Satyr's eyebrows pulled together. "It absorbed a shade's magic?"

"*If* that's what it was, yes," Fael said, not looking at her.

"You think I'm wrong," Leo said, cross at having been so easily dismissed.

"I think you're in shock and we have too little information to start making assumptions."

The orc cleared his throat, interrupting her heated reply. "There won't be much time," he said gently. He nodded to the sword. "What is its name?"

"Camhaoir."

"The Breaking Dawn." The orc hummed and pursed his lips in thought, the action at odds with his tusks. "I couldn't say. Though it does remind me—" He studied the blade as his voice took on the rhythm of a practiced storyteller. "In an earlier age, ancient eyes opened. Suddenly, the giant, having spent his life sleeping, woke, caught in a nightmare. He spoke with a voice ragged from centuries of slumber, and scribes labored to pen the bleak prophecy that spilled from his lips. Its final words shook the very mountain—

"Darkness is coming.

"Compelled into madness, the old one did as no other Sleeper has since done—he vowed to never dream another dream, to never sleep again. Instead, he spent the rest of his days forging blades to arm against the coming dark. Blades that demanded from him, even as he willed them into existence. From the very moment of their creation—taking. As they were born to take. With every weapon forged in the tears of his mountain, the magic of life inside him dwindled until he gave his life for their purpose. After his death, his legacy carried on, the technique passed down by a very select few who guard its secret religiously. Protected, but rarely, if ever, used—it's cost deemed too great. These are the legendary blades rumored to consume magic. Some stories say they hold on to it, store it. To aid the wielder when they need it most." Satyr offered the hilt to Fael, who accepted it with reverence.

"I've read about the Sleepers before, but there are so few written accounts. That was excellent." Leo bowed her head. "And thank you for"—she glanced at Fael, unsure how much she should say—"everything."

She couldn't stop herself from smiling when the orc's booming laugh shook his belly. The openness of it made her lighter, and it made her ache. The soldier wasn't immune either—a hint of humor creeping into his worried eyes.

"Fael pays me well for my hospitality, miss. That, and many other things. But what's more, he brings me his stories. Sometimes"—he winked at her—"I get to play a part in them myself."

Leo felt a surge of fondness for the innkeeper. She could understand that well enough.

Immediately, Fael's expression darkened, and the tension returned. "You'll need to be extra careful over the next few weeks."

Like a punch to the gut, Leo realized what he meant. Now they were both implicated in her escape. The reality of her situation poured in, threatening to drown her. Anyone who helped her—it didn't matter if they knew who she was—anyone who helped her would fall under suspicion. It would be treason.

She wasn't sure if the stricken feeling showed on her face, but Satyr lifted his tray of bandages and motioned to her to take a cup steaming on the side. Finally, he left, and she wondered if he or any others would pay for her crimes with their life. And Sebastian—

Later.

Later, she would wonder if he made it to the healers. She would question if she'd seen his chest rising and falling. She would chastise herself for not checking for the tug of magic. Why had the shield been so taxing on him? The blows weakened him too fast. It wasn't consistent. It took too much from him. Then there was the dagger. She could only hope the bolt was meant to incapacitate, rather than kill.

"Our ride is here." Fael stood by the window. He already carried his bag, her satchel over a shoulder, and her sack in his hand. He'd shed his leather armor and weapons, as well as his elaborate cloak. "It's time to go."

With a nod, she brought the cup to her lips, hoping its warmth would carry her into the long night ahead.

The aroma made her pause, brows pinching, as she wondered at the coincidence.

———◈———

She hadn't expected a carriage, but never considered it might be a merchant wagon modified to transport illegal goods.

She'd balked, but Fael insisted.

"You said it yourself; they're likely searching even now." Naturally, he offered no explanation for the hidden compartment they now lay in.

He was still as stone, his rigid body pressed against her in the cramped space. She wondered which of them suffered most. He took up the lion's share of the room with his wide chest. The wood of the compartment had threatened to slam on his nose unless he turned his head. She had little space and no choice but to wiggle in sideways between his shoulder and the frame of the box, their legs tangling together along with their bags. Arguing seemed pointless—she'd wanted out of the city, and here was the chance to escape undetected. Thankfully, the space warmed quickly. She'd never had trouble with small spaces, but when the wagon stopped and the driver loaded it down, she tensed, thoughts swirling. They would never be able to push the compartment open, not from this side, and not with the added weight that caused the middle to sag toward their prone bodies.

They listened to the squeaky wagon wheels and the clomp of horses for an indiscernible amount of time. Wouldn't they go out the front gate of the city? There was no market noise to suggest they headed in that direction. Her shoulder burned. She leaned into the soldier, trying to adjust.

"Sorry," she whispered, placing a hand cautiously on his chest to give him time to protest. When he didn't react, she pressed into him, trying to stretch her aching shoulder behind her.

Someone shouted from outside the wagon. "Halt!"

Leo jolted and sucked in a sharp breath. Fael's arms curled around her, pinning her waist and wrist. In any other situation, she'd protest against the brazenness. But this wasn't the time. She wasn't a princess anymore; she was a fugitive. A caged rabbit ready to bolt blindly, but Fael wasn't the man she was fleeing. No. His message was obvious. Don't move. Don't panic.

When she stilled, he loosened his grip but didn't let go. Voices carried over. Apparently, the king ordered all exiting carts and carriages to be detained to search for any persons matching a certain description. The driver complied with minimal complaint, though he protested as the guards broke open the bigger boxes he carted.

The tension in her body ratcheted higher. Her lungs burned for air. The boards over them squeaked, their weak middle straining under the weight of a guard. The stress pushed the boards low enough that light slipped through the cracks as it warped.

Even after the wagon moved again, they didn't. The minutes ticked by until the rumbling of the wheels muffled, having moved from hard stone to dirt. They sighed in unison. His hands fell off her, and she rolled away, pressing herself against the frame of the box to give them both the breathing room they needed.

"How far will he take us?" *How much longer will we be in here?*

"He is going to Lamel Village to the west of Arnell. That's a three-day trip."

She winced. Three days like this? "Can we ride up top?"

"I don't recommend it, Princess. No point in escaping, only to be found again."

She rolled her eyes.

"I could go up," he said. "It's unlikely I'll be recognized. You'd have more space."

She worked her jaw. The frustration made its way into her tone. "It's not the space I'm worried about."

His silence compelled her to go on.

"I can't just do nothing. I can't lie here and wait for something to happen. Or even for nothing to happen. How can you stand it?"

"You assume I spend a lot of time lying in secret compartments?"

"Don't you? You are a purveyor of information for some person or another. You spied on me. You had my room searched. You knew of the impending engagement before I did. You sourced the shady wagon through a really, really nice innkeeper who openly admitted you pay him handsomely and just happened to serve me my favorite tea. It's a very odd combination, you know. You're trained in fighting and wealthy enough to afford that lavish cloak and an enchanted Tuskalan sword. You hold yourself like a soldier, but you don't speak like one—if you speak at all. Not to mention you gained an invitation to a royal engagement ball."

He shrugged. The motion rocked against her. "My father is a noble. I used his name to get in."

"Is he?" she challenged. "Anyone I'd be familiar with?"

"No. Just a rich man with a troop of bastards and too much pride to let them wallow." There was an awkward silence. "And the cloak and sword were combat awards. They have nothing to do with wealth. And," he pressed, "are we going to ignore how you used your spells to trap me in an unlawful interrogation? Or that you asked me to attend your party armed so you could pilfer my cloak and dagger?"

"It's not the same," she hissed.

He laughed. "Really? Okay. How about the wizard back there? Do you think your betrothed noticed the way he looked at you? Don't nobles usually wait until after you're married to start extra-marital affairs?" There was something in his tone, something beyond righteous indignation that set her on edge.

She prodded him hard in the ribs. "What I do and do not do in my bed will be no one's business but my own. And the prince wasn't after my heart. He made it clear I was free to give it to whomever I chose."

"That's a lie, Princess." His voice softened so slightly she may have imagined it. "We never get to choose."

Leo crossed her arms and closed her eyes, turning to face the wood behind her as much as possible. She didn't want to talk about Sebastian. Not when the memories were still so vivid, so real.

The wheels and her mind went on and on and though Fael snored softly, sleep did not offer her a respite. Vague images haunted her nightmares. A winged beast, a monstrous, bleeding forest, screams that turned to laughter, and her father standing tall, imposing, with eyes flooded, black as the night.

Chapter Eighteen

FAEL CALLED OUT TO the driver, and a weight shifted against him. Restless and plagued by nightmares, she'd turned toward him in the night. He shook the arm that splayed out across his chest and she woke, peeling herself away, self-conscious. The wagon was still. After an eternity of listening to boxes being unloaded, the man lifted the compartment and blessed sunlight scorched their eyes. The princess all but leapt onto the ground, and he climbed out after, grabbing their bags.

"I'm going to attend to some lady business." Dark circles ringed her eyes. He marked the direction as she hurried out of sight.

"Not an easy ride, I wager." The driver was wiry under well-fitted clothes. His amiable smile no doubt served him well in Satyr's service.

"Easy wasn't what we needed. They paid you?" Fael asked, as they loaded the cart with the twice-disturbed boxes.

The man nodded. "When we loaded up, I sent it along to my family. Just in case, you know."

Fael understood. As they bid each other farewell, the princess reappeared. She glared at him, suspicious of the cart rolling away. Instead of fighting his grin, he put his back to her and made a show of kneeling down to check their bags.

"I thought we were to ride for three days."

"I never said that."

She ripped her bags away from him and donned her satchel. The violent movement wasn't enough to disguise the tension that fell from her shoulders. He didn't blame her. He knew the ache of inaction. His own motivations, however, had little to do with being stuck waiting.

This was a mercy for him. The way she pressed against him, the scent and softness of her. Her fear. Instinct drove him to protect, and his body had a hard time remembering she was the enemy when she was so close. It would be better this way.

"So, you mean for us to walk? Did it occur to you to discuss this with me?" Her arrogant tone heated him as quickly as her nearness had.

"We can't use the road." Logic. Logic was his defender. "The cart was a risk. We'll be better off in the forest." He stalked toward it, not bothering to see if she followed, but relieved all the same by the sounds of small, angry footsteps behind him.

His tension seeped away as they entered the shadows of the trees. Arnell, Umbri, it didn't matter. The forest whispered its welcome. Though it was harder than usual to hear it—

"I've led scores of men who didn't make as much noise as you, Princess," he called back without turning so she couldn't see the humor behind the bored tone. Cursing, she yanked at her skirt, yet again tangled in brambles. It would be in shreds by the time they made it to Lamel. If he were alone, he wouldn't bother stopping, but she wouldn't last long in what she was wearing, not with the chilly nights, and there was no telling what she'd packed in that pillow covering. She'd need a real bag.

"Oh, I'm sorry," she crooned. "Forgive me if I sully your name, oh King of Subtle. Wait. Perhaps I did that already."

"Perhaps." How was he going to spend days alone with this woman? "You should find another way of entertaining yourself besides berating the person who single-handedly rescued you from an engagement to whatever that creature was."

"And why, pray tell, did you do that, Great King? I'd so love to hear about your own motivations in all this."

"Why did you save the thief?"

"Why did you save me from him?"

He turned, his restraint slipping. She squared herself, jaw clenched and eyes narrowed. The smallest, sturdiest wall of willpower he'd ever seen.

"It's who I am. It's what I do," Fael said.

Not anymore. He grit his teeth and shook his head at the thought, and at her, before turning to continue. An iron grip stopped him, the delicate fingers were so at odds with their vice-like strength.

"So you say." Her dark eyes flashed. "Then why is it so hard to assume my reason is the same?"

"You," he said pointedly, "are a Princess."

"I am much more than that."

The forest had gone quiet as they quarreled. Still enough that he cast his eyes about, weary, but their only company was a breeze that snaked down his spine.

"We should keep moving."

"There isn't even a path here," the princess whined, squeezing past the crowded underbrush. "Where are we going?" She walked several yards behind, unable or unwilling to match his pace.

He stopped, allowing her the opportunity to catch up. "Through the forest," he answered.

She stopped too, refusing to get any closer. "You are infuriating."

He let half the smile show this time. "You're welcome to go back if you'd like. It's a straight shot."

Her lips became a thin, bloodless line as she contemplated him. "You wouldn't have made us get out of the cart unless you had a different destination in mind."

He crossed his arms. There was no way she'd agree to go to Umbri, yet. He needed time. "We are still going to Lamel. You need clothes. We'll need to restock by then. But no, there is no path, that's why we're here. Paths mean people. Who we are trying to avoid."

"Lamel is the first place they'll look."

"After, we will go to my uncle's farm. He lives near there."

"You say it like you're certain I'll agree to go with you."

Fael began to walk backwards, letting his instincts pull him past the bushes and brambles. Just as she was out of sight, he heard low cursing, and more tromping. He waited, hidden, until she was near.

She gasped, startled when he stepped out in front of her. He met her growing fury with an even look.

"Now that that's settled," he said, and turned on a heel to continue on their way.

The princess didn't speak again until they made camp. In fact, she'd gone suspiciously quiet. He'd whipped back in worry on more than one occasion, but each time she was some distance away, ready to look down on his concern. How was she suddenly so silent?

He expected her to complain about the tent—nothing more than hide sewn cleverly together so that he could prop it up with its thin, sanded posts.

And small. Nearly as small the smugglers compartment the night before.

Thankfully, she climbed in without protest. A new tiredness edged the movement—dull eyes, ashen skin. Had he pushed too hard? No doubt she'd be too prideful to admit it.

He hadn't even considered slowing his normal pace.

Tomorrow he'd pay more attention. He sat outside for a while, stalling. But if she made nothing of it, then neither would he. With a sharp exhale, he gathered his courage and climbed in. She used his cloak as a blanket, obviously having pilfered it from his bag, and was already asleep. The exhaustion was concerning, not least of all, because they'd have to push hard if they didn't want to be overtaken by those who might follow.

Fael left as much space as he could, but it was inches or nothing. Would the nightmares come for her again? He shoved the troublesome image away.

That thought and many others circled as the night wore on. Most, he dispelled. *Just stick to the plan.* It would work. He'd cracked his sending stone in the fight with the Corsarian prince, but in Lamel he'd contact his king. She wouldn't like it, but he would convince her it was best they seek his sanctuary. Fael couldn't be completely honest, though. There's no way she'd trust him if he gave too much away too soon.

She was safe. It was the only thought worth focusing on for now.

In the morning, the princess stretched on tippy-toes, groaning at stiff muscles. Light filtered through the canopy and lit her hair like fire. He looked away, focusing on his breakfast, but his fae hearing caught the grumbling of her stomach.

"Did you bring food?" he asked.

"Yes, I brought food," she snapped, glaring at him. He didn't take it personally; he happened to know she hadn't slept well. At all.

Her mood lifted as she went through her bag, exclaiming that her friend from the kitchen packed extra food. The spark died quickly as she withdrew a thin leather bracelet set with a round stone the color of the moon. He watched, snared by the tragic expressions that played over her face, wondering if she would rather he didn't.

He couldn't have looked away if he tried.

When she struggled to tie the bracelet on, he offered his hands. She averted her face, but held still, allowing him to tie it for her.

———◆———

It didn't take long for things to start going wrong. As they ate, his senses sharpened, realizing the birds were silent. He broke camp as quickly as possible, claiming they needed to get an early start. Instead, he pushed them in a wide circle, bringing them back around to the campsite.

They were being hunted.

Paw marks dissected the space, and he found many more behind bushes on either side, where the creatures had watched and waited. There were at least three separate beasts. Whatever they were, they worked together. Not far away, he found fresh scat, definitely that of a predator.

He'd already been carrying his bow—a quick aim often meant a hot meal—but now he drew his sword, carrying it at the ready.

"Keep that dagger handy, but try not to impale yourself with it."

"What's going on?"

"Something is following us. Trying to decide if we are worth eating." He left the explanation there, and they walked on. The princess kept closer to him, deciding against the usual distance, or maybe he slowed to keep pace with her.

Bracing himself, he turned. "Don't try to use any of your magic if things go bad. We're days away from a healer and there's no way I'm carrying you if—" he stopped, stunned into silence by two lithe, four-legged creatures sprinting toward them on silent paws. Oblivious, she raised her eyebrows at him, but he launched past, sheathing his sword, slinging his bow into his hands and knocking an arrow in a single, fluid motion.

He missed.

Then the third cat pounced.

It slammed Fael from the side, the force of it sending him and his attacker rolling, and his shoulder stung as its claws ripped free. He leapt to his feet and dragged the princess behind him. Her eyes were closed, brow furrowed in focus. She hadn't even moved.

They faced three feline creatures, each half the size of a man. Their coats were brindled black and gray, but his focus caught on their double sets of eyes. Large red eyes glinted in the sunlight, blinking independently of the normal eyes below them. He drew his sword again as the one on the left sprang forward, but its body bounced off an invisible barrier in the air. He stole a quick glance at the princess. Her eyes remained shut, brow furrowed in effort. The stone on her bracelet glowed.

As they attacked the wall, Fael noticed blinking red in the brush beside her. In unison, he and the ambushing creature leapt, meeting in the air. Camhaoir slipped smoothly through flesh and bone, but a claw snagged Fael's forearm and ripped. The pain burned through him, further narrowing his focus. The moment he landed, the princess turned to him, eyes wide with frozen panic, and he knew. The three remaining cats prowled closer, testing the unguarded space before them. Her wall had fallen.

Bracing the borrowed dagger in trembling hands, she backed away. One beast matched her step for step and two circled, trying to surround them.

With a roar, Fael swiped wildly, trying to keep their attention. A stone flew, smacking one on the face. It flinched and he lunged. The cat moved faster, but even as it darted away, his sword caught flesh. Another stone went wide, missing the second beast before them. A shock of adrenaline speared through him—the third had disappeared.

Instinct sent him rolling to the side, and he brought his sword up diagonally to shield against the weight that slammed down. Savage jaws caught in the flat of the blade, inches from his face. Using the momentum, Fael surged his arms up over his head. The beast hit a tree with a bone shattering crunch. It wailed in pain but did not rise.

Its comrades looked at each other and fled, deciding they weren't worth the fight after all.

Chest heaving, Fael watched them go. The princess stood nearby, hands clenched over her arms. After he was sure they were gone for good, he stalked to the immobilized cat and put it down, his sword a kinder death than its broken spine.

The princess watched, near frozen, and though he shouldn't, he grazed a finger along her blood-spattered face, urging her to look away from its corpse. She looked at him instead, and the depth of vulnerability was startling. Where was the fire now? Where was the passionate fighter who fiercely guarded this fearful heart? The wall of stubborn determination had collapsed, leaving that fear unguarded.

It built in her eyes again, brick by brick, and he withdrew.

. . . The dragons mourned our creation, shunning
Atlas for his vanity. Still, each wept when he fell.
In time, his children came after one of their own,
greedy for the power that spilled before. That
day, we were abandoned. Left to live in a godless
world of our own make.

-Gods and Giants, One and the Same

Chapter Nineteen

SHE PULLED AWAY, UNABLE to stomach the pity. "What were they?"

"They're kalawaras," he said, wiping the blood from his sword. "They used to keep to the Leywinn forest, but they've been pushing their territory farther out for the last few decades."

Leo swallowed. If she had been alone . . . Yet, the thought bothered her less than what she'd seen.

"I watched it die." Her voice shook. Why bother to explain? Maybe because he was the only person around for miles. Or that he had now saved her on three separate occasions. Or because he hadn't pushed her to talk about . . . well, any of it. Even now, he saw her reluctance and turned his attention back to his work. "In the magic you can—can *see* life. Everything glows with its own—vitality." It wasn't the most accurate word. She wouldn't be able to explain it in a way he would understand. "You can see it dim. It just—It pours out." Her arms ached where her nails dug in, chipped and dirty from wrestling the forest.

He sighed and sheathed his weapon. "I should have warned you. I can't leave them suffering." He bounced his palm against the pommel.

"No, it—not that one." She glanced briefly at the broken cat, but let her gaze focus beyond his shoulder, trying to put distance between herself and the words she spoke. "It was the one that surprised us. I held the shield, but I had to hold the magic too. I could sense all the creatures while I casted—the soldiers from the alley. The ones you—" She swallowed. "*They* were gone before I brought up the wall. But when *that* creature died, I watched its life force fade and it—" It was no use. He wouldn't understand the heart shattering realization that it—"It became nothing. Just nothing." The essence had dispersed, joining with the rest.

Leo's eyes wandered over his face, and a small hope in her faded when she found he'd carefully schooled it into neutrality. Disappointed, she clicked the door shut in her mind—the one that led to a room quickly filling with the horrors of the last week. Just as his mouth opened, she spun, cutting him off. "We should keep moving."

Thanks to Sebastian's focus bracelet, it was easy to maintain the silence shield. Somehow, he must have learned about Leo's stow-away bag and snuck the focus into it when Elaine wasn't around—the cook wouldn't have let him near it.

But if Sebastian knew, why hadn't he told the prince and stopped her long before she had the chance? He had been adamant that she not act on the information they had. He'd stopped her from going to her father when he needed help and neglected to help her father himself. Clearly, he had no plans to stop his cousin from kidnapping her and forcing her to marry him. Was he a coward, or just selfish? Neither rang true. Not when he'd given his focus to her and still used his magic to protect her from the cursed prince, possibly burning out in the process.

Her heart squeezed. For a week—a single week—he'd seemed sincere and flirtatious and taught her more about magic than she could have learned in years of isolated study. She'd nearly kissed him—nearly left her home, confident that at the very least she'd have a mentor. A friend.

And what of Callum? She'd warned him to be wary of their father, but there was no way to know if he'd be enchanted by the shade as well. Did fleeing put him in danger?

You wouldn't have done him any favors by staying.

It was true. What could she have done? Sebastian was right about that at least—she wasn't strong enough to protect anyone yet. Callum could handle himself.

Leo pushed the thoughts away and focused on changing the shield as she went. Silent shield, physical shield, then a mix of both. She kept the physical shield close, only an inch from her skirts. The barrier stopped the snags, pushing away briars and wily branches as she passed. The silent shield she kept an arm's length away, grateful that it made up for her clumsy hiking skills. She'd had enough needling. Before, the magic had sapped her, but with a focus it was second nature to draw in and channel her intent outward.

The forest was more beautiful than she could have ever imagined—and more terrifying. Kalawaras? She'd never even heard of such a creature. For her, beasts weren't a focus of study or leisurely interest, but Callum would have known what they were. Still, the towering trees created a breathtaking sky above—one where each canopy of leaves reached for the other, but never touched, creating a puzzle snaked through with blue. The underbrush forced their path to wander, but Fael always righted their course, guided by a sixth sense she assuredly didn't possess. They passed fruiting bushes, but Leo was too proud to ask the soldier which were edible.

That afternoon they got lucky, their relative silence and Fael's quick bow skills providing an opportunity for a hot meal sooner than either of them expected.

"We should go ahead and cook it now," he said over the sounds of the forest.

"Is it safe to stop?" Surely it was better to continue on if there were predators somewhere behind. Though, without the protection of the lawstone there were likely threats on all sides.

"It's safer to stop than it is to carry a carcass around. We don't need to give anything else a reason to follow us. Here, move that log and I'll clear this side."

Leo didn't argue. Her stomach had kept up a constant hymn, the magic demanding despite the focus on her wrist. The soreness and hunger twisted together, weighing her down. Sheer willpower, or perhaps pride, kept her going, but any opportunity to rest was welcome. Little insects skittered away as she moved the log nearer to where he'd cleared space.

"Go ahead and start the fire, I'll get this cleaned." He dropped his bags and turned away, rabbit in hand.

Leo stared at his back for several seconds before reaching for the nearest branches that littered the forest floor. Once she'd assembled a pile that seemed sufficient, she whispered the spell over her fingers and pressed it to the wood.

"That's not going to work," he said, peering over his shoulder.

"What exactly makes you say that?" she said without hesitation, but disappointment sank in as she realized he was right. The flame wasn't catching. Her efforts were rewarded only by smoke.

"The wood is too green. And you have to stack them." He sighed, and the sound set her teeth grinding.

"They seem perfectly stacked to me."

"You have to stack them correctly, so there's enough air for the fire to breathe. When it's all piled like that, it will just smother itself. Find pieces like this." He handed her a small limb, old and lighter than it looked.

She scavenged around, trying to find ones that were similar. "You'll have to forgive me if I'm not as proficient at being a fugitive in the woods as you seem to be. These aren't exactly skills Arnell requires."

He didn't deign to look at her. "I'm sure plenty of your citizens know how to start a fire."

Once he'd finished with his own task, Leo stood, rigid, as he scraped her pile away. "Here, watch." His voice softened, but only a fraction. "This will be good for you to know."

He waited, refusing to continue until she'd knelt next to him. He'd tugged up his tunic sleeves over his forearms while skinning their meal. The rabbit's blood still spotted his hands.

With practiced ease, he set drier, smaller chips in the center, and then balanced the shorter limbs over it. "Start small. Once it catches, then you can add the bigger pieces. If they're too green, they won't light. And it's usually better to avoid adding too many leaves. The more smoke you make, the more likely you are to be spotted." He produced the flint and steel, and a sharp crack later an eager spark took to the fuel. It grew as quickly as it could find purchase. "Hand me one of yours?"

She did, careful not to let their fingertips brush. Soon the flames flickered merrily, and he stood, brushing his hands together.

"Feeling up to cooking?" The question appeared rhetorical, as he hoisted a skewered portion of meat on a stick. "The trick is to keep turning it."

Despite the disturbing thought of the meat having once been adorable, the scent as it cooked was mouthwatering. Fael huffed a laugh as her stomach grumbled, all but consuming itself in its eagerness. Hunger outweighed her self-consciousness, and she bit into the greasy hunk with relish. He sat on the opposite side of the fire, leaving the entirety of the log to her and opting to rest on the ground instead.

Through the smoke, he caught her eye, grinning.

"What?" she asked, covering her mouth with a hand. The forest suffered from a distinct lack of napkins.

"Nothing. I'm glad you like it."

She'd expected sarcasm, perhaps 'Imagine the king's face if he saw you eating like that.' But the words had her face flushing all the same. She likely looked haggard and wild from their trek. Politeness was the last thing on her mind when her stomach clawed at her from the inside.

When she said nothing, he went on. "Have you ever had rabbit before?"

Leo nodded. "Almost certainly. Elaine, our cook, likes to try her hand at any dish she sees fit."

"And Elaine would be . . . the one from the kitchens—who held your bag?"

"I'm not sure that's information you need," she said sharply. Elaine would be under enough scrutiny just for being her friend. Escaping was supposed to be Leo's burden alone, and already she had a mountain of reasons to chastise herself for creating a situation she couldn't control.

They fell into silence. She got the distinct impression he wouldn't speak again until she did, whether because he was offended or wanted to give her space, Leo didn't know.

Once finished, she threw the makeshift skewer in the flames. "Will your family miss you now that you've disappeared?"

"No." He'd turned his attention to a small journal, going over whatever notes were inside.

It was her turn to wait for him to speak. After a moment, he sighed. "Bastard, remember?"

"And what of your mother?"

"She was human."

Was. Leo ignored the old ache in her chest.

"Brothers and sisters?"

"I have many, though we aren't close."

"Is that why you became a soldier?"

"Yes."

She surveyed the forest. "And who was it that taught you how to survive out here?"

He sighed again and began throwing dirt over the fire. "Perhaps I shouldn't have fed you. It seems it has only given you energy for more interrogation."

She stood and retrieved their bags. "I still want to know who sent you to intrude on my privacy."

"I still want to know why you'd put yourself at risk by wandering through Arnell alone."

"I told you. I was retrieving the grimoire."

"You know that's not what I mean."

Did she? "Enlighten me."

"Why did you want the grimoire? Do you not have enough?"

The accusation clanged through her, an echo that joined other voices. A lifetime of being told to be cautious of her weakness and being shamed for the way she fought anyway. He continued speaking, but a roaring in her ears drowned it out. "Why yes, I have had quite enough. Thank you." The dismissal was lackluster at best, but she gathered her bags and set off again, wanting nothing more than to be alone, and terrified of the thought all the same.

⊗

Three more days, he told her that night, absently turning his coin in a hand. Three days until they made it to Lamel, and Leo wasn't even sure she would be able to enter the village. Fael planned to scope it out and make sure it was safe, otherwise he'd have to get what they needed and move on. Afterwards, they'd continue their hike, aiming for his uncle's farm between Umbri and Arnell. Leo balked at the continued assumption and told him her father had a vacation home he hadn't been to since her mother died, but he waved away the idea.

"That's exactly where they'd expect you to go. My uncle's will be safe while we decide how to move forward."

Inwardly, she balked at the word 'we,' but it was hard to deny she would have been either captured or killed without his help, so Leo stifled the irritation. If she needed to break away from his plan, she'd make sure to be prepared.

Chapter Twenty

By the next afternoon, the sky had turned a stormy grey. The air was thick with the promise of rain and her skirts clung to her legs with every step.

As they walked, she practiced. She laughed out loud the first time he turned around to find her holding a ball of flame, like the reading light, in her circle of silence. Making a fire that warmed but did not burn had proven more challenging than expected, and she still hadn't got it right. Fael tensed at the sight, hand twitching by his sword. She let it die, smiling with wicked amusement. He kept those predatory eyes on her as the power receded, the glow of it dissipating. They stared each other down and something sparked in him. Just a hint of challenge. Of amused approval. The wolf turned away, deciding she wasn't a threat. She stuck her tongue out at his back.

S. Wilford Abadacus's grimoire was only half forgotten in all the chaos. On Sebastian's recommendation, she'd disregarded many of the spells, but since she could no longer rely on him to teach her, it was time to move forward. Surely, some practice would count for something—and she had a focus now.

She'd taken to reading as she walked, grateful that the silence shield stopped the soldier from hearing each time she tripped due to her inattention.

There was a spell called "Wave" which was meant to be used with water, its force determined by the strength behind the spell. Unfortunately, they hadn't crossed a single stream since they began.

The next spell that piqued her interest created a magical hand, with the size being similarly determined by the amount of power used.

Half a thought had her pulling and chanting. The draw didn't seem too much for what she wanted—a hand the size of her own. It manifested as a softly glowing, corporeal light. Satisfied, she sent it forward to pick up a twig. It lifted neatly in the air, but judging the grip was challenging, and it quickly snapped in two.

Fael spun toward the sound, but she dutifully ignored him. Out of the corner of her eye, she watched him cross his arms. Fighting a smile, she allowed the broken pieces to fall. Next, she turned her attention to a larger branch, envisioning the hand grasping not-too-firmly, and pulling it up. It didn't move. She'd grabbed it perfectly, but a soft pull did nothing. She tried a little harder, imagining the hand simply backing in her direction. The drain on her magic became a more intense. It felt odd to mime its motions with her own hand. Grab, lift. The limb relented, rising into the air, but her concentration wavered as Fael approached and she let the silence go as it fell again.

She sucked in air as the connection dissolved, feeling like she'd run a mile, surprised by the amount of control it required.

"You're not going to hurt yourself, are you?" The question seemed genuine.

"I wouldn't dare inconvenience you."

He huffed a laugh. "Just keep in mind my medical skills are middling."

"Wouldn't you rather I practice so the next time something attacks we stand a better chance? There could be more kalawaras. Or other monsters. Bears."

"The bears here are pretty low on the food chain." If he was teasing, it didn't show on his face. "Monsters are easy. We'd have infinitely more trouble if we came across other people."

She let the implication sink in. Anyone hiding in the forest wouldn't want to be found, likely for more nefarious reasons than theirs. Even if they seemed kind, there would be no way to know their intention. Worse, Leo couldn't imagine killing anyone, even in self-defense.

"And if we do meet others?" Clearly, he was capable of more than she. It had worked in her favor so far, but—

"I don't kill without reason," he said, interrupting the memory of soldiers felled by white-feathered arrows. His face had gone blank, tone flat.

"I see." She waited for her gut to turn, but fear did not spear through her as she expected. Instead, she nodded. "Then I suppose we're as dangerous as anyone else we may encounter."

For just a moment, it seemed as though his shoulders lightened, but he said nothing, only turned on a heel and carried
on.

. . . but Atlas was slain, and the giants banded together, seeking revenge on their father's killer. They twisted what should create, to bring destruction. The living nightmares that prowl outside the lawstone's protection are punishment for sins none alive can remember.

Verdas Merlin Harringbon, a Wizard's Life Before Death

Chapter Twenty-One

FAEL FOUND THE MAIN road and kept them parallel to it, but hidden in the forest. Eventually, they came across a cluster of houses, a little hamlet too small to appear on a map. Many of them were deserted. They agreed to pass it by, realizing there'd be little chance they'd find what they needed.

But it pulled at her. The foreboding feeling seemed so familiar her gut churned, and she reinforced the shield, trying to use it to block her scent too. Whatever it was . . . it wouldn't be good to be found by it. Dread curled a beckoning finger, and like a cursed fool, she followed. Fael hissed under his breath and tried to overtake her, but she silenced his irritation with a desperate finger to her lips. Warily, he drew his sword and looked around, searching for the threat.

How could he not feel it?

The unease only strengthened as Leo guided them into the center of the village. They passed one empty house, then another. The animal pens were empty too, their fences mangled. Her bile rose. Bones. Bones and blood stains, dried in the watery spring sunlight. Something had smashed several doors in. Shattered windows. At the center, the despair edged to a fine point.

A man.

A black dagger stuck in his chest.

He lay over the lawstone, sacrificed. His blood ran down in thick streams and dried, darkening to a red so deep it was black. His chest gaped open, its cavity revealing a rot that spread unnaturally fast, exposing the bones around the evil blade that claimed his life.

And under him—

Under him, the lawstone was cleaved in two.

Something had ripped apart the ancient spell that created a circle of safety, allowing all manner of magical beasts to invade.

Corsair had claimed the alliance with Arnell was necessary because they feared an attack from Leywinn, asserting the desecration of their lawstones was systematic, meant to weaken them before waging war.

That rot had finally crossed to Arnell.

But it wasn't Leywinn. The conviction of it steeled her shaky heart. This was evil, dark magic, yes.

One she had felt before.

A crash tore through the air behind them. Leo swiveled her head back and forth, trying to find its source. Fael put his arm out, motioning for her to stay still. He crouched low, footsteps silent as he creeped to the alley between two buildings and peered around. Nothing. Leo fought panic, some obscure wisdom reminding her that running from a predator made it chase after you, anyway.

Fael crossed to search the other side of the building.

That's when it attacked.

The beast hurtled out of the house on all fours, the door already splintered. Its body was a swirling shadow given form. There were no eyes, just a gaping mouth full of serrated teeth that hung open as it galloped. Its body was grotesquely thin, emaciated, but all four limbs ended in deadly claws, and when it neared her and reared up on two legs, it stood larger than a man.

She should be running. Instead, Leo stood frozen to the spot and allowed it to wrap her in the crook of its elbow, wrenching her off her feet.

Fael shouted from behind as it ran.

"Yes, she will be pleased. It does well," it said, the words leaving her mind feeling slimy.

"Let me go!" Leo battered its thick forearm with her fists, to no avail. Fael chased them on foot, but the monster had a head start and a longer stride.

"It has done it. It does well."

Realizing she wasn't going to be eaten immediately, Leo forced herself to assess the situation, blocking out the dull ache of the beast's grip. She breathed, grappling for focus, but the magic surged wildly with her fear. Gritting her teeth with resolve, she opted to do the only thing she could.

The words squeezed out of her, rushed, and the air erupted.

The chaotic gust tore her from the beast's hold, but savage claws sliced into her, and Leo flew, airborne, until colliding unceremoniously with a stone fountain. The world spun and a moment later, pain shockwaved through her chest and head. She huffed against it, every breath a slice in her lungs.

Hissing, the beast recovered, its irritation filling her mind. *"They think, they always think. But it is not so easy to destroy, no. It destroys. It does well."*

Her head lolled as she tried to find Fael.

The creature roared, the sound filled with pain. *"No. It will kill this one. It will kill them both. She will understand. She would not want it hurting."*

There he was, the glow of his sword caked over with black blood. Leo stood, then fell to her knees and heaved. The monster swiped with its unnaturally long arms, lightning fast. Fael rolled out of the way, dealing another slice to its legs before skipping backwards.

Leo reached an arm out, but the movement sent agony through her middle. She couldn't focus, and if she sent another uncontrolled blast, she wouldn't survive the recoil. Helplessness snaked around her.

Fael fought like the wind, keeping the creature moving on its bloodied legs. The beast snarled, thick saliva dripping from its maw. If it grabbed hold of him, he wouldn't stand a chance against the deadly bite.

Then Fael stumbled, his energy flagging. It propelled Leo to her feet. Pain was a drumbeat against her head. She clenched a hand over her ruined side as she walked, every step more painful than the last. With her other hand, she palmed the borrowed dagger. Fael faced away, and she was glad he couldn't see, couldn't stop her. Once he dodged another severing arm, he leapt forward in a roll, getting behind it again, taking another stab at its legs. With the monster between them, he finally noticed Leo. His face flooded white instead of angry red, but the beast had turned as he did, expecting the maneuver, and took advantage of the hesitation. Fael hardly had time to bring his sword up to deflect the claw that came up to gut him.

With its back turned, it didn't see as Leo took a few jarring strides and leaped. Something tore inside her as the dagger caught fast in the beast's back. She was the living embodiment of agony as gravity jerked her body down. Groaning, she collapsed, and it whipped its head around, one enormous claw casually flicking her onto her back and clamping over her waist. She coughed, a warm wetness coating her lips.

"That one cannot hurt us," it gloated.

She spit in its face, her blood speckling the serrated yellow teeth. Its grotesque pleasure assaulted her until a shadow fell over them both.

She grinned, tasting the blood that coated her teeth as well. "That one can."

It cocked its head back in time to watch Fael sever its body in two. The scrawny torso fell forward, and the legs collapsed. Black gore puddled on the ground beside her.

"Leo," he cursed at her bloodied clothes. "What the hell were you thinking?"

She coughed up blood in reply, pain spiking and leeching away just as quickly. He scooped her up and flew to the nearest house. The door hung off its hinges, but there was a bed. "Alright, Princess," he held each of her shoulders, "you're going to have to heal yourself. I can bandage your ribs, but I think one of them is broken. It's punctured your lung. *I can't fix that.*"

Leo nodded, but shock and adrenaline had her spiraling around and around. She coughed again, the sound rattling in her chest. Fael lowered himself to his knees at the side of the bed and slipped an arm behind her shoulders. "Leo." He held her jaw in one big hand, forcing her to look into his eyes. "You have to do this. There is no other option."

Breath wouldn't come to her. She couldn't.

"You have to."

She wasn't sure she said the words out loud.

"Fight, Leo."

Voices echoed in her mind, arguing it would be easier if she didn't.

The feeling in her legs went first, then her shredded insides became remarkably numb. Her vision swam with every labored breath, though she knew with increasing clarity that if she closed her eyes, they'd never open again.

Fael gripped harder, his hands sticky with blood. He shook her. "Leo. Open your godsdamn eyes. It's time to stop being a spoiled rotten royal who's never had to fight for anything."

Her eyes flew open as fiery anger shot through her, and with it, a fresh wave of pain.

"Don't like that? Well, Daddy isn't here to save you. Your servants aren't here to dress you or wipe your ass, and I'm sure as hell not going to coddle you. This is what you asked for. But here you are, dying. Disappointing everyone—the king, your brother, the cook." He shook his head. "Imagine how your wizard would feel. You and I both know they would all say you should never have left the castle—"

Leo rallied enough strength to shove at him, but he didn't budge. He just changed his grip from her face to her hand, holding it to his chest, the arm around her shoulders so gentle compared to the words that raked her. The iron in his eyes wavered. Almost like tears.

"Please, Leo. Just fight."

Chapter Twenty-Two

For several terrifying moments she just stared at him. When she finally tried to sit up, Fael slipped his body into the gap between her and the bed's headboard, clasping a hand over each of her arms. Once settled against him, Leo put her hands over her stomach.

Then she went still.

Her heart pounded into his chest, and he clung to it as time stretched, unable to tell if anything was happening. She coughed. It sounded like death.

After a helpless eternity, her hands began to glow. A sickening pop sent her flinching into him, and she cried out, the light dimming immediately.

He rubbed her arms. "You can't stop there."

Fael's heart leapt in triumph as the light returned, as the rise and fall of her breath became deeper. Magic illuminated the dim room, bringing more details into focus.

Pink accents decorated the walls, and wooden toys lay strewn in a corner. On top of the short bookcase sat a row of stuffed creatures, the kind sewn from flour sacks and spare buttons. Closer to the door there was what looked to be a shattered decanter, the glittering pieces scattered alongside a bloody smear.

Since before the Great War, lawstones had protected populated areas. It was a testament to their strength and longevity that none were destroyed in the battles that raged, magical or otherwise. Without one, any beast might wander in, killing for food or pleasure. For one to be broken there had to be great, insidious forces at work. They shouldn't be here.

The light petered out again and her body went limp against him.

"Leo?"

She didn't stir.

He extricated himself and laid her back against the pillows, checking her pulse, but she only made a small sound of protest and rolled away.

Asleep. She was asleep.

He peeled back the rips in the dress, disturbed by the still open wounds he found over her ribs. They, and the feverish warmth of her body, had him swallowing bile. With trepidation, he pressed a hand to her forehead, her cheek. It wouldn't be a true fever, not this fast. Memories flashed, of his arms raw and red, burned by her overtaxed body.

He would have to take it from here.

The kitchen was built in a small horseshoe, with a short bar under a window that looked out to an overgrown garden. Rummaging through the cabinets produced a variety of hand-painted bowls. After he filled a couple with water, he grabbed the soap bar from the sink, but thought better of it, choosing instead to use tools he was familiar with. Everything he needed would be in his bag—the bandages were fresh and folded, and he sent a silent thanks to Satyr for the foresight to replace the ones he'd used in Arnell. He frowned at the remaining king's laceflower as he palmed what he needed.

The princess didn't move when he ripped the side of her dress the rest of the way. He leaned a bit on her shoulder, bracing them both, before raising the small brown bottle and pouring liquor over the injury. Fael grimaced as she bucked under him, spitting curses and fighting with a blind, animal aggression. He caught and pinned her other shoulder too, spilling the antiseptic.

"Leo." She battered at his arms. "Be still or you're going to make it worse."

She stilled under him and glared, chest heaving.

The rock in his chest uncoiled, and a wayward smile spilled out. "The worst part is over, Princess. All that's left is bandages."

With a nod, her eyes drifted shut. His hands were clinical with the dressing, especially as he slid them under her dress and over the smooth warmth of her stomach to wrap it. Luckily, the blanket acted as a cover, allowing him to work blind. By the time he finished, she was sleeping soundly again.

Fael carried the bowls, one of clean water and one filled with a pink tinge that contrasted against the bowl's white and silver coloring. Once he dumped both in the sink, he spotted a sponge, and this time grabbed the soap bar before filling the bowls again.

The blood on the floor was old enough to have dried and flaked. Fael scrubbed well, but it'd had plenty of time to set into the wood. Surveying his work, he opted to drag a woven rug from in front of the fireplace to hide it. As an afterthought, he gathered the toys as well, and moved them to the master bedroom, which he locked before closing. That room would take more soap than he had.

Fael considered scouting the rest of the town, but if any creature lingered, they'd have either fled during the commotion or, more likely, would have already appeared, drawn by the scent of blood. Instead, he dropped into a chair in the sitting room and let his face fall into his hands.

They should have ridden in the cart. Predators rarely bothered him when traveling, or maybe they did, he just wasn't used to it being disastrous. Having her in tow was like leading a deer that welcomed being eaten. He groaned—and yet, if she died wouldn't it be a weight off his back? His king was a proud man. Fael would have to talk quickly to justify his decision to go against his orders, but if Corsair's prince was under the thrall of dark magic, it changed things . . . right? All he could do was get her to Umbri safely and trust that she was worth more alive than dead. After all—perhaps Arnell and Umbri should consider a marriage alliance, to gird themselves against Corsair's scheming.

Fael shoved away the image of her marrying any of the most eligible men in the Umbri court. The king did not have an unmarried son, but he had a nephew or two. Even a marriage to some of the higher nobility might hold enough weight. Never mind that Fael knew and detested every one.

She coughed again, the sound lighter, harmless enough.

He checked on her anyway.

Later, Fael scoured the garden and returned with full arms, his efforts rewarded by a plethora of root vegetables still in the ground: carrots, beets, a few small potatoes. Trips to his uncle's farm had made him familiar with their foliage, with context at least. Soon, a stew simmered in the pot over the fireplace. The beast's corpse lay unmoving in the street, but it did not tempt him. Whatever it was, it didn't seem good for eating.

Not that there was much meat on the thing, anyway.

"Fael?" Leo clung to the threshold of the kitchen, eyeing the stew. He'd had to cut the sleeve on her dress as well, and the severed piece hung over the arm that clutched it together, revealing a birthmark near her collarbone. Just a coin sized patch of skin that was darker than the rest. He pulled his attention from it as he crossed the room and locked his hands around each of her arms, pushing her back toward the bed.

"You shouldn't be walking around."

She pouted, furrowing her eyebrows and pursing pink lips as she took reluctant steps backwards. He would have laughed at the expression had he not been so irritated she risked opening her wounds instead of calling for him. "I'm starving."

He opened his mouth to argue, but a step later she stumbled and hissed in pain as her heel caught in her ruined skirt. Luckily, Fael caught her before she fell, tamping down the frustrated growl that rose from deep in his chest. Without thinking, he pulled her into him, and for a moment their faces were too close. She blinked, attention fluttering between his eyes and his mouth. Wisely, she didn't protest as he looped an arm under her legs and carried her the rest of the way. Unwilling to be swayed by the smell of her, he held his breath, hoping his heart might stop its reckless pounding.

Their eyes caught, though, as he lowered her to the bed. His aggravation fell to relief, and perhaps he was too slow to reclaim his arms.

"So," she said as he made to leave, "you wrapped me up?"

He threw a cautious glance her way. "I told you I would. It seemed like there was little choice." A phantom warmth lingering over him, one that was delighted he hadn't gotten away to easily.

"And my dress?"

He felt his face pinch with confusion. *The dress?*

"What I mean is . . . thank you . . . very much." She tilted her head to him, overly formal. Pink splotches already glowed high on her cheeks, probably from the lingering pain. "But this was all I had to wear."

No. She was definitely blushing.

It quite suited her.

Reigning in his traitorous thoughts, Fael stumbled over a quick apology. "The houses nearby will have clothes. I'm certain most didn't have time to pack before—"

There was no need to continue. Subdued, she cast her eyes about the room, and he was grateful for the rug on the floor. Her attention caught on the flour-sack dolls on the bookcase.

Don't look.

"Bandages first."

She whipped her head back to him. "I beg your pardon?"

He gave her an indolent smirk. "You got up. Alone. Then fell. Like a newborn fawn. First, I check your bandages. Then I will bring you soup."

"I'm. Fine." The words were muffled behind gritted teeth.

He crossed his arms, more than happy to argue with her.

⊗

Thankfully, the injury wasn't worse for wear, and she polished off two bowls of soup before Fael finished one. He'd either have to hunt in the morning, or hope some of the neighboring homes had abandoned gardens as well.

The princess fell back into the bed, self-consciously covering herself with the blanket as she lay down. That was his cue to leave.

It took him little time to gather the clothes he could find, unsure what size or style she would prefer. Many of the residents packed light or didn't pack at all as they fled. Some, unfortunately, were mangled skeletons scattered in the alleyways he passed.

By sunset, he'd set up a makeshift bed on the floor in her room, barring it with his body. The house itself had no door at all, and it seemed prudent to have a lock secured against whatever might hunt them next.

Little good it would do.

But the sounds of her even breathing eventually lulled him to sleep, and nothing disturbed them until the sun itself peeked over the horizon in the early hours of the morning.

"Princess." Fael prodded her thigh. She grumbled at him. "Hey, wake up. We need to get moving today." He waved the plate of charred root vegetables and venison under her nose. *That* got her attention. Once she was up and eating, he launched into their plan.

"We can't stay here. It's asking for trouble—and we have to restock," he spoke, and she nodded into her venison, utterly unaware of what she was agreeing to. He paused.

"No eye roll? No glares that could cut glass?"

As if on cue, her eyes became daggers. "Is it wrong to defer to someone I trust?"

"No." *Trust?*

"Or perhaps you'd rather I ignore all your advice and make this journey harder for both of us. After all, I'm just a blundering, useless, good-as-dead princess who should have never left her castle."

Fael winced. They weren't breezing over that, then. "I just wanted to—"

"Oh, I know what you wanted to do. And it worked. So, no harm, no foul—right?"

Her eyes said something different, but he couldn't lie and say he was sorry. "I would do far worse to protect those under my care."

Her expression hardened into something she could hide behind. Fael knew the feeling well. He waved a hand in a flourish toward the clothes he'd collected before gathering his things and leaving to wait outside the door.

Nobles.

⸻ ◈ ⸻

By mid-morning, they were trudging through an amount of underbrush that made Fael hope she'd finished healing herself before they left. Icy silence stopped him from asking. Clearly, she felt well enough to be upset with the way he'd spoken to her and, though he slowed his pace, she kept her distance.

By the afternoon, he wondered if he'd been too harsh. If he'd merely traded one kind of wound for another. Did she believe what he said? Did he?

It didn't matter.

But the thought ate at him.

Trust?

The olive branch was shaped as a question called over his shoulder.

"So what books do you like to read?" He'd seen plenty of different titles at the library.

Surprised, the princess didn't stop when he did, and allowed her steps to bring them even. He fell in stride next to her. She considered for a moment, looking sideways at him from under lowered lashes.

Fael shrugged. "What."

"You feel bad, don't you?"

"What? No, I don't."

Her eyebrows lifted. "What *books do I like to read*?"

He kept his attention to the wandering path. "Forest is big. Been a long, quiet day."

She hummed in disbelief and the silence stretched, though she didn't check her speed to get away.

When the princess finally spoke, his shoulders lightened. "Hmmm. Anything related to magic, of course. I also enjoy adventures, retellings of old myths, romance." She pulled her shoulders square, as if she expected him to berate her for it.

Instead, he shook his head, smiling. "I've never been much of a reader, but—" He cringed at the thought of admitting it out loud. The princess watched him with suspicious curiosity. "I've done my fair share of poetry—No really!" he said when she scoffed. "I first started because there was a girl . . ." The nostalgia was almost painful. "Well, it's almost always a girl that inspires a man to poetry, right?" He couldn't help a nervous laugh.

"I wouldn't know," she said, but he caught her fighting the corners of her mouth as they tried to turn up.

He fiddled with the stone in his pocket as they walked. "Anyway . . . promise you won't tell anyone? My cousin Markus would die laughing if he knew."

That finally got her to laugh, but she winced and held a hand over her ribs. She hadn't healed them, then. Fael slowed his pace. Why hadn't she let him know she was hurting?

This is what you asked for. But here you are, dying. Disappointing everyone—

He'd said it for a reason. He willed forward a bit of distance, a bit of the good soldier, putting it between him and the painful truth of their entire relationship: It would be over the second he handed her over to Umbri. And Fael couldn't regret that in the same way he couldn't regret hurting her.

It was the only way he could spare her life.

They camped early, and Fael tried not to notice the way the princess favored one side, or how she grimaced as her pack fell to the floor.

"We should have stayed at the house longer," he said. "I shouldn't have pushed you."

She shook her head. "I didn't want to stay there either . . . Do you think anyone got out?"

"It's possible." *Unlikely.*

"It doesn't make sense that the lawstones are breaking. How is it happening? They've worked for this long and now they're failing one by one . . . It's intentional."

The man's body draped over the broken stone was enough to convince Fael of the same, but he said nothing.

"Corsair says it's Leywinn," she said.

Fael shook his head.

"The histories of Arnell say they protect," she went on, "but other sources say they also act as a magical water wheel, able to focus a vast amount of magic. Some theorize each stone is connected to the others—" She hissed and held her side.

Something in him thrummed with the need to address it, frustrated by her pain and the way it made him restless, the way his gut dropped with every sign—"Why don't you finish healing that?"

"I will." she said, easing down to the ground. "I tried this morning. But I pushed too hard yesterday. I feel . . . raw. Chafed. Healing is demanding, and I haven't practiced it often. Only once, actually." The princess lifted an eyebrow at him and tucked an unruly lock of hair behind one ear.

Fael turned, setting the tent poles into the ground, hiding his grin. At least she'd forgiven him enough for the jab. "I barely scratched him," he said, draping the supple leather over its frame.

"You hurled a knife at a child. It was only a scratch because you missed."

"I didn't miss." He could feel her eyes roll, but deflected. "You know I'm going to have to change those bandages, right?" The lack of rebuttal made him turn at last to find the princess sitting with stiff, courtly posture. "*And* once you're able to heal yourself, we'll have to start our training." It was an effort to keep his features schooled as he watched the royal irritation rise.

"I beg your pardon?" she said. "I will do no such thing."

"You froze with the Kalawaras. And you blasted yourself along with the shadow creature."

"That was on purpose. I won't subject myself to whatever it is you have in mind."

"You will." He sat, stretching his legs out and leaning back on his hands. "Because if you don't, I'll leave you alone just long enough to prove how badly you need it."

She seethed, but it was the familiar, withdrawn anger of a noblewoman unwilling to risk making a scene. The kind that meant Fael had pissed her off by making a perfectly valid point.

Chapter Twenty-Three

A PREDATOR STALKED HER. *She ran, but it flickered at the edges of her vision, its sleek form a shadow never wholly in view. A man's body appeared, a griffin feather arrow in his heart. Her knees scraped on the forest floor as she knelt beside him. The broad plain of his chest already festered with a corrupt darkness, but his face—she took his face in her hands and did not hide the tears as she pressed a mournful kiss to his cheek.*

Looking up, she locked eyes with her hunter, unsurprised at the familiar challenge they held.

"How could you?" she said in a pained whisper, enraged that the beast could live, while the man lay cast away before her.

The wolf bared its teeth and advanced, its low growl promising death.

The perspective shifted and, from afar, she watched herself realize the well inside her was empty. Watched herself realize she was powerless. Again.

"You," the corpse between them sneered, "are a princess."

She flinched, and the wolf lunged. An angry scream ripped her throat as its teeth tore into her arm and held fast, pinning her to the cold ground.

"Look at me, Leo," the dead man called. She did, eyes wide, but the wolf-

"LEO."

Leo jolted awake and wrenched out of the soldier's grip, nearly taking their tent down with the recklessness of her escape. Watery light streamed through the open tent flap and Fael raised his hands, as if she were a frightened animal.

She may have been. Her pulse thrummed alongside the pounding ache in her chest. Air, it seemed, wouldn't satisfy it, but her eyes flickered over his body, whole and unmarred, and the evidence was enough to ease the serpent's squeeze of a panicked heart.

He was okay.

Fael withdrew, mistaking the sharp look for an assessment of threat. "I'll be outside," he said stiffly, before promptly sacrificing any dignity he'd mustered by crawling out of the tent.

Leo sighed, slumping back into the blankets. The nightmares didn't seem to be getting any better. That one had felt so real . . . She took a few breaths, but it was no use—she'd feel better in the sunlight.

Outside, he was already packed and ready to break camp.

"How do you always wake up before me?" Leo asked. She rummaged through the pillow sack, pursing her lips at the crumbs and stale bread that had seen better days. The cured meats Elaine stowed away had gone quickly, of course. After sinking so much energy into healing, she'd consumed anything remotely palatable.

"It's what my body's used to." He rolled up the tent, shoulders tense, not looking at her.

"Fael," she sighed. "It was just a nightmare. It wasn't you. I needed to make sure you weren't . . . hurt."

One fist clenched as he took a deep breath, rippling the muscles in his arm. "You don't have to explain." He went back to his work. "I . . . I'm sorry if I scared you."

The unexpected apology sent a pang through her chest and settled just below her ribs, warm and achy. He didn't seem to notice.

"If it's between the two of us," he went on, adopting a tone that was too unaffected to be anything but bait. "I'm not going to be the one that gets hurt." With his back turned, she couldn't see his smile, but knew it was there. It was as familiar to her now as the canopy that crowned the forest, that safety net of leaves and limbs that barricaded them from the rest of the world. She struggled through the tangle of sudden emotion, grasping for the lifeline of their familiar sarcasm.

"Well," she said primly. "At least if I were to die, you'd have excellent fuel for your poetry."

He looked over his shoulder, raising an eyebrow. "In that case, by all means . . ."

She rolled her eyes. "I need to send a message to my brother once we make it to the city." His teasing turned to silent disapproval in an instant. "I won't say where we are," she said, pulling leaves from her shirt—at least there weren't hours of preparation in the forest, "but they need to know about the lawstone, and we are far enough away now. You have a sending stone, don't you?"

"It's broken." He sighed and sat next to her. "I can take the letter into Lamel and send it through the post. Don't you think they'll know about the broken stone already?"

"I also want him to know that I'm safe." The soldier didn't give voice to whatever argument was causing the tightening in his shoulders, which meant he was learning.

"Oh," he said around a mouthful of their usual dry biscuit, "I forgot to give this to you." He tucked his journal into his pack and produced a small leather-bound book. The spark of warmth in her chest took her by surprise as he handed over the old grimoire.

Well, it was hardly accurate to call it a grimoire, since it mostly contained some obscure wizard's ramblings—part autobiography, part theory, part history, and only a few spells slipped haphazardly within, but it had been her first and only magical guide before luck allowed her to buy S. Wilford Abudacus's the day she met Fael.

It fell open to the binding spell she'd used on the very man seated next to her.

"Are you sure you want to give this to me?" Leo offered her best court smile, fluttering her lashes for good measure.

Fael shook his head and laughed, low and husky. Pleased by the reaction, she studied him, her faux-grin falling to a fond half-smile. He ducked away from the attention, making a show of dousing the fire.

"Call me a fool," he said while he worked, "but I'm thinking if you wanted me out of the way, you would have done the job by now."

She squinted. "Was that a compliment, soldier?"

Grinning now, Fael reached for his leather belt. "Well, Your Highness." His hands moved with graceful fae-born efficiency, strapping it and ensuring all his weapons were secure. "I can't say that it wasn't."

It felt like a victory.

Leo did agree to train, irritated he was right, and relieved he hadn't been dense enough to suggest she learn real swordplay. They began the next evening, having stopped well before nightfall to set up camp.

"Good. Again." In slow motion, Fael approached from behind and grabbed the collar of her shirt, exaggerating the movement as he twisted his fist to subdue her.

"Foot," he commanded. She stomped halfheartedly on his foot. "Elbow." She may have elbowed him harder than necessary. "Head." Her head thumped against his chest.

"This won't work if my attacker is as tall as you," she said.

"They may not be. Now what do you do if you're armed?"

"Politely ask them to let go so I don't have to stab them?"

"No."

She reached back and tapped twice against the soft parts of his stomach.

Though soft wasn't the word for any part of his body—which she'd learned in the last hour, as part of her *training*.

"Good." His breath spirited over the sensitive skin of her neck, sending prickles down her spine and a wave of suggestion through her middle.

She stepped away. "Good," she mimicked.

"We also need to make sure you can use the dagger you stole." His face remained blank, but Leo forced a practiced smile.

"Oh, did you want that back? I couldn't hear your protests over the beast I distracted from severing you in half."

The scar on his cheek flickered, but he said nothing, and she let the false cheer fall. She stared at him, impassive.

A breeze touched the forest, spiriting through the leaves, bringing awareness to the litany of wild sounds that came in the silence that followed.

Fael couldn't know that Leo had played this game with her father since she was old enough to talk. Presenting a steel spine was the best choice for both friend and foe in court, and while her insides may rile and an anxious heart betray her, Leo had sculpted her impassive stare over half a century. Fael had the same self-assured cockiness as any soldier. The kind that made them think they would never be the one who died—obligatory for the profession. But if she could go head-to-head with a king, she could go head-to-head with a soldier.

She stepped into his space—people were often cowed by less—ignoring that it forced her to look up at him.

When Fael didn't take an appropriate step back, she blinked, surprised. One corner of his mouth twitched. While at the house, he'd shaved, but hadn't since, and the stubble growing in didn't quite hide the scar on his cheek. Her fingers itched to brush over it. Once, she'd nearly asked how it happened, but after the kalawaras, perhaps it was better not to know—at least until they were somewhere safe. Surely, she'd faced the worst already and survived. Barely.

Thanks to his wretched mouth.

Ass.

Why did men always get the most delectable looking lips? Leo licked her own and swallowed, mouth suddenly dry. His bright eyes flashed and caught on the movement—they were the exact shade of the sun kissed leaves that framed him now, a potent green that traced her mouth with languid desire.

They'd been in this forest far too long.

Allowing her head to fall, she curtsied, hiding the blush and silently conceding. Fael's attention weighed on her as she fled back to the safety of the camp.

But when she dared to look again, he was gone.

Endlessly, they walked. Leo used some of that time to craft stories in her mind, aching for parchment to record them. Eventually, they stayed side by side, letting the sound barrier surround them both. He became a wealth of information on the forest and seemed pleased by her interest, but every now and then, when he caught himself smiling, his face would fall, and the shadowed look would be erased by a now familiar, forced neutrality. She was conflicted, too. How bad were things now that she'd fled? Sometimes the monotony of their hike lulled her, but just as often it left her mind free to worry. All the same, it became Leo's secret mission to draw out his smile each time they spoke. They could both use the distraction.

Every night, they set up camp and trained before settling down to eat. Why they waited until after, Leo couldn't fathom, but it was frustrating to no end. A few days later, he gave her a lazy grin and an infuriating explanation.

"Because it motivates you."

She swung, blood boiling over. It was only a pathetic stick—of course he wouldn't let her come at him with a real weapon—and he chuckled, skipping away. His tied up hair and that devilish grin only sharpened the fae angles of his face.

"You're a bastard." She said, swinging again. Fael stepped away, only to step back in on her downswing. A warm hand wrapped around the fingers of her weapon-hand and held fast.

"Bastard, at your service, Your Highness." His other hand pulled back on her opposite elbow, pressing their bodies together. She slammed a heel down, nailing his toes. He didn't flinch.

"There it is," he said, a hint of satisfaction coloring the words.

"There's *what*?" She yanked herself away, irritated by the way his words and approval danced over her skin.

He stepped forward, overwhelming in his size, but she refused to give him ground. "There's. The fight. We need." He threw an arm to the side. "You probably won't ever have the luxury of being evenly matched with your opponent. You are small, but you're also holding back. Believing you are weak will get you killed. You're not at home anymore, Princess." He pointed at the ground between them. "This is the place for the savage parts of you."

Leo rolled her eyes, and he just stared, arms folded. Instinctually, she accepted the challenge, but broke away from the intensity immediately, disarmed by the luxurious heat that speared down to her navel. "Fine," she said. "You'll have my earnest effort—but only if from now on we include magic training."

He blinked, the only sign she'd taken him by surprise.

⚬

Naturally, Camhaoir shattered the shield on impact. The runes that ran along the side lit up. It wasn't a language she recognized.

"It's really never glowed like that before?"

"No. As far as I knew, it was just a glorified heirloom."

"It did light up with the shadow beast, though."

He pondered the blade for a moment. "I've slain many beasts. None caused the sword to react before the prince."

"Do you think it's related to Satyr's story?"

Fael shrugged, lifting Camhaoir again and nodding for her to draw up another shield.

Leo shook her head. "You'll have to grab a branch. The sword saps my magic in a strange way."

When he approached again, he wielded one like a club. "Ready?"

Leo nodded. The drain as the club bounced away was manageable with the focus. After a couple more test swings, he attacked in earnest, and she countered by reinforcing it before it could dim. Sweat beaded at her temples by the time the club broke. Fael tossed the kindling toward the fire and brushed his hands together.

"That went well." Moving across the campsite, he drew Camhaoir again. "Next, try to attack me."

"What? No." Her voice had risen an octave.

"Think I can't handle it?" He grinned and waved the longsword like it was a toy. "Enchanted blade, remember?"

She fought the curl of her lips in response.

"I'm a soldier. Attack me, and if I get hurt, heal me just enough to keep me alive, and leave the rest—so I'll suffer for my stupidity."

Leo's mouth fell open. "That's *barbaric.*"

He winked, clearly keyed up at the thought of the challenge, bouncing on the tips of his toes. She drew up two of the book lights. Harmless—but he didn't know that. His eyes narrowed as they flew, approaching from either side. He caught the first with a sideways slice and danced away from the second. Leo darted it up high and meant to drop it down on top of him, but at the last moment, he rolled. It vanished under his blade in an instant, and he smirked as she brought forth a handful more.

He met or maneuvered away from each one, impossibly fast, effortlessly aware.

Utterly fascinating.

She'd never seen anyone move with such brutal grace. Pressing harder, she eventually caught him in the back of the head with a cheap ambush from around the trees. He whipped around and caught her grinning.

He laughed. "What was that? That didn't even hurt!"

"Technically, I don't know any offensive magic." Amusement shouldered its way past the embarrassment of looking at him. His face and neck positively glimmered with sweat. His chest heaved. The look in his eye had something ferocious and victorious in her rising to meet it. Fael sheathed his weapon, eyebrows knitting together.

"But you used it to get away from that beast."

"*That* is not what that spell is supposed to do. It's just what happens when you try to use the power without concentrating."

He shook his head. "But why didn't you concentrate?"

Leo huffed at the ignorant question and went to sit, prodding the fire with a long stick until the embers flared up to claim the offering. Just the thought of the beast encounter threatened the peace she'd had since they left the creature in two pieces behind them.

"Some of us aren't fearless, soldier. What was it, anyway?"

"I'm not fearless." He plopped down and dug through his bag for a waterskin. "And I don't know. Though if I was the one about to get eaten, I might not have been able to concentrate."

"I don't think it was going to eat me," Leo said, disturbed. "It said it was delivering me to someone."

Fael choked on his water. "It *said?*"

"You couldn't hear it? Saying my weapon couldn't hurt it? Or that it was going to take me back to the woman that sent it?"

"I did not hear that," he said, suddenly impassive. The coin—though up close it looked fatter than a coin—appeared in his hand and he rubbed his thumb over the engravings, refusing to look at her.

The tone had her hackles rising already. "What?"

Silence.

"You don't believe me."

"I did not say that," he said, voice never wavering.

Her blood heated, anger rising as her eternal guard, but sudden exhaustion tempered the indignation. She stood. "I'm tired. Night."

"You haven't eaten."

"I'm not hungry."

"That's a lie."

Leo ignored him and crawled into the tent, squeezing as close to one side as possible. Luckily, she didn't mind the smell of leather. There was a small sound at her feet. A hard biscuit and a soft apple had appeared in front of the still-swinging tent flap. For a moment she considered leaving them, and in a different life perhaps her bitterness would have won. But she was hungry, and reluctantly grateful. The tart apple disappeared in a flash. The biscuit took some gnawing but did the job, and she lay down, mood lighter.

She still hadn't found sleep when Fael joined her. He pretended not to notice, careful to keep to his side. For some reason, she remained unsettled long after his breathing became deep and even. When she adjusted for the umpteenth time, her hip accidentally brushed against him, and she bit down a yelp as a huge, sleepy arm hooked her waist, clumsily pulling their bodies flush together.

"Shhh. I've got you," he whispered, voice thick with sleep.

Leo froze, waiting for the rush of adrenaline that would send her heart into a tailspin, but Fael heaved a deep breath, nestling his cheek against her head.

Then he snored.

Instead of succumbing to surprised panic, she grinned into the darkness. He was asleep. He was asleep and she should move away and save him from the embarrassment he'd no doubt feel upon waking—even if her smile broke wider at the thought of his mortified expression.

When she tried to ease away, he groaned in protest. The low rumble against her ear, and the commanding arm tightening around her waist sent unexpected shockwaves down to the tips of her toes, all but melting her into the floor of the forest. Gods, he really was blessedly warm. And he smelled good too, like pine and . . . something sweet and earthy that she couldn't place. She breathed deep, eyelids already heavier, her own exhaustion warring with her good sense.

Maybe his mortified expression would be worth a little mortification of her own.

it is a law of nature
that if you do not feed something
it will die

so i don't

i Starve the warmth
i do not feed its hopeful embers
its curious fingers of flame
whose feather-light touch has seared
a brand over the ice
that is my chest

i Starve it
so that the innocence
does not turn to ruin
does not wreck
this man
whose home has never been anything but wood

i would not survive the blaze

im not certain i will survive the hunger

Chapter Twenty-Four

———➤———

THANK THE GODS THEY would make it to the village today, because Fael wouldn't last much longer. Not if he were alone with her. Not if he had to watch her light up with the magic she commanded or watch her lips curl into the satisfied smile that often followed. Not if he had to spend one more night as a guardian keeping vigil as she slept, waiting for the telltale signs of the nightmares that meant the walls of her mind had finally come down, allowing all the darkness and terror she'd carefully kept at bay to sweep in. If, again, she curled into him and found peace. If, again, he had to untangle them as the sun rose and feign an early start to spare her pride or her modesty.

Sometimes his own modesty . . . often his own modesty.

Gods, he was a mess.

Despite his body's eager reaction, none of it mattered. None of it. She was grieving, traumatized, and floundering.

And he needed to stick to the plan.

Fael couldn't quite call it luck, but encountering the broken lawstone before they made it to Lamel was good timing. He'd seen nothing like the obliteration they'd passed on the way here—an entire settlement of people vanished, consumed.

The silence of it.

Whether any could've fled, he didn't want to consider. The shadow beast and the kalawaras attack were proof enough that travel came with its own risks, and unarmed village folk would be prime targets for any hungry forest predator.

If he could find the cause, Umbri would have time to prepare. How, he didn't know. It wasn't his job to find solutions anymore. His job was to report. The king needed to know about the Corsairan Prince and his apparent possession, about the princess's rejection of his proposal and the alliance, and about the broken lawstones. Greater minds than his would work together to puzzle out any connection, and Fael would continue to ensure the princess didn't end up in enemy hands.

They set up camp long before the sun went down.

"You'll stay here while I scout ahead." He waited for the stubborn set of her jaw, or the cross-armed glare, but she just continued creating a tent of twigs the way he'd shown her.

"Okay," she called over, "see you before nightfall?"

"Yes." He shifted on his feet. Leo whispered something he couldn't hear, and a spark of flame grew sticky on her fingertips. After the fire caught, she rubbed her hands together, smothering the unnatural flame. He cringed. Why didn't it burn her?

"I thought you didn't know offensive magic?" Fael was stalling, and he knew it.

She glanced back at him, warm eyes crinkled in a half-smile. "I don't."

"Why not use the fire?"

She scoffed. "And burn down your forest?"

Fael bounced his hand on the pommel of his sword as she grabbed that old leather-bound book and used her pack as a pillow, settling into the forest floor like it was a plush mattress. The ends of her newly sheared hair curled unevenly around her chin—did Arnell's princess know there were bits of the surrounding woods captured in it? Neither of them had bathed for days, yet she wore the shredded leaves like a crown. They contrasted against her pale skin and full, freckled cheeks, giving her the aura of a royal woodland nymph.

She arched an eyebrow at his attention, and offered a slow perusal of her own, eyes roving from his supple boots to the worn leather armor. A blazing heat trailed after her gaze, and, with it, a rush of satisfaction.

Until the look caught on his scar.

Fael turned on a heel and marched away, making a considerable amount of noise, mood souring with every snap and sweep of brush.

<hr>

An hour later, Lamel appeared. It mirrored its capital with tall buildings and bright colors, but where Arnell smelled of the sea, Lamel had to make do with fountains. They grew from every available space, sometimes emerging right into the middle of the main cobblestone road. People gathered around each one, reading or talking. Some sat on their edges, playing instruments for coin.

Most large cities had a post system. It took a few days, sometimes longer, but a broken sending stone meant there was little choice. There were stiff consequences for tampering with mail in all three kingdoms, but it was still too much of a risk to get in contact with King Treveri with information about the princess while still in Arnell. Fael handed her letters over and, with assurances that they would find their recipients by the end of the week, the young man slipped it into a full bin being sorted by workers who paid Fael little mind. For a fraction of a second, he lingered. It might be a mistake, but that wheel was already in motion.

Outside, the streets became more crowded as the evening drew near. Lamel, like Arnell, was dominated by humans and fae. Still, a couple of gruff dwarves argued as they passed. A giant-kin towered over the crowd that split before her. She was at least three heads taller than the tallest fae and trailing after a group of finely dressed nobles that wrinkled their noses at a pantless faun playing a pan flute for coin.

He'd read Leo's letter, of course, and she, like him, had included no damning evidence of their plan to go to the farm. It both relieved and ate at him—the blind trust the princess readily extended to those around her. Gods knew there were plenty of threats waiting for that exact opportunity.

His temper flared, fingernails biting into his palm as he squeezed a fist to crush the thought of how others might take advantage of their situation. If he were optimistic, he'd claim she had an intuitive knack for deciding who was trustworthy—but he'd been on his way to assassinate her when all this began. Only luck or some divine intervention caused him to fail and whether he was thankful for that or not, he couldn't erase the attempt with a jaunt through the woods, no matter that he protected her now. No. She had zero self-preservation. Had likely never needed to cultivate it, royal as she was. He needed to be the eyes and ears for both of them if he expected her to survive.

Fael chose the busiest tavern in the area. A woman in a low-cut blouse and stained apron greeted him fondly before shepherding him to a table in the densely packed room. "First time visiting Lamel?" she asked over the din.

"No. I have family that lives this way. Shame what happened to the village down there."

"Isn't it just awful?" She shook her head, lips pursed. "Our Emilia, she works here too, she grew up there. She hasn't heard from any of her family."

"Has the king said what he will do about it?"

A group of men at the next table looked over, not bothering to hide their interest. One of them sneered and spat. "I don't think the king much cares. With the princess kidnapped and all. What's one small village when Arnell is looking to war with a whole nation?"

Fael didn't have to pretend to be uneasy. "Why would the king want to go to war over the princess's disappearance?"

"Over her *kidnapping*," the man enunciated over a missing bottom tooth like Fael didn't quite understand. "The Umbri champion is the one that done it. Ya heard of him?" The man dropped his voice to a dramatic whisper. "The Wingbreaker."

A hush fell as more tables turned at the name. Fael willed his body to still, to ease into calm anticipation.

"I'll get you that drink." The woman winked as she moved away. He flicked his eyes around the room, marking the exits.

The man's eyes glittered with glee as those around him looked on, some with rapt attention, some with weary fear. "They say he snuck into the engagement ball and stole her." He snatched his hands forward. "Right out from under the Corsairian prince." He grinned. "And the nose of her kingly father, too." There were a few nervous laughs. Some swiveled their heads, looking to see if the wrong people were listening. "They found her dress ripped to shreds in the castle gardens. Guards, dead. Griffin feather arrows in their throats. The people saw em' spiriting down the street, his gold n' white cloak flying behind em' like the spirit of the legendary beasty was on his very heels. Corsair's own prince came through here, searching for his lost love."

"And how would you know that, Hartman? You can't possibly have seen him. You never leave that stool." A fae woman dropped a tankard in front of Fael and raised a skeptical eye at the storyteller. The handkerchief tied in her hair did little to hold back the puff of tight curls. Her dark skin flickered in the light of the blazing fire as she held his stare in warning.

The man only turned back to his table, subdued, and slowly normal conversation stirred up around them.

"Don't let him scare you off." How she could tell Fael was more than ready to leave, he didn't know. He ordered food and kept his ears open, but no one brought up the rumors again. On a whim he asked if they kept any desserts around, and exchanged enough coin for the meal and a thick slice of fruit cake. He wrapped it up, thinking it might help soothe any disappointment the princess felt about being left behind.

The general store had what they needed. The sapphire necklace the princess offered to help pay was more than useless, but he hadn't told her that. No shopkeeper here could afford to buy it, and trying to sell the piece would scream suspicion. Just asking would put a target on their back. Still, he bought another set of trousers and a warmer shirt—gods he hoped they'd fit her—and a bag she could carry on her back.

When he left the shop, the sun was touching the horizon. A few guards walked in pairs, too alert to be casual, the royal crest glinting on their armor. Whether they guarded this city's lawstone or searched for the princess, he wasn't sure, but Fael had no plans to find out. He cut through Lamel toward the forest, perpendicular to the main road, but stopped short. Pinned to a notice board beside one of the many fountains, was his likeness, and that of the princess. In her illustration, she smiled, the crown and long, braided hair the vision of royal perfection. Juxtaposed beside the portrait was his own scowling face. They'd drawn his brows more angular, and his eyes held an aggressive intensity. Of course they thought he'd kidnapped her.

He bared his teeth at the hefty sum below the posters and moved on.

Dread turned his gut, knowing she was alone as dark clouds crept overhead. He met the treeline and fell into the shadows of the forest, blending with them. Moving *toward* his target, not away. This time, he made no sound as he ran, letting instinct guide him. Scent, and sight, and sound and all the little nuances that became useless and overwhelmed in a crowd came forward to take charge. His fae heritage gifted him superior senses, but most of all, what truly made him known was the way he could move. Soundless. Following a trail no other could see. He never manifested the magic of the fae and had no desire to wring it from tattered books.

This was his gift. Carving himself into an apex predator had garnered his reputation, his name.

The Wingbreaker.

Once, he'd used it to ensure the safety of his home. Now? Now he was part idol, part mouthpiece, part assassin.

Teeth grinding against the burn in his legs, he pushed harder, leaping over fallen trees, dodging tangled thorns. He didn't flinch at the cries of startled animals. By the time he made it back to camp, chest heaving and covered in sweat, his thoughts had sorted themselves into a semblance of order. They would continue west, avoiding all settlements on the way to Umbri. Then rest at his uncle's farm, sort out the kidnapper nonsense, then move on to Umbri proper. Finally, once the princess was out of the way, and safe at the castle, Fael could check all the towns and villages on the border to be sure their lawstones hadn't been targeted as well.

The rain started just as he arrived back at camp. The princess had banked the fire, though the smell of burning wood still hung in the air. A sudden anxiety wrenched him and a few strides later, he threw open the flap of the tent.

Leo gasped and sat up, clawing his prized-cloak-turned-blanket to her chest. "Fael!"

He grinned at the admonishment, relief loosening the coil in his gut. "Miss me?" he said, squeezing into the space next to her.

"You're so sweaty!" She batted him away. "Did Lamel not have baths? And you didn't have to sneak up on me like that!" Her annoyance was edged with the same relieved humor he felt.

"I'd be afraid without me, too," he said, pulling his wet shirt off.

"I almost stabbed you." She displayed his dagger braced in a slender fist.

He shrugged. "You could have tried."

She just fixed him with a bored look that was meant to remind him she'd have no problems stabbing him in the future.

Fael held her stare, still grinning. Her bored look folded into a reluctant half smile before she looked away. It could have been the darkness, but he could have sworn the most interesting pink tinged her cheeks. Huffing, she threw the cloak around her and lay down, facing away.

But the beast of the forest hadn't released its hold yet. Fael's eyes locked on the curve of her shoulder, trailed up her neck. Reaching out, brushing her short hair aside, he bared the soft column of skin, relishing the surprised hitch of her breath as he leaned over, close enough to feel the warmth of her on his lips. Gods, her scent had his voice coming out lower than he intended.

"I brought you a slice of fruit cake."

And he really shouldn't have.

Because she sat up, beaming like the fucking sun.

And he was lost.

Chapter Twenty-Five

FAEL PUSHED THE PACE, and the forest seemed happy to see them through. It would take at least another week to get to the farm, and they needed to put as much distance as possible between them and the—

The wanted posters. He'd said there was an official bounty on their heads. What did Father think? Did he barrel into a rage? Blame her? If he could tell magic swayed his actions, there was no indication. Surely, Callum, at least, would resist the idea of bounty hunters dragging her home. Without the enchantment, Father would come to realize she'd made the best decision for everyone. Wouldn't he? Leo sighed for the hundredth time—she'd really hoped to go into Lamel, eat something more nuanced than a hunk of meat on a stick, sleep in a bed.

Bathe . . .

Unfortunately, that dream was long gone. They planned to avoid all populations of people on their way to his uncle's. So when Leo finally heard rushing water, she pushed past to jog toward the sound, magic keeping her steps silent as he followed behind. There was a wide creek, hardly a foot deep, but thankfully it ran fast and crystal clear.

She squealed when she turned to find the soldier already undressing.

Fael laughed. "There's no modesty in the woods, Princess," he said, shirtless, well-defined, and neatly unfastening his belt. "Baths here are to get the job done, not to *soak*." How he made the word sound like an insult she didn't know. Gods he was beautiful. "We get in, rinse, and get out. It's too cold for anything more than that." He jerked his chin at her clothes, urging her to get on with it. The thick belt hit the ground, then he tugged at the laces of his trousers. Seeing her petrified look, he smirked and turned away, as if that would be enough to spur her forward. It only served to put the broad muscles of his back on display and gave her full leave to appreciate the sculpted nature of his arms. Fate was unbearably cruel, she decided, as the clouds parted to cast light over his excellent form and shaggy, shoulder-length hair, illuminating the hues of blonde and gold. He stepped out of his trousers and boots, turning to her, hands held out as if to say *"It's not that big a deal, right?"* At least his undergarments left something to the imagination. Hardly anything.

Not that there was *hardly anything*.

She glued wide eyes to his sun-kissed face, as if they weren't just devouring everything about him. His own gaze glittered with challenge as he backed into the water. Chin up, she watched him go.

She swallowed once.

Twice.

Absolutely not.

Crossing her arms, Leo stomped upstream, Fael's mocking laughter ringing as she fled.

A few strides later, there was a splash, like he'd let his massive, body fall into the water. How long do you have to traipse around the woods to look like that? Banishing the image, she moved faster.

The stream widened. Once out of sight, she paused and tugged at the laces of her new bottoms, wanting to get the whole thing over with. Further ahead, water rushed heavy enough that curiosity, and a tug low in her belly, had her moving again.

A waterfall. Not enormous, but easily three times the height of a fae male. It cascaded into a round pool in front of her, the dark, still waters betraying their depth. Carved bricks marked its edge, now overgrown in some places and missing in others. Lazy fog drifted over. A kernel of feeling bloomed in her gut. The atmosphere was . . . almost spiritual. Crashing water drowned out the noise of the forest, leaving an unwieldy sense of calm. She touched the water, surprised to find that it was warm. Elated, and unwilling to question good fortune, Leo undressed quickly, fetching the vanilla soap from her bag. With a sigh, she lowered herself over the edge, slightly disturbed that there was no shoreline to speak of, just an immediate drop. The warmth soothed away any concerns, however, and the small feeling grew. As she dipped under, a sixth sense caught the edge of . . . she wasn't sure. Something familiar in the water's embrace. The sensation was so familiar that she kept her eyes closed as she broke the surface, and allowed herself to sink, not into the water, but into the part of her that could see what eyes couldn't.

It was a pool of . . . magic? The water was there, yes, but the magic flowed just the same, settling here, in this place. Why? Leo dragged herself back up, the density of what flowed in making her feel too-heavy. Had she opened herself to it? No, but couldn't quite keep it out either. It was potent and invigorating. Warning bells went off in the back of her mind, but her eyes were too heavy to open now, and the heady feeling coaxed a rich, blissful smile to her face. She'd never felt like this—strong.

Was this what it felt like for Callum? For her father? Leo would never have the Blood of Kings, but this raw power claimed her with every pump of her steady, steady heart.

Suddenly irritated, she scowled at the unease that tainted the feeling. Shooing it, as if it were a nagging fly. Mirth exploded a second later, and she laughed, twirling in the middle of the pool. The water carried her, cradled her. She could stay. Here. No cursed prince, no secrets, no bounties or broken lawstones. Only this place. It was hers, after all.

It was hers.

Distantly, the forest splintered. A wave of sound rushed closer, and both Leo and the power stilled, readying to pounce. She cocked an ear over her shoulder and waited for whatever thought to come forward with a challenge.

She didn't need to look, or even turn, to see it. Its essence glimmered, a spirit in shades of blue, taking such detailed form she didn't need sight to know a giant-kin approached. No. Not a giant-kin. A true giant. Bigger than any she'd ever seen.

Without seeing, she saw the scowl on his face, the angry fist at his side. His other hand clenched something, perhaps a weapon. This was more than the life force she could usually sense. This was his essence—what made him.

Leo was fully naked under the water, but as the magic continued to pour in, there was no space left for embarrassment, or shame, or fear. She squared her shoulders and did not deign to turn and acknowledge the intruder as he stopped short, glowering from the shore. The stillness grew, her magic an adder ready to strike.

His voice carried over like a landslide. "Get out."

She attacked. Rage like she'd never known scorched her from the inside out, ripping her eyes open at last. She felt their glow, her entire body illuminated, barely holding on to the power that continued to seep in. Wordless, formless magic condensed, and she wielded it against his mammoth form. The giant held a massive obsidian shield and appeared only mildly surprised as she continued to throw bolt after bolt. The blasts that would annihilate him bounced off its shimmering surface. A blood-curdling scream razed her eardrums, and the water rose. Magic poured as it was spent, an unending supply lapping eagerly at her skin. The pool continued to solidify until she stood on a rippling tower tall enough to bring her face to face with her opponent.

Their eyes locked, and she wiped the astonishment off his face with a blast that slammed him back. As he staggered, she laughed again, the sound warped in roaring ears.

"Leo!"

She whipped around at the shout. Had to pull back, hard, on the reins of magic that rejoiced in finally being found. Hesitation had the power coalescing as the current pushed through, insistent. She was a dam against the raging flood, trying to place the familiar figure that stood, mouth gaping in fear and bewilderment, on the shore below. Memories stirred. But who—

Something smacked her and exploded into a cloud of dust. The force knocked her over the edge of the pillar and she plunged, careening toward the pool below. With a shudder, her lungs solidified, magic now as rigid and chill as a block of ice.

Absently, she knew that the tower of water, severed from her control, would fall. Knew that, if she couldn't stay oriented as the wave shoved down, she'd be forced to swim blindly. The chill crept down her limbs, and Leo rallied against it, readying herself to fight the pull of the water.

But in the end, she hit the surface like it was solid ground, and did not wake when the world crashed down around her.

Chapter Twenty-Six

WATER THUNDERED DOWN, THE pool overflowing in waves. Fael watched where she'd gone under. Waited for her to pop up sputtering mad.

One breath.

Two.

The water still roiled with her impact when he leapt in.

The soldier plunged into a darkness that snaked around his arms, dragging him into slow motion. He fought to the surface and sucked in as much air as possible before shooting back down. Painful pressure built in his ears as he sought the bottom. Too soon his lungs ached, forcing him up, but alarm blared through him over the sluggish response of his body. He'd never find her. Not like this. The surface clung, as if it didn't want to break. With a final desperate surge, Fael pushed through, gasping. He drew in a sharp breath as a shadow loomed over him, intending to dive again, but a mammoth hand hooked around his torso, plucking him from the water.

"Be still, man of courage," the ancient voice said as Fael struggled against the giant's grip. "She is here, too."

At the shore, the giant let him slip unceremoniously to the ground, and his legs collapsed, body trembling from the exertion.

She was here. He brushed his thumb over her freckled cheeks, wiping the water away.

Pressing a finger to her neck, he leaned close to listen for the breath that whispered out of her. With a sigh, he sat back, relieved, if not confounded.

She was okay.

A completely new feeling washed through him a moment later, godsdamn him.

Fael swept his cloak over her and leapt up in search of her clothes.

Glowering at what was no doubt the largest giant he'd ever seen, Fael quickly retrieved her pack from the edge of the pool. The frigid air and his wet clothes already sapped the embarrassed flush from his body.

"What did you do to her?"

The giant knelt at the edge of the clearing, looking harmless enough now, one six-fingered hand securing the huge obsidian shield against the tree beside him. Fael saw no weapons, but a being his size wouldn't need one.

"It is called a Maik Morta," he said, watching Fael with steady eyes. The soldier studied him in turn. The male's red hair fell over a simple brown and patchwork fur cloak, the braids long enough to reach his stomach. "It is an enchanted powder that stills the magic flowing through one who wields it."

"No such thing exists." If it had, the Great War wouldn't have been as devastating as it was. War wizards, according to the histories, were a one-man garrison. During that time each kingdom kept at least a handful, with more pushed into training to replace them. A concoction that stopped a magic user would have been invaluable, well known, and used on a mass scale.

"It does." The giant paused, reading Fael's silence. "There is magic in all of us, man of courage. Maik Morta would be a weapon that leaves no victors."

Leo didn't stir. Uneasy, he stood, stepping over to put himself between her and the giant that studied her too-curiously.

"What is this place?" A statue stood by the waterfall, overgrowth making the likeness of the god Atlas almost unrecognizable. A pair of iridescent wings waved slowly on the cliff side, and it took Fael a while to recognize that it was a moth half as big as he.

His attention was torn away as the giant dipped his head. "I will answer when she wakes. You will carry her?" He stood, long legs carrying him up, at least five times the height of a man.

"Where are we going?" Fael shouted. "How long till she wakes?"

"If you do not follow me," the giant called down as he strode into the trees, "she will not."

Chapter Twenty-Seven

IT HAPPENED SLOWLY. FROZEN veins thawed. Her hands prickled painfully as feeling returned. The warmth intensified, becoming more insistent. It moved down her throat, settling somewhere in her middle to burn through layers of ice. A silent crack resounded and Leo gasped as her lungs broke free, the scent of sweet, smokey air accompanying the flood of awareness.

"Leo," Fael sighed. "You had us worried."

It shouldn't make her smile that he'd used her real name. *Wait. Us?*

Her eyes settled on the giant behind him.

Leo tried to rise, but the swimming in her head and the gentle press of his hands carried her back down. "Easy," he murmured. There was a small cup in his hand, and a sickly sweet taste in her mouth.

"Another, man of courage," the giant said, motioning Fael over. He stirred a pot—large enough she could have bathed in it—but filled the cup from a much smaller pitcher on a table towering with ingredients.

The cup trembled in her still-thawing fingers, and Fael braced a warm hand over hers as she tipped the tonic back. She winced at the cloying taste. When he set the cup away and turned back to her, their hands collided on the bed, but instead of pulling away, he reached for the other and drew them together, cocooning them in his own.

"Your hands are freezing," he grumbled. His pupils were dilated in the dim light of the cavern. Torches and the giant blazing fire lit the room well enough, but complete darkness hugged the spaces beyond. They were underground. The giant continued fretting over his stew, adding a tableful of vegetables before dumping what she could only guess was an entire deer into the pot.

Fael's attention hadn't wavered. He watched with an intensity that confirmed the feeling that something had gone very, very wrong.

"What happened?"

He released her hands and huffed. Actually huffed, and looked backwards, annoyed, at the giant male who merely lifted the index finger of one hand while spooning a sample of his stew to taste.

"We will discuss it over dinner, it seems. How are you feeling?" he asked, brushing her hair back. The casual gesture pierced her heart.

As close as she'd been to crumbling lately, her first instinct was to pull away. She willed her body into stillness, preferring the strength of rigid stone over the puddle she'd become if allowed to dwell on why, exactly, someone might seek to offer any substantial comfort.

He froze and sat back, face shuttering, but she followed, pulled in as he pulled away. The fur blanket tickled her fingers. She and Fael occupied a small portion of the biggest bed she'd ever seen. Hoping she didn't look as dead as she felt, Leo mustered a bit of inner royal and gave him a slow perusal. He sat, cross-legged, damp shirt clinging to his chest, hair hanging in wet clumps around his face.

"Did your clothes have a bath too?" she croaked, her throat ragged.

Fael crossed his arms and lifted one unimpressed eyebrow. "Is it the thought of me bathing that makes you blush like that?"

"No!" *Yes.*

He smirked, clearly pleased enough to forgo the sanctuary of steely remoteness.

But what had happened in between a shirtless Fael and here? She'd fled. There was a pool of water. Leo racked her brain, unable to summon any memory beyond that hope to bathe.

But something had happened. Her limbs were heavy with exhaustion, and her stomach gnawed at her with fervor—both pointed to magic. A hundred little hurts made themselves known as she moved, the worst being her neck and shoulder. Fael, too, seemed exhausted.

Behind him, the giant approached, aiming for the foot of the bed. When he sat, they popped up slightly with the shift of the mattress. He held his own giant-sized bowl. His voice rumbled through the cavern, "I would serve you, but . . ."

Fael dropped to the side of the bed, rummaged through their bags, and returned with a hearty fae-sized portion for each of them.

"This is extraordinary, Lord . . .?" Leo prodded, enjoying a heavy spoonful while waiting for the answer.

"I am Tor. Son of Skir."

"I am honored, Lord Tor. I can only assume you've done my friend and me a great service in welcoming us into your home." She never imagined a giant might live in a cave, though it seemed cozy enough.

"It is my duty, my lady." He dipped his head. "You are not the first magic user I've wrested from the Pool."

"The Pool? I don't . . ." she trailed off, glancing at Fael. He wore an odd expression.

"The Well of Atlas, or one of them. I am a guardian." Tor faced her head-on, as if he expected the revelation to stir something in her memory.

Leo gave him a blank look.

His head cocked to the side. "You do not know about the Wells?"

Fael still wasn't looking at her. Leo shook her head. "I know the story of Atlas though—that when he was killed, it released his magic into the world."

Her chest rattled as he cleared his throat. "It is not a story. It is a history. Now, magic lives as a sentient, nebulous, all-encompassing creature. Wizards like yourself prefer to believe it is a resource ripe for the taking, but it has its own desires beyond your own."

Sebastian hadn't said anything like that—only that emotion influenced magic. Although, now that she considered it, Leo often felt the eagerness or restlessness of the energy she pulled in.

"It," Tor continued, "like all living things, needs care and nourishment. It flows like the wind, settles like water into wells—many undiscovered. In the past, they were molded into a sanctuary where the essence might rest before continuing on its way.

"Once, worshipers came to make wishes, to treat the ill, but over time the magic became unpredictable, dangerous. It stagnated, reluctant to move on. Over time, the worshippers forgot, and wizards came for it—though never for altruistic reasons."

Leo flushed. Did he think she sought the place he guarded? "We stopped to bathe—I didn't know . . ." she said, wide eyes beseeching Fael.

"We're only passing through to Middlewood," the soldier confirmed.

Tor wasn't so easily convinced. "Only a fool would choose the forest over the main road."

Neither Fael nor Leo cowered at the unspoken challenge, both rushing to speak at once.

"I'm fleeing an arranged marriage—"

"I don't disagree—"

She grinned at him, and he returned it with an incredulous laugh. "Fleeing an 'arranged marriage'?"

Leo shrugged nonchalantly, fortified by the grin that continued to widen on his face. "Among other things." His laugh echoed on the wall, cut off by Tor, who cleared his throat. They both whipped their heads back to the giant.

His eyes flicked between them, and Leo flushed deeper as his gaze lingered over the blush on her cheeks. "I'm inclined to believe you. Those who seek this place now—they hope to harness the well, to tap a source of power that, in theory, would never run dry. They flock to it, entranced by the prospect of its power, but in the end, none can withstand the force of the magic as it rages. Over the years, I've pulled eighty-four wizards out of that pool. Mine is like most tales of the wells and priests who guard them. Where once we protected the spring, we now guard others from its volatile nature."

Fael's wet clothes, the raw ache inside her, the hunger, all pointed to—"I went to the pool? Like the others?" Leo clutched her empty bowl, trying to remember.

Tor did not answer until she looked in his eyes, fixing her with an even stare. "You are not like any of the others," he said. "You survived." The words hung on her shoulders. She'd never been so exhausted in her life.

Tor looked to Fael. "As did the one who leapt after you, of course." Leo looked to the soldier, who pretended not to notice. "The favor of Atlas," Tor continued, "is rare to appear, but I do not doubt it. The Well rejoiced for you, and you seemed equally eager to join with it. Magic will always amplify what's inside of you."

Fael gathered their bowls, leaving Leo to face the giant alone. "But what does it mean?"

"Perhaps nothing. Many who carry the favor of Atlas become exceptional wizards of their generation. The power consumes others. Where you will fall is up to you."

Fael returned, and she thanked him as he pressed another helping of stew into her hands.

"I would urge you to listen to the voice of Atlas, as I feel your . . . plight is not random chance. Change is on its way, flowing in with the currents and riding on the wind that embraces the forest. Talented as you are, you may find yourself sought on multiple sides. You would do well to prepare for it."

Leo shivered at the truth of his words. Did he know who she was? Or what they were hiding from? Fael wouldn't have told him.

"And finally," Tor said, almost reluctantly. "I feel compelled to point you toward Bastion, home of the Sleepers and the Echos—a month's journey north of here. It is among the last fortresses of the Giant empire, a keep atop the fields of Skalreign. There, you'll find tales of a Sleeper who woke to speak a prophecy of great darkness. Whatever role you will play in the coming days, I hope you seek his words and heed them as well." The giant rose, rubbing a hand over his stomach. "I'll ensure you have rations, though it will mostly be meat, as it's all I have cured."

"We would be so grateful. The stew was really excellent," Leo said. "Do you grow your own spices?"

"No." He smiled. "I am not so reclusive as it may seem. I do travel into town."

"Oh! I didn't mean—" Leo fumbled for words, having honestly assumed the giant would choose to avoid modern settlements.

"Be at ease, Lady . . .?"

"Leo." With a relieved sigh, she clasped her hand over his offered fingertips.

"A mighty name." He bowed his head to her, then looked to Fael. "Guard her well, man of courage. It is rare that we are called into the service of something so much greater than ourselves."

Leo's stomach flipped, the words reminding her of her station and the task ahead. Fael hesitated, but gave the male a quick nod all the same.

Tor cleared the table, gathering the vegetable scraps into a large bowl. "I will leave the bed for you two this night."

"We have a tent," Leo said, suddenly aware of the knee that brushed against her folded legs as Fael got up. "We can't take your bed."

"*You* can. You need to rest." Fael stepped down, taking their bowls to rinse and pack them away.

"I insist. I do rarely get company. Allow me this." Tor smiled, gathering a giant-sized bag and a shimmering obsidian shield. "I am no stranger to sleeping under the stars. I'll return with the dawn and ensure nothing bothers you until then."

Tor exited through a tunnel she could only assume led outside, leaving the space even more cavernous with his absence.

"So . . ." Leo said to Fael's back. It was time for some straightforward answers. "He said he pulled us both out of the water?"

Fael turned. Nodded. Leo's stomach clenched at the reluctance that edged every movement. "Yeah. You were—you fell . . . and went under."

"Fell?" It explained why her entire body ached.

Fael took a deep breath and climbed up to settle himself against the headboard, stretching his long legs out.

"I heard Tor first. It sounded like the entire forest was splintering, and I just knew it was you, somehow. I shouldn't have let you go alone."

"It wasn't far—"

"In this world that doesn't matter. Anything could have found you."

A spark of irritation flared. "I'm not completely helpless." She had the barrier, and her fire was stronger by the day.

He smiled. "That seems to be true. By the time I got to you, you 'd pitted yourself against a giant."

The bed was *too* big. Leo insisted Fael sleep in it too, since there was so much space, and all the other furniture was wooden. Even though they lay together, it was far from the cramped space of the tent, where she could feel the heat of him. Here she could reach an entire arm out and find nothing. Did that bother her? She'd slept easily enough on her own before all of this.

Before her father had been enchanted and promised her to a man under the thrall of—or possibly in league with—a corrupt magical being.

Before she ran away, and the man beside her had killed for her.

Before the two of them had faced horror upon horror.

Before she nearly died.

Leo fingered the focus bracelet on her wrist.

Once everything calmed down, she'd contact Callum. Once they left, the enchantment on their father would fade, she'd return and get answers. Would that mean parting ways with the man next to her?

"Why are you helping me, Fael?" Leo whispered into the darkness.

She heard, more than saw, him turn to look at her. "Why did you heal the boy?"

She smiled. "Because it's who I am," she said, using his own words against him. Rolling sideways, she allowed an arm to stretch in his direction, knowing he was too far to touch. "Your turn. Why?" she asked again.

"Because." He hesitated, then sighed, and the blankets shifted. Lightning coursed through her at the unexpected, feather-light sensation of his fingertips brushing hers. "It's who I want to be."

⬦

Leo watched a mirror image of herself struggle in the grip of a faceless soldier, glaring at her captors over the man's scarred hands. The prince remained cold, his face tired and drawn, but where Dimitri succeeded in frozen detachment, Sebastian failed. He stood next to her, hands tucked in his pockets. Stiff with restraint, but hopeless anger revealed in the set of his jaw and the raging ocean of his eyes. Fael claimed to notice the desperate look before, yet she hadn't. She'd hardly allowed herself to look at him at all that day.

Shouts rang out and she turned in time to watch a white-feathered arrow bloom in the throat of a soldier. Two more lay nearby, their wet attempts at breathing flipping her gut. Fael leapt into the chaos, and the man holding the dream version of her let go. Fael risked a glance, searching her for injury before stepping forward to draw his sword against the prince. She took one step forward in his wake, arm outstretched. Sebastian took that step as well. His brow furrowed, eyes flickering between the dream versions of her and Fael. Her eyes stayed pinned on the two men who battled between them, trading impossible blows.

The prince groaned and clutched his injured side.

"Do you feel that?" Dream-she had grabbed Fael's arm, eyes wide. He tore his gaze away from her to look.

Leo knew what would happen next, and she willed herself to wake up, but the feeling, so similar to dread, grew in her gut, and this time she knew it was dark magic. Somewhere, her father began to scream.

"It's so nice to finally meet you." The corrupted prince said, the unnatural female voice riding his own. Then he angled his *head toward her and raised an arm. This time, the black dagger shot into her chest and she fell back. Sebastian fell next to her. Two more thuds indicated that Fael and her doppelganger went down as well. Coldness swept through her chest and down her limbs. Thick, inky darkness took its time creeping over their bodies.*

Sebastian's eyes remained open, sightless. Their deep blue dragged her in like a current and she fell, splashing into thick, warm water. Her fingers tingled as sensation returned. She surfaced, gasping for air, and her head rose to see Fael sitting at the inn. Satyr stood before them, his eyes pooled with black ink that spilled out, streaking his face like tears. Leo clawed Fael's arm, ready to pull him away, but he wore a broad smile, one that threatened to crack her wide open. Calloused hands slid gently up her arms, but she flinched as his fingers tightened like manacles. From one blink to the next, his eyes went black, smile poisoned, something worth fearing. He yanked her forward, bringing his lips to her ear as a lover might.

When he spoke, it was not his voice.

It was the voice of eons.

Of life and death.

Of magic and unmagic.

The voice of a prophetic giant.

The voice of a god.

The words seared like fire, and she screamed, branded, even as she grasped for their meaning.

"Darkness is coming."

. . . and thus they swore themselves into the monk-like service of Atlas's life force, shepherding its natural flow over the world. Where it pooled and became strong, they built shrines for worship, and many brought offerings in exchange for healing in their blessed waters. Time and mysterious pollution appeared to taint these places, however, and some who would be healed instead went mad at the water's touch. Over time, the wells became feared, shunned, and eventually forgotten. Many historians now consider the wells to be myth, while those I've spoken to claim they were lost to the sudden, magic-driven expansion of the Leywinn forest that followed the culmination of the Great War.

-Gods and Giants, One and the Same

Chapter Twenty-Eight

Darkness. Leo blinked, trying to focus against it, but the shadow remained impenetrable. The throbbing in her chest beat in her ears too, reacting to the terror of the dream, and now this utter blackness, like the eyes of warped friends. Leo panicked, trying to sit up, to draw a shuddering breath, but a body pressed to hers, a binding weight over her stomach. Struggling to heft it away, she craned back to look, but there was only the inky dark. The weight tightened. Then a familiar, woodsy scent washed over her and with it came relief.

"Fael?"

They were still in the cavern. The fire must've gone out.

A deep breath sighed against her skin, the caress so unexpected she nearly leaned into it. "Sorry," he mumbled, voice ragged with sleep. The arm that held her lifted as he scrubbed at his face. Before he could leave, she twisted, hands grappling his shirt. A warm hand wrapped around her wrist, felt the tension there, the trembling.

"Leo?"

She closed her eyes against his voice, its softness striking like a blow. Everything slammed in at once: the tears, the overwhelm, the enormity of the problem she faced, with no clue where to start.

Breathe.

Fingers threaded gently through her hair as she went through the familiar cycle, the sensation anchoring her. The soft fur of the blanket, the coarse cotton of his shirt, the scent of safety in quiet woods.

"You okay?"

"I find myself in great need of a distraction. Just . . . keep talking to me."

The silence was tense, but as his rough voice finally rumbled, her clenched fist unraveled to splay fingers over his chest.

"You asked why I'm helping you." She could feel when he tried to retreat from the words. The hand tangled in her hair stilled, but his grip on her wrist tightened, holding there, as if he sought an anchor as well.

"They said I was lucky to know the man who sired me." The words came out laced with reluctance. "My mother and I lived on his estate—far from the main house, closer to the road on the edge of the property. She worked there, where the lord and his real family lived." The hand in her hair returned to its gentle ministrations, a pleasant distraction from the melancholy that washed over her at the way he said *real family.*

"The lord was proud of his brood. We had governesses. Never went hungry. Not like the beggar children on the street or the working poor. And certainly not like, as we were often reminded, the true nobility." She winced at the venom in the words, even if it wasn't meant for her. Though, perhaps it was. The impenetrable dark remained, keeping his face hidden.

"There was a girl there," he went on. "I guess she was my sister—the lord did not encourage his children to get along. Instead, we . . . vied for his attention. Rewards went to those who pleased him, and cold indifference afflicted the rest. He was a harsh master and swiftly rendered justice for any wrongdoing. This ensured we didn't *disturb him.* Neither his praise nor his ire often fell on me. I only wanted to be out of the way, but she—Willow . . ." Fael huffed a laugh. "She fought. Made trouble with the governesses. Riled the other wards, often to the point of violence. Each time, the lord would punish her, and she would wield his own cold, indifferent expression against the blows that were dealt. Willow did anything to spite him, claiming he often punished her mother, a beautiful fae woman, to please the vanity of his jealous wife. Willow was older than I, and when she was close to aging out of his care, she'd go on about how she was going to convince her mother to leave with her."

"But her mother grew mysteriously ill. Died. The lord lost any hold over Willow. There was nothing to stop her from leaving. But first, enraged by her mother's suspicious death, she went to the main house, and dressed him down in front of company, availing them of all of his ruthlessness."

"Later the servants would say how the nobles laughed at her. How they reminded her she was nothing. Lucky to have anything. They told her she'd be crawling back." Fael stilled again, and she traced an idle pattern over his chest.

"They arrested her before the end of that first day." He cleared his throat. "Something was stolen from the main house, or so they claimed. She fought the guards, and they dragged her back to the estate, already bloodied. My other siblings and I watched their approach and I . . . I followed. They didn't stop me. Didn't stop any who came to witness. By then she could hardly walk. The men kept her standing until my father met them on the lawn. They read the charges. And my father paid them to ensure he could handle it himself, with discretion. She didn't try to run, couldn't. He told her he was a magnanimous, kind master, and wanted to prove her scathing lies wrong. 'You have two choices,' he said. 'You can stay and owe a life-debt. Work for me, as your mother did. Or you can meet the same fate all thieves find in Umbri, in time.'

"She spat on him." Leo could hear Fael's smile. "His face. Oh gods, there was blood speckling his perfect fucking clothes, and she'd *spat* on him. That was her answer. So, he stepped forward with the knife . . ." A tremor betrayed how he battled with the truth that wrestled its way forward.

"You can't stop there." Leo said, but when she spoke, it was his voice that she heard, echoing what he'd said after the shadow beast ripped her apart. It was him—a brace as the pain and fear flared alongside her magic, threatening her control.

She caught the back of his neck his hand fell down to her waist, wrapping over it with strength. Security. His hair was dry now, and silky, as it brushed over fingers that meandered over his neck, his head, his ear. He finally moved, letting his own hand trace between her wrist and shoulder.

To the darkness, he whispered, "I was too weak to save her.

"I tried. I put myself between them. Me. A helpless, stupid child. The lord flew into a rage at the challenge. Struck us both down and made me watch while he gutted her. She died slowly. And all I could do was wait for the end. After, he laughed and beat me to within an inch of my life. Sliced my face while her blood still wet the blade. Forbid healing, ensuring the scar remained to remind me and everyone else what happens when you start a battle you can't win."

Oh my gods. "Fael—"

He cut her off. "Don't. I wouldn't change it, Leo. I'd do it all over again, even knowing I couldn't save her. She did it. She proved he was who she said he was. None preened under his attention again. My mother grew old and died, and I had no reason to see him. And I never will. I joined the royal legion as soon as I could, along with several of my brothers. We were all well trained. I had a natural affinity training, tracking, fighting, but none of that mattered in the face of our birthright, so each of us started as foot soldiers with little chance of advancement. That moment—it made me who I am. I trained harder than anyone, honed myself as sharp as any blade to become the person she needed. To help those who need it. I've saved hundreds of lives." He spoke with the conviction of a man who had spent years reciting the words. "Mine is a small price to pay."

In the silence that followed, it was a wonder he couldn't hear her heart breaking.

Then the anger rushed in.

"You will tell me the name of this lord. The king won't tolerate abuse of his people." Leo would single-handedly tear him apart, actually, and when she was done, there'd be nothing left. There wouldn't be a person in Arnell who hadn't heard of his crimes before he went swinging on the end of a rope.

"Your father isn't his king."

"What?" But something else bothered her too, something he'd mentioned about the fate all thieves find in—"Umbri?"

Fael had gone rigid under her fingers.

"You're a soldier. And you're from Umbri." She withdrew and propped herself up on an arm, cursing the dark, wishing she could see his face.

"Yes," he said, warily.

Unease rippled through her. "And you were gathering in-formation, searching my room on behalf of *interested parties*."

"Yes." He barely managed the word. "But Leo—"

She stiffened, bracing herself as steady stone crumbled be-neath her feet. She should have known. "You may address me as *Princess Madeline.*"

The mattress shifted as he sat up. "You never would have let me help you if you knew."

"And are you? *Helping*? Or just getting me as far away as possible from Arnell?" She ripped the blankets away, allow-ing the air's cold bite to fully wake her before moving out of the enormous bed, ignoring the sudden dizziness at the movement. Knees jarring, she landed on the ground, briefly surprised by the warmth of the cave floor. "Why did I trust you? You gave me every reason—"

"Listen. Leo, I—"

"*Do not* interrupt me." The princess of Arnell fully returned, the girl in the woods banished for her tender foolishness. Of course, Fael was just another player on the board. A pawn. "You may report to your commander that I escaped you in the woods. I am sure *Umbri* will be relieved the alliance was foiled, so consider your job well done and kindly leave me alone." She walked blindly, trying to outpace the sounds of Fael following. By some miracle, she found the fireplace and, a whisper later, tried to light it.

Fael came up, laying a hand on her sore shoulder.

"Please—" his voice broke on the word.

"Don't *touch me*." The stinging feeling in her heart spiked into rage, wrapping vengeful fingers around her power and calling for more. It ravaged her, but she relished the feeling, happy to trade one pain for another. Fael fell back, shielding himself against the flames that erupted over her entire body. Good.

She continued, skin unscathed, to the opening in the cave, struggling to calm the fire and grab her bag. Everything was raw. Walking ached, breathing ached, listening to his voice ached too. "Just let me explain." The words echoed down the dark tunnel.

"You've had miles of forest to explain, Fael." She didn't look back. Of course, she was as much to blame. It had never crossed her mind that he worked for another kingdom. After the marriage alliance was proposed, she should have been able to connect the dots, but she'd been so consumed by her upended life.

The cave split abruptly, and Leo took the sharp incline that tasted like frozen air rather than the narrow passage that continued on. The dark of the forest was so different from that of the cave. Slowly, night sounds erupted into the chatter of birds. By the time she burned through her anger, sunlight touched the leaves, which was good, because she chattered from the cold. As the sun rose, she aimed for it, hoping to make it back to Lamel, where she could hire a ride to the royal summer home. It was as good a plan as any at this point. Except that the towering trees swallowed the sun throughout the day, and by evening she discovered she'd been heading more north than east, and everything looked the same in this gods-forsaken forest.

She had food, for now, but Fael had the tent. She'd started packing his cloak into her bag since she was always the last one to wake. Wrapped in white and gold, she watched the campfire die. A stick cracked and fear had her seeing shadows where there were none. She shouldn't have left. Tor would have been willing to guide her to the village, had she waited. There was no way she'd make it back now.

The forest went silent as the flame sputtered out. Leo was a fool. For so many things. For everything. Tears welled in her eyes, but she willed them back, refusing to let them fall.

Chapter Twenty-Nine

SHE THOUGHT OF HIM before her eyes opened. Memories laced with anxiety sent her heart racing, taking her breath before she'd even greeted the day. It was still dark. With little to pack, she set out, eating dried meat as she walked. The magic still chafed as she cast, but continued rest wasn't worth the risk, so she raised the shields, anyway. At least she could manage that.

By the second evening, the cold snap had settled in, and she wore Fael's cloak over her clothes during the daytime too. From morning to night, she walked, trying to create a fire that would float along and warm without burning. By the end of the day, a little flame floated nearby, but it barely took the edge off. Fingers numb and too stiff to shiver anymore, she consumed the last of the food. Purple bunches of berries grew in tangled patches, but Fael had cautioned against a poisonous look-alike. Hopefully she would find Lamel before she had to test them. How many days had it taken them to reach the Atlas shrine? She didn't remember. It seemed like another life entirely.

True rest was elusive, yielding to every noise or whisper of the forest. The exhaustion wore on, and she could feel her progress slowing as the long day continued into a longer night.

An animal darted into her path, and, too late, Leo wondered if she should try to kill it—to eat it. Her stomach rumbled in protest as it scrambled away, though it was difficult to make the connection between a furry animal and the satisfaction of a full belly. Resigned, she practiced throwing a tiny flame like a dart. Fael said she'd wielded magic offensively in the pool, though the memory of it remained evasive. He said a lot that made little sense, actually. She shook the thought away. To hunt, she had to focus. Now it was second nature to pull magic as she spent it, and the focus bracelet allowed for experimentation. Hunger overrode caution, and her dart turned into a spear, hot enough to burn through the trees.

Her thoughts flashed to a body wreathed in flame. How easily anger wrenched the power from her control. She could have really hurt him, could hurt anyone, without meaning to. She cringed, for the first time wary of her talent. Odd, after so long striving for it. She'd found sanctuary in the dream that she could become more than what fate had denied her at birth. To be concerned, now that she'd succeeded, was laughable.

She was lucky, really. Lucky her life hadn't been like Fael's, lorded over by a man who viewed his children as what? A collection? Leo shuddered.

Luckier than Sebastian, too, whose family sent him away for his safety, and while he'd gained a wealth of knowledge she could only dream of, he'd missed his human mother's entire life. He'd returned only as a pawn, a weapon to be owned.

And sweet Elaine, whose remarkable talent for cooking led her to the castle's own kitchen, but whose life dream—one she'd stowed away to guard a ravaged heart—had already caused her lifetimes of loss and pain.

The king had tried to shape Leo into who she should be, and the molding chaffed—suffocating as surely as the storybook walls and baubles that decorated the castle's third floor. It only grew worse as time went on. Her wayward desire to experience another life, through books or otherwise, threatened him. He'd cleared the castle library of suspect material, loaded her down with escorts and guards, claiming her relative powerlessness would make her a target. Callum, unsurprisingly, never found himself similarly burdened.

"Your brother can handle himself," he'd said a hundred times over. The Blood of King's ensured that.

She speared the fire through a tree.

"There are many who hunger for a life like yours."

Two more found their mark.

Leo had no space for complaint, not really. And the truth of that shamed her. Who was she to desire more—something other?

She stumbled, distracted, and the flame went wide. Cursing, she flung herself at the little fire and stomped it out, careful to mind the hem of Fael's cloak, sloppily trimmed with the stolen dagger.

As she tended to the errant flame, she reached to steady herself on a tree, but caught in something invisible and sticky. She tried wrenching her arm back, but the strands had adhered firmly to the arm of her tunic. With a jolt of alarm, she realized it was an impossibly large web—a spider web. How had she not seen it? The strands were thin enough to be transparent, but held fast like iron shackles. Fighting panic, she used her borrowed dagger to cut the snared sleeve and used flame to burn away what stuck to her skin.

Skin pebbling with gooseflesh, she paced away with haste. The spider that made it must have been enormous.

Suddenly, something skittered across the nape of her neck and she shrieked, slapping at her back and tossing all of her bags to the ground. Her hand cupped a fleshy lump, and she flung it away, shuddering when a spider the size of her palm hit the ground and gave her a remarkably reprimanding look before scuttling up a nearby tree.

The spider moved up and up and up and Leo tipped her head back to watch it go.

Then something shifted in the air and the forest went quiet.

And the shouts began.

Diving into her power, Leo spotted the faint glow of bodies not far off. Five encircling one. She should hide, but worry drew her forward. Ensuring the shields were strong, she tried to slip past the vegetation, not wanting their movement to draw undue attention as she came upon the group and her fears were confirmed. Of course he'd followed her.

"That's him alright!" A large man grinned, showing a scrap of parchment to those closest to him. Facing them, stood Fael, shoulders relaxed, gorgeous blade glinting in the speckled light of the trees.

"If he's here the princess won't be far, now will she?" His friend said, pointing a cruel-looking club at Fael. "Have you had a taste of her then?" He licked fat lips and dangled a second parchment, one with her likeness on it. "I'd like to get a bite myself." He laughed with his friends, and his eyes still glimmered with the taunt when Fael leapt, fast as lightning, and speared him in the gut.

Chaos erupted. Fear tore the breath from her lungs in a startled gasp as two men jumped at him from behind, each wielding short swords. At the last moment, he spun, dodging and deflecting each strike. The metallic clash of blades shattered the air and her stalled heart leapt into a frenzy before she could bring up the bubble of silence. She sucked in a breath, willing herself to settle into the quiet even as the fight continued. One man baited Fael, and a second closed in behind.

Leo didn't hesitate. With the physical shield up, she sprinted forward, causing the man's sword to bounce harmlessly to the side. Teeth grinding at the impact, she hurried to reinforce the barrier. The attacker looked surprised for only a moment before attacking again. The shield weakened rapidly under the onslaught, and as a last resort, Leo changed tactics. A dart of flame seared through the man's hand as well as any sword, and he dropped to his knees, cradling the spurting limb. Fael whipped his head around, and his sword flashed, ending the man's agony as an afterthought. He threw a panicked look her way before being engaged again.

Their leader stepped back to scan the forest while the three remaining men continued to engage Fael. His mouth moved, giving them orders, but Leo couldn't hear the words. When he found her, his face split in a slimy smile. She took an involuntary step back and froze, pinned by the victorious look in his eye. Sounds of battle erupted as she faltered, further suffocating her concentration. Clumsily, she conjured another shield, but it popped weakly as he moved in for the kill.

Then Fael was there again, his body a wall in front of her, but the leader drew a wicked-looking dagger and the three remaining bounty hunters worked in expert tandem. Fael bared his teeth in frustration as two of the men doubled down, forcibly occupying his attention. Their leader kept his eye on her as they batted him away.

Leo bolted.

The trees sent clawed branches into her path, whipping her face for running blindly. The foliage tangled in her legs. She fell, ripping her hand from a bramble before rising to run again, but didn't make it more than a couple of paces before a vicious kick sent her sprawling. A spike of agony flared at her temple. With a cry, she rolled to a stop, clutching her bloodied hand.

The man wrapped long fingers into her hair and dragged her up. He was of medium build, but taller all the same. His clean-shaven face shined. Someone had patched his overcoat in several places, and she tried not to breathe too much; the stench of stale ale overwhelmed her nervous stomach. The magic bucked wildly, fear pushing it far from her reach.

"There you go," he purred as he patted her down, searching for weapons. The lingering touch turned brazen, gripping her backside. Wild fear whipped into anger as she dug chipped nails into his arm, aiming a knee between his legs for good measure. Chuckling, he shoved forward, his whole body crushing her against a tree. One long, bony hand wrapped eagerly around her throat.

Reality narrowed to a single desperate need for breath as he squeezed. Even as spots formed in her vision, she could see the glint in his eye. "You fight for him." The accusation seeped through a growing film of half-consciousness. "A far-cry from the kidnapping sob-story they're telling . . . Is it worth the war between our kingdoms? The love of the Wingbreaker?" Panic returned as he nuzzled his face into the crook of her neck, his chest pressing into hers as he inhaled and sighed. Satisfied. He uncorked a vial of dark liquid with his teeth and lifted it to her lips. She shook her head, struggling uselessly against the solid weight of his body.

"Shhh." He pressed the veins in her neck and the world disappeared, her legs giving out as she slipped toward unconsciousness.

"Don't fucking touch her."

The man grunted in surprise as a force abruptly tore his body away. Leo gulped glorious air, vision clearing with every breath. Fael had tackled him to the ground. The force of it sent them rolling, but each came up with a weapon in hand.

They traded murderous looks and began pacing in half-circles. Fael forced the man to switch directions to stay between them. Sparing her a glance, his eyes swept over her before turning back to his opponent.

"You're a dead man," Fael said, though he looked haggard already. His sword arm was bloodied, his shirt sleeve soaked in red and clinging to the wound. Leo's chest hollowed out as blood dripped from the pommel of his sword. He'd lost too much already.

The bounty hunter, fresh and hardly winded from the chase, just offered a pointed smile over Fael's shoulder. He didn't doubt how this would end.

Fael took the bait, and swords clashed, the peal of metal deafening. They traded blows for an eternity and Leo begged her body to calm, but the magic remained restless inside her, stirred to madness by her friend's blood and her own useless fear.

But Fael wasn't as exhausted as he appeared. He matched the man blow for blow and then some. First, he forced him to give up ground, then feinted and doubled back, slashing open the skin over his ribs.

A moment later, the bounty hunter's sword clattered away, and his eyes went wide for a moment, expecting a killing blow.

But Fael sheathed his sword and wiped his bloody lip on the already ruined sleeve.

The man looked relieved for a moment before Fael lunged and he found his body lifted and slammed onto the forest floor. They wrestled, trading punches as they rolled. The hunter fought, but Fael fought harder, roaring and mad with rage. Once he gained the upper hand, he didn't lose it, instead using his hands to pummel through flesh and bone.

"Fael." The sick thud of knuckle and flesh slowed. The man had stopped moving long ago. "Fael. Please." Her voice broke.

The battle hadn't yet left his eyes when he finally looked away from the dead man beneath him. Blood spattered his neck and face, wild eyes blinking slowly as the rage gave way to something else. Shame? Regret? His chest heaved, and he stared, as if waiting for her to look away.

She didn't.

Far away, something fumbled through the underbrush. One of the bounty hunters fled, barely discernible through the thick trees, a hand pressed to a wound at his side.

"I'm going to regret that." Fael groaned, shooting up to follow, but his eyes unfocused, body wavering. "I need to make sure they don't send more after us." His words slurred—he'd lost too much blood.

Leo rose to meet him just as he crumbled to his knees.

i never learned to be cautious
no.
i was enchanted
by the flame:

by its fervor
for a short life,
spent wanting

and here she is now
the sun beaming down
like a blessing
the forest in her hair
like a crown and

on my knees
in supplication,
hands outstretched
in hopeless offering,
i can do nothing but wait
for the beginning of the end

and wish that I had learned

when i still stood a chance

Chapter Thirty

FAEL GROANED AND CLUTCHED his arm to stem the bleed-ing. "More will come if word gets back to Lamel they've sight-ed us nearby." Leo pressed into him as he tipped forward, sav-ing him from crashing face first into the underbrush as vertigo washed in again. The blood loss was a problem on its own, but the bounty hunters had laced their blades with poison.

Without it, the prick wouldn't have even had the chance to touch her.

Leo flared with light, and she placed a soft hand over his. Cool tingling caressed the agony of his poisoned wound. Whatever it was, wouldn't kill him—they weren't stupid enough to risk killing them before collecting their coin.

"There's something . . . wrong with it." Leo's raspy voice made his blood surge all over again. The handprint ringed her neck like a collar.

Over his dead fucking body.

"I don't know how to handle this," she said, her face pulling into a concerned pout. The magic glow lingered, and it was all he could do to look away, to focus on getting her out of here. Fael didn't like their chances of escaping a second time.

"It's a paralytic or a sedative of some kind." Fael examined the wound. She'd healed the skin itself, but the stupor of the drug continued to worsen, making his limbs cumbersome, unwieldy. Swimming vision turned his gut and he groaned again, fighting the bile that threatened. No, they couldn't stay here. With one great heave, he stood, and nearly toppled over again.

Leo secured his arm around her shoulders and groaned, pulling him forward. One step. Two. "You're heavy. One too many sticky buns, soldier." Her breath was labored already, her scratchy, cheerful tone too light for what happened and what remained between them. "They're my favorite too." She babbled. Another labored step. "A mountain of sticky buns for both of us." Another. "Just have to make it to the other side of this damned forest." She cursed as they tipped precariously to the side, but still pushed forward, west. Good. But she couldn't keep this up for long.

"If you go ahead." His words slurred. Hopefully it wasn't obvious. "I can catch up."

She laughed, the bright sound tinkling through the haze of the drug. "I'm not doing this alone again. No. Just . . . hold on." Trembling, she lowered him. He made some unintelligible sound in protest as the ground came up to meet him, and the air whooshed from his lungs.

"Secret Umbri spies," she panted, falling beside him, "don't get to complain."

She shook him awake.

"Here. Use this," she said, shoving a thick branch in his hand. Fael shot up, the world spun. Was the sun lower now? They needed to move out immediately.

His pack lay open, emptier than he remembered. "Did you eat my rations?"

"*Our rations*," dual images of Leo admonished, "if I'm to carry you." The healing magic must have exhausted her, then.

Fael blinked hard, dragging the world into focus. "You're wearing my cloak." He grinned, the drug muffling his good sense. He hadn't felt this drunk in decades. Then he frowned. "You cut it."

She gave an indulgent spin. "I rather like it this way. Besides"—uncharacteristically uncertain, she ducked her head and tucked tangled hair behind an ear—"it got cold. And I couldn't have it dragging behind me."

She should never have been alone. Not here. "I'm . . . sorry." The mournful words slurred over the voice in his head that warned him to shut up. "I never wanted to hurt you."

She avoided looking at him, though. Gods, she was so pissed at him. Grateful for the branch, he dragged himself up, wobbling.

Instead of tearing into him, she brushed leaves off his sleeves. "We will discuss that later, and at length. *Wingbreaker*."

He winced.

"For now, I need silence. The spells to hide us require concentration and I'll be using most of that to keep you up. One day I might be able to float you along, but for now I think that's out of the question."

Oddly, the surrounding foliage moved out of their way, pressed against a barrier he couldn't see. After the past few days of tracking her, he had to assume the sound barrier worked as well, but there was no way to confirm. Every heart wrenching snap under their labored steps wore him down—he'd be useless if anything came for them now. After a time, the worry ebbed away, eased by the scent that wrapped him alongside the arm at his waist.

Tracking her had been easy, because she didn't bother to be cautious with her footsteps. Every broken stick or crushed leaf may not make a sound with her magic, but it left a trail. And it wouldn't take much skill to follow the one they left now.

After an hour or so—he really couldn't tell how much time had passed—she stopped, panting. "I need you to stay awake," she said.

He hadn't realized that he'd been dozing off.

"Fael."

He jerked his head back up. The drug fought to drag him under again. A sharp pain shot up his leg as she slammed her heel against his foot.

"I'm awake," he said, words still slurring.

"Stay that way," she commanded.

They walked in silence until she abruptly brought him back by elbowing him in the ribs.

"Are your arrows made of chicken feathers?" she asked.

The question swirled in his head. "Chicken feathers?"

"Yes. I heard a rumor the Wingbreaker's arrows were made of chicken feathers. That the griffin slaying was a fabrication."

"No, I . . . the griffin feathers are real," Fael said, shying from the memory.

"How? Did you slice its belly with a longsword? Snare it in a trap after hunting it for days?"

"No." He wobbled and nearly fell, causing her to hiss as she tried hard to steady him.

"Then what's the real story?"

"I got lucky."

She laughed. "It takes more than luck to slay a beast like that."

Fael swallowed, tongue thick and dry. It wasn't something he liked to remember.

"It killed my friend," he finally said.

Leo's silence invited him to continue.

He took a deep breath, focusing on putting one foot in front of the other rather than on the words. "We were tracking a pack of kalawaras." They took a step. "Our second night in the woods, Ptolemus came down. He never ranged that far. His realm was the mountains. There had been sightings—but he came down that night." More silence. "I wasn't hunting him. And we weren't prepared for something of that caliber. Roan was the first one to die. He leapt in front of three other men from the neighboring homesteads. They'd joined us, simple folk, hoping to do their part in protecting the life they'd carved out. Kalawaras would be scary, but no real threat. If anything, the beasts can often be run off to find new hunting grounds—as you saw. But Roan knew they'd be no match against a griffin." Fael tried hard not to heave, forcing them to stillness before Leo pulled him on.

"In the end, it was for nothing. And there was nothing I could do. I'd gone to double back on our steps to ensure we weren't being hunted." Fael laughed at the bitter irony. "All it took was a talon to gut each of them beyond saving. Roan and another were gone before I got there, and the third was bleeding from an artery in his leg. The fourth had fled with Ptolemus in pursuit."

Leo still said nothing as he sucked in air.

"I think the screaming is why it didn't hear me. Camhaoir may have made short work of a griffin, but normal steel has a hard time doing any damage. Their feathers are like razors." There was no way she really wanted to know, but still the story poured out. "It was tearing large chunks of the man, eating him, when I leapt at its wing—the only thing I thought might actually work. It was stupid and desperate, but in that moment, all I wanted was to end the beast that killed Roan. I didn't expect to survive.

"The feathers ripped into my hands, my arms. Shredded me. But griffin bones are hollow, and the joints snapped as easily as any man's. And then he ran away."

"What?" Her voice was strained.

"The griffin fled."

"But the stories say you killed him."

"I returned half-dead. And I was still unconscious when they found the body. By the time I woke, the tale of my victory had spread far and wide.

"He was at the bottom of a cliff. Everyone assumed he'd tried to fly and succumbed to his injuries. But I think he lost the will to go on. Wings broken, taken from the sky, I think he lost what made him. I think the ageless Ptolemus, Terror of the Thunderwell, had chosen his end. But it wasn't the drop that killed him.

"It was heartbreak."

⁂

As the spring sun went down, the air became cold enough to chill even their over-exerted bodies. A warm little flame manifested, and while he was wary of the light, it and the heat let them press on long after the sunset. Finally, when they were ragged with exhaustion, their eyes sunken with their efforts, she called for a halt. Relieved, Fael collapsed. He couldn't imagine what this dose would have done to a smaller person. It was a surprise he hadn't puked with how his head swam. He almost wished he would. It might help. Between one long blink and another, she set up the tent.

Before going in, Leo paused to study him, lips turned in a frown like she wasn't sure what to say, guarded eyes flickering in the light of her flame. He waited, trapped in vicious nausea and exhaustion and regret. He didn't dare speak before he knew where they stood. But Leo only smirked at whatever expression he wore, the tilt of her lips dipping into shadow as she extinguished the magic. The tent flap swung as she went inside.

Leaving him alone in the dark, with little else to do, but follow.

———◦———

"Every part of my body hurts," she groaned the next morning. For the first time since they'd separated, Fael was relaxed, comforted by seeing her on the opposite side of their little fire.

"Why do you always carry that coin?" she asked.

Fael caught it as it came back down and held it up, pinched between his thumb and forefinger. He hadn't realized that he'd pulled it out.

"It's a Cairn Stone. They're made out of Umbri stone and iron. Every soldier gets one—a holdover from the Great War." He held it up, so the sun illuminated the triple spiral pattern in the center. "One side represents the joining of land, air, and sea. And the other side depends on the soldier." He flipped it and tucked it back into his pocket. "We each have one. So no matter where you fall, it can be brought back to your village and added to the Cairn. Speaking of soldiers, consider that soreness part of your training." Fael picked up his skewered rabbit and pointed in her direction.

Another eye roll. He lifted an eyebrow.

"I'm serious. You still have a lot of work to do. Plus . . ." He threw out his arms, indicating *everything,* then bit into breakfast. Gods it was delicious. Had rabbit always been this good?

She lowered her own food. It had been oddly normal when he'd left before she woke, and returned to find the tent packed, and a fire ready. At the time, she seemed remarkably happy that he felt well enough, and hungry enough, to hunt this morning, and Fael was happy to fall into their routine.

But the warmth that had shone in her eyes then was certainly gone now. "It hardly matters at this point. Nothing I've learned made a difference," she said.

She was serious.

"When that bounty hunter locked his sights on you, you froze." He tried to keep the ice out of his voice. It wasn't for her, but she needed to realize—

"That hesitation almost got you killed."

"Fear. It always breaks my focus—and I'll never match up in physical combat. I don't want to hurt people, anyway."

"You saw me being attacked by several men and jumped in without thinking. You leapt onto the shadow creature after it already half-killed you. You weren't afraid."

She scratched the dirt with a finger. "I was. I'm just more afraid of some things than others."

His gut bottomed out. "What does that mean?"

"Fael," she sighed his name, exasperated.

"Leo."

Her lips twitched but her eyes were heavy. "I am less afraid of bounty hunters or monsters than I am of you getting killed. Besides, I was angry. That helps."

He stared at her for a moment, mulling over the admission. "The physical training will help you stay grounded even when you're afraid. And you *will* learn to protect *you*." She looked away, but he pressed on. "Martyrdom isn't useful in a fight."

She whipped her head back to him. "You're ignoring that I'm a fair bit of the reason you didn't get killed. It sounds *useful* to me."

"In the end it was a distraction."

"I wasn't aware the esteemed *Wingbreaker* could be distracted," she sneered, but instead of standing to stare him down in righteous indignation, she pulled her knees into her chest, as if to shield herself. Too late, the alarm bells in his head rang. He hadn't expected this—and that damn ache cinched his chest again.

He leaned over, trying to catch her eye. "Leo. I would have told you sooner."

"You had every chance." She laughed, the sound stinging and bitter. "And why would you have? It would only have made your task more difficult." She stared into the flame, refusing to meet his eye.

"Retrieving you was not my task." No matter that his task had been far more deadly. "I . . . reluctantly admired your drive to escape. You needed help, so I helped."

"And what was your task?"

His blood went cold at the answer, the memory.

"I was to retrieve information about the marriage," he said, wondering if she caught the careful neutrality in his voice. "That Umbri benefits from the alliance being called off was a . . . coincidence." He flipped the cairn stone in his hand.

"Except now it's not benefiting Umbri, is it? Arnell is saying I was kidnapped by the Wingbreaker. That Umbri's renowned griffin slayer walked into the engagement ball and spirited away Corsair's bride, a trail of dead guards in his wake." She looked at him at last. Devastated.

She whispered, the words barely there, as if speaking them aloud might make them true. "The bounty hunter said they're going to war."

Her voice cracked on the word, and he willed his body to be still. To resist the urge to draw her in. His comfort was the last thing she'd want right now.

"We can fix this."

"I have to return to Arnell."

They'd spoken in tandem, but Fael recovered first, blood roaring in his ears.

"You what? After all this, you're just going to go back? Do you have any idea what they'll do to you? What the corrupted prince wants with you?" No, he couldn't accept that they'd fought their way this far—for nothing.

"It's not important." Her voice rose as she stood, and he followed, relishing the spark in her eye. *This* he could handle. All she needed was a brick wall to throw herself at. Release. And all he had to do was prove they'd both leave this unscathed.

"I can't let you go back." He stepped toward her, crossing his arms.

"Don't want to disappoint your king, soldier?" She squared herself to him. It would be funny, with how small she was, if he hadn't seen her entire body cloaked in angry flame.

"Best-case scenario, you marry the cursed prince. Worst case, they kill you for treason."

"The worst case is our kingdoms go to *war*. What do you think *your* king will do? Because if he doesn't want to war with my father, he'll hand me over."

Fael felt the blood drain from his face. "We would tell him about the prince," he hedged. "There's no way he'd allow Arnell to be allied with a kingdom that has that creature as its eventual ruler."

"Not even to avoid a war with both Arnell and Corsair?"

"He'd see the threat as it is, but your power would force him to see you as an asset."

"I don't want to be an asset." She poked a hard finger into his chest. "I didn't want to be a tool for my own kingdom to marry off and I won't be a tool for Umbri either."

An image snaked into his mind: her, naked, blindingly radiant on a pillar of water, throwing enough raw energy to stagger a giant. Pressing a hand over hers, he splayed it flat, only half-hoping she wouldn't feel the way his heart raced underneath. "You'll always be on the board, Princess. If not a pawn, what will you be?"

"I don't want to play at all. Not like this." She deflated. "All I wanted was to be my brother's equal. Worthy of my crown, my bloodline. I'm tired of being told I am both too weak and fight too much. I don't fit where I was put, Fael. Not the day I was born, and not now."

Her head fell with the weight of the words, but he caught her chin with a hand, bringing her eyes to his. He expected tears, but there was nothing, the fiery anger extinguished with her confession. The emptiness swallowed him whole, and for a moment he swam in water that was too thick, too dark, his limbs too sluggish to respond in time to stop him from drowning, and she was burning and radiant and unstoppable.

"Fael?" He startled as she spoke, but he answered with the conviction of a man who held the world in his hands.

"You will never be weak. You give freely to thieves and defy royals. You dive into feral magic wells and battle giants." He cleared his throat against the tightness in his chest as an errant, blessed spark teased its way past the sadness in her eyes. "You've faced down monsters and monstrous men . . . Not least of all me." She laughed leaning her face into his palm, the sound easing the weight on his shoulders. He smiled too, gently, and her umber eyes grew round and unguarded in a way that shifted his every instinct toward protection.

Toward claiming.

Before he could damn himself with that mistake, he slipped his hand around the back of her neck, daring only to lean in and press his forehead to hers. "I'm sorry. Whatever I was meant to do before—I . . ." The words were a noose. In every way. She grasped his other hand, bringing it around her waist in a silent request, and though it was yet another on the long list of bad-for-him choices, he conceded, wrapping her up with both arms, relaxing inexplicably into her scent and soft curves as she pressed her face to his chest. He wanted to believe that, if he was willing to give up everything, there could be more.

But he was the only option for comfort in this gods-forsaken wood.

And he knew better than to offer more than he could afford to lose.

When he backed away, the step felt like miles. He bounced a palm on Camhaoir's pommel. "We really should get moving. We lost a lot of time yesterday."

She wiped wet eyes and crossed her arms, suddenly wary as reality crashed back in.

Well done, Wingbreaker.

"Where?"

"To the farm. We can decide from there. Once it's safe."

Leo pursed her plump lips as she surveyed him, no doubt trying to divine his intentions.

Good.

With a nod, she started forward, though she didn't deign to meet his eyes.

He swept into a bow as she passed.

"Your Highness."

Fael was a selfish, masochistic bastard.

She'd never brought up their nighttime charade. He wasn't sure if she even knew, or if, at this point, he should have told her. Despite everything, it continued: their subconscious habit he tried hard to separate from his day-to-day thoughts. It would end soon. They'd arrive at the farm in three days. Two more nights—and each would go as the others had gone.

The birdsong would start with the first light of dawn, and he'd wake. Still, the sun would take its time meandering over the trees, and she'd remain, her sweet face relaxed in sleep, her soft curves nestled against him. She always rose soon after he left, so he would stay as long as he dared, as long as he could bear, before peeling away, as he did every morning. Every. Single. Godsdamned. Morning. It was his own personal brand of torture.

And letting go got a little harder every time.

The dappled sunlight illuminated the tent with little pockets of muted color. He could map her freckles like constellations now, the lines of her sleeping face even more familiar than his own. At first, it was a matter of survival. The nightmares sapped the energy she needed to make it through the forest. Then it was a given. They'd fall asleep apart, only to tangle together in the night, some secret need met in the vulnerability of sleep.

Now it was an unwelcome need. Something in him refused to be at ease without her. She mumbled, caught in a dream, and, again, he wanted nothing more than to wake her. To ask: If she didn't *need* it, would she *choose* it?

He wanted to.

And the truth of that clung to him, even as he pushed away to spare them both the weight of all that it implied.

Chapter Thirty-One

OVERALL, THE FARM REMINDED Leo of the garden and kitchen at home—of Elaine. Thoughts of her friend brought unbearable melancholy, but it was hard to avoid with the spring veggies ripe for harvesting and the familiar herbs growing alongside bright leafy greens. The farm style house, with its open rafters and braided onions, reminded her of a love story. Romantic. Especially with the large window on the far wall of the living area, where a black dog lay surrounded by puppies, her pointed ears and dappled paws twitching.

A week after the bounty hunter attack, they'd arrived, filthy and unannounced, and Fael barged through the house's heavy front door. The warmth that erupted from inside was shocking. An elderly human woman threw her arms around Fael, her frail body dwarfed by the massive arms that gently wrapped around her. An elderly man, bent deeply over a cane, limped into the sitting room at the commotion, and Fael opened an arm for him to join.

Awkwardly to the side, Leo squeezed clammy hands together, a strange prickling in her eyes. It was the casual hospitality, she'd decided. That and the knowledge that this kind of welcome did not wait for her at home.

Gods she was tired.

Watching Fael with his family was both an ache and a balm. He smiled openly, as he'd rarely done since she'd known him. Something pinched her chest and she set herself against its implication. He was cordial enough most of the time. And there had been . . . moments. But, for no reason at all, his genuine joy—that grin—took her off guard.

Took air from her lungs.

Fael caught her faux smile, his expression wavering. The pinch in her heart sharpened to a stake. She didn't know him, not really. What she did know was they'd never be this close—this honest. Too much lay between them already. Two entire kingdom's worth of distance and maneuvering. Secrets. She'd be getting in contact with Callum as soon as possible.

He struggled with words as he introduced her. "Aunt Cynthia, Uncle Rodrick, this is my . . . friend . . . Leo."

She blanched when they giggled at her curtsy and instead drew her in for a hug as well.

"Any friend of Fael's," Aunt Cynthia said, "is family to us." Her gray hair was pleated elegantly over a shoulder, eyes sparkling with what she knew—or suspected.

Now they were admonishing him for not visiting sooner, and he expertly hedged when asked how long they'd stay. Jesse and Markus, their children, nodded their greetings to Leo and embraced Fael next, both adults, both human as well. The girl shared his golden hair—though neither had the same forest-morning eyes. Uncle Rodrick, his smile bright against his dark skin, took Leo's hand and pressed a chaste kiss to her fingers. They all quieted as he gave his nephew a serious look. "It's about time," he said.

The blush was quick, heat reaching for the tips of her ears as she spied the redness that crept up Fael's neck too. It was an innocent assumption.

Neither corrected them.

After they begged for the mercy of a bath, Aunt Cynthia showed them to the guest room. Dominating one side was a large double bed, though it was hard to consider any bed large now that she'd slept in one meant for a giant. A dried lavender wreath hung over the headboard. One corner of the room harbored a wardrobe and floor-length mirror, another corner, a small writing desk. Cozy. Perfect. The woman cheerily informed them dinner would be ready in an hour, and that they'd find the washroom down the hall.

"I'll sleep on the floor." Fael said as soon as she shut the door.

Leo couldn't roll her eyes hard enough. "You're going to miss the opportunity to sleep on a bed for the first time in who knows how long, all because sharing a bed with me is somehow different from sharing a tent?" She tried to rub the chill out of her arms.

"It is different." Fael said, dropping his bags and moving to the fireplace.

"You didn't seem worried when we stayed with Tor."

He struck the flint and stone together. The spark didn't catch. "You were sick." His tone was final. The stones struck again.

"They already think we're together," she said, unable to tell if the thought still affected him too. "If they find you on the floor, they'll ask questions."

Fael remained silent. Ignored her.

"Fine. What a shame—a bed to myself." Breathing words that brought fire to her fingers, Leo squeezed her body in front of him and placed a lazy hand on the logs. Slowly, they ignited, and the fire grew. She twisted and smiled, shamelessly preening over the tiny success she'd worked so hard to achieve, but—

Oh gods.

She sat on the ledge of the hearth, and he knelt before her, leaving them eye level and too close.

Leo made to move, to voice an apology, but a hand shot out to grip her hip, pushing her firm against the brick. Her breath hitched at the delicious, unexpected pressure and it was too late to hide it. The warmth of the fire kissed her back, but the languid heat pulsing in her now made her eyelids too heavy, made her lips part to feed the sudden demand of a racing heart.

And, as if he knew, he studied her, eyes dark even as the light behind her grew. Unbidden, her curious fingers traced the tattered sleeve that let the cut of his muscular arms peek through. The idle movement drew his attention, and her skin pebbled as it dragged up her arm, along the curve of her shoulder, so heavy she could feel it like a breath on her neck, like a whisper in her ear. Slowly, so slowly, his gaze traced her lips, too. Then his eyes flicked to hers, freezing her in place.

Softening, he reached to tuck her hair back. "How are you so beautiful?"

She wanted to close her eyes, to lean into the touch, but there was such resistance to his movement. Like he was a moth, and she was an inevitable fiery demise.

Instead, she watched him take a measured breath, entranced by the rise and fall of his chest. The intensity suddenly dropped by a mile and, with a smirk, he plucked a leaf from the crown of her head. Then another, and another. She drew herself up to hide the too-late embarrassment, but his grin only grew as she flustered. Arching an eyebrow, she fought her own traitorous smile. Another leaf came away, then a gentle thumb went to her jaw, no doubt rubbing at a smudge of dirt. The touch sent electricity skittering to the back of her neck, down her spine. She shivered, and he stilled, eyes narrowing again in predatory focus.

They leapt apart as a knock split the air.

"I brought towels!" Jesse called from the hallway.

Leo huffed a nervous laugh, but Fael's face was stone again, and she fought the urge to bring a hand to the lead that settled in her chest as he gathered the collection of leaves.

"You get first wash, Princess."

The farm may as well have been a castle. Nothing could top the ecstasy of the first real wash after weeks in the woods, and she was even able to trim the awkward edges of her new hairstyle—not that cutting it had provided any camouflage. What a waste. No words could describe the relief of knowing they'd be able to rest for a while, though she'd never say so to Fael. For now, she was content to sit cross-legged on the bed, needle in hand, patching the rips in his clothes. Anything—anything but walk another step.

Or ogle the shirtless male in front of her.

"Is your family going to be at risk, now that we are here?" she managed to say. They were both now gloriously clean, but Fael was struggling to find a shirt that fit, as he was a bit broader than his cousin. Despite his shirtless-ness and a remarkably distracting, recent memory, the worry still spun round and round in her head.

Fael blinked once before his countenance darkened and he turned to inspect the contents of the wardrobe tucked in the corner. For the third time. She shouldn't have said anything; surely, he'd considered the possibility too, but his steely silence was starting to turn her gut, so different from the flash of affection before.

"The king doesn't know about them." Fabric and wood muffled his voice.

"He doesn't? How?"

"They're my relatives on my mother's side. As I became more valuable, my father stepped forward to let the king know I was . . . To tell the king he sired me. The king knew better than to ask who, exactly, my mother was. And I never mentioned it.”

She followed him as he left the room. “But still, he might know. Might think to look here?”

A sharp cough sent them whirling savagely toward the interloper.

“Nana found this,” Jesse said in a rush.

“Thank you.” Fael pulled the moth-eaten shirt on, and walked past her, stiff with the tension that still hung in the air.

Leo offered Jesse an apologetic smile and strode after the Wingbreaker. Then they were in the dining room, and his family erupted in greetings. The amiable smile returned, but his eyes remained shadowed. Leo tried to turn as many questions as she could back to the family, but they plowed forward with their lighthearted interrogation anyway. Yes, she was from Arnell. She and Fael met at the market when he brought in the Umbri traders. She worked in the library and lived in a room there. Sadly, her human mother had passed, and her father lived in Arnell as well, but was very, very busy. Yes, she had a brother, but he was working hard with her father to take over their business one day. It was a bakery. No, she did not have any fae magic, but her brother had a talent for water magic like some of the fae they employed. Fael did not contradict her, instead studiously focusing on the lean meat and mountain of vegetables on his plate.

Aunt Cynthia tutted. “That must be very difficult for you. Your brother being primed to take over, and your father paying you so little mind.”

"It's how I prefer it, actually. My father can be intense."

"Is that why you ran away with Fael?" Jesse asked, and the table went silent.

Fael looked to his uncle, his brows pulled together. Jesse hissed as Markus elbowed her under the table.

"Did you think we wouldn't hear the rumors, boy?" Uncle Roderick coughed deeply.

"Uncle, I didn't know where else to—" Fael went quiet as the man lifted a hand.

Roderick turned to Leo and pointed a long, crooked finger in her direction. "First, if you need to get away, we will help you."

Fael sputtered even as Leo's heart constricted at the man's kindness. "I did *not* kidnap her," he said.

His uncle continued. "Second," he bowed as much as he was able, "it is an honor to welcome you to our home, Your Highness."

"The pleasure is mine, Lord Roderick. Oh, you don't—" She resisted the urge to cover her face as the rest of the family bowed seriously. Fael alone remained upright, shaking his head softly.

"Why did you—I . . . I'm so sorry for lying to you all—" Leo began.

"Uncle, if I could speak with you privately for a moment." Fael stood without hearing the answer and found sanctuary elsewhere. His uncle excused himself before creeping slowly in his wake.

"Don't apologize, dear," Cynthia said, "it was easy to suspect, but hiding who you were seemed more comfortable for you. There was no reason to press. Do you prefer 'Leo'?"

Leo nodded dumbly, chest tight, forever taken off guard by the strangers in her life who gave more than they realized.

"How did you meet Fael?" Markus leaned over his plate eagerly. His skin wasn't as dark as his grandfathers, but his hair had the same springy curl. Jesse put her fork down in hopeful expectation. She wore a finer dress than when they'd arrived. Aunt Cynthia had changed too. Realizing they'd each dressed for the occasion, Leo was suddenly made shyer by her worn tunic and wild hair. The older woman admonished their questions, but the words seemed to ring in deaf ears before she, too, smiled softly, waiting for the answer.

But what to say?

Leo laughed. "It started with a book. Foolishly, I went to retrieve it alone. When I took a wrong turn, a thief grabbed me."

"Oh dear." Cynthia's eyebrows rose, and the cousins swapped excited looks.

"But a man stopped to help. He walked me to a carriage, never expecting to see me again, and I never expected to see him again, either, which is why I was bold enough to plant a kiss on his cheek," Leo ducked her head, "fancying myself a damsel rescued."

Jesse's eyebrows shot up, her mouth hanging open. "And that was . . .?"

Leo nodded. "Things only got worse from there. Then I met the man again. And again. All the while, my world turned upside down and he remained a constant, a pestering image, an anchor for my mind—this stranger who had become the keeper of my greatest secret. I can't explain it.

"He's saved my life more than once. He's seen the worst of me—known me. Not the title, but who I am when it's gone. A person I only hoped existed. One that's afraid and angry, yes, but free . . . He's been my ally, and I have been his. He's the only one who knows the true reason I had to escape, and while many would have fled at what we discovered, he is helping me—and is making a great sacrifice to do so. I can only hope they absolve him of these false claims. I'd hate for him to regret getting himself involved."

"Never," Fael's voice was rough, from where he stood in the doorway. "I'll never regret it."

truth
like poison
made potent
with every stolen smile
doom comes to the frog that boils
doom comes to the scorpion

forgive me
it is in my nature

it is in my nature

Chapter Thirty-Two

"Leo," Fael said, voice tight as he walked over and tugged on her hands. She only looked up with a glowing smile that dropped his stomach to the floor. "Come on," he said, tugging harder, wrenching her up.

She ripped away from him, "Fael. What are you doing?"

He didn't stop to see if his family noticed what sent him looping a hand around her middle and tugging her toward the door. She stiffened but didn't make further argument until they'd made it to the bedroom. Once there, she tore herself away and whirled.

"What has gotten into you?" she hissed. "I get a little sentimental and you have to drag me to the nearest bed?" She'd crossed her arms, never failing to keep that barrier between them. "I didn't even know you were listening." Fael gaped in stunned silence for a moment, his mind going into overdrive at the memory of the way her body felt when he sank his fingers into it. He sputtered, the sound half amusement, half irritation.

"Is that how it works in your books, *Leo*? Or—" His blood heated, threatening to boil in an instant. He stepped into her space, lowering his voice, battling his wilder nature as it tried to break through again.

"Since you're being so forthcoming with what's on your mind, I have to caution you: I require more than warmth, more than *a little sentimental*." He drew a finger over the pout of her lips, relishing the way her eyes darkened. "I want you mad with need for me, Leo," he murmured. "I want time. I want everything. So mid-family-dinner would be the last moment I'd choose to *drag you to the nearest bed*."

She didn't answer, only composed herself, tilting her chin up at him in that too-familiar way. The movement alone had him envisioning his hand gripped over that delicate jaw, in that auburn hair. Teeth grazing over her pulse, trailing kisses over those flushed cheeks.

Godsdamn it.

What was he doing? This would end badly for the both of them, worse if he didn't put a stop to it. He ripped himself from the thought of her, chest thundering. This reaction. This unbearable feeling. He'd experienced nothing like it. To feel it was to mourn it.

Because it wasn't meant for them.

For once, Fael looked away first, too consumed with his thoughts to enjoy the surprise and triumph lighting her face, followed swiftly by concern.

Light. That's why they were here.

"You were glowing." He tried to keep his voice even, but exhaustion weighed him down as swiftly and completely as the drugs that had ailed him. Was that only a week ago?

He fell on the bed and scrubbed at his face, ran a hand through his hair.

He was a mess.

The mattress shifted. Her concern weighed on him, made him feel strange—vulnerable. Like a starving animal refusing food, unable to trust that such kindness could exist in its world. Fael knew there was something splintered in him, always had been.

In a way he wished he'd never met her at all.

Not because he'd lose his position if he couldn't keep his head straight—or even because he'd be on the run until he was absolved or executed by the enemy. It was that being near her sent that splintered piece inching toward his petrified heart. Every time he caught her watching, every time his hands itched to reach for her, that jagged pain and the scar on his cheek would remind him that love was earned, not given.

And that, for some, the cost was too great.

The fire in their room warmed the stone floor, the solidity of the ground welcome as he wrestled with warring thoughts. She'd fallen asleep long ago, the evenness of her breathing only audible over the crackling fire because of his fae hearing. The memory of her skin was still kissed to his lips, to his hands. The soft shine of her eyes had taken him off guard at the time, but now he contemplated how he'd reacted to the way she'd spoken of him. Like a friend.

Like more.

It didn't change what he needed to do.

With one last heave of willpower, he stood, moving on silent feet to the bags by the door. The clothes she patched lay over-top of them—it was enough to still his hand, just for a moment.

He inked the report by candlelight at the kitchen table. Straightforward, with as much information as was safe. It was the best option before them but—

His heart skipped at the sound of footsteps, but it was only Markus. His cousin jerked his chin up in silent greeting before filling a cup from the tap. "Couldn't sleep?"

"Just some business."

"Think things will settle down soon?"

Fael sighed, rolling the parchment and tucking it into his bag. "I hope so. Just some things to clear up."

"If it comes to it. I'll fight." Markus flexed his sun-tanned hands, lightly scarred and heavily calloused.

Fael's brows lifted in surprise. The Umbri garrison didn't conscript soldiers, not anymore. "Really?" Markus loved working the farm, loved the animals. Had a talent for it. Not gifted like the fae, but who needed magic when you had passion? "You'd leave?"

Markus ducked his head. "Jesse can manage it all, and we've got the help. I wouldn't be missed . . . There's nothing here for me anymore."

Ah. When Fael visited last year, Markus had a young woman on his arm. Their smiles bounced off each other—one would start and before long the two were stuck grinning like fools. Nauseatingly sweet.

"What happened?"

"She decided I wasn't the best match. And now, with the deliveries, I can't do my job without interacting with her family."

"I'm sorry." Fael said, knowing the words wouldn't ease the ache. "It gets better."

After filling the glass again, Markus raised it in a toast and slammed it back like it was alcohol, and Fael repressed a grin. Markus was so young, barely twenty. He had a long life and a lot more heartbreak coming his way.

"I won't tell you not to, but if I do my job correctly, there won't be a war," Fael said.

His cousin snorted.

Fael leaned back against the kitchen chair. "What?"

"You'd let her go?" The question rang between them, but Fael wasn't sure which meaning his cousin intended. Would he let her go back to Arnell to face the cursed prince, or drive a wedge between them by presenting her to his king? His answer was the same, regardless.

"Yes." The word sounded hollow even to him.

"You know she's going to get you killed." Markus scrubbed the cup and put it away. "She seems nice, stiff, but nice. I just can't imagine you wanting to be with a—with someone . . . like her. Do you even know her? You're thinking with your head, right? Not with your—"

"Markus."

Markus put a palm up. "Whether you see something in her or not, I don't understand why you'd stick your neck out this far for Arnell's princess."

"No one else seemed willing to do so."

His cousin huffed and shook his head while Fael managed the cooling in his veins, the necessary distancing of himself that meant his mind switched into focus mode. Into fighting mode.

"I see that."

"See what?" Fael managed through clenched teeth.

"That no-shit-taking face. That scary fae look you do."

The side of Fael's mouth curled upward. "Scary fae look?"

Markus deepened his voice and puffed up his chest, "I'm the apex predator," he said with a scowl.

That earned an unexpected laugh.

"I thought I heard you get up." Leo rubbed her eyes as she entered, feet scuffing on the floor, lazy with sleep. Her tousled hair stuck up at odd angles and Fael's heart leapt into his throat at the sight. Why hadn't he heard her coming? Had she used magic to shield her approach? Did she suspect him?

Leo stretched, the motion putting her and her borrowed sleep shirt on display in a way that redirected the blood in his body. It was wrinkled and big enough to fall off one shoulder, letting that birthmark peek out before she tucked it back into place.

"Water, Princess?" Markus had already turned to the cabinet.

She chose the seat next to Fael, and crossed her legs, letting her knee settle against his thigh.

"It's Leo." She gave Markus a sleepy smile, accepting the glass and taking a delicate sip.

"Of course, Princess Leo." Fael couldn't tell if Markus was serious or being an ass.

As the silence stretched awkwardly, Leo's eyes sharpened, narrowing in on Fael's bag and the rolled letter resting conspicuously on the table. Finally, she took in his borrowed cloak and belt. He'd intended to deliver the missive and be home before she woke.

"Where are you going?"

"I wanted to get a read on the city. If there are posters here too it's better I go at night."

"I haven't seen any posters," Markus supplied.

"I'd rather see for myself." Fael pressed his lips closed in the awkward silence that followed, suddenly nauseous at the thought of Leo finding out about the letter. Her eyes flickered between him and Markus.

"I've interrupted something," she said. "Please, you'll have to excuse me." Leo stood and made her exit, wearing the rigid grace she donned when her own mind prepared for battle.

"Leo," Fael was already standing.

Markus raised an eyebrow. *You would let her go?*

Pulling himself from his cousin's silent gloating, Fael followed.

⟡

"Into Middlewood?" Fael repeated the words the next morning, hoping they would make sense coming from a more reasonable mouth.

Leo just put her bags on, all but ready to stroll out the door.

"What if there's wanted posters here too? What if the bounty hunters checked this far?"

"Markus said there aren't any. And Middlewood is technically an Umbri city." She put her finger in the air. "I'm assuming that's why you glossed over its name when we first discussed our plan."

Fael ignored the jab. She was still upset from the night before. She knew he was hiding something, and this was her taking matters into her own hands. It *was* an Umbri city, that was part of the problem. Royalty did not casually explore rival kingdoms. It wasn't done. He grabbed his bag, already knowing how it would end before he followed her down the hallway.

"Oh, you're going now?" Jesse perked up from her spot in the sitting room. "Let me get my things."

Fael glared at the back of his cousin's head. "This was her idea, wasn't it?"

"No. It was my idea. Jesse just wants to get some things for your aunt's birthday."

"We can't be seen with them," he reminded her.

Jesse walked back in the room and Fael spoke to her instead, "You can't be seen with us. It's too risky."

Jesse slumped enough that guilt nudged its way in.

But he wasn't wrong.

"She can't be seen with us, but she can be seen with me." Leo plopped a bright red hat over her red hair, tucking it neatly underneath. "And, if you must join us, you may trail behind at a respectable distance. Oh! You should wear a hat too." She walked out the door. Jesse gave him an apologetic shrug he didn't believe for one second before following.

Cursing under his breath, he grabbed a cloak from by the door. His uncle watched, grinning from where he sat by the fireplace.

Was anyone on his side?

Fael gave him a salute before following them into the sunny morning. He allowed plenty of space between them, and to his increasing annoyance, Leo didn't look back to see if he followed.

The city was packed with people, but the bright hat she wore made them easy to find. Jesse led the way, with Leo craning her neck this way and that, taking in the stocky stone buildings. The muted colors, he knew, were very different from the variety she was used to. In the center of the larger, circular crossroads, cairns towered, stacked proudly by friends and family of the those who were lost serving Umbri in the years since the kingdom was founded. The buildings were slightly bigger as well, to account for the larger population of giant-kin.

Many lived along the kingdom's southern border, in the Thunderwell, a valley nestled in the peaks of the Silk Mountain. Orcs and other giant-kin towered over fae and human, though many of the recent generation giant-kin barely stood a foot taller than an average orc at this point. Certainly smaller than Tor.

Slowly, Fael let his shoulders relax. There were no wanted signs here. Any guards patrolling were half-asleep, not on the hunt.

It was more than just color that made Leo contrast against the gray of her surroundings. She leaned into Jesse conspiratorially, and the two erupted in laughter. A fist gripped his heart. He should send the letter. Its presence carried too much weight in his bag, dragging his shoulder down, throwing everything that he was off balance.

Not yet.

He couldn't step away from them, not on this first pilot run into the city. He could return another day. They could stay at the farm a while—the rest was necessary for them both—though her continued presence was a blessing and a curse. He could let them have this. He could have this.

For just a little while longer.

Where did that hat go?

Fael cursed. He'd lost them. They were just at a stand offering fruit that had seen better days, but they'd disappeared. He popped his head into the clothing shop next door, eyes darting around, but the seamstress gave him an odd look. He gave her a polite nod and left before she assumed he meant trouble.

Relief washed over him when he spotted Jesse stepping into a building labeled "Herma's Beadery." Trotting over, he found the whole room draped in earth-colored fabrics that concealed the stone walls. Jewelry and bizarrely embroidered cloth lay over several tables and hung behind the counter. Jesse was already haggling animatedly over a long necklace of turquoise and clear stones.

"Jesse," he said, with growing concern as his eyes swept the shop. "Where's Leo?"

She flipped a casual hand. "She said she'd meet me back at the bakery."

He stilled.

"She's a grown woman, Fael. She's fine."

Blood roared in his ears, drowning out the conversation that went on despite the pit of fear that grew in his gut. He stepped out of the shop, fighting the urge to shout her name and draw more attention to himself. He let his eyes unfocus, let them land anywhere they caught. A couple kissing, a dwarf caught in the current of the crowd, the dilapidated wooden sign of an old tavern whose door kept opening, spilling voices and raucous music that had his teeth grinding.

Then a bakery. There had to be a dozen bakeries in Middlewood. There was every chance this wasn't the one.

He flew into the squat building and collided with Leo.

She gaped at him, pastry now smeared over the lower half of her face.

"Um . . ." She covered her mouth while she chewed and then thrust a second pastry under his nose. "This one's yours."

He took it awkwardly, the apology stalled on his lips by absurdity and embarrassment. Footsteps and poorly smothered laughter told him his cousin had found them. Jesse's laugh must have been Leo's undoing, because she giggled as she wiped at the sticky icing that smeared over her face instead of coming off. Jesse broke into a cackle, no longer able to hold it in, and Fael huffed a laugh that was amusement and relief and despair all in one.

Leo tried to push him. "I told you to keep a respectable distance."

He made sure he didn't move an inch, the challenge, the touch, and her faux indignation cradling his heart and setting it at ease. He swung out his cupcake hand and bowed.

"King of Subtle, remember?"

Chapter Thirty-Three

LEO HUFFED UNDER PARCHMENT, ink, and a mountain of books she'd borrowed from Middlewood's library. Returning home seemed to take much longer, but at least Fael carried the other half. Luckily, he hadn't argued or tried to reason with her, just rolled his eyes in a poor attempt to hide his smile.

Jesse chattered animatedly the whole way, as she had done throughout the entire tour. It was a miracle Leo was able to find time to visit the post building alone, but everything had gone to plan. Evergreens speckled the rolling hills around them. Bright pops of color waved, petals reaching for the sun. The city hadn't been quite what she expected. The people seemed reserved, somehow. Maybe they could tell she was an outsider. Overall, it was . . . sturdy.

Before Leo could voice the thought, she spied a group of figures coming toward them on the road. It was too late for Fael to drop back, but she still had her hat, and Jesse seemed unperturbed, still going on about Markus's nasty break up with one of her friends. Still, Fael's eyes narrowed, determining the threat. The group, thirty or more soldiers, armed and bearing the Umbri crest, nodded politely as they passed. Fael's eyes tracked over them. The tension cleared as the clamor of footsteps and armor faded. Jesse finally noticed the worried silence and turned around to give the group another look before Leo stopped her with a whispered command.

They walked the rest of the way in silence, each stuck in a concerned cycle of who the men might have been and what their presence might mean. Leo would ask, but not in front of Jesse, not when she'd finally made a friend who carried a modest amount of books home herself. Who called her by the name she preferred—without a reminder.

Fael refused to let her catch his eye, however, and that alone meant the soldiers' appearance did not bode well.

⸻⟨◉⟩⸻

"It was likely one of several parties the king sent out in response to my warning about the lawstones. There's no way to know if they'll stick around or move on after seeing things are well here." Fael hardly moved, but she recognized the undercurrent of stress that buzzed under his skin. She could nearly feel it under her own.

"And if they stay?" She shuffled the books around, making space on the small writing desk before arranging the ink and parchment.

"It may affect nothing. I'll return tomorrow to gather what I can."

Equipment or intelligence, he didn't specify, but she suspected it would be both, considering the possibility they were to be chased out of their resting spot so soon. Neither of them brought it up, and she assumed he'd be even more regretful to leave than she.

"Do you think they recognized us?"

"If they did, they wouldn't have let us pass."

She looked up, catching his terse tone, but the fight seemed to rush out of him all at once. He let himself fall back onto the bed, the opposite end bouncing under his weight. Even as he stilled, she could feel the worry pouring from him.

"I'm going to do whatever I have to do, Fael."

"Me too."

Should she go to him? He threw an arm over his face, revealing a very interesting strip of skin above his waistband.

I want you mad with need for me, Leo.

She jumped as someone passed their open door on their way to the washroom.

The sooner Leo left, the sooner his family would be safe.

She'd done what she could about their situation—sending a letter to her brother, asking after her father's condition and the status of Corsair. Fael wouldn't have agreed to the amount of information she'd included, or with giving away their location, but it was her last chance before deciding what to do. She'd told Callum if it would stop a war, she would return. Being forthcoming was not Fael's strength, and while she trusted him to see her safely through the woods, he'd spoken little of what they'd do now that they were safe. Leo didn't divulge her plans to him, either.

She stared at the blank page, her mind swarming in a way that would only calm once it was spilled onto paper. The memories were painful though—raw, as they poured onto the page, forcing her to realize the kind of horrors they'd endured. True, she'd been debilitated by fear, and, at times, in need of protection, but she'd also been strong.

Maybe it didn't have to be one or the other.

A while later, bleary-eyed, Leo looked up to where Fael stood in the doorway. "I'm sorry?" She flexed and stretched her hand absentmindedly.

"Aunt Cynthia called us to dinner."

Oh. The sun peeked through the window in the same oranges and reds that spread across the horizon. She grimaced at her splotched sleeves, but capped the ink and followed Fael to the dining room. Aiming straight for the sink, she scrubbed the hard bar of lye over her skin. It didn't help. With a defeated sigh, she sat at the table next to Fael, across from Jesse, with Rodrick and Cynthia at either end. A small vase of fresh flowers decorated the carefully sanded wood. Modest. Steadfast, like much of their home. Like the family themselves. They dug into their food with open appreciation, discussing potato deliveries, and how many cows would calve.

Leo marveled at how very different this table felt from the one at home. Fael seemed as knowledgeable about the farm as any of them—his earlier mood resolved. Did he often come here to escape his own duties, to find peace?

Peace. Her heart flinched at the word and picked up speed, dragging the air from her lungs. A couple of controlled breaths later, Fael twisted in his seat, a question on his lips, but she stood abruptly.

"Just need a moment." She beamed his way without meeting his eyes.

The heavy door scraped hideously against the floor as she wrenched it open. The sound grated against her frayed nerves, but sunlight and the cool caress of a breeze beckoned her out, feet moving of their own accord. Her steps carried her into a field of green, growing things, following the rows until they ended. She continued, cresting the hills into open farmland, unable to outpace the thoughts in her head.

How naive had she been to think she'd solve anything by running away? Everything had gone from bad to worse because she chose her own peace instead of that of her kingdom. She'd always done so: abhorring the demands of her station, ignoring all the while how it might affect those she was supposed to lead. Surely, she could garner support to handle this? Not the Umbri king. She wouldn't throw herself at the mercy of a rival kingdom. That would be beyond foolish, but perhaps someone in her own court? Sebastian seemed the most obvious one to question, though he'd shown where his loyalties lay. If nothing else, she was stronger now. If nothing else, her return, consequences be damned, would stop Umbri and Arnell from going to war.

Foolish. For being here at all. For play-acting a simple life while behind her loomed catastrophe. This wasn't for people like her. This was selfish. Shortsighted.

She sat on the newly green grass and laid back, resting her head against her hands, drawing focus to her breath. The blue sky. The puffy white clouds. The weeds tickling her skin. The rush of irrigation. The sighing wind. The crisp scent of spring mingling with rain soon to fall. Slowly, her heart eased, lulled into the rhythm of life around her. Magic came easy, then. Flame wrapped her fist, licking the air, greedy for a life of its own.

For fuel to burn.

———⟡———

Fael met her on the walk back. He seemed to swallow his questions as she smiled.

"It's beautiful here."

He looked around. "It's very . . . open."

"Not enough trees for your taste?"

He grinned. "It's a good reminder that we are close to the edge of the lawstone's protection."

Leo turned back to eye the distant tree line. How different it was in the sphere of protection. She'd lived her whole life knowing the danger, but before, it was a faraway thing. Now, she shivered, imagining what might be looking back.

Nothing escaped the Wingbreaker's attention. "You're cold, we should head back."

Once they'd returned, she retreated to their room to flip through the grimoire. It seemed wise to prepare for her return, but a spell she'd brushed off before suddenly stood out—"Change color." Aptly named. She frowned. It would likely have helped to have used it on herself before going into town. "Lasts up to twelve hours."

Seemed safe enough to try.

Leo scurried to sit on the floor in front of the mirror, leaning in a dusty corner. Her reflection gave her pause. She looked thinner, older, but there was life in her face. The unruly mop of her hair had no maids to tame it, and the sharp gleam in her eye was new. The point of her ears and full cheeks were the same. She tugged at the auburn locks, failing to smooth them down.

"Who are you now?" she asked the disheveled, keen-eyed woman in the mirror.

She didn't answer.

Leo blew a quick breath and readied herself for the spell. When she opened her eyes to speak, she startled at the sight of her eyes glowing. Quite odd. Diverting her gaze to the page, she focused hard on her intention, picturing it as clear as day in her mind. A stir of warmth passed over her head, and the hair itself glowed before fading, revealing itself to be exactly the color she imagined.

Abruptly, Leo fell over, clasping a hand over her mouth, trying to cover the laughter lest someone come to investigate. Tears leaked down her cheeks. An entire minute passed before she recovered, but the laughter returned the moment she glanced at her reflection.

When she spoke to release the spell, nothing happened. A second failure had her scouring the page. "Lasts twelve hours"

Then in the margin, in a frustrated scrawl "Cannot be changed for twelve hours***". Leo laughed again, the sound tinged with despair.

Footsteps carried down the hall, sending her racing to the bed to throw the blanket over her head. The door opened.

"Leo did you—" Fael stopped short. "What are you doing?"

The blanket was her second mistake of the last half hour. She pulled it up, scooting it over her head to wear like a cloak.

"Did you want to finish your dinner? My aunt saved it for you."

Leo swallowed, embarrassed that she'd fled, and embarrassed that she most certainly could not appear now.

She gave him a sheepish grin. "Would you mind bringing it to me? I'm famished, but indisposed."

Fael regarded her critically, clearly trying to read what was wrong. "Indisposed how?"

"A proper lady never tells." She almost laughed at how his eyes widened. What could possibly go through his mind? Jerking his head in a nod, he about-faced out of the room, shutting the door behind him. She raced to the crimson hat she'd worn to Middlewood and leaped in front of the mirror, arranging all her hair neatly underneath.

Not a moment too soon, she turned to the door as he returned, her hands delicately folded. "Thank you," she said as he placed the plate on the desk.

"Are these . . ." His attention had gone to the scattered parchment. "About us?"

. . . Some wizards were slower to leave than
others. Among the bold was the great Ellesida Northrow, who passed in a tragic house fire
shortly after she began spouting about the end of
the world. Personally, I think the husband did it.

-Tales from Umbri's Anonymous

Chapter Thirty-Four

🔥

His genuine, hesitantly curious smile tugged at something in her chest. He reached for the top page. "Do you mind if I . . .?"

"No . . . Go ahead." It wasn't anything he didn't already know. He'd been there after all.

He lifted it and skimmed quickly, brow wrinkling behind a curtain of untied golden hair. "I should have given that man a slower death." Mouth set in a grim line, he replaced the parchment and padded over. One hand wavered in the air, but he stopped short, crestfallen, as if he couldn't bring himself to touch her.

"I'm sorry, Leo. It's my fault it happened at all. I was supposed to keep you safe and instead I let us get separated. I failed. I chose to go through the forest when the cart would have been better, safer. I put you at risk because I didn't want to be cramped up and I thought that you didn't want . . ."

She wrapped her arms around him, clasping her hands and squeezing hard. Sighing, he let his arms slide over her back, enveloping her with the scent of sweet, earthy pine. Gods, Umbri made the best soap. With her ear to his chest, she recognized the worry in a heart that beat too fast.

"You were right. I didn't want to stay crammed there with only my thoughts to keep me company."

He placed his chin on her head. "Your thoughts and yours truly, you mean?"

"I didn't know you too truly then. I couldn't confide in you."

"You can now."

Naturally, Markus appeared in the doorway and Fael stepped back, leaving her in the cool space of his absence.

"Oh, uh, sorry. Did you still have time to—?"

"I told Markus I'd help him finish his stable project," Fael said.

"Is there any way I can help?"

"Possibly. What he really needs is company. He seemed upset that he was avoiding going into town while the rest of us had a grand time." Markus shook his head in mock offense, but Fael pressed on. "I tried to tell him all *I* did was keep watch, but I'm happy to listen." Fael lifted an eyebrow. "If he needed to talk."

Leo pursed her lips to one side. "Jesse mentioned the . . . situation. It does help. I can vouch for that."

Fael gave her a half smile. "Me too."

Her heart lurched against her chest at the unexpected admission.

To Markus's quickly reddening face, he said, "New training exercise," while digging in his bag and procuring a flask. "You drink. You talk." He took a swig.

"I'm sorry?" Leo said.

His grin was lethal. "You drink. You talk, Leo."

Leo ignored the way he said her name and looked to Markus for clarification. "And how is that a training exercise?"

With a long-suffering sigh, Markus sat at the foot of the bed, but he smiled, holding his hand out to Fael for the flask. "Age old technique. Really important." He took a drink and Leo laughed as he sputtered. Then Markus held it out to her, and she glared at each of the men in turn. Fael's wicked grin had her taking a too-long pull, and she lifted a hand to hide her cringe as the alcohol burned its way down to her gut. She still hadn't eaten.

Fael retrieved the flask and drank again before speaking.

"She was a human. Beautiful. Tough—fierce, really. I met her in training. For a while, she was better than me. Not stronger, but crafty. Every time she put me down, I fell a little more in love. But—" He sighed. The sound edged with melancholy. "I was a fool. I thought I'd get her attention. Instead, I nearly got her, myself, and two of my friends killed trying to take on a pula that was terrorizing local food stores. Commander told them to heal us, of course, but not too much. A few days later, she looked at me—bitter that the worst of my injuries were well on their way to healing. It took longer for her, without the fae blood." Another drink softened a grim smile.

"Anyway. I was changing her bandages and our eyes caught. I thought . . . well. It didn't matter what I thought. Because what she said was 'I really wish you were human.' And that was that. There was never even a chance. She didn't want to be with someone that would survive what she couldn't, who would outlive her by lifetimes. The fear of being replaced, maybe forgotten? It raised a lot of hard questions for me. Imagine living and dying with the one great love of your life, only for them to move on and find that *their* greatest love was the one they found after you were gone."

Leo sat in stunned silence for a moment. The thought made her nauseous. Had her mother regretted the life her father would live, or had lived, without her?

"Don't be sad, Your Highness. I've had lovers, sure. But like I said, we don't get to choose who we give our heart to."

Had he given his heart away since?

Leo avoided voicing the question by swiping the flask and throwing herself on the bed. Back against the wall, clutching a pillow to her stomach, she said, "Well, *my* heart wasn't nearly so dramatic," She fluttered her eyelashes at Markus, who chuckled. "Naturally, a handsome, well-dressed, well-bred boy was put in my way—as often happens when you're a princess—and we seemed to have many of the same interests. I, young and moon-eyed, was enamored with him from the start. Just bold enough, always charming. And did I say handsome?"

Leo drank to hide her blush as Fael scoffed. Markus's laugh echoed out the room, down the hallway, clear and high. Her cheeks heated, from embarrassment or the alcohol, she didn't know. Regardless, she plowed on, counting her points on her fingers. "He catered to me, never riled, was always agreeable. One day I was miffed over something, and he didn't defend himself, didn't engage me in any way and I realized—he'd been parroting everything I said back to me. Every interest, every whim. And since decent *bedtime skills—*"

Leo stopped—lifting an eyebrow as Markus failed to shove down some kind of sputtering sound. Fael remained carefully neutral, as if she would miss the way his lips fought to curl.

"As I was saying," Leo said pointedly.

The men nodded sagely.

"Since that kind of talent can't be a whole personality, I decided he must not have one at all. Dismissing him is what finally got an honest reaction, apparently. A few good rumors came out of it—each more embellished than the last." She sighed. "Alas. So, then I went the other way and wound up with a secret lover. He didn't recognize me, and I never told him who I was, but that didn't work either, because he wanted me to be the one to parrot *his* interests back to *him*, and his only conflict solution was aggression." The alcohol burned a little less this time.

Choosing to ignore the weight of Fael's scrutiny, Leo passed the flask to Markus, who sighed, his long legs braced wide against the stone floor. His softer face and round ears reminded her how young he really was.

"Drink and talk." Fael reminded him.

Resigned, Markus drank.

"She is the daughter of the noble merchant we supply. I handle their orders and deliveries. She's beautiful. Stunning, honestly. And I was interesting enough, for a time. But I am not a noble. Her mother had told her they were looking for good matches. And I am not one of those. She's not self-seeking like the—" His eyes flickered between Leo and Fael. "She's different. But she loves her family. She's committed to doing what's best for them. Announced her engagement last week."

Silent now, each of them contemplated the floor for a while before Markus said, "Decent bedtime skills," and started chuckling. Fael shook his head and groaned, rubbing his eyes, but he was smiling too. Leo giggled into the pillow to hide a face as crimson as the hat she wore.

"We should go before it's too late," Fael said, trying to rein them in.

Markus wiped a hand through the air. "I'm good." He still smirked as he shrugged. "I just needed the company."

Chapter Thirty-Five

THE FIRST QUIET LIGHT of the morning streamed through the window, illuminating Fael's second cup of tea.

"Oh no, I'm late!" Jesse stampeded past him in a rush of cloak and bags.

"Late for what?" Fael called after her.

She answered from the sitting area, clearly struggling with her shoes. "I told Markus I'd take the meeting with Lord Gerund about the potato sales. His daughter is the one Markus—well. Anyway, I don't know why they want to do these meetings so early in the morning, and they serve the daintiest breakfast!" She popped her head in the kitchen. "See you later."

"I'll be in town later, but Leo is staying, so you'll see one of us at least."

His cousin shouted something back, muffled by the drag of the front door. Everyone would be awake now, if they weren't already.

Using the still-hot kettle, Fael brewed another cup and carried it down the hallway to where Leo slept. His back ached from the nights on the stone floor, but he'd never admit it. It seemed her nightmares hadn't stopped, as she still tossed and turned in the night, though she didn't admit to that either. Maybe he could mention joining her, just for one night, for the sake of his aching joints. Just so she could get some peaceful rest. His heart picked up at the thought as he opened the door and—

"Is your hair BLUE?" Fael froze, his mouth dropped to the ground. Leo was still messy with sleep, her face lined with the kiss of her pillow.

And every strand of her wild, chin-length hair was corn-flower blue.

Her eyes widened, and she tumbled out of the bed. The blankets fell after her and she crawled on all fours until she faced her reflection.

In the mirror, she pouted. "It said it only lasted twelve hours."

Once the laugh started, it wouldn't stop. She swung her head around to glare. And he really did try to stop it, but it erupted, full bellied, and soon his chest ached. Her own bright laugh broke through his gasps for breath and he placed the tea down lest he spill it.

"What did you do?" He could hardly get the question out.

On the floor, she pulled up her knees. "It was a color changing spell! I thought it would help me blend in. I didn't realize it wouldn't let me change it back." She scrubbed at her hair in the mirror as if she could wipe it off.

His aunt and uncle were up, bustling around the kitchen. Fael closed the door and set the lock.

"Well, try it again—they can't see you like this." Every time he dared a glance, he chuckled a bit more, threatening another laughing fit.

She stood and crossed her arms. "Maybe I like it like this." Her smile belied the challenge.

"It looks so real," he said, having crossed the room to tug at the strands. He ran his fingers through, watching the color catch the light.

"Ow," she said, as his fingers caught in a tangle. "Your hair pulling could use some practice, soldier."

His focus zeroed in on the too-innocent look on her face, hyper-aware of every inch between them and the prim lift of her chin that left her neck gorgeously exposed. Fael wasn't the best hunter in Umbri because he was rash or impatient.

But this woman.

From the other room, the sounds of morning grew louder, and he withdrew. "I'll cover for you. Just try." Once he had the door safely shut between them, he took a steadying breath.

A chorus of good mornings later, he was cutting sausage and frying eggs. Aunt Cynthia's hands were giving her trouble, so he shooed her to go sit at the table. Markus tossed a jar of honey, a plate of butter, and a few thin slices of bread on the table.

The peace here used to surprise him. They'd never visited when he was a boy—his mother didn't receive enough funds or time to travel this way, but once they met in Umbri City proper, and had lunch. That was before his cousins were born, of course. The toddler who'd been with them was Markus and

Jesse's mother. Even then, she'd been a handful. Unsuited for farm life, they'd all said.

Fael's uncle creeped in on his cane, "Smells good, boy." Fael reached to pull out a chair, but the man waved him off, choosing instead to scoot it slowly, an inch for each tug. Fael's heart twisted.

"Breakfast is ready," he called out the door, and served his uncle a plate. Aunt Cynthia stood, but he only scooped a good portion and hefted her breakfast onto the table as well.

"Aren't you going to serve me too, Wingbreaker?" Markus seemed rosy cheeked this morning. Fael clapped his cousin on the shoulder. "You'll have to fight me for the last sausage."

A ruckus of pushing and shoving later and Markus cursed Fael in relief that, despite losing, there were still plenty left.

"Save some for the princess," his aunt tutted.

"The princess is here!" Leo announced as she swept in. She hugged his aunt and his uncle, the latter of which pressed a kiss into her hair. She flapped her fingers at Markus. "Good morning." She was all cheer. Red graced her hair again, perhaps a shade brighter than it had been. "Thank you." She curtsied to Fael in a dramatic flourish before snatching his plate out of his hands, throwing a wry look over her shoulder as she sauntered back to the table. Markus stuffed his face to hide his amusement.

"Where's Jesse?" she said as she sat across from the empty chair.

"She's handling the Gerund meeting today," Markus supplied quickly.

Leo hummed over her food in answer. "This is spectacular, Cynthia. Thank you."

"Actually, Fael made breakfast this morning."

Fael stiffened.

"This is excellent, Fael. Really, some of your best. Thank you." She took another hearty mouthful.

"Of course." He'd cooked plenty for her on their trek through the forest. Why would he be nervous about it now?

Later, Leo occupied the large window in the sitting area, engrossed in a book. Markus was out managing animal bedding. Aunt Cynthia had gone to lie down and his uncle soaked in the warming sun as he surveyed one plot or another, making notes on what needed to be done. Slow, but dogged.

Out the window, Fael could see him talking to one of the farm hands—fae-touched, if the point of his ears were any indication. There were a lot of workers on any farm, split between the races. A few fae or giant-kin were often worth the higher price of employment. A sick plant might choose to be well in exchange for a song. Pests might find other places to feed, encouraged to move on by the gentle enchantment that flowed in their veins. And one giant kin could do the work of several human men. Nevertheless, the wage disparity could be a point of contention for those without magic, especially humans.

Despite these differences, Uncle Rodrick managed to keep his workers happy. Instead of employing one race or another as some chose to, he ensured there was camaraderie, and that plenty witnessed the benefits a fae or a giant-kin could bring;

better production meant better profit after all, and his uncle passed around the surplus, keeping only what the farm needed.

"Anymore and it would be a waste," he'd said once, when Fael questioned him, used to the greed of nobility and kings.

The Wingbreaker watched with a sad, swelling pride. Soon, Jesse would have to follow the old man's lead.

Chapter Thirty-Six

"I'M GOING TO LAMEL," Fael said as he headed for the door. "I'll likely be back in the morning."

"It's nearly sundown," Leo argued from her perch by the window.

"I know. It'll be easier to do what I need to do."

Leo leapt up, one arm clasping the elbow of another. "You'll be careful?" It was an absurd question to ask the Wingbreaker of Umbri, but with the set of his shoulders and the events of the previous day, it was obvious he felt nervous about investigating the group of soldiers they'd passed. It worried her too. What if he ended up outnumbered again? Or poisoned?

He wrenched the door open and turned. "I will," he said, hesitating.

The timid expression was so unlike him that laughter bubbled out of her, part nerves, part amusement. "What?" she asked.

"I don't know how to do this." Fael shook his head, smiling.

Her stomach dropped. "Do . . . what?" Was he blushing?

He ran a hand through his hair, throwing a glance toward the laborers in the field. "Say a proper farewell?"

Oh, he was definitely blushing.

"Do you need to?" Unease fluttered in her stomach. He was coming back, right? He stiffened. "No. No, you're right." He turned to leave.

"No wait," she caught him with a hand on his arm, too slow to pull it away. "A proper farewell," she said, ignoring the way her heart quickened in anticipation. For once, he seemed more uncertain than she, and it was too easy to drop her chin, offering him a few enamored blinks. "Alright. You're supposed to offer your hand."

He did, palm up, and she laid her own on top of it, skin tingling where they touched.

"Now, you bow," she said. Inexplicable nerves tangling in her gut. "Then place a kiss on the back of my hand."

Fael's warm lips lingered, sending a thrill down to the tips of her toes. He kept his eyes on her, watching her hesitant breath. When he straightened, the shadow was gone. Now, the very male smile on his face oozed arrogance, so when he tried to let go, she held fast. "Not yet. Now *you* say, 'I am grateful for your time, Princess Madeline. You are as enchanting and pretty as they say.'"

Fael didn't balk. Only contemplated her for a moment, tracing a thumb over the spot he'd kissed. A single step forward brought him so close the heat of his body radiated through her clothes. She fought the urge to lean into it.

"I am grateful for your time, Leo," he murmured. "I am certain they don't know how enchanting you really are." His eyes sparkled with amusement before dimming to something bolder. "And pretty is an overly modest way to describe you." He lifted her hand again, turning it to press a kiss to the tender spot on the inside of her wrist.

Leo pushed the edges of her smile down and lifted her face to the sky, but it was no use, there was no stopping it. "Flattery will get you nowhere, soldier," she said, her grin revealing the lie.

With a tug, he pulled their bodies flush together, hooking her around the waist. "I wouldn't entertain the thought, Your Highness." Every inch of him was like hard flame, burning where they touched. Her lungs couldn't decide if they needed to suck in breath or hold it in anticipation. When he spoke again, his voice was a low caress over her skin, causing the most remarkable need to melt where she stood. "I do remember quite a different farewell, though." With agonizing slowness, he pressed his lips to her cheek. The touch was unbearably, heartbreakingly gentle. Like he was too aware of the violence in him. When he pulled away, her mouth hung open. For once, incapable of words.

"Was that right?" he murmured.

She tucked her hair behind her ears, nodding and smiling like a fool, unable to contain the swelling feelings in her chest.

"You're glowing, Princess."

Surprised, she surveyed her arms and willed the magic down with a laugh. "I don't know why that keeps happening."

He just smiled, eyes intense enough to make her stomach flip.

"I'll see you in the morning?" she said.

"See you in the morning, Leo."

She watched him go, relishing her name on his lips, tilting her head to bathe in a stray beam of light. When it retreated, she threw her body against the heavy door to close it.

By late afternoon, only the crisp sound of turning pages filled the now-empty house. Empty except for the dapple pawed pup who stretched beside her now, graying nose tucked into Leo's side. She'd borrowed "The History of Atlas, Giants, and Their Kin" from the library, and found it fascinating, if a little grim. The author of the book had an honest, but dismal, outlook on modern Giant culture.

Unfortunately, there appeared to be little mention of what it meant to be Atlas favored or why the well of magic reacted so extremely with her, though perhaps she'd gone mad, as the text suggested.

Sighing, she picked up another book—this one much thicker—detailing Orc history. Leo's eyes swam at the lengthy account of blood lines, occupations, and locations. She blinked hard at the page, attention already glazed over.

Someone shouted outside. A muffled background noise suddenly came into focus. The window offered no clue, and the door wailed as she tugged it open, briefly drawing the attention of Markus, who stood a little way down the road. Beyond him, a pair of horsemen raced toward the farm, a familiar figure in pursuit. A group of armored men followed behind, also on horseback and gaining quickly. Leo watched as the last group loosed an arrow at the man, only missing him by a foot.

Adrenaline lanced its way through her, forcing her body into action. She ran, drawing magic in with every step, every breath. "Go inside, now!" she told Markus, who called after her in fear and confusion.

An arrow tore through the neck of one of the closest soldiers, and the rider fell from her seat, the horse under her shying from the path.

Leo let her fire spread over her body, burning through the fear of who the pursuers were and what she had to do. Fael's lips moved as he shouted now too, but she couldn't hear him, because she needed to focus, and the shouts of men and clatter of horses could overwhelm her as easily as any real threat. The welcome silence already embraced her.

The second rider was nearly to the farm. She felt the first dregs of panic rise as they locked eyes. He smiled and drew a shortsword, yanking his horse around suddenly, aiming for Fael.

Fael stopped short, lifting his bow to take the man down, but an arrow speared out from the group behind him and sank into his shoulder. The horseman kicked his steed into a sprint, sword raised high.

She didn't feel it when she killed him.

The flame punched through his body effortlessly, leaving a gaping hole of cauterized flesh. Soft tendrils of smoke wafted from the wound as he convulsed and fell forward, sword falling to the ground.

The horse veered away from Fael, who winced as he continued toward her. He was trying to say something, but she couldn't hear it behind her shield.

Another arrow sailed past him and he turned to look, letting her see the first arrow still stuck fast in his shoulder.

Anger rushed in and Leo strained as she raised a whip of connection. Magic funneled through her as flame grew on its end. The horses balked, some veered away entirely, but still some continued, confident in the face of battle.

Almost there. Fael kept running—running and . . . waving a hand? They were nearly upon him. One man nocked an arrow. She spared Fael a single glance just before she let the fist of fire pummel into their ranks, but his eyes were wide in fear, fear of her. Confused, she studied the shape of his lips, felt her face and concentration waver as she looked behind him to search the horses.

At the back of the group, one guard held Jesse, gagged and bound.

Leo rallied and, with an angry yank, splintered the blunt fist into flaming lances that readied themselves at her back.

She gritted her teeth, magic bucking wildly against the restraint.

The first shot speared clean through a soldier, his body falling in the way of the horses behind him.

Her second attack went wide. Fael made it to her, but if he spoke, or stood, or continued past, she didn't know. Her third and fourth attack killed again and again. Arrows flew from behind her, and more soldiers fell. Jesse's face crumpled in horror, her body wracking with silent sobs. The soldier ripped her head back and held a knife to her throat, his meaning clear.

Leo growled in frustration and let the silence fall. The spears of flame hissed as they dissolved. The attackers advanced to the clanking of metal and Fael's labored breathing at her back. Several soldiers lay still, white feathered arrows decorating the spots their armor didn't reach. Leo risked a glance behind, ensuring anyone outside the farm fled or found shelter. Fael stood only a step behind, pale, the bloodied arrow from his back on the ground now.

"You should run." His voice was hoarse. "It was an ambush. They threatened my aunt and uncle and . . . and Jesse told them where to find you." His voice broke.

Jesse? The young woman still sobbed, her bottom lip bleeding and already swollen. "Can't you shoot the man holding her?"

"I won't risk it."

"I'm done running. And I'm not going with them."

Fael nodded and stepped to her side. A touch of breeze sent goosebumps up her arms.

He drew his sword. "As soon as he dismounts, I'll—" his head whipped sideways at the hiss of an arrow.

Pain lanced through her thigh. Fael angled his weapon down, clinging to her with both arms. The pain ebbed away and numbness spread. She stared at the arrow in shock. They wanted her alive, didn't they?

Dread washed over her, but the Wingbreaker met her wide eyes with a resolute stare of his own.

They wanted Fael alive. Didn't they?

A few soldiers dismounted. "Wingbreaker. I have something I think belongs to you." He gestured to Jesse. Then, looking at Leo, he said, "I'll be taking this one to the king. He's quite curious to see what motivated you to go against his orders."

Fael's arm tightened around her as he swung his sword out at the approaching soldiers, but Jesse squeaked in pain as her captor tightened his hold and let a crimson tear slip down her throat. Slowly, Fael's arms loosened and rough hands dragged Leo out of his hold. She cried out as a bolt of pain cut through her numbed limb. The world wavered as the poison took hold. Another guard dismounted, dressed finer than the others, and Leo loathed the tenor of his voice as he spoke.

"Did you think I wouldn't spot my own little brother? You're famous, Fael." The men behind him laughed at the bitter words. The captain had darker hair, but he and Fael shared the same broad shoulders and irritating smirk.

"Oren," Fael said, his voice barely more than a growl. The man stepped close, but Fael didn't move as he was disarmed, and his bow was tossed to the side.

"Not going to fight now, Wingbreaker?"

The twist of Oren's lips warped to a sneer when his captive remained silent, refusing to be baited.

"Leave him alone." Leo's voice was soft, slurred. Fael didn't look at her. He kept his eyes locked forward, hands clasped behind him, at attention.

The man threw Fael's pack on the ground and motioned for the remaining soldiers to search it. They all let out a soft whistle as he held up the Corsarian necklace Prince Dimitri had given to her. Next came a sealed letter, and the captain raised an eyebrow at Fael before breaking the wax.

"Fael—" She tried to speak again, but a dusty, calloused hand clamped over her mouth in warning. Ever more distantly, she was aware she should fight, but the most curious sensation afflicted her entire body. She wasn't sure she would have the strength to lift any single limb, weak as she was, or heavy as they had become.

Why wouldn't Fael look at her? It made her stomach churn. There was something foreboding in the way he stood motionless, not even the bleeding wound on his shoulder seemed to affect him.

Oren studied the letter, pursing his lips. "'I have her," he read aloud. "And information pertinent to our situation. Rest assured, she will be more valuable to Umbri this way. We await orders in Middlewood.' Hmm. Seems you have some self-preservation after all. It's odd, though. All of this"—he swung his arm around, indicating the scene—"would have all been avoided if you had killed her, as commanded."

The words punched through the fog of her mind with horror in swift pursuit.

No.

She must have resisted the idea aloud, because the Captain turned to her then.

"He is usually a very reliable dog, I assure you."

The next item was a half-full vial. The captain sniffed it. "Ahhh. King's laceflower. Spies said she'd been poisoned, but the castle healers foiled the assassination. Not willing to get her pretty blood on your hands, I assume? Well, it's evidence in your favor, at least. With that and the letter informing the king where you waited with the girl, I think you stand a chance of not being beheaded. Though." The man put a hand to his chin in mock contemplation. "If you intended to give her up, why race to save her? Why kill your brother-in-arms?"

"You threatened my family," Fael growled. Jesse's sobs doubled. "And I will be the one to present Princess Madeline to the king. Alone."

"Oh, you'll be there. You'll have quite a bit of explaining to do." His tone was downright cheery for a captain with several of his men dead behind him. "You're off to a good start," he went on, tapping the parchment on the Wingbreaker's chest, "from her demonstration today, I can vouch she'd be more valuable to Umbri alive—with the right motivation, of course."

The captain's hands rummaged again, this time coming out with more paper to read, her handwriting scrawled over half of it.

Her mind spun with fractured thoughts, trying to piece together truths that didn't fit.

'Retrieving you wasn't my task.'

'If you'd have killed her as commanded.'

'She will be more valuable to Umbri this way.'

Leo lurched, bile rising, and the soldier let go. Snide laughter followed her down to all fours. This time. This time she would die. Her heart barreled forward, propelling her lungs and her mind, and her chest seized, caught in the bind of an invisible serpent. Squeezing.

He'd been sent to kill her. Assassin turned collector. For the good of a kingdom. After everything.

Of course. *Of course.* What was she? The spoiled princess he could hardly keep alive. The reason a bounty was placed on his head. No one compared to his family, or the name he spent centuries building after being born without one.

They continued to speak, but she couldn't hear because her pulse pounded in her ears as the world spun around and around and around and—

He remained as stone.

When Fael finally deigned to glimpse at where she kneeled—blindsided, defeated, and utterly broken—it wasn't her friend, but the enemy soldier who stood witness to her angry devastation.

This part of him was glacial, unflinching in the face of her pain. Cruelty masqueraded as survival. Loyalty molded from lean seasons by those who would offer to feed him, for a price.

The Cairn Stone fell from his hand and rolled, spinning to a stop beneath her. Her gaze narrowed in on the etching. He'd said one side represented the elements; the other, the soldier.

This one was a wolf.

And she'd laid her heart at its feet.

Chapter Thirty-Seven

C OLD STONE.

Leo struggled against heavy eyelids. Why was she lying on the floor? Sitting up drew a rasp of pain from her broken throat. Water. She needed water. Absently, she noticed bare knees and the bandage over her wounded thigh.

But it was the iron bars that truly commanded attention.

Few details of the cell stood out in the darkness—only a thin cot.

A bucket.

The frigid stones burned now. It had to be late in the night to be so cold, but there were no windows to tell. No guard to ask. Leo pressed her hands into the ground, trying to shift her weight, but her vision swam as the dull ache in her leg protested with a sudden stab. Even after she slid to the cot, no strength remained to lift herself up. Weak arms and legs wobbled uselessly, and nausea came as the world spun with the exertion—the poison still held her. It was all she could do to wrest the heavy blanket down.

Its silky texture was a shock after weeks away from home. A fine pillow sat on the cot as well, and a mad laugh bubbled out of her.

A princess—even as a prisoner.

The laugh echoed off the hard spaces, mocking and unfamiliar. The sound went on. Warped.

The walls wept, too, in their turn.

An angry stomach woke her an eternity later—twisting in a comforting, reliable pain. She'd used a lot of energy in the fight, and likely used even more as her body burned through the foreign substance in her blood. Even as she slept, her heart raced. Even as she shivered, she perspired under the heavy blanket.

The cell bore no sign of how much time had passed. After hours, she made it to the cot. The wound on her leg opened under the strain, blood seeping through to discolor the bandages. They'd taken her clothes and replaced them with a man's shirt that didn't even reach her knees. Useless indignation and shame fueled an attempt to reach for magic, but they'd taken the focus bracelet, too. She could barely feel the brush of it under the film of the poison. Over and over, she reached down. Time wore by, but was it hours or days?

A voice startled her awake, grating, like a door on tortured hinges. "Hello little mouse." A woman stood in the cell across from her, clasping the bars, running idle fingers over rough iron. "I don't often get company of a lady sort down here." She giggled, thin shoulders bobbing with the motion. Long, blood-red hair fell around her shoulders, its oily length matted in inseparable chunks. "What can a mouse have done? I watched them drag you in here. The man, he wailed, but you? Slept like a babe. He called for you, you know."

"A man? What did he look like?"

"Oh, you know the man. Or . . . he knows you. He sang so sweetly. Such longing. And you?" The woman mocked her, laid her head on clasped hands and rocked, feigning sleep. She laughed again.

Leo's skin pebbled at the sound. "That's enough."

The mad woman's cackling only grew louder.

"Shut up!" A man jeered from far down the hall of cells. Leo bent her face into the bars, trying to see if she could tell where the other prisons were. Who else might be down there.

"He's not here." The woman said, suddenly subdued.

"I know." It stung, admitting it out loud. He wouldn't be here. She was the captive; he'd merely been her retriever. Leo fell back into bed as a roaring began in her ears and exhaustion swept in.

The woman retreated as well, mumbling. As Leo fell asleep, the prisoner whispered. "We are sacrifices in the game of kings."

"I won't be sacrificed." Leo didn't open her eyes, speaking as much to herself as to the madwoman.

"Never listen. Never *hear*," the woman chided. "The raging beast?" She laughed. "A mouse in the eyes of the ocean. Little paws race and race and *race*. The wave is faster. Might is nothing. The wave is mightier. And we are in awe. And we cannot condemn. Even as it drags us under, we admit its nature. We shook the earth. We birthed disaster. And it will drown us all."

"Shut your trap, Ellesida!"

The woman laughed again, a screeching wail of delight.

"I'm not a *mouse.*" Leo said, unsure what else to say as unease prickled her spine.

"I did not name you, little mouse. She did." The woman tittered. "She who sends the beasts."

Leo shot up, confused and frustrated. "How do you know about the beasts?"

"I saw them, in the web. I went down, down, down. Never came up. They were there. And now they are here."

The words sent chills over her skin. "Who are you?"

"I . . ." The woman sat on her bed and rocked, suddenly distraught. "I am one they did not heed."

Footsteps echoed down the hallway for the first time, forcing Leo to lay back and wrench the blanket up.

"Some food will help you feel better, Miss E." An armed woman slipped a tray through the iron door. The man stood behind with a short sword in hand as the gate rattled open and closed, the threat clear.

"Alright, she's next." The guard jerked a chin to Leo's cell. "Then we can do the rest all at once."

Leo winced and when they returned, she closed her eyes, heart pounding as she listened to the rattle of keys and the slide of the tray. If she was going to escape, it needed to be during transport to the Umbri capital. Even if she overpowered them and got out of this cell, she had no clue where to go. The door closed; the lock clanged in place soon after. A strange flurry of disappointment and relief flooded through her as they walked away. With an angry stomach rebelling against caution, she crawled out of bed, keeping low, to retrieve the food—hard bread and even harder cheese, but she was famished enough that her tongue sang with the first bite.

The woman had gone quiet, a blissful smile on her face.

Leo's chewing slowed, unease settling in her stomach alongside the first bite.

She spat and threw the rest to the ground. "They drug it?"

The woman ignored the question in favor of whatever daydream carried her now. Pallid skin stretched strangely over one side of her face and neck, like a burn. Layers and layers of clothes hung off her gaunt body.

Leo retrieved the mess from the floor and retreated to the bed, tucking the evidence into the folds of the blanket.

She did the same for the next meal. And the next.

As her body expelled the drug, the magic became more substantial. It continued to slip away, her grasp weak from overuse and lack of food. For hours she lay on the cot, arms draped over her stomach, trying to remember how it felt to reach it without the focus. Time meshed together, her meditations peppered with the ravings of a madwoman, the jangle of keys, and the blessed silence that always followed. The same guards appeared every time. Leo feigned sleep, giving them no reason to doubt their assumptions.

After several meals, the hall door opened outside of rotation. Fresh air spilled into the space, following a single set of footsteps.

A male voice called down, "The king will be here in an hour. Make it quick."

"It is in Umbri's best interests to assure Arnell its princess is well. That evaluation will take as long as it takes. Assuming this *arrangement* is to continue." The door slammed shut.

Leo flew up at the voice, the ache of her injured leg forgotten in the rush that carried her to the bars.

A long shadow stretched eerily in the torchlight. Had she thought wrong? Was this a stranger, a trick? Why would he come? Her mind raced with the possibilities, bouncing between hope and despair. The steps grew closer.

Then he was there.

Hands in his pockets, he peered into each of the cells. The stark angles of his face half-hidden by the contrast of the sunless room.

"Sebastian."

He hesitated, brows pinching. Leo had no pride or indignation to muster as he took in her sheared, disheveled hair, or the shirt that exposed her body all the way to the bloodied wound at her thigh. Days of not eating, of reaching for the magic regardless, had surely given her a gaunt, desperate appearance. She felt like a madwoman, herself. Might be one, actually, if all she could offer his devastated expression was numb apathy. She had nothing else.

Without a word he stepped forward to wrap his arms around her through spaces of the iron bars. The world spun and opened around her in a blink.

"Hello, Cub." He pressed a chaste kiss to her head before stepping away. They'd reappeared somewhere in the city, outside an imposing stone building.

"Your bracelet." She croaked after him. Probably the most useless thing she could have said.

"Shh. Later. Walk with me." He'd gathered a pair of cloaks stashed at the side of the building and wrapped one around her and then himself.

He murmured under his breath. A single blue earring glowed dimly as it dangled with their steps. Another focus? His long legs propelled them forward, and she allowed him to tow her along with an arm. They took several turns, her mind struggling to catch up with this turn of events.

"Where are we—?"

A warning bell clanged, sending fresh panic through her bewilderment.

Sebastian cursed and forced them into a sprint, aiming for the center of Middlewood. Its lawstone was smaller than the one in Arnell.

Before the stone, he gripped each of her shoulders, speaking slowly, as if worried she might not understand. "I'm going to need your help."

The sound of clanking armor closed in from two different directions.

He braced a hand on the lawstone and reached another out to her. "Leo, do you trust me?"

"No." She shook her head. Her voice was hollow. It was too much. Everything was too much.

"Leo. Please." His eyes darted around, catching on the soldiers that approached from behind her. Shouts rang out, and the sound increased tenfold. Absently, she wrapped herself in a blanket of silence. Sebastian's lips still moved. Faceless soldiers stood behind him, spouting commands she couldn't hear.

This was a dream. Just another nightmare.

He took one of her hands in his and placed the other on the stone. There was a sluggish pull on her power as it leaked into him. Too slow. The lawstone illuminated, but whatever was happening was too slow.

Sebastian's body strained, veins in his neck and arm standing out, illuminated by his glow.

An arrow whizzed past, nearly spearing him in the shoulder. The lawstone flickered, the thread of connection weakening.

Why? All the parts were there. She could see in—the shape of the spell that surrounded the lawstone—and its cost. The ancient enchantment all but sung with the hope of being remembered.

Another soldier raised a bow behind Sebastian, mouth moving with a command. They'd kill him if he didn't get away. Leo clawed her fingers into his clothes and pulled him to the side, severing his connection with the lawstone, just as another bolt passed through the space he was in.

He gaped at her.

She fixed him with a level stare. "Don't let go."

Then she slammed her palm against the lawstone.

Her body ripped, stretched with the force of the power that blasted through her. A geyser funneled into rock. She rose onto her toes, neck bared to the sky, fist clenched against the sensation of overwhelm that swept through.

A few weeks of practice meant nothing as she came apart. The barriers of her magic flaked away. The walls fell, one after another, gaping open until the only thing left was the one beneath her. The foundation.

It wasn't enough. The lawstone took and took. Would it kill her? She gave everything, but still it wasn't enough. Any second, they'd be apprehended by the guards, and he'd be condemned. There wouldn't be a second try.

In a desperate move, she shaped her will in that sacred space inside, forming it into a weapon. She rammed that last barrier over and over again until the floor splintered and gave way to cracks that shined with blinding radiance. Once the fissure was made, it spread of its own accord, splitting and crumbling until, a breath later, it burst. The rush of power was well beyond her control, and she was gone. Lost to divine light, with nothing left to wonder *who*, or *what*, she'd become. Consumed. Compressed.

And then tossed into salty air.

She lay on hard flagstone in a courtyard next to her unconscious friend, fingers still gripped in his midnight jacket.

⊙

Leo woke in bed. *Her* bed. They'd transported to Arnell, but she had had no memory to fill in the gap. The windows presented her city in the thrall of night, still with sleep. Shoving out of the blankets, she rushed, fumbling, to the door.

Locked. Had Sebastian merely retrieved her too? Dimitri must still be here, if this was their destination, if they'd locked her in.

A discreet cough outside revealed the door was guarded. She fought the panic that threatened to take hold, but cried out in alarm as flame enveloped her body. With intentional breath, she willed the fire away, and back again. That shouldn't happen. She hadn't summoned it. The magic shouldn't act without an expressed command. The walls had returned, but seemed flimsy, pliable, now. Her eyes flicked to the heavy armchair by the fireplace. Foregoing the incantation, Leo raised a commanding finger in its direction. With a single flick, the magic obeyed, and the armchair sailed over, bobbing, as if floating in a current. Effortless.

She waited for the sense of triumph. Shouldn't she be happy? Everything she'd worked for, her wishes, granted. And yet the seed of disquiet remained, firmly lodged in a hollow void that usually housed her tempestuous emotions.

Here she was, back in Arnell, locked in her rooms, once again a prisoner in her home. She could fight. Gods knew she could fight, could sunder it all, make them regret caging her. The thought was spurred on by the swirling eagerness of the power that eddied around her, kissing her skin, pooling at her feet. This wouldn't stay. How she knew, she couldn't say, but it seemed to recede even as she coaxed it forward.

But it wouldn't need it for long.

Chapter Thirty-Eight

A FLICK OF HER chin blew the door off its hinges. The guard shouted as the splintered pieces erupted into the hallway. She stepped out, bare feet poking under the long, thin nightgown they'd dressed her in. It should be frigid this time of night, but the cold did not touch her. Not with the fire under her skin.

Her head swiveled to the man who now brandished a sword, the confusion plain on his face. "I do not wish to kill you," she said, softly. "But if you raise a hand against me, I will."

A vague worry sounded in her mind. She buried the errant voice, used it for kindling.

He dropped the sword, and the clatter had her jaw clenching as she fought the impulse to lash out. "Your Highness, it's you! I thought perhaps—"

Her walk down the hall took on a dreamlike quality as Leo left him to puzzle through his thoughts alone. She found herself on the second floor. Unsure which door belonged to the prince, she chose one at random. Locked. This is what she should have done all along. She backed away and extended a hand, willing the spears of flame to life, but before she could strike, the door opened. Sebastian stepped out in loose, white sleeping pants. His upper half was bare. She blinked, distantly processing the rows of thin scars that decorated one side of his ribs. One was bright red, fresh and scabbed over. His face didn't change as he studied her and the magic poised to strike. Should she feel something over the fire in her veins? Hurt? Perhaps relief?

"I can't let you hurt him. You'd have to kill me first, Cub."

Her fingers twitched against the delay. Ridiculous. But she couldn't pull herself from the neat scars. "Who did that to you?" They'd die too.

His eyes bore into hers. "I did."

She shied away from the truth of that, but the magic spilled out of her hold, wrenched, as it so often was, by unexpected fear.

"Why?"

He took deliberate steps toward her. "I suspect you know something of the allure of self-destruction, seeing where you stand. What you're now prepared to do." She backpedaled until her body pressed against the wall and Sebastian closed the distance. "Do you think the shade will allow you to harm him? She is more powerful than you and I combined. You're *asking* for death." He was angry. At *her*.

"Better than complacency," she spit the words at him, grateful for the jolt of feeling that pushed past the indifferent resolve. "How dare you send the focus bracelet when you *just stood there* while he tried to spirit me away? How dare you be angry with me for accepting the only hand that reached out to help?"

"I tried!" he shouted, the sound echoing off the walls. "I tried. But I couldn't oppose him outright. He would have pushed me away, and then what could I have done for either of you?"

A sound down the hallway made both of them twist around.

"Leo." It was Callum, in a wrinkled shirt and feet as bare as her own. He surveyed Sebastian, who took a cool step back.

"Your guard woke me," her brother said, slowly. "What happened?" Not what happened to the guard, but what *happened*.

Leo looked at Sebastian, speaking low, "Have you checked him for compulsion?"

"Even if I hadn't, the thorn he's been for everyone the past month would prove he's on no one's side but yours."

The relief was a tidal wave. She hadn't realized how badly she needed to know he was okay.

A closing door echoed down the hall.

"Come on, into here," said Sebastian, gesturing for them to follow. He locked the door behind them, but stopped short, suddenly awkward as he watched them look around.

It was a disaster.

Books and parchment littered every surface. Half-full tea mugs found homes anywhere a flat space presented itself—book stacks, armrests, the floor. Clothes lay crumpled by the bed, the ones he'd worn today, she imagined.

Sparing her a glance, he raked a hand through his hair. "It's a mess. I don't let the maids in. They . . . disturb my system."

"Your room doesn't bother me. It—it makes sense."

"Always the flatterer," Callum said, but the jest didn't meet his eyes. He looked haggard.

"First," Sebastian began, "I'm sorry—"

She cut him off with a look. "It doesn't matter, Sebastian. Nothing matters now. Except stopping whatever that thing has planned."

"I have an idea for that," he said in a rush.

You'll have to kill me first, Cub.

"Why are you protecting him?"

"He's my family. He's been influenced by the shade for too long. I didn't realize, and I should have—I . . . please. I need your help." And damn her if the pleading in his eyes didn't strike a chord.

She sighed and stalked to his bed. It was the only place with space left to sit. The soft blankets smelled like quiet nights and enchanted breezes. Like a blanket of stars reflected over the ocean.

The night was only getting longer, but at least they had Callum here, too. At least it was time to stop hiding. Leo sagged into the bed. Her body begged for sleep, her stomach for food—"Sebastian, could my brother and I have a moment? Perhaps you'd find us all something to eat?"

The lord nodded reluctantly, and the instant they were alone, Callum whirled on her. "Leo. What. Happened?"

She picked at her sleeve. "I woke up. And decided to kill Prince Dimitri. But I didn't know which room he was in." She gestured around, eyes catching on details that hadn't stood out before. The wardrobe hung open, filled with thin, wrinkled pajamas tucked under pristine black suits. A delicate comb rested on a hand mirror on the side table. ". . . I chose wrong."

Callum blinked several times.

"I'll explain everything when he comes back, but first. Are you okay?"

"No."

The honesty shouldn't make her smile. "Me either."

"Did he hurt you?"

"Not once," she said, failing to distance herself from any memory of him. "Has father been acting strange?"

"Well, I'd imagine so, considering he believes his daughter was kidnapped." He gave her a level look she couldn't decipher.

The door opened on silent hinges as Sebastian returned. "I found someone. They'll leave the tray at the door."

Leo thought they'd discuss Dimitri immediately, but both men insisted on beginning with her version of events.

She went on about the first time she encountered Fael. They bristled at the theft. Then they grew exasperated that she'd taken him to the library instead of the guards.

"You shouldn't have tried to interrogate him alone," Callum said.

"*He's* the one who sent that letter?" Distracted, Sebastian sourced a dark cotton shirt and pulled it over his head as he spoke, hiding the scars that still warred for her attention. Most were faded, all but that one line of angry red. When? Why?

Callum refused to look at her as she discussed Dimitri and her plan to escape. "You should have told me."

"I tried! Well, I wanted to try. I—I didn't know who was safe."

They remained carefully neutral as she discussed the shade's appearance and the flight through the forest as the shadow of the Wingbreaker. Naturally, she left out quite a few of the more private details.

Sebastian grew restless at her description of the Atlas Well and dropped his head into his hands before fetching parchment and ink. Callum scowled at the part the bounty hunters played. But neither interrupted again. She skipped most details about Fael's family and discussed his betrayal in a dull monotone.

By the time she'd finished, Callum was as stone, and Sebastian had a lap full of illegible notes. They asked several questions, rehashing the story again and again.

Exhaustion took her stillness as an invitation to weigh in. It fell all at once, smothering any remaining vitality.

Sebastian took the floor—he seemed unable to confine himself to a chair. As he spoke, he referenced several texts, leaving them open at the foot of the bed. They were certainly not from the castle's library, or Arnell's city library. The thought tugged on her, and she couldn't decide why.

"... when a wizard is powerful enough, they're able to sacrifice the life of a person they love to become immortal, for lack of a better word. They preserve a shadow of themselves in an object. This is actually a way many items get cursed. If the wizard fumbles the spell or isn't strong enough, the item just becomes imbued with a dark power that isn't necessarily sentient but warped and certainly malicious. They had a lot of cursed objects in Galen actually—"

He'd put on a pair of reading spectacles. The book in his hand fluttered its pages in protest of the way he brandished it like a gavel in emphasis. She tried not to think about the scars, though it was clear now there existed a version of him that wasn't defensively confident or crafted for court.

"The lawstones themselves were made by encapsulating spirits of the fae. The magic protects an area, but they also—"

"The lawstone . . . How did that happen?" The questions multiplied as the fog of reckless apathy cleared. "How did we *get* here?" And how long had it been? Surely, no more than a night. Would Fael have spoken to his king, yet?

"The lawstones used to do many things, but much of their purpose has fallen out of memory. One thing I know for certain is that they can be used to travel from one stone to another, as we did. The stone holds the enchantment, but it takes a lot of power to activate it."

"The last thing I remember was a soldier about to put an arrow into your back."

Callum sighed as if he'd aged a decade.

Sebastian halted so abruptly, her head spun. "You don't remember the spell?"

"What do you mean?"

Finally, he sat. ". . . I honestly don't know. By all accounts, what happened shouldn't have happened. I was foolish and drained myself getting to you, and then my theory of joining our power didn't work. You shouldn't have been able to activate the stone. Not without the incantation, not after so little instruction."

"But how did you know where to find me?"

"I didn't. Not at first. I . . ." He gave her a sheepish look. "When I realized you were sending letters to Callum, I set up a way to intercept them."

Callum jerked himself upright. "You *what*?"

Leo had stilled. It was too easy to forget whose side he was on.

"You still got every one that was sent," Sebastian said quickly. "Don't worry. I . . . I just needed to make sure she was okay."

"I was."

"Yeah."

"Then you came to fetch me?"

"I didn't *fetch* you. No one knew I left. I didn't intend to bring you back if that's not what you wanted, but I wasn't sure how much information was getting to you about how things were escalating here. When Umbri sent word of your capture, they seemed to believe they'd keep you—your father went mad with rage. You'd told Callum you were in Middlewood. So that's where I went. Obviously, I'd learned a lot about my cousin's ensorcellment that you should know. And," he went on in a peculiar tone. "Like you said, you didn't know the man who . . . the man that aided in your escape. When it came to light who he was . . . I was concerned. We were all concerned."

Leo bristled, the memory of Fael burning as well as any flame. "Well, clearly, you needn't have been." Sebastian pressed his lips together as Leo plowed on, "Don't claim this was for noble reasons. You still brought me here. Back to your prince."

His quiet answer confirmed the truth she knew but denied. "It was your spell, Cub. You brought us here. With the power you used, you should have been able to go anywhere."

And she took them home. In the end, this was still home.

Leo turned to Callum. "Father. He was upset they had me?" The thought gave her some inexplicable measure of hope. "Does he believe I was kidnapped?"

"Yes—"

"No," Sebastian shook his head and he interrupted. "He and Dimitri decided it would look better if no one knew you went willingly."

Callum's eyes went distant. Leo's stomach may never make it back from how far it had fallen. She busied herself with smoothing the blankets around her. "So, he's still firmly under whatever power the shade used then."

"I . . . I haven't seen any evidence of it," Sebastian said, cautiously. "That kind of compulsion . . . it's complicated. It's incredibly specific and only triggers when certain circumstances are met. And it doesn't last long."

That was . . . good, right? That the compulsion wasn't as powerful as she thought. It could have worn off, even now.

"Do you think Dimitri used compulsion to get him to say I was kidnapped?"

Sebastian ran a hand through his hair. "It was King Galentya's idea. Sariah didn't have to get involved." He paused. "That's the shade's name. She spoke with me."

Leo eyed him warily. "And who's to say you aren't being compelled by her now."

He laughed. "You can learn to guard against it, like any spell. But she hasn't tried . . . she doesn't have to." He shrugged. "She has Dimitri. Until I can get that damn band off of him . . ." Sebastian trailed into regretful silence.

Leo didn't understand. "What does he *want* with me?" The fact that she was still alive meant he assumed she would still be useful. "He can't think I'll marry him."

"We just have to play along until we can break the shade's hold."

"You think we can?"

"I wasn't sure at first, but I have a theory."

Sebastian launched into monologue again, and only when her eyes drooped of their own accord did they move away to discuss in hushed tones, long into the night.

Later, she flinched awake as the lord laid her on her bed.

"I'm sorry. I thought you'd prefer to avoid any scandals so soon after your return." She couldn't make out his expression in the darkness, though she could hear the wry smile in his voice.

"It was a nightmare." She murmured, wrapping herself in the blankets and turning away. "You're in a lot of my nightmares."

A soft brush of wind let her know he had gone.

"Elaine!" Leo squealed when her friend delivered breakfast the next morning.

The cook spoke low, hurried. "I tried to check on you last night, but they refused to let anyone see you. Are you okay, did they—" She stopped. Leo didn't know what a fitting punishment would be for a runaway princess, either. "They're saying you were kidnapped by the Umbri scoutmaster?"

"I wasn't, but"—Leo pulled her further into the room, wary of the guards listening outside the broken doorway—"he helped me escape too. I think it's better for you to pretend you don't know that, for now."

Elaine nodded.

"I thought about you so often," Leo said as they embraced. "I couldn't bear it if anything happened to you. Are you okay?"

"Am I okay?" The cook laughed nervously. "Are *you* okay? When I heard you'd—*returned*—I feared the worst. I'm fine, Leo . . . though there were some . . . interrogations after you'd left."

Leo's stomach dropped to the floor. "They questioned you?"

Elaine nodded. "I think . . . I think there's something wrong with Prince Dimitri."

"There is," Leo agreed, "and I think it's best you consider taking some time off. Things may become dangerous soon."

"But what about you? I can find a way to get us out of the city—"

"I have to do this, Elaine," Leo said quickly. "I can't run away again."

"But—"

"Elaine. Please. Trust me." Leo took a heavy breath. "Now. Tell me something good?

"Something good." Her friend laughed, red creeping up her neck. "Well . . ." She grinned, brighter than Leo had seen in a long time . . . There was something different—

Leo gasped in false indignation. "You met someone? I fight the forest for weeks and you're falling in love!"

Her friend leaned her crimson face into both hands, chuckling in despair. "I wouldn't say I'm *in love*."

Leo pulled her to the bed, wrapping the blanket around both of them. "Tell me everything."

Her friend sighed. "It's still so new, really, it might be in my head."

"Elaine, you're clearly enchanted, so—" Leo wiggled her shoulder suggestively and laughed as Elaine groaned.

"It's not like *that.*"

"Oh, it's like that," Leo teased, relieved a small slice of life hadn't changed.

"I met him in the market. We reached for the same spice and our hands got all tangled up." Elaine ducked her head, fiddling with her apron. "He's strong. He offered to carry my things, and we spoke the whole way. And then he invited me over to cook with him. Says he's curious about my renowned cinnamon rolls." When she finally looked back up, she was beaming from ear to ear.

There was no resisting the contagious glee, and Leo grinned too. "They *are* excellent cinnamon rolls." Elaine was *happy*, but, even as Leo basked in the warmth, a solemn ache tried to creep into her own heart, but it couldn't matter. Especially not now.

There was a polite knock on the splintered door frame. "Your Grace." The maid bowed. "From the king," she said, offering Leo the message.

Be prepared for a public appearance at noon.

Leo pursed her lips, the dread that waited in the background of her mind solidifying into her gut. She'd wondered why he hadn't come to confront her about escaping. She'd expected him to thunder into her rooms, roaring mad, but there'd been nothing but expectant silence. He hadn't come to visit, hadn't acknowledged her at all—until now.

This was going to be some kind of punishment.

Elaine watched closely, eyebrows pulled together in concern.

"He wants everyone to know I'm back safe, I assume," Leo said, clearing the bile in her throat. "The whole charade must continue if he's to save face."

"You're worried?"

After crumpling the note, she aimed it at a waste bin by her desk. And missed. "Not at all." The lie was easy, like slipping into an old, trusty outfit. She'd woken up completely normal. The well of magic was replenished, but encapsulated once again by barriers she'd found no way past. She willed the helplessness away and smiled again. "Now, back to this *muscular* man."

Elaine all but swooned. "He said he has a decades-old family recipe for roasted duck that makes the meat so tender it falls off the bone. You should have heard him talking about it." Her tone turned wistful, and she shrugged. "If nothing else, I think we'll be great friends."

After Elaine left, Leo ate, flipping through a tower of books stacked on the couch, lack of restful sleep making the task more difficult. There'd been a folded note on the top.

"See you tonight."

She scribbled her own message and sent one of the guards to deliver it. There were several now, all different from the night before.

Woodworkers came to fix the door. None asked how it broke. She imagined her father selected them for their ability to be discreet, hoping to shield others from the unease any rumors or truths might bring.

Chapter Thirty-Nine

By noon, they'd reinforced the door. New and familiar faces spoke uselessly, overly-kind as they avoided her eyes and helped her dress. She played along.

After they'd finished, three guards escorted Leo down the hall. Her father and brother waited at the main entrance, but the king did not acknowledge her, instead leading them out the main entrance to join the group from Corsair. Leo studied Prince Dimitri from under lowered lashes, peering closely at his sleeve, trying to make out the band underneath. If the prince noticed, she couldn't tell, but he did not deign to glance her way. Sebastian stood ramrod straight at his back, and King Nathair wore a scowl, facing the amassed crowd. From below the steps, they cheered for their royalty, the sound deafening.

All went silent as King Galentya raised his hands.

"Today is a great day for Arnell. Our princess has returned!" Another cheer. "After being kidnapped by the renowned Wingbreaker, who presumed to end the Corsarian alliance without the order of his king, the clever and quick action of our Corsarian friends led to her rescue." The king gracefully stepped back, allowing the applause to rain on Sebastian and company. Leo's stomach churned, her gaze unfocused over the crowd. "As a show of good faith, Martin Treveri, King of Umbri has cast away his usurping pet. The Wingbreaker is being sent here as a proof of goodwill, chained, and ready to face the justice of Arnell."

No. Fear speared down to the tips of her toes, but Callum bumped her shoulder, a reminder to acknowledge the good news. The best she managed was a nauseated grimace, the expression frozen as tears finally welled and began to fall. Fael was supposed to be safe with them. He was on their side. He'd intended to give her to his king. It wasn't his fault she'd escaped.

But the crowd roared in bloodthirsty celebration.

Across the balcony, Prince Dimitri glanced over, his expression guarded. He knew. He knew she'd run away willingly. She shook her head, silently begging. But he faced the crowd once more.

Her father continued. "Today is a day of celebration!" her father continued. "Let the work day end. Return home to your daughters and your sons. Be grateful today, for none may know what tomorrow brings."

They exited the balcony to exuberant applause. Leo outpaced Callum, aiming for the king. "You can't do this, Father."

He whirled and her heart skipped a beat as he stared her down. "I am your sovereign. I may do as I please."

"And this pleases you?"

"What *displeases* me," his voice grew loud enough to echo in the large hallway, "is my daughter thinking she may disobey me! There are consequences for your actions, Madeline!"

"So you're going to kill him?" She shouted the question, hating the way her voice broke.

"And Arnell will be better for it!" the king thundered back. "Umbri will lose an icon. As they should, seeing how they thought to snare you into their service. His life is a small price to pay to subvert a war. One life for many. He delivered you to his king. What reason could you possibly have, Madeline, to grieve for an enemy soldier?"

She said nothing.

Victorious, he smiled as the echo faded, leaving only a volatile silence.

"When they found you in the square," he said, his voice soft now, "you were barely alive. You've proven time and time again that you cannot take care of yourself, cannot be trusted to make the correct decision for you and your people. Your mother rolls in her grave over the danger you've put yourself in and if it takes his death for you to finally learn, to finally listen. Then so be it." His cape swept up as he strode away, disappearing down the grand hallway that felt so foreign now. Leo hugged her arms around herself, clinging to the last vestige of hope that retreated, inch by inch, to reveal that yawning pit she'd never escape. A tender hand brushed her shoulder, and she flinched.

"This can't happen, Callum."

Her brother paused, studying her face. ". . . Why?" he said, gently. "Leo. You said it yourself, he tricked you. He acted like your friend, and then he betrayed you."

"He was doing his job." The thought made her heart ache impossibly more, but she should have known better than to trust him in the first place. If she'd been capable enough to escape on her own none of this would have happened.

"His *job* was to assassinate you. At the engagement ball. And he tried to. The search party discovered a glass, discarded by the gown you left behind. The healers identified the king's laceflower. The only reason we knew you were even alive was because Dimitri—" he broke off.

She shuddered. Secrets and more secrets. If she allowed herself to fall apart, she'd never go back together again.

"So you won't get him out," she said flatly.

"I am a prince, but even I am bound by laws. I'd do anything for you, Leo. You know that. But for him . . .?" Callum's arms enveloped her and gave a reassuring squeeze. "Fael wasn't who you think he was. He never intended to help you, only himself. He protected you, to protect himself. He may be a good man in Umbri, but he was never on your side. Not really."

Not even her brother could understand how irrelevant that truth was. Fael rescued her before he ever knew who she was. He bolstered her, taught her, demanding she fight in a way no one else had.

"Isn't," she said. "You mean 'he *isn't*' who I think he is," she said.

Leo ripped away from the embrace without another word. Stealing into a servants' passage, she made it back to her room in almost-privacy. With an urgency that bordered on frenzy, she touched each torch with flame, illuminating pointless pretty trinkets and hollow memories. The space became stifling with the heat of the fire, but she couldn't stand the shadows that haunted her room. It shrank around her. It didn't fit, it never had. And now it never would.

Fael was going to die.

⬦

That evening, Leo waited for Sebastian on the couch by the fire. The air shifted with his arrival.

"This says we can interact directly with the cursed object to break its hold," she said, by way of greeting.

"It does." He took his place on the floor, leaning back against the couch by her legs. Leo shifted to give him more space. "But we'd have to pull the shade out first." He went on, "She originates in the wristband and uses it to occupy him as if he were the object. The only other way to get rid of the cursed wristband is to give it away and have someone willingly accept it."

A polite knock made him pause, and Callum entered. Sebastian raised his eyebrows, but she shrugged in response. Leo hadn't wanted to be alone with him, and her brother wanted in on the plan to confront Prince Dimitri.

379

"Whatever power helped us in Middlewood is gone," Leo said, still mourning the walls that rebuilt as the gift waned. Whatever it was, it was temporary. "I'll need a new focus if I'm to be of any use."

Sebastian sighed. "I don't have another, and they aren't easy to find outside of the college."

"Well, what do you suggest?" Leo asked, as Callum took the armchair.

"There's little choice. I have one focus, and I think we can manage. If we can coax her out of Dimitri long enough, we may be able to hold her until I can remove the band, which she would return to once she became too weak to exist outside of it."

"That sounds deceptively simple," her brother said darkly.

Sebastian winced. "It is. We'd have to fight her until we can bind her. She'll be less powerful outside of her host, but in order to get her out, we'd have to be pretty convincing. And there are risks to holding her too."

"But you have a plan for that?" Callum's sarcasm showed just how loath he was to trust the lord.

Sebastian paused. He'd foregone the spectacles this evening—seemed to have reigned himself back into the typical mask. "Technically, she wants to possess Leo."

Leo felt the blood drain from her face. Callum's demeanor became positively thunderous.

Sebastian went on. "Dimitri was able to negotiate for a few . . . perks . . . and his side of the deal was to provide a female body, a fae, for the spirit to take over." He stared distantly into the fire. "So," he continued, "he marries you, she . . . moves in, and becomes his queen. In exchange, he'd be granted a lifespan as long as hers, and some enhanced abilities similar to what the fae naturally have. Extra speed, strength, that kind of thing."

It's so nice to finally meet you.

This was so much worse than she thought.

"And he just volunteered all this information? That he bargained with a shade. In order to become a—"

"A warlock," Sebastian confirmed.

"You knew this, and you didn't tell me before. You didn't let me end this. Why?" Leo ground out between clenched teeth.

"He's my family, Leo." He paused, staring her down.

Leo. Not Cub. Not for this.

"Nearly the only family I know. He's too far gone to pull out of it himself. He needs my help—our help. King Nathair may think of me as a weapon. The humans in Corsair may despise me. But I helped raise Dimitri. He grew up watching me, believing he would do magic one day. I didn't think he'd go this far. I don't know how the armband found him. But he's a good kid. This kind of dark magic isn't something anyone could just brush off. And he's worn it long enough, it's likely his will isn't entirely his own even when she hasn't fully taken over. Besides, if we attack him, she may become incredibly destructive. She'd gotten stronger. At this point, she may even be strong enough to move into an *unwilling* host. She's been—"

"Breaking the lawstones." When the idea snapped in place, she didn't need Sebastian's solemn nod to know it was true.

That's why it felt so familiar. The rot had started in Corsair, and followed the Prince to Arnell.

"That's my theory. I just can't figure out *how*. It would take more power than she has. One thing is certain—she has to be ancient to know the ritual that breaks them. It hasn't been used in centuries."

"That and everywhere it happens more monsters pour in." Leo massaged the spot between her eyebrows. "How do we trick an ancient evil wizard into doing the one thing that shows her weakness?"

Sebastian eyed Callum before launching into his explanation. It risked everything. Familiar numbness circled at the thought, and she welcomed it, but Callum swore, refusing. Afraid. He knew that once the idea was in Leo's head, nothing would stop her. Sebastian's eyes were tumultuous as she considered, but he didn't try to sway her in one way or another.

I suspect you know something of the allure of self-destruction.

What was she worth if she couldn't protect her people—those she loved? What wouldn't she give up to do so? She'd throw herself into the fire, be forged by it. Prove she was made to be more than the helpless sister of a future monarch, a sacrifice in the game of kings.

Callum stormed out when Leo agreed. He loved her, but couldn't see how she'd grown so quickly after being freed from her cage. He couldn't understand. Concern for his anger faded as the door slammed behind him, and she and Sebastian made finalizations. The air was dense with his regular enchantment, but the tension between them was far from the languid warmth that existed the last time they were alone in these rooms. He seemed on edge, though confident he could manage the shade once Leo had her distracted. Leo, thankfully, felt nothing, until the air softened and she finally lay alone in a bed that was far too big.

She could nearly feel him next to her. Solid and fearless in a way she would never be. He'd anchored her with intent to drown.

And she was, drowning.

Anxiety-fueled images of his hanging body caught and snared her mind. Her grounding process failed, though she tried again and again. The single image morphed into a vision, vivid to the last detail. His death flashed behind every blink and Leo lay wide awake, helpless to quell a racing heart. The soft blankets bound her, suffocating. No matter her rage, no matter her power, she would always be useless in the face of this. Fear. It used the night to torment her, and left her bleary-eyed, unable to bear the sun's first kiss of the morning.

As noon approached, Leo allowed the maids to dress her. Though it wasn't their fault her father insisted on keeping up appearances, Leo's fingers kept curling themselves into claws at the thought of seeing Prince Dimitri. Thankfully, subtle inquiry confirmed Sebastian would act as chaperone. She hissed as the ladies pulled the corset taut. There was no good reason to be this over-dressed for brunch. A chorus of tittering and apologies flowed around the room. Three ladies' maids attended her today, all faces she didn't recognize. They'd switched the guard again, too.

When the time finally arrived, she found Sebastian waiting for her at the arching rosebush that framed the garden entrance. It burst with pale yellow blooms. Any other time she'd feel relief at the promise of warmer weather, but not today. The prince sat at the table and didn't stand to greet her. A muscle flickered in Sebastian's jaw at the slight and Leo opted out of greeting the prince as well, helping herself to breakfast in silence: egg-cooked toast with sweet syrup, glimmering slices of pork, and apple juice sweetened with honey. She'd really missed this food.

Unfortunately, the silence didn't last.

"I hope you enjoyed your trip," Dimitri said, spearing the toast. Guards stood at every corner, and every exit. "A pity they caught your dog. Tell me, should we be concerned about fleas in our bed?" His tone remained cordial, but he gave her a slow assessment, not bothering to hide his disgust. An errant tendril of magic reared up, but she yanked it down. It wasn't time.

"No concern for your kidnapped betrothed?" Leo asked, patting her mouth with a towel, making a show of smoothing it over her lap before smiling at him. She wouldn't be the one to break first.

"None at all. You surprised me at our last meeting, in fact. They led me to believe you were rash and shortsighted, but harmless enough." He waved a hand at Sebastian. "I've instructed my own court wizard to assess your magical talents. Curious that none mentioned it before. Though it could be that the power is so middling as to be unremarkable, like the rest of you."

Immediately, she turned to the lord, and she didn't have to fake the suspicion. One side of Sebastian's mouth twitched up, just barely. But it was enough. She stabbed a slice of pork, pursing her lips.

"An unremarkable bride, was that the criteria you set when you sought me out?"

"I sought only what was best for Corsair."

"Consider me wooed, Prince."

His eyes were lifeless. "I assure you, Princess—wooing you is low on my list of priorities."

"I understand. You seem to prefer a darker magic than mine."

"I'm certain I've no idea what you mean."

They regarded each other in a beat of silence.

"This would go much easier for you if you gave up on whatever ideas are whirring in that plucky little mind of yours. You and I both know that, alone, you'll be easily handled either way."

"You betray your own ignorance, Prince." Leo stood to leave, no longer willing to act as entertainment. "I've never been easy to handle in my life."

Chapter Fourty

Two days later, Fael arrived. Leo pulled open her city-side windows as crowds lined the streets, waiting to jeer or throw rotten produce at the cart as it passed. The king had stationed extra guards for the occasion, warning them to keep her inside—or be hung alongside the Wingbreaker. Leo clenched the nape of her cloak, wondering if she'd live long enough to feel the guilt of their deaths.

And then she leapt out the window.

Fear had proven, time and again, its ability to steal her focus, causing her power to fail in times of need. She spent hours weighing the other options, but this was the only choice.

It turns out there comes a point when you have to decide what you're afraid of most.

There was a moment of weightlessness before the sensation of plummeting stole her breath away. It was three stories down and if she could have breathed, she would have screamed. The ground rushed toward her, impossibly fast. She cried out at the sudden drain as the shield met the earth, halted her in midair for a fraction of a second before it shattered, but it was enough to slow her descent.

A little.

The impact jarred every bone in her body and she wheezed, curling in pain, but the watch would pass this way on their rounds soon. The ground was soaked from the rain, but she'd lived, at least, first task done. Adrenaline helped her to stand, and with a groan, she limped along the wall until turning the corner to pass through the kitchen garden to the courtyard. Any thought of complaint was swallowed by the crowd that waited in a haze of fog.

Its clamor set her on edge. The shouts rose to a deafening volume as the cart wheeled to a stop, forcing her to summon silence. A driver and two guards marched back to lift the rusted metal that barred the door. The rest of the transport was solid wood. No windows. No bars. It had to be stifling. How many days had he been in the dark? As the driver eased the door open, the guards held their weapons at the ready. Leo almost missed her chance when a nobleman shoved in the way, but she dealt a savage kick to the back of his leg and pulled the spell just as Fael disembarked. Miming with a hand, she guided its phantom counterpart to grip one of the guard's swords and ripped it forward, spearing the driver in the leg.

The man opened his mouth in a silent scream, and a chaos of movement erupted.

Sweat dripped down the back of her neck as she forced two flaming spheres toward the carriage. The space inside her guttered, the walls held firm. This was all she had. It had to be enough.

She let the fire fly into the faces of the soldiers, battering them away.

Now. Go!

But instead of escaping, Fael turned, his wide eyes searching the crowd. His mouth moving as he shouted something she couldn't hear.

Her stomach twisted at the purple that ringed one eye. Blood dried over a swollen lip. Her flame grew, fed by her anger, and she gritted her teeth as it tried to break from her. The crowd roiled as watchers tried to flee. More soldiers poured in, some trying to direct the panicked crowd, others aiming for Fael. The paths she cut through their ranks only closed in behind him. In another moment, he'd be surrounded. His hands were bound, but he could do it. He could run.

Yet he didn't.

The flames weren't enough to distract all of them. The silence faded. The overwhelm of the crowd set in as her magic dimmed to nothing, and her fire extinguished as well.

"Run Fael!" The tumultuous sea of the shouting crowd drowned her pleas. He couldn't hear her.

"Leo!" He searched the ocean of faces in a frenzy and didn't notice as a group of soldiers rushed in until they grabbed him from behind. She tried to claw her way forward, but the panicked sea of people swept her back as the guards began to corral the chaos.

As they dragged him away, Fael shouted with the intensity of a madman, struggling against their hold. Three more guards leapt on him as he broke away.

"Leo! King Trev—" One of the soldiers twisted his fist into Fael's hair and kicked at his legs. Combined with the weight of the others it was enough to force him down. "LEO—" The guttural cry clawed at her insides, but was severed short as the pommel of a sword knocked him into unconscious silence.

She cried out, but the sound only mingled with the pandemonium.

Cheers erupted. Some murmured, excited about the magic, some looked around in fear, whispering about the person he'd called out to. But she had no concern they would link the name to her. Not here.

"Out the gate!" the guards continued to shout, using their arms to direct the flow of bodies. A man next to her shoved through in fear and was quickly stunned by a blow from a frustrated watchman. A barricade of armored bodies assembled, some of the guards spoke gently to those who were injured in the rush.

As they hooked their arms over Fael's shoulders and carried him to the castle, his head lolled, neck limp. His boots scraped against the hard stones, and she clung to the sound as he disappeared from view.

A new plan already forming, she bared her face to the nearest guard. His eyes went wide. It appeared the entirety of Arnell was aware of the orders to keep her confined.

"Princess. Allow me to escort you back to your chambers."

Their steps echoed, as everything did, hollow, against the towering walls. Her father's voice boomed from ahead, "I want every available man searching for the attacker!" He was moving up the stairs. He may not be able to tell anyone else, but she'd be suspect number one. Three flights and he will have made it to her room.

"We have to hurry, Your Highness." The soldier pulled Leo to the side and pressed his hand against her back, shifting a curtain aside to reveal a servants' stairwell.

Leo ripped away, suddenly wary. "What are you doing?" His young face glistened with nervous sweat. He craned his neck to look over his shoulder before giving her a pleading look.

"Please, Your Highness." He nodded toward the stairwell again, giving her a brazen push this time. The tone of his voice thinned. How young was he? If the roundness of his ears was accurate he couldn't be more than sixteen. "My brother is on your rotation today. If you don't get back, your father will—"

Oh.

Oh.

Leo flew up the stairs. He matched her pace, and they sprung, breathless, into the third story hallway.

"Archie?" one of the guards said, his face pinched in confusion.

Her heart dropped at the familiar voice. "Ellroy, get the door open!" Leo said in a fierce whisper.

"*Princess Madeline?*" he responded in horror.

"Hurry, the king is coming up!" the young guard, Archie, said.

The others guarding her room blanched. Ellroy fumbled the keys on his belt, trying to turn several new locks. The first key didn't fit.

"Go faster," the tallest guard said in a nasal tenor made worse with panic.

The second key didn't fit either.

Leo threw a hand at the door. "Break it. Then restrain me."

But it was too late.

Ellroy stiffened as familiar footsteps thundered around the corner.

Leo slammed herself against him and shouted, beating his chest with her fists. "Let go of me! I had to help him—please!"

"MADELINE LEONORA." The name echoed off the tall, salmon-colored curtains and sea green walls. Dread did its familiar dance, skittering over her stomach, down her legs.

She struggled against the soldier. He held her, but reluctantly. His breath hissed when she put a heel to his toes and a sharp elbow into his gut, forcing him to tighten his hold. Then she hung her head, listening to the gait of the king's frustration, waiting for the familiar rage, the twin to her own, but he only sneered in disgust at the men around her.

"Which of you thought to hide your failure by spiriting her back here?"

Leo jerked her head up, "Father, you can't—"

"For gods' sakes Madeline for once, *be silent!*"

Archie trembled, eyes wide as the king looked at each guard in turn. They exchanged nervous glances.

Her father drew an intricately wrought dagger. "Your king asked *which one?*"

Ellroy's heart beat into her back. His chest rose, went rigid. Then she felt, more than saw, him jerk his chin in the direction of the tallest guard beside them.

The man didn't see, but it wouldn't have mattered. Ellroy's grip went featherlight as she flinched away from the blade and blood sprayed, adding crimson freckles to the ones on her cheeks and the bridge of her nose.

"No!" Leo lunged for the man as he hit the ground, intending to heal him, or to try, despite the empty well inside her, but as her fingertips brushed the Arnell-coral uniform, the king chained her with an iron grip on both arms. He wrenched her up, eyes boring through her shock and shaky devastation, ignoring the dying sounds of the man whose neck gaped open at their feet.

"Why would yo—"

"YOU MADE THIS CHOICE," he roared, shaking her, bruising her arms with the strength of his fury. Leo's heart seized before thundering forward, fear as powerful and damning as it had ever been. If there were any magic left, it would have been impossible to guide. There was nothing she could do now. She'd been carved down to her most vital parts, still bled from the wound of it. And this is what remained. A person capable of killing or sacrificing others, if it meant protecting the ones she loved, no matter the ache or the shame that lived in her now. Leo *had* made this choice. For a half-hearted, desperate plan.

Her soft shoes became soaked with a repulsive warmth.

"I would do far worse to protect my people," she said, the words a quiet admission, almost a lament. There was no bluster, no challenge. She did not meet his eyes, instead letting her attention fall to the man at their feet. His eyes were open in shock over a wide nose. Fae ears. How many more hundred years could he have lived?

"Your people," the king sneered and addressed the guards. "Get that door open!" He pulled her that way, her feet squelching with each awkward step. "You have no people," he said as locks turned. "You're incapable of taking care of yourself, much less anyone else. The magic you use is pure vanity—party tricks. You're the first in memory to be passed over for the Blood of Kings, why do you think that is, Madeline? You are not a daughter, you are a curse." He shoved her across the threshold.

"The Wingbreaker's hearing will be in the morning," he continued. "If he is found guilty, he shall hang by sunset tomorrow. Your lack of self-control leads me to believe it is better that you don't attend. After, the alliance to Corsair will go through *as planned*. Try not to kill anyone else before then."

The slam of the door jolted her entire body, inexplicably sending another bolt of fear and shattering the cocoon of adrenaline that kept his words from sinking in. The locks slid in place, but curiously paused, and after an expectant silence the slithering sound reversed, and the door inched open again—

Ellroy's head popped in. "Are you—"

"I'm fine." She held up a hand, but it trembled, and tears tracked down her face. She picked up her hem, dripping red, and slipped off the ruined shoes, gaze catching on the bloody footprints that now marred her woven rugs.

"Your Highness." All three guards crowded her open door.

Leo nodded, dropping her cloak into a puddle at her bare feet.

Ellroy and the boy that guided her up could have been twins. Ebony skin, with hair that puffed straight up. Rounded faces. The only difference was that the chubby cheeks of youth still clung to Archie, while Ellroy's face was sharper with age. "And—um, this is our friend, Jamie." He clapped the third guard on the shoulder, a fae with tan skin and narrow eyes, dark hair cropped short. Nervous silence stretched between them.

"You escaped," Ellroy said.

Leo crossed her arms and lifted her chin. Gods, she was tired.

"I did."

Ellroy's eyes seemed haunted as they fixed on the open window. His face pinched, and he shook his head, coming to his own conclusions about the course of events.

"The Wingbreaker's only crime was helping me when I needed it," Leo said, defensive and raw enough that tears sprang to her eyes as she spoke, "and clearly you understand the impulse to protect one life over another."

Archie's eyes cut to hers. "Are you going to tell the king?"

Leo shrugged. "No." She meant it. "I don't want any more blood on my hands."

The men relaxed a fraction.

". . . What was his name?"

Ellroy's voice was a whisper now. "His name's—*was* Silas."

Nodding, Leo stepped gingerly to her wardrobe. She draped a fresh nightgown over the back of the sofa and went to the fire on still-shaky legs, tugging at the laces of her ruined dress. "I would have done the same thing for my brother."

The guard ducked his head, before impatiently dashing tears away from his eyes. Commotion down the hall pulled his attention, probably whoever was sent to clean up the body. "We will . . . keep you updated, Your Highness," Ellroy said, and the door clicked back into its reinforced frame. Several bolts slithered through the wood again. Then silence.

Updated. On Fael's trial, of course.

It was more kindness from them than she deserved.

⬦

"What were you *thinking,* Leo?" Sebastian barked the moment he appeared in her room. She startled and his expression fell, taking in the bloodied rug. The dress burned in the fireplace.

"What happened?"

"It was my fault," she whispered, voice cracking.

"What happened?" He asked more insistently, kneeling by her knees, searching for injury. "Are you okay?"

No. "Yes."

"Were you hurt in the panic? Why didn't you tell me you were going to—"

Leo shook her head, too tired to hold in her mirthless laughter. "Why *should* I have told you, Lord Sebastian?"

He looked away, pressing his lips together.

"I want to do it tomorrow." Leo stared him down, trying to impress her seriousness upon him.

"Do what tomorrow?" he said warily.

"I want to confront Dimitri. I want this to be over one way or another."

He stood, sighing, and shoved his hands in his pockets. "We won't be ready, Cub. Look at you. You're already white as a sheet after today." His forced smile faded when she didn't give in and began to pace the room. "You know what happens if we fail, right?"

Death. Or worse.

"It's the last chance Fael has," she said. If they could publicly prove the prince's corruption, Fael would be absolved of the false accusations. He had to be. "Regardless, I'd rather have it done before I'm forced to marry Dimitri."

Sebastian didn't seem to have heard her. He'd stopped abruptly at the open window. "How did you get out of this room?" he asked. Careful. Too neutral.

"I jumped," she said, flatly. "I used the physical ward to—"

"Gods DAMMIT, Leo—" he strangled his shout, her name coming through gritted teeth. He slammed his hands on the windowsill.

"I have seen where *your* loyalties lie," she said, tone rising as her body flushed with angry heat. "Forgive me if I disregard any comments you may have on my own."

"This isn't about loyalty, Leo."

"Of course it is. When the lines are drawn you are not on my side. You can't be. It would be absurd to change so quickly, to allow one person to shift your allegiance so much in so little time."

"Yet here you are," he said.

The challenge settled something inside her.

"Yet here I am."

"He handed you over to his countrymen."

Images flashed through her mind: griffin feather arrows decorating Umbri soldiers, a cairn stone discarded in the dirt of the road, Fael's crazed expression as he searched the crowd instead of fleeing. The agony in his voice. The good soldier, the stone, sundered. Screaming her name.

LEO

"Leo, he—"

"I don't care," she whispered fiercely, because it was true. Because speaking any louder was impossible with this weight on her chest. Because even if she wasn't sure what the facts were anymore—"I don't care." She cleared her throat and used a breath to steady herself into detached logic. "And I don't need him to care. I just—I need him to not die. Not because of me."

and
for the first time
i'm mourning
the silence

Chapter Fourty-One

⟶

"YOU DISOBEYED A DIRECT order."

"I made a decision in the moment. New information present-ed itself."

"They're calling for your head. We nearly had a war on our hands."

"I understand, but killing her was the wrong call."

"You presume to challenge me?"

"Apologies, Your Majesty. But the situation was bigger than you could have known. If we can protect her from—"

"Protect her? No. You'll finish what you've started, or you'll trade your life for hers. Do you understand me, Wingbreaker?"

"I'll trade, Your Majesty."

"You . . . what?"

"I'll trade."

Fael ached, stiff with cold. Blood pounded through his head in waves of pain to the point he could barely stomach squinting against the sliver of light that streaked through the Arnell dungeon's tiny window. The thin scattering of hay hardly softened the jagged edge of uneven stone that formed the floor. He winced as he pushed himself up to sit against the wall. The guard standing watch shifted on his feet, turning to eye him wearily.

Fael couldn't suppress a groan as he rested his head back against the wall. He definitely had a concussion. Probably from—

The memory flooded, clear and vibrant. Leo had come for him.

Why?

The letter damned him. It would have saved him, if he sent it. But the look on her face as she discovered he'd planned to betray her to King Treveri was carved into his heart, festering. He wrote it in a panic after realizing the truth of his situation—he didn't want to become a traitor, and the things he had done for her, the things he was willing to do for her . . . They were treasonous.

But he hadn't sent the letter. And somewhere between writing it and all hell breaking loose, he'd realized what a colossal ass he'd been for thinking he ever would.

She didn't know that. She had no way of knowing that. He'd laid waste to any hope for him. For them. Worse, he'd ruined his chance to warn her. He'd called in one last favor in Umbri—for any information that concerned Arnell or Princess Madeline.

His king had dispatched three men to finish what he was unwilling to.

As soon as the enchanted flames flew in, he knew she intended for him to escape. After everything, she fought for him. This was all he could do for her.

"You need to tell them she's in danger." His thick, dry tongue wetted with warmth as he spoke. His busted lip had opened again. The guard didn't turn around.

Arnell's prisons looked much the same as Umbri's. Fael hadn't hoped to learn that in his lifetime, but if he was honest, it wasn't surprising. A tray of food lay at the foot of the makeshift bed, but he eyed it wearily. That first night in the Umbri dungeon, he'd attacked it with fervor, welcoming the drug that would bleed his days and nights together into oblivion. And then they threw him in a carriage. How many days had it been? The trip had been a hurried one. They changed wagons several times to keep the horses and drivers fresh. Arnell's princess had returned, and Umbri was smart enough to toss her kidnapper at their feet to avoid the retaliation that might come after suggesting they had her—and planned to keep her.

Fael wiped the blood from his chin. A few of his carriers thought he needed a bit more retribution. Or perhaps they were happy to see the Wingbreaker fall. Many despised that he, bastard as he was, could find such prestige among his betters.

The issue never arose with his own men, but the rivalry stirred anew with his betrayal.

It seemed he couldn't be faithful to any one thing. The thought tore at him, and yet, his own king had tossed him aside just as easily. There'd been no chance for discourse, little opportunity to explain. He'd been fooling himself to think he had any true sway in his position. He was a set of ears, and sometimes a sword, but nothing more.

Looking back none of his logic made sense. He'd been consumed, blinded by the desperate idea that he could reconcile what he wanted to do and what he needed to do. He would die for it. But she wouldn't.

He shook his head, leaning heavily against the wall. Despite his fae healing, his knee still hadn't recovered after a particularly bad beating.

"Did you hear me?" The words weren't more than a rasp. Food and water sat untouched. He could drink it. But first, he needed to know they'd protect her. "King Treveri is sending three separate groups to make sure she doesn't solidify the marriage alliance with Corsair. They'll kill her at the first opportunity. They may already be here." The guard didn't respond. Frustration speared through him and he rattled the bars of the cell. "You have to tell them."

"Nothing you say will bring you pardon," the guard said coldly.

"I don't want a pardon. Just—a letter. Can I write a letter?"

The soldier shifted uncomfortably on his feet. "No—"

The dungeon door opened, cutting him short. A warm breeze blew in and sucked out the tiny windows set high in the cell walls. The scent of the fire that warmed the room beyond billowed in. The new guard rotated in with a cordial nod.

"About time you made it here, Ellroy. Good luck. He's been restless. Moaning and spewin' shit, trying to get a pardon."

Godsdammit. Fael resisted the urge to slam the bars. They were wasting time. Who knew what the corrupted prince had already done to Leo, and now there was even more danger on its way. He had to get them to listen.

The new guard eyed him warily. He was tall and thin, his dark skin made darker by the lightless space. After the first guard left, he stood and stared directly at Fael. Fael repeated his plea, but the guard shook his head. "It doesn't matter if what you're saying is true or not. They'll never listen. Not to you."

Fael let himself sink back against the wall, his knee protesting at the weight. He rested his head back and despair leaked from his eyes, tickling his ears. Of course, they wouldn't listen. His word meant nothing. To anyone.

Fael had witnessed beasts eviscerating men. Had seen the gruesome deaths that afflicted those that wandered too far from the safety of their village lawstones. He'd battled the griffin, Ptolemus, that terrorized the rocky mountains of Umbri for centuries. He'd served, protecting others as a twisted penance for his childhood crime of helplessness in the face of the world's rampant cruelties.

But now he could protect no one. For all he had fought for, he was cast down in an instant.

No. That wasn't true.

Death had snaked its way around him silently these last few weeks, but he'd refused to see the trap until he so thoroughly tangled himself there was no hope of escape. Repeatedly, he'd made the choices that distanced himself from the life he had before meeting Leo. He'd welcomed it. He still did. In another life, maybe he'd spend less time trying to choose where to lay his heart. If he'd decided, things might have been different, but regret wouldn't change anything now.

"I need to write her a letter. Just one. Please. For all the rest of this, I won't fight. I'll go easy. I promise. Let me warn her. Let me apologize."

He'd listened to men beg at the end of their lives. Pleading to unhearing gods, to loved ones who were miles away. He'd seen those who remained stoic, refusing to cling to life, believing their silence was dignified.

There was never dignity in it, in dying. And Fael would die. It was a minor miracle they hadn't beheaded him on the castle steps the moment he'd arrived. No, surrounded by iron and a castle's garrison, there was no way he'd get out of this alive.

After a long moment, the guard nodded, so slightly Fael might have imagined it. The Wingbreaker closed his eyes against the pain of his injuries, letting himself bask in the smallest, briefest moment of relief.

Chapter Fourty-Two

"THEY DECLARED HIM GUILTY, Your Highness. He is to be hung at sunset." Jamie stood awkwardly in her doorway, clearly loath to be the bearer of bad news. Their voice was gentle.

"Thank you, Jamie."

They bowed deeply. "Ellroy asked us to deliver this." As Leo accepted the small, folded parchment, she glimpsed unfamiliar faces trying to peer past the open door. Ellroy wasn't among them.

Had they changed the guard again?

It didn't matter.

After the door snicked shut, she opened the missive. The familiar handwriting sent her pulse into overdrive—overly neat, careful, as if he refused to let any evidence of his injury or fear show.

Leo,

I've been barely outpacing my fate since that day in the alley. Inexplicably drawn to you. Caught, for good, with the triumphant smile on your face when you snared me in the library. I was never truly unbound, and I could feel it in our every interaction. It frightened me—and with good reason. You've shattered my arrogance, made gray my morality, and forced me to face parts of myself I'd intended to ignore for the rest of my life. And though mine is over, I am grateful to have played a part in your story. I'd do it all over again, if only to give you this warning:

King Treveri will not stop. He's already sent three more to do what I couldn't. My mistakes and assumptions are innumerable—and damning.

I won't ask your forgiveness.

But please be safe.

Fael

Leo smiled, but tears fell, the letter trembling in desperate fingers as relief and despair fought for purchase. He did care for her. He did care, and it may not matter. It may already be too late. For him. For them.

Callum flew through the door without knocking. A moment later, Sebastian transported into the room, his face drawn, eyes ringed with dark circles.

Her brother didn't flinch at the lord's sudden appearance, only took in the silent cascade of tears that fell down her cheeks and crossed the room to wrap his arms over her. "You've heard?" he asked softly.

Leo nodded, throat too tight to form words, the ache in her chest at war with a nervous stomach. She pulled away and held out the letter.

A line appeared down Callum's brow, noting the sender. "How did he get this to you?" He went on before she could answer, his eyes flying over the text. "Three more assassins? They could be here, waiting in the throne room, even now. Leo . . ." He stared at the text again, fear creeping into his voice. "The words say he . . . he cares for you, but please tell me you aren't still going to go down there. This could be a trap. We don't even know if he wrote this."

"I know his handwriting. I'm definitely going down there." She snatched the paper away and tucked it into a fold of her dress. "We need to prove the shade's existence to an audience, to enough people that there will be no choice but to believe I was safer away from the castle."

"You can't, Leo," her brother said, an edge to his voice.

She whirled on him. "Are you going to stop me?"

"No, but—" He clamped his mouth shut, but defiance and irritation flashed in his eyes.

"If we *are* going," Sebastian said, "it needs to be now. The ending remarks will be over soon." He stared at her, face drawn, shoulders uncharacteristically slumped with fatigue.

Leo gave Callum a parting nod, hoping he would forgive her if their plan failed, and went to grip the lord's jacket. Sebastian hesitated, lifting a thumb to catch a tear, brushing it over her cheek. "Are you sure this is what you want?"

The question felt loaded, but Leo nodded, not trusting herself to speak. She wanted to end the shade. She wanted to save Fael. And if she broke now, she'd be no use to anyone. Sebastian wrapped a firm hand around her waist and the room spun before they materialized in the hall that led to the massive doors—big enough for Tor—that led to the throne room.

"I'm not going to let anything happen to you, okay?" Was he speaking for her benefit? Or his own?

"You're worried?"

Sebastian's conjured smile didn't fool her, but he spoke before she could call him on it. "My only worry is how many more men will be trying to enchant you once they see you in that dress."

She huffed a laugh, wanting to believe the false confidence. "Sebastian . . . whatever happens—"

"Don't, Cub. I'm not saying goodbye to you yet."

Leo nodded and took a moment to steady herself before walking down the hall. She approached as a queen would. Head held high, regal. The guards threw open the throne room doors. Waves of jewels and brightly colored sashes turned her way—hundreds of people crowded the throne room—all nobles who attended the indictment. That would make their plan more dangerous. Briefly, she was grateful Callum hadn't arrived with them. At least he was safe.

Sebastian cut through the crowd to one side. He would begin once everyone was distracted.

King Galentya halted his speech, realizing it was she who approached. Only Leo would hear the subtle warning in her father's tone. "Princess Madeline. I'm glad to see you are well enough to join. We were just about to celebrate the sentencing of the criminal who abducted you."

She continued toward the dais in long strides. The weight of the dress train pulled as she ascended the stairs. She'd dressed for the occasion, intentional in selecting the shimmering gown; white with golden embroidery reflecting the light from the tall windows.

A dramatic choice, but necessary if she was to use her title as an advantage. Few, if any, would recognize the similarities to Fael's cloak. No—they would see the royalty they were meant to see, but the parallel gave her strength. It was time for her to fight.

Leo turned to Prince Dimitri, who sat on a makeshift throne by his father.

"Unfortunately, King Galentya." She bowed deeply, then rose to look him in the eye, projecting her voice so that all could hear. "We have made our judgment in grievous error. I accept full responsibility, as I've been too cowardly to come forth with the truth. But I cannot accept the condemnation of an innocent man." The crowd of nobles gasped, and she turned toward them, away from her father's quickly reddening face. "I fled this castle the day I learned my betrothed was under the ensorcellment of dark magic." She paused as the crowd reacted. Some laughed, and her eyes flicked to them, marking their faces. They swallowed their amusement.

"Unfortunately," she continued, "it has become more of a priority for the three kingdoms to posture than to keep house."

Her father stepped forward, the charismatic mask breaking. "Madeline you cannot—"

"Fael—the Wingbreaker, as you call him—also witnessed the prince come under the influence of another entity, a shade—a wizard who thought to preserve her soul in an object until happenstance put her in the path of someone who would make a bargain." Searching the crowd, Leo spotted Sebastian moving in from the back, his black clothes contrasting sharply against the vibrant pastels of Arnell's upper class. He lifted a tattered book and his lips began to move.

An eerie silence fell over the throne room as Leo turned with finality to Prince Dimitri. "You sought me, Sariah." The name bounced off the high ceilings and glass windows, while Sebastian's low chant hummed underneath. Leo straightened, tilted her chin up in what might be her last act of defiance. "Here I am."

One heartbeat.

Two.

The air sang and then shattered as the protective power of the lawstone came through the window, condensed into a swirling current. Leo grinned, awed despite the clamor of fear that rose from the crowd. Sebastian had done it. Nobles shouted as it writhed and flowed, graceful, before spearing into its target. Dimitri screamed as it slammed into him, arching back to reveal the outline of emaciated ribs.

The prince shuddered and hunched over, the light of the spell spider webbing like tendrils of lightning over his body. Then he and Sariah laughed, the dissonant sound sending chills crawling down her neck. When he looked up, he wore a too-sharp smile. Cocking his head, Sariah said, "You truly think you can beat *me,* mouse?" Wide eyes glittered with inky blackness against the sallow color of his skin. King Nathair looked at his son in horror, then scurried away toward the side door of the dais.

"I intend to try," Leo said, conjuring silence to cut off the fearful clamor of the crowd that ratcheted up as the foreign king fled. A thick hand dug angry fingers into her shoulder, but she threw herself into the magic and let the flames embrace her instead. Her father was the least of her concerns now. Leo didn't look back to see if he fled, too.

Chapter Forty-Three

"BY THE ORDER OF your Crown Prince, stand down!"

Fael stood at the commotion. Startled, his guard only watched as the prison door swung open to reveal a tall man, dressed elegantly in a blue jacket and salmon colored sash. Behind him, two other guards gave incredulous looks, one silently mouthing his confusion.

As the man strode in, his long legs covering the distance with purpose, Fael stood to attention. There were no other prisoners that he'd seen. The castle prisons weren't for petty criminals.

His guard bowed deeply. "Prince Callum. The prisoner is secure, and we've sent the kitchen his request for his last meal. The king has forbidden visitors . . ."

The prince nodded, "I assure you, Ellroy. I'll be just a moment."

Ellroy shot a glance at the guards that waited by the door, then gave Fael a long look.

"Of course, Your Highness."

Wearily, Fael watched the prince as the guard left. Nothing good ever came from royalty visiting when one is locked in a cell. He was probably here to do a good brotherly job of kicking Fael's ass.

As soon as the door closed, the prince's determination faded. His shoulders fell, and his eyes deadened—exhausted.

"She gets the same look when she's struggling," Fael said before he could stop himself. He definitely had a concussion.

The prince blew out a breath. "She needs your help."

Fael's stomach dropped onto the dungeon stones. His instincts, laid to rest over the last week, filed themselves to claws. "What happened?"

"I'll explain on the way."

"On the way where?" Fael growled.

The prince chastised him with a look that reminded Fael so much of Leo that a hopeful pang assaulted his desolate heart.

"Stand back." He produced a wicked-looking knife and set the blade against his palm. Red pooled in his cupped hand, dripping down to steam off the dungeon floor.

Once Fael backed away to the opposite wall, the prince slammed his blood onto the stones.

The ground beneath his legs shuddered as the earth fissured. The floor under the door broke apart, widening until the iron bars warped and the hinges snapped under the strain. The entire hallway crashed with the sounds of ripping metal and stone.

The Blood of Kings.

"Hurry. I'll clear the way, but keep your guard up."

By the time Fael managed to squeeze through the gap, the previous soldiers had opened the door with weapons drawn, stark fear on their faces. "Your Highness are you—" They saw Fael behind him. "The prisoner—"

The prince raised his bloodied palm, as the men charged forward and a roaring wind tunneled toward the group, bowling them to the ground. One lay forebodingly still, neck awkwardly angled against the wall, two struggled to rise. "Stand down, men," the prince said. "The Wingbreaker does not die today."

One soldier adjusted his grip on the sword, looking uncertain. Fael's guard, Ellroy, stood just behind. A tense moment passed.

The guard's voice trembled. "King Galentya ordered—"

Ellroy slammed the back of his partner's head with the butt end of his sword, knocking him unconscious.

Prince Callum cleared his throat and adjusted his sash. "Thank you, Ellroy."

Ellroy looked down at the two men on the ground before giving Fael a sad smile. "She jumped out a window for you. Don't make me question the judgment of my princess."

Of course she would jump out a window. Gods, she was reckless. Fael grinned, hardly able to feel the agony of his split lip.

Callum huffed a breathless laugh and shook his head. "Don't celebrate yet, Wingbreaker. Come on. They're in the throne room." He pointed to a chest against the far wall. "You'll need your weapons."

Chapter Fourty-Four

Sariah attacked immediately. Leo didn't shield it, knowing that without a focus, it would take too much. The magic bounced off a glittering barrier to collide with the back wall, shattering one half of the stained glass window. Sebastian. In chaotic silence, the crowd scrambled over one another to flee.

The shade's wicked smile didn't falter as she sent another blast.

Every thin spear of fire Leo hurled in retaliation missed its mark. Sariah lazily batted them away with a hand, but Leo continued the assault, taking cautious steps forward, advancing. At the edge of her vision, Sebastian fought through the madness of panicked bodies, his face strained. When he nodded, she began the spell—one that was both new and familiar. She wouldn't make the same mistake twice. The shade hurled attacks at the shield, but the fear in Leo wasn't enough to mangle her concentration this time.

Prince Dimitri's face twisted in ire as the magic bound his body. Sebastian's shield dropped. He remained on the edge of the room, a grimoire in his hands. Leo was nearly drained already—but she only had to hold the shade until he finished. Alarm whipped through her at a distinct tugging sensation deep in her middle. The shade slammed against the invisible restraints.

"I can't hold her!" The spell pulled too much. Sweat slipped down her neck as she began to shake. It was going to start pulling from her life force. Did Sebastian hear her?

Prince Dimitri faded in and out, the ghostly form of a woman occupying the same space as his body. Another sudden drain brought Leo to her knees. She cried out, gripping desperately to the magic that rapidly dwindled. Sebastian's lips continued to move at lightning speed, his eyes glowing faintly with the magic that coursed over his skin. Leo closed her eyes as the spell reached for her life force, but she didn't let go.

You're mine, little mouse.

"SEBASTIAN."

In an instant, a sharp prick in her hand let her know she had what she needed.

The shade slipped in during Leo's weakest moment. The binding spell fell, and Sariah's shadowy presence filled the spaces Leo had emptied.

Exactly as planned.

The focus earring in her hand broadened the magic immediately, sending power coursing through her body. She inhaled it, became it. Letting the silence fall, she funneled everything she could into a shield. A kind she'd never built before. Instead of keeping things out, this one kept things *in*.

What do you think you are doing?

Once the shade was bound, Prince Dimitri collapsed. Sebastian knelt over his limp body, struggling with the cursed armband over his forearm.

Pain lanced through Leo's skull.

You think I'm so easy to contain?

Another slam. She should have boxed Sariah in tighter. Why hadn't she considered this?

The bloodless princess. You're nothing. The disappointment of three kingdoms. Leo gritted her teeth against the pain. Somewhere, a familiar voice called her name, but the sound was distorted, like the light shining in through the broken stained glass over her family's thrones. She hit her knees, throat constricting against the air that sawed in and out of her lungs.

You don't deserve what you have. You're ungrateful. Spoiled.

Leo relaxed a fraction, and some of the pain eased.

They'd be so much better off without you, wouldn't they?

Her hands found the cool welcome of the marble floor. A drop of sweat landed next to her splayed fingers.

Dear thing. I know. It's alright. We can fix all of this.

When Leo tried to bring her head up, the room spun. Sebastian moved frantically over his cousin, the fear clear in the slope of his shoulders. Suddenly the armband came off, clicking apart into two pieces. His wide eyes met Leo's.

I can make you worthy.

Her vision flickered, focusing closer and then farther away. Colors vibrant, then faded.

We can prove them all wrong.

Sebastian screamed her name.

We'll never be afraid again.

No, it wasn't Sebastian, it was—

Fael slammed his sword into the gut of a guard who stepped in his way. More of Arnell's guard flooded in after him, fighting Callum. Her brother blasted the men back with a gust of wind. Fael cut down another who was too hesitant to attack the prince. Leo blinked, confused. But the image didn't stay in focus.

"So delicious of you to join us," she heard herself say. Then the world moved. She stood as Fael advanced. Sebastian still sat on his knees next to Prince Dimitri. The two halves of the armband lay next to the grimoire as he flipped through its pages.

"Leo." The Wingbreaker held her face in one hand. "Leo, can you hear me?"

"Aw," she heard herself purr. *"You're always a half step behind, hunter."*

"Let her go."

"No." The shade pressed Leo's finger into his chest. *"I don't think I will."* Magic erupted from the touch, dark and angry and Fael flew backward, rolling haphazardly to a stop. Inside, Leo reeled from the pain the dark magic demanded. Instead of being bound up in life, this kind of power was born of anger, of devastation. It ripped at who she was, demanding the pieces in exchange for something more potent than life.

Callum stepped forward, already haggard. Blood dripped freely from the fingers of one hand. The shade set her attention on him.

No. Leo struggled against the too-tight space inside her. She sank her claws deep into the foreign consciousness, ferociously satisfied when it shuddered. Memories that weren't her own washed through their mind.

"Be grateful I've allowed you anything."

"It's unnatural. This isn't right for a woman."

"How do you live with the shame?" "Why can't you just be happy?"

"Mother, what did you do?"

"Mother. WHAT DID YOU—"

Don't. Another spike of pain lanced through Leo's mind.

Fael rose. He limped heavily, but held his sword at the ready. Sariah tossed lazy handfuls of power toward her friends, but Fael caught each one with an elegant swing. His blade glowed, the unfamiliar script blazing with a golden light that illuminated his face, savage and angelic. He advanced again, and Leo fought hard to plant her feet so the shade was a half-step behind in her retreat.

Her vision wobbled again. "Fael." It was her voice this time, but there was no strength to it. Sebastian, still on the ground by his cousin, noted the change and gave her a desolate look. The armband and grimoire lay forgotten on the ground. He shook his head. A dull roar filled the throne room. Callum stood behind them, pale, his eyes unfocused, maintaining the savage cyclone of winds that sealed them in, preventing the garrison from pouring in. A rhythmic banging on the door meant they planned to batter the door down, anyway.

Sariah gripped her again and grinned wickedly at Camhaoir.

"Here to finish what you started, Wingbreaker?" Leo's eyelids fluttered as the spirit crooned. *"Oh, if you could feel the way she wars inside. The way her heart leaps and drops. Hope on the heels of devastation."* Leo felt her face twist, simmering with disgust. *"She'd have wasted herself with you."*

Fael stepped toward them, his voice pained. "Leo. I'm so—"

The distraction worked. Magic speared forward, and his sword rose too late to stop the black dagger that embedded itself in his chest.

Fael dropped to his knees.

Leo screamed, throwing herself against the walls that closed in, but the shade sauntered past him, her sights set on Callum.

"Perhaps I chose the wrong royal, after all. Pity. I imagine you'd have put up a more interesting fight than this one."

Callum stood like a statue, blood still dripping into a growing puddle beneath him. Sariah drew a delicate finger over the hard planes of a high cheekbone, down his chin.

"Would you desire me, Prince? I could give you so much more than this. With your blood and my power, I could make you a king among kings. One kingdom, not three. And it would be yours."

Callum leaned forward, blinking slowly as he registered her words. The shade pressed against him to whisper in his ear.

"Anything you wanted, Prince."

Callum grabbed her arm as Sariah moved to pull away. She peered up at him with a coy smile.

"I want you to get the hell out of my sister."

A force impacted Leo's chest, frigid. Ice. She couldn't say if it was her or Sariah who screamed as the agony ripped into them.

They fell to their knees.

Sebastian appeared in her peripheral vision, the image flickering. His disheveled hair and wild eyes betrayed his desperation. Fear ruled through Leo's pain at the sight of what he held. But the fear wasn't for her. Sebastian pressed the tip of Camhaoir into her gut.

"This will end you, you know it. Return to the armband or you're gone forever."

"*You won't do it.*" The spirit's voice was weak against the binding ice that wrapped around Leo's magic.

Warmth spread across Leo's belly, a relief even accompanied by the savage slice of the sword as it pressed deeper. Sebastian bared his teeth. "*Try me.*"

"Sebastian!" Callum drew his attention to a point behind Leo. The sword pulled away, but only slightly. A man groaned.

In a burst of hope, Leo turned in time to see Fael beside Dimitri . . . wrapping the band around his arm.

The soft click as it sealed together shattered her.

Sariah's shadow careened into Fael, his body going rigid, head thrown back, chest lifting as the shade's curse, freely accepted, poured itself into him.

when the lines are drawn
you'll see sorrow in my eyes

not regret

Chapter Fourty-Five

IN THE END, THE choice was already made. Every step brought him here. For this moment. Leo was right, and her words echoed in his mind.

Whatever came over him. It was dark magic.

The savage fury on the wizard's face convinced Fael the man would use Camhaoir to end Leo's life, rather than let the shade have her.

Perhaps some kind of curse. I fear it was a shade,

Perhaps it was a mercy,

but a bargain with a shade must be freely accepted.

but Fael couldn't let it happen.

He grabbed the band. There was a breathless moment as it fit itself over his arm.

Without warning, the force clawed into him, as savage as any beast. But the initial impact ebbed just as suddenly, retreating.

Shocked, he sucked air into his lungs. Leo glared at him. Not the black eyes of the shade, but Leo.

"Don't," Fael begged. But he couldn't stop her.

Her face contorted, and she raised outstretched arms to guide the invisible pull. The darkness stretched, pulled taut between them. She tugged hard, but the spirit surged anew, making him cry out.

"Cut it!" Fael shouted as Leo tried to wrest the curse from him. Camhaoir was forged for this.

The wizard understood his meaning. He raised the shimmering sword over the whirling current of darkness that stretched between Fael and Leo. The blade trembled in his hand, from weakness or adrenaline the Wingbreaker didn't know. Sebastian slammed the sword down once.

Twice.

Chapter Fourty-Six

It wasn't going to work. Sebastian cleaved at the dark magic, but it held fast, each blow sending shockwaves into the marrow of their bones and a searing pain through her wounded middle. Sariah and Leo wrestled over control even as the cursed armband fought to drag the shade away.

"Don't," he'd said. But he straddled life and death, shoulders bowed, golden hair hanging limp around his bruised face. The evil, black-magic blade buried in his chest remained, greedy in its hunger and if he took on the burden of the shade, Sariah would use his body to destroy everyone or get Fael killed in the process. Camhaoir slammed down again, each attempt growing weaker.

"Seb." Leo's voice was hoarse, but it was her own. "Do you trust me?" She smiled sadly at his morose expression. "I need you to hold her." Leo only had a moment to register his incredulous, fearful look before she dove.

The walls that bound the magic inside her were as solid as any other, but she'd tasted the allure of what lay beyond. Had given herself over to it once before.

She'd bathed in a legendary wellspring of magic and lived to tell the tale.

She'd faced monsters, and monstrous men.

She'd risked crumbling the boundaries between who she was and the power she wielded, and would risk it again and again for the people who waited for her return.

She was Princess Madeline Leonora Galentya. Atlas favored.

Leo.

And there was no cage that could hold her.

As her consciousness fell into the ether, magic swept in.

She awoke in deep ocean. Suspended in warm water that claimed and sought to be claimed. Tranquility. Silence.

The giant eye of a sea beast opened, piercing her with a staggering awareness. Eternal. Unfazed by the tumultuous waves raging above.

Atlas.

"What is your truth, child?" The voice came from all around, a grumbling storm.

"I need your help."

"That is not your truth."

"You've helped me before. You gave me the power to use the lawstone."

"I gave you nothing. The power is yours."

If she stayed too long, Sebastian would burn himself up binding Sariah.

"Please."

"You must state your truth."

Leo's heart squeezed. "I don't know what that means."

"Your truth is what shapes you."

"My . . . my family? My station?" It didn't make any sense.
Silence.

"Knowledge?"
What did he want her to say?

"The truth."

Anger gripped her, enhanced by the well-spring of magic that surrounded them. "I have *told* you the truth!"

"For the thrice and final time I ask—" The storm boomed suddenly, sending her pulse skyrocketing. Leo may as well have been drowning as the tendrils of panic wrapped around her chest. *"MADELINE LEONORA, WHAT IS YOUR TRUTH?"* As always, the thunderous cadence of her name sent dread skittering over her stomach and down her legs, binding her in panic. Again.

Sebastian was probably dead now, burned out for trusting her.

Fael would be taken by the shade, forced to watch from inside while Sariah used his hands to eviscerate them all.

Callum would end up fighting alone, slaughtered, damning her with his last breath for thinking she could do this. She'd failed. Just like in the woods, just like every time—every time—she froze. Every time she'd panicked. Every time her heart raced in fear of threat both real and imagined. She couldn't help anyone. Couldn't even help herself. She was powerless. Selfish. Worse than every truth the shade had spoken.

The overwhelm fed the heat in her blood as she raged at the god. "The truth is I'm afraid!" She choked down a sob.

The ocean quieted, welcoming the salty tears she brought home.

"I'm afraid every second of every day. I'm terrified of what it means that the Blood of Kings ended with me. I'm scared that they're right, that fighting is useless—that the way I was born is the way I must be."

"Fear." The voice hummed. *"This is what shapes you. You seek to banish it, to conquer it. To become so powerful, it no longer binds you. Sometimes your anger is a guard, sometimes your bravery may overcome. But it is your truth. And neither the Blood of Kings nor my favor would save you from this.*

"You will always be afraid."

No.

No no no no.

When Leo opened her mouth to speak, the water closed in, shoving itself down her throat, up her nose.

"Many have made it here, child. Strength lies in finding the way out."

The awareness dissipated, leaving her alone.

Leo writhed, trying to swim toward the surface. She wasn't going to make it. The thick water dragged at her limbs, and she was too far from the light to return.

Light.

A whisper of remembrance brushed over her, over skin that burned not like fire—but starlight.

She'd been in this water before.

Leo twisted a clawed fist and commanded the sea to obey. With a jolt she was rising, frantic with the need to breathe. The column of water shot into the air and as she broke the surface—as she raised her head for a shuddering breath—the throne room returned. Sebastian still looked at her, horror morphing to hope as she stared back, completely in control. Sariah reared in surprise at the sudden shift, and Leo didn't hesitate. Power zipped in from around the castle, from the city of Arnell, from her beloved reefs. There was no delay as it swept in. No waiting for it to gather.

The room erupted in blinding radiance as she wrapped the entire force around the possessing spirit like a maw.

And bit down.

Sariah writhed, but condensed. As the darkness sputtered down to a single thread, Fael gained enough control to lift an arm out, and Sebastian tossed the sword. As the Wingbreaker's hand closed over the hilt, Camhaoir lit in a glorious, fiery blaze, its dormant magic called by fate or desperation, she didn't know. With a roar, he slammed the blade over the darkness that linked them.

With a deafening splinter, it severed the bind.

The loss of connection sent Leo stumbling, sending a spike of pain through her stomach, but she let herself fall onto her back, too busy with the battle that somehow still warred inside. How was the shade still fighting? Her body convulsed, but she gritted her teeth, holding onto control as Sariah continued to weaken against the assault, shrinking, until all that remained was like a single drop of seawater, buried at the very bottom of the wellspring of magic inside Leo.

The world rushed back in waves.

Glass and rubble rained down, weakened by the force of Sariah's fury. Cracks spiderwebbed over the giant windows, some broken through, ushering cold air that licked over Leo's fevered skin. The mother of pearl throne that once crowned the space lay in jagged pieces over the dais. Broken tiles dug into her shoulder blades, and her middle spiked with white-hot pain as she tried and failed to sit up.

Sebastian knelt and pressed her back down, his brow pinched so deeply she could have laughed.

Then Callum, his pallid features and weary eyes less predictable.

As she turned to look for Fael, Sebastian gently pulled her face back, not allowing her to see. He and Callum studied her, touching her pulse, peered into her eyes looking for any trace of the curse that lingered. Their mouths moved. Confused, she reached for her ear, and cringed against the protest of an angry muscle in her shoulder. Her fingers came away bloodied.

"She's gone," Leo said, but couldn't hear if the words rang with truth. "She's gone. Go, help Fael."

Sebastian smiled softly and laid a warm, radiant hand on her belly. He brushed a thumb over her temple in comforting strokes. His expression broke into something pained as he continued to speak, eyes earnest.

But she couldn't hear him.

And then the light faded, and it was just her and the dark.

. . . and really, what are we, if not the culmination
of every person we have ever loved?

Wallflower, Blooming

Chapter Fourty-Seven

S UNLIGHT STREAMED THROUGH THE window, kissing each of the overstuffed pillows piled around her. Leo shifted against a warm weight. Fael sat in a chair pushed flush with the bed, an arm under his head, face softened by sleep, fingers tangled in the blankets over her lower legs. As she sat up, he mumbled before returning to easy breathing, deep and slow. She tore her gaze away as the door opened, panic overriding her relief.

"Rise and shine, Cub." Sebastian came in carrying a tray laden with food. "Elaine has been glaring daggers at me every time I set foot in the kitchen, I think she—" He paused, noting the studious attention she gave to breathing. "You okay?"

Her blood raced, warming her body to discomfort. "I just thought—" She looked around at her remarkably normal room. At Sebastian. At Fael here, in this part of her life—at ease.

It wasn't real.

She breathed, trying to master her panic, and Sebastian dropped the tray down at the foot of the bed, perhaps a bit harder than necessary. Leo flinched when Fael jerked up at the sound, and his sharp eyes pinned the wizard with a defensive glare. Sebastian just looked at him impassively, like they'd done this before, then offered her a lopsided smile. Fael whipped his head back, concern falling to a painful tenderness that stopped her galloping heart completely.

Sebastian murmured something about going to find Callum and the door snicked shut behind him.

They stared at each other, too far gone for words. Then, as if realizing his hand was clamped over her leg, he withdrew suddenly. "Good morning, Princess."

The title clanged through her and his face blurred.

He leaned forward, clearly torn. "Look, Leo—"

"How *could* you?" Her voice was ragged, her throat shredded along with the rest of her insides. She pressed a hand to her aching belly, but there was no wound. There'd be no scar, either.

He didn't hide the naked grief in his expression. "I was a glorified soldier, Leo. Following orders. Proud to—to serve. I thought that made me good, but—"

"I don't mean that," she snarled, frustration warring its way to the front of the myriad of emotions that vied for release. She wrapped a trembling hand around his long sleeve, a poor attempt to hide the band on his arm. "I mean this." It pulled at her, the smallest thread linking them together. How much worse would it be to wear it?

Fael's eyebrows shot up. "It's nothing. We destroyed her. She's gone." He caught her hand in his own. "She's gone Leo. Whatever you did." Something flashed in his face. Pride. "It worked."

It worked? Then why did she feel—

Weariness crashed in, the weight of everything too much. Lying back down, she held on to his hand. "I need you to stay. Here. In Arnell."

"Leo." He seemed conflicted, the look on his face rife with meaning. Her stomach dropped as he pulled away, disappointment cleaving an already raw heart. Coming out of the chair to kneel at her side, he placed a fist over his heart. "Princess Madeline Leonora Galentya, my life is in your debt. As payment, I offer my unwavering loyalty. I offer my diligent service. I swear to stand without fear before your enemies. From this moment on my strength, my perseverance, and my hope lie with you, unto death."

Reaching an arm out, Leo caught a finger in the collar of his shirt. Already, her face burned, but after everything she had faced, what was one more fear?

The words were barely more than a whisper.

"You could have just kissed me."

His bright smile could have broken her all on its own. Her eyes flickered between his lips and his eyes as he inched closer. A calloused hand brushed careful fingers over the skin of her cheek. He hesitated, like he wasn't sure he could trust the words.

She met him halfway.

He tried to make it sweet, brief, but when he tried to pull back, she followed, fist in his shirt now, demanding. He let her pull until his chest fell over hers, catching himself on an arm that pressed into the bed over her head. Just the weight of him elicited an appreciative moan, and he grinned, uncertainty and cautious enchantment warring on his face.

"Leo. I—" She pressed a finger to his lips, unable to bear the shadow for now. She kissed him again, fingers tangled in his hair now too as she moved her body to maneuver them, guiding him fully onto the bed to settle between her legs. When she pulled away, chest heaving, his pupils were so dilated only a sliver of green could be seen around the rims. Maddeningly, he only watched her, still as stone.

Leo raised an eyebrow at his restraint, then lifted her chin. A memory. A challenge. He smiled, thank the gods, and her heart soared in triumph as he lowered his lips to trail a series of sweet kisses from her temple to her collarbone, each spearing a new flame down to the tips of her toes. She gasped when he nipped lightly at the soft, sensitive spot under her ear.

The sound seemed to be his undoing.

Encircling her waist with one muscular arm and holding deliciously tight, he nipped again, and she let her body react, arching into the touch, baring her throat and more in an unspoken offering of any other part he wanted to explore through the thin nightgown that did nothing to hide how eager she was.

"You're perfect, Leo." His voice vibrated in her chest as he rose, eyes devouring the flush of her cheeks, her lashes, heavy with blatant desire. Seeming suddenly inspired, he tugged the collar of her nightgown down, pressing a gentle kiss to the birthmark it revealed.

"You have no idea how long I've wanted to do that."

She laughed, the sound swallowed by a kiss that quickly moved from sweet, to claiming, to desperation in the space of a few breaths. He began to tremble, and his breath hitched.

"Fael?"

He tucked his head into the crook of her neck. "I'm so sorry."

His body shook softly, but words wouldn't move past the lump in her own throat. Instead, she wrapped her arms around him, squeezing, then tracing circles across the sculpted plains of his back. After he'd stilled, she pressed gently against his chest and kissed his lips, then the wetness on either cheek. Gods, his eyes were so beautiful. All of him was beautiful. In wonder, she brushed his silky hair back, revealing that scar, shining silver in the unbroken light of the window. When her lips found it, he went rigid, but she pressed small kisses down to his ear all the same.

"I want everything, Fael," she whispered to the devastation on his face.

"Everything." He agreed, and cautious hope battled its way forward before he pressed his mouth to hers, trailing his tongue over her lips in a silent request. She opened, and he moaned as he tasted her, sending a shock of thrill spearing for her middle. The kiss deepened, and her body sung as he ground himself against the sensitive spot between her legs. But her mind wasn't there yet.

And she froze.

"Leo?" He'd already pulled away, already let himself drop alongside her on the bed.

"Everything," she panted, turning into his chest. "Just not .
. . everything *today*."

He laughed, the worry easing off him. "Your pleasure is mine, Your Highness."

She scoffed and shoved him, but he snared her arms, wrapped her up and squeezed her into him, grinning at the squealing protests that were betrayed by the way she wiggled her body into his. She settled, enraptured by the cocoon of strength.

"I'm never letting go," Fael whispered, almost to himself.

Then he pressed a kiss to her cheek.

—◈—

A sharp cough startled them both awake. Fael untangled their bodies, and she watched him cut across the room to the discreet bathing room door before acknowledging her guests.

"You've been asleep for days," her brother said as a greeting. Sebastian stood behind him, gazing out the far window.

"I'm glad you're okay, too." Leo's words had no bite. She looked him over, eyes lingering on the arm he'd bled from. "*Are you okay?*" His body seemed healthy. The healers would've seen to that, but his face was drawn with fatigue.

"It was . . . a lot," he said. "I imagine it'll be awhile before many of the soldiers stop flinching when they see me."

" . . . Thank you." What else could she say? The cost of using his power was great—hard on the body, harder on the mind. The Blood of Kings might give the people a sense of

438

security in their monarch. It might be cheered on at festivals and coronations, but as much as the power was respected, even coveted, it was feared and—behind some doors—condemned. Callum had turned his powers against their own people.

Some might never forgive him.

He nodded and jerked his head at the bathroom door.

"The charges against him have been dropped. Father is hiding in his rooms, refusing to see anyone. Prince Dimitri and King Nathair left in the night. No one is talking about it, not openly. I made an official statement this morning that Fael rescued you from a would-be assassin at the engagement ball and was wrongly accused before being able to see you safely home. Arnell intends to extend a public apology. We will hold a ceremony, officially welcoming him . . . and instating a guardian position that I've only just made-up in my mind." He gave her a soft smile, a bit of mirth returning. "I trust you won't mind having him around rather often?"

His smile broke wider when she rolled her eyes, but Leo couldn't fight the corners of her mouth from twitching. "I suppose that would be fine. Prudent, even, considering the rumors of assassins."

"They aren't rumors," Fael said as he returned and bowed. "Prince."

"We will take every precaution," Callum said, sobering again. "I trust you won't balk at being assigned chief bodyguard of Arnell's princess, Wingbreaker. I'll fill you in on the details later. We will announce at noon today, before Father has a chance to step in."

Leo's eyes grew wide. "He doesn't know? But what if he—"

"I'll handle him. The rumors of my involvement in the death of our own soldiers has brought another truth to light." Darkness clouded Callum's eyes. "Silas. The guard he killed. Why didn't you tell me?"

Leo's gut twisted at the memory. "It was my fault—"

"Don't. Leo," her brother said. "He's been going downhill for years. You can't keep protecting him like this."

"I don't protect him," she said, wrapping her fists into the blankets.

"Then why didn't you tell me." His tone and his eyes were flat.

Because it was my fault. "We don't know that it wasn't part of the compulsion," she insisted.

"It wasn't," Sebastian cut in. "I watched his anger when he discovered you'd escaped. I watched him try to grab you in the throne room while you confronted the shade. Whatever violence we've witnessed—" His eyes cut to Leo's and softened. "I don't believe it's the first time. And after some thought, I believe you might have noticed already."

Leo's heart constricted, her ability to respond strangled by the dread that rose up to bind her. They weren't wrong. He'd always been fearsome when enraged, but ever since their mother's passing he'd gotten worse. There was silence for a beat before Fael's eyes flicked over her and then back to the other two men. "This conversation needs to wait for a better time. You." He threw a chin at Sebastian. "Why are you still here?"

Leo let out a breath, relaxing a fraction.

Sebastian straightened. "My cousin has made it clear in no uncertain terms that I am no longer welcome in Corsair."

"That kind of thank you seems accurate from what I know of his character," Leo said, forcing the light sarcasm. After everything Sebastian had done, after the worry and heartache and risking his life, he was rewarded with abandonment. Dimitri was a selfish, spoiled child. One day she would make sure he saw the gravity of the situation he'd caused.

How much worse it could have been.

"Will there be no repercussions for him?" Fael said.

"Our hands are tied, for now," Callum said. "Certain kinds of magic are hard for people to handle on a good day. To admit that our princess was nearly wed to a prince possessed by a shade, or admit she herself was possessed—no matter how temporarily—would stir panic and unrest we can't manage." His eyes seemed to lose focus as he spoke. "Things are bad enough right now."

"I can leave," Sebastian said, quietly. "If you want."

"We want," Fael said.

"*No we don't*," Leo hissed.

"He tried to kill you!"

"So did *you*," she said, trying not to laugh at the absurdity of it all.

Fael nodded, crestfallen, and rearranged himself to stand at attention.

"Let's remember not to admit these things too loudly, if you don't mind." Callum said in a familiar, suspicious deadpan.

Leo whipped her head back to him, squinting, fighting the curl of her lips and failing. Her brother finally broke into a chuckle, and the bind on her chest eased, relief beckoning the tears that stress always held back. They were going to be okay. All of them.

"Each of you," she said, looking at the man in turn, "has saved me, in some way." She could never be grateful enough that they'd all come out alright in the end. With new, invisible wounds, but alive. That was enough for now. They prevailed together, and would go forward in the same way,

"You saved us too, Leo." Fael said, and Sebastion and Callum both nodded in agreement.

Leo called out for the guard at her door and beamed, for once, at a familiar face.

"Yes, Your Highness?" the man said, dipping his head down low.

She huffed in false indignation. "Ellroy, how many times do I have to tell you to call me Leo?"

Ellroy grinned, bowing again, "Perhaps we can agree on 'Princess Leo'?"

It was certainly progress. "That will do, Captain Ellroy."

"Just Ellroy, I'm afraid I haven't made captain yet, Your Highness."

"I disagree. You've done so just now. Isn't that right, Prince Callum."

"I believe so, Princess *Leo*. Though I hope the new captain doesn't mind playing royal guard for a little while longer."

"Of course not, Your Highness, thank you, Your Highness .
. . Highnesses," Ellroy said in a rush. "It's truly an honor."

"Captain Ellroy," Leo said seriously, "would you please send
for Elaine? I'm afraid I promised this man a mountain of sticky
buns." She gestured to Fael, but when their eyes met, she found
she couldn't look away, caught in the grin that brightened his
face. He studied her in turn, and soon they were both smiling
like fools. Leo laughed, her face hot.

Callum coughed. "Now if you'll excuse me, I need to return
to overseeing the *remodeling* in the throne room. Sebastian,
may I have a word?"

As the men left, Leo turned to Fael, patting the space on the
bed beside her.

"Now. Where were we, Wingbreaker?"

Epilogue

SHE WAITS FOR YOU, mouse. Two sides of the same coin. Like drawn to like.

This wasn't the forest she knew. The trees loomed over, black and twisted. Red eyes blinked, peering through the darkness, there and then gone again. She reached out to press curious fingers over ash colored bark, but flinched back, surprised by its sinister glee.

Yes. It is hungry. Always.

"You can't be talking to me." Leo spoke aloud, the words deadened by heavy air. "We destroyed you."

Did you? The voice was faint in her mind, but there was no mistaking it. The canopy swayed, creaking.

The forest drew her in like a winding chain, calling her deeper into its web. The trees gave way to a clearing, where a towering image stood vigil.

It was lined with starlight, barely discernible for what it was. But she knew.

Time skipped, and it stood before her. A spider creeping up one side. She ran trembling fingers over the sundered stone. With mounting dread, she looked around—gut churning, prisoner to the need to discover whose life it had taken, even when so many more were now in peril.

The body lay next to her, the crown not far away. Blood, nearly black, congealed on her fingers, dripping from the wicked knife in her hand.

A pinprick of ice made itself known within her, the size of a raindrop. Deep in the well of her magic, it writhed, eager for her attention. She dropped the knife and held her stomach with pebbled arms, body wracked with cold as it reached out wriggling tendrils, grasping at what it could reach.

The corpse's sightless eyes followed her, and she knew what he saw. What he'd always seen.

A little spot of darkness.

Leo jerked up with a gasp. Fael already rubbed a hand over her goose-fleshed arms. She took several deep breaths and allowed him to wrap a steady arm around her, tugging their bodies together, the sensation a reminder they were safe. They had won.

The embers in the fireplace glowed a muted orange. The dinner they'd ignored was cold on the tray by the door. The stars through the large window were distant witnesses to the nightmares that continued to plague her.

Soft blankets, plush pillows, his heartbeat.

Even breathing that tickled her ear. And there—faintly, the ocean waves crashing along the coast of her city.

She turned into him, and her heart eased with the scent of earth and pine.

He adjusted, and she hissed as the frigid metal of the band bit into the skin of her arm. Why wouldn't it come off? The dream flooded back, and the fear did too.

"Hey," Fael said. She'd gone stiff, heart picking up speed. He lifted her face to his, his expression tender. "It's over."

"I'm not sure that it is."

He stilled, studying her face, clearly trying to weigh the sincerity of her words. "I'm not going to let anything happen to you."

Her stomach tightened, a whisper of pain slithering over her insides.

That was the problem.

She was pretty sure something already had.

Acknowledgments

GAH. HOW TO WRITE this without writing a second book? I have endless appreciation for the Coven. Jemma Croft, Sarah C. Davies, Lex Veia, Stephanie Beverly, Ana Miki, and Ellen, literally you guys changed my life for the better. This book wouldn't exist without you. I'm so grateful to be surrounded by talented, loving authors that have taught me the magic of memes, donuts, hoses, and beta readers.

Thank you, Sarah C. Davies and Alyssa Murillo, for being my first ever beta readers and following this book as its grown into what it was meant to be. Thank you, Cody King for telling me to ignore the rules of poetry—it wouldn't be in there without you.

Thank you to Shawn, Pebbles, Atlas, Nander, Ole, Alex, and every single person in the writing community. I only know I can do this because you encourage and teach me every day. I'm grateful to follow in your footsteps. Thank you to Atlas for Indie Author Connect, and for letting me shamelessly copy your every move when it came to publishing!

Thank you to my husband Landon for being my biggest fan and for letting me use the D&D world this story is based in.

And for being all in with every change I made even when it dominoed and created chaos. Oh, and for being patient with the endless pendulum of excitement and self-doubt! Never once have you questioned my capability, and that is a gift.

Thank you to our two babes R and E, for remaining patient and encouraging while I lost my mind diving into this world of paper and ink.

And if you're still reading, thank you. I wrote this for you. I hope you like it.

Megan G. Mossgrove is the author of The Sundered Stone series. She's a line editor, loves writing poetry, and writes as part of the team for The Long Rest, a fantasy audio drama. When not absorbed with writing, she grows flowers and plays videogames with her husband and their two feral children.

Scan for Socials, Website, and More!